D0190314

# THE EYES HAVE IT

"Return me to the ballroom immediately."

She tried to duck around him, but he trapped her against the railing with his arms braced on either side of her. "I'll let go if you answer one simple question, Lady Olivia."

Olivia had no choice but to accede. She could only hope his question had nothing to do with the robbery. It didn't.

"Are you as innocent as you claim?"

"How dare you!" she cried as she swung her hand back and delivered a well-aimed blow to his face. He reeled backward but did not release her.

"What have I done to deserve this kind of cavalier treatment from you?" Olivia demanded. "Why would you ask such an insulting question?"

"I want to be your lover," Gabriel returned, "and I avoid virgins like the plague. I saw you talking to Palmerson. His unsavory reputation surpasses even mine." He shrugged. "I just assumed . . ."

"You assume too much," Olivia protested.

Gabriel stared into Olivia's angry green eyes and felt a strange sense of familiarity. Something tugged at his memory but the sensation was too vague to retrieve. He had gazed into those same emerald-hued eyes before, he was sure of it. Where? When?

# The Rogue
## and the
# Hellion

# CONNIE MASON

LEISURE BOOKS  NEW YORK CITY

A LEISURE BOOK®

June 2002

Published by

Dorchester Publishing Co., Inc.
276 Fifth Avenue
New York, NY 10001

ISBN 0-8439-5020-X

The name "Leisure Books" and the stylized "L" with design are
trademarks of Dorchester Publishing Co., Inc.

Printed in the United States of America.

Visit us on the web at www.dorchesterpub.com.

# *Chapter One*

London, 1817

The elegant black coach rattled through the moonless night along the turnpike to London, its coal oil lanterns casting an eerie glow through the thick fog blanketing the countryside. Inside, the Marquis of Bathurst's dark head lolled against the rich velvet squabs, his legs sprawled in exhausted abandon.

Pleasantly tired and sexually sated, Gabriel closed his heavy eyelids as he recalled the pleasurable hours he had spent in the Countess of Barrow's bed. When the countess had invited him to her country manor, Gabriel had accepted with alacrity. It hadn't been the first time he'd been invited to share Leslie's bed while her husband, the Earl of Barrow, was at his hunting box in Scotland, and it probably wouldn't be the last.

Since the earl was returning tomorrow, however, Gabriel had thought it prudent to take his leave, though it

1

had been difficult to extract himself from the warmth of Leslie's clinging arms. Leslie had coaxed him back to bed for a final goodbye and one thing led to another, which resulted in his late departure.

A slow smile stretched Gabriel's sensuous lips as his erotic thoughts lulled him to sleep. His last vision before slumber claimed him was of soft white breasts, clinging arms, and open thighs. Too bad Lord Barrow wasn't away from home more often.

Two horsemen waited along the deserted dark road, shrouded by damp mist that rose up from the ground in thick, suffocating tendrils. Covered from neck to heels in long cloaks, caps pulled low over their foreheads, they were barely discernable in the darkness.

" 'Tis late, Ollie. Time to go home. No one seems to be abroad tonight."

Ollie sighed regretfully. "So it seems, Pete. We'll try another—"

Pete cut his partner off in mid-sentence. "Hark, Ollie, perhaps luck is with us after all. I hear a coach coming down the turnpike. Remember now, caution is the word. There'll be hell to pay if I let anything happen to you. You're to ride away at the first sign of trouble."

"What can go wrong? We've done this before and probably will again."

"No doubt you're right, but I don't have to like it," Pete grumbled.

"You're far too protective," Ollie complained. "Don't worry, nothing is going to happen."

Ollie peered into the darkness, waiting for the coach to round the curve, every nerve ending tingling. When the vehicle finally came into view, Ollie hissed, "From the looks of the coach, the pickings will be good to-night."

"Remember what I said, Ollie," Pete warned as he reined his horse into the center of the road and withdrew his pistol. Ollie followed, taking a stance beside Pete, a pistol clutched in fingers gone numb with tension.

Gabriel was dreaming when his coach jolted to an abrupt stop, hurling him to the floor. He shook his head to clear it of the last remnants of sleep, returned to the seat and pulled up the shade. Seeing nothing beyond the glare of the coach lights, he reached for the door handle.

"Stand and deliver!"

Gabriel's hand froze. Highwaymen! Wide awake and alert now, he scrambled for his pistol.

"I wouldn't if I were you," the highwayman ordered in a low growl.

The pistol aimed at him through the window was long, large and lethal.

"Toss your weapon out the window."

Cursing beneath his breath, Gabriel removed the small pistol from his pocket and threw it out the window.

"Now get out. Don't try anything—there are two of us, and my partner has your coachman covered."

Gabriel descended cautiously from the coach. He wanted to do nothing to endanger the life of his coachman. His relief was palpable when he saw Jenkins standing beside the horses, alive but closely guarded by the second highwayman.

His attention snapped back to the highwayman waving a pistol in front of his face. Though the situation

3

wasn't humorous, he wanted to laugh. He could discern nothing threatening about the bandit.

"Empty your pockets," the highwayman ordered in a gruff voice that sounded forced.

"You'll get no more than a few pounds," Gabriel drawled as he pulled several banknotes from his pocket and offered them to the highwayman. "You've held up the wrong coach this time. No jewels, no cash box, nothing but a man on his way home from an assignation."

Gabriel's midnight-blue eyes narrowed as he peered through the darkness at the highwayman's face. The bandits had picked their night well, he thought. Obscured by clouds and mist, the moonless skies provided scant light, and the highwaymen's faces were all but hidden by their cloaks and caps, making identification impossible. But the impression of a slim build and youth was strong. And once, when the highwayman lifted his face, Gabriel saw a flash of green and a hint of red beneath the brim of his cap. A green-eyed, redheaded bandit; the clues were mounting.

For the space of a heartbeat their gazes met and held, and some indefinable emotion passed between them. Gabriel barely had time to think about what it meant when the highwayman said, "Is that a ring on your finger?"

Gabriel's fingers curled spontaneously into his palm. The ring had belonged to his dead brother, the one who would have been his father's heir if he had lived.

"Give it over," the highwayman hissed.

"You can't have it."

The pistol lowered perilously close to his privates. "Give it over, I say. Which would you rather part with, your ring or your . . . family jewels? Make no mistake.

4

I will stop at nothing to get what I want."

Gabriel hesitated but a moment before working the ring off his finger and placing it in the highwayman's outstretched palm. The man sounded more desperate than dangerous. His voice had risen several octaves and he appeared nervous. He also spoke rather well for an ordinary highwayman. Gabriel stored all this within the chambers of his memory. He wouldn't rest until he saw the highwaymen swinging from the gallows on Tower Hill. No one robbed the Marquis of Bathurst and got away with it!

"Are those diamond studs in your shirt?"

"Will you leave me nothing?" Gabriel drawled in a deceptively calm voice.

"If you are rich enough to wear diamonds for buttons, the loss will cause you scant grief. Hurry."

"What's the problem, Ollie? Is he giving you trouble?"

"Everything's fine, Pete. I'm just waiting for his shirt studs."

"Shall I bind the coachman and help you?"

"I can manage," Ollie called back.

Gabriel removed the studs and placed them in the highwayman's eager hand with a contemptuous flourish, wishing he had thought to strap on his sword tonight, but he'd had no need of it in Leslie's bed.

"Anything else?" Ollie asked.

"That's it," Gabriel replied. He shot the highwayman a curious glance. "Your voice is changing, Ollie. Aren't you a bit young for this kind of work? And your speech; 'tis rather refined for a highwayman."

"Get back in the coach," Ollie ordered.

Gabriel wanted to protest but thought better of it. His wasn't the only life in danger. Though he sensed no danger from the lad, his partner was another matter. He watched through narrowed lids as Ollie backed away. A moment later the highwaymen mounted their horses and quickly disappeared into the swirling fog.

"Are you all right, Jenkins?" Gabriel called as he leaped from the coach and searched the ground for his pistol.

"That I am, my lord. And 'tis sorry I am for allowing this to happen. Bloody highwaymen. They came out of nowhere. I had a devil of a time getting the horses under control."

"It's not your fault, Jenkins. Help me find my pistol. It's too late to stop the bandits, but I'd hate to lose the piece. It belonged to my brother." And so did the ring, Gabriel thought with a surge of anger.

The pistol was found in short order, and Gabriel returned to the coach. Jenkins picked up the reins and the coach rattled off down the road. Drumming his fingers on the seat, Gabriel sat back and reviewed the clues the bandits had let slip, few though they were. Their names were Pete and Ollie. Ollie was young, possibly with green eyes and red hair. Gabriel hadn't seen the other one close enough to note any identifying aspects of his appearance.

Gabriel closed his eyes and tried to picture the younger highwayman again. Something uncomfortable stirred in him when he recalled Ollie's green eyes; the feeling that Ollie was something other than what he pretended clawed at him.

The following evening, Gabriel stalked into Brooks's Club on St. James's Street, still miffed over the previous night's robbery.

"Bathurst, over here!"

Gabriel saw his good friend and fellow rogue, Ramsey Dunsford, Earl of Braxton, motioning to him from the doorway of the game room and swerved in his direction.

"Westmore and I missed you last night," Ram said in greeting. "We looked for you at White's, then headed to Crocker's gambling hell. We both lost a fortune," Braxton grumbled.

"I need a drink," Gabriel said, summoning a dignified, black-clad footman with a wave of his hand.

"Something's happened," Ram guessed. "Don't tell me until Westmore joins us. I want him to hear this too."

"Are you looking for me?"

Lucas, Viscount Westmore, strolled over to join his two friends, his eyebrows raised in question.

"You're just in time, Luc," Ramsey said. "Bathurst is about to regale us with his misadventures last night."

"Misadventures?" Luc drawled.

"Nothing short of calamity would bring so ferocious a scowl to Bathurst's face," Ram vowed. "I haven't eaten yet; shall we repair to the dining room? Bathurst can relate his tale of woe while we eat."

Anger simmered inside Gabriel as he followed his friends into the dining room and ordered a meal of roast pheasant, trout and potatoes. He had been so busy trying to track down his midnight bandits that he had forgotten to eat today. He had even hired a Bow Street Runner to find the bloody bastards.

Gabriel regarded his friends moodily. Both were the best friends any man could hope to have. Blue-eyed Luc had deep auburn hair and classically handsome features. Luc had fought beside him at Waterloo. Dark-haired, silver-eyed Ramsey had been his friend since Eton.

"Well, out with it, man," Ramsey goaded. "What woman is bedeviling you? Where were you last night?"

"In Lady Barrow's bed. And she's not the one bedeviling me."

"Her husband caught you tupping her!" Luc said gleefully. "It's not like you to be so careless, Gabriel."

"Barrow most certainly did *not* catch me," Gabriel retorted. "And you don't have to act so bloody smug about it. For your information, I left the lady's bed shortly after midnight."

"Something happened, that much is clear," Ramsey said.

"Indeed," Gabriel allowed. He took a healthy swig of the brandy the footman had set down in front of him and slammed the glass on the table.

Ramsey's upper lip curled in amusement. "You seduced a virgin and her papa called you out. When will you learn that virgins are off limits?"

"Bloody hell!" Gabriel groused. "Will you leave off? You know I prefer experienced women. I want nothing to do with cringing virgins. A pair of highwaymen stopped my coach on the turnpike last night. They took my brother's ring and the diamond studs from my shirt."

Ram suppressed a chuckle. "They probably didn't know you were a war hero. It's not like you to be caught off guard."

"I fell asleep," Gabriel muttered.

A brief silence ensued as a footman placed their food before them. "Lady Barrow is a legendary man-eater," Luc claimed as he picked up his fork. "Hell, even I would be exhausted after a few hours in her bed."

Gabriel slanted him a sardonic look. "You're tireless, Westmore. Not even I can keep up with you."

"Now there's a lie if I ever heard one," Ram laughed. "There isn't a willing lady whose charms we haven't sampled, a bordello we haven't visited or a gaming hell we haven't frequented. We're called the Rogues of London with good reason."

"And proud of it," Luc added. "Tell us about the robbery, Bathurst. A pair of unlikely highwaymen accosted Lord Trowbridge and his wife a few weeks ago. They're probably the same ones who robbed you."

"Highway robberies have been occurring with some frequency of late," Ram mused.

"I heard about the robberies," Gabriel admitted, "but never thought I would become a victim. I've set the Bow Street Runners on them. I know their names and aim to see them brought to justice."

"You know their names?" Ram asked, all agog. "Rather careless of them, wasn't it?"

"They call themselves Ollie and Pete. Careless or not, it's a damn good clue."

Their meal arrived and they ate in silence, but Gabriel's mind churned as he chewed and swallowed without really tasting his food. Something about one of the highwaymen bothered him. The younger bandit's mannerisms and voice were distinctive. If he saw the fellow again, he most certainly would recognize him.

"Forget the rascals, Bathurst," Ram said as he sat back and lit a cigar. "The law will deal with them. Sooner or later they'll make a mistake and end up on the gallows."

"Who's for Crocker's?" Luc asked. "I aim to win some of my money back tonight."

"I think another type of entertainment is what Ga-

Connie Mason

briel needs to take his mind off the robbery," Rum suggested. "Anyone for Madame Bella's?"

Gabriel grinned. Madam Bella's sounded just the thing. "Madam Bella's it is," he said. "Eat hearty, we'll need the energy for tonight's activities. I hope neither of you want the tall, green-eyed redhead with the fancy name, for I plan to monopolize her all evening."

Now why had he said that? Gabriel wondered. Red hair and green eyes had haunted his dreams last night, but they belonged to a man, not a woman.

"You mean Fifi," Luc said. "You're welcome to her. I prefer petite blondes with big, pillowy breasts."

"Let's be off, then," Ram said, rising.

The infamous Rogues of London strolled off, intent upon their usual pursuits of wenching, gambling and drinking.

Stifling a yawn, Olivia Fairfax entered the kitchen to fix her breakfast a good three hours later than was her usual wont. It was nearly ten o'clock, and Peterson, their only full-time servant, stood beside the hearth, removing something from the wall oven.

"Good morning, Peterson," Olivia greeted.

His brow wrinkled in concern, Peterson searched Olivia's face. "Are you all right, Miss Livvy?"

Olivia smiled brightly . . . too brightly. "Of course. Why shouldn't I be? Have you seen my aunt?"

"I'm right here, dear." A diminutive woman of middle years bustled through the door. Save for intermingled strands of gray, her hair was the same deep rich red as her niece's.

"Good morning, Aunt Alma," Olivia said, mustering a smile.

Olivia didn't feel much like smiling, and with good

10

reason. The slim pickings the night before weren't nearly enough to pay the day help and make the repairs on the roof, much less pay her brother's fees and expenses at Oxford. And the arrogant man she'd encountered in the coach had given her an uncomfortable feeling in the pit of her stomach. Intuition told her the man was trouble, and she would be wise to be wary.

"Good morning, Livvy." Bright blue eyes peered intently into Olivia's face as Alma's tiny, birdlike hands fidgeted with her apron. "You look exhausted, dear. You know I don't approve of what you're doing. And Neville, poor lad, would be appalled should he find out about his sister's . . . unusual activities."

Olivia blew out a sigh and plopped down heavily into the nearest chair. "We've been over this before, Auntie. I do what I must to provide for my family. Neville deserves a proper education. No one but us is aware that Father left nothing behind but his title, and that's how I want it."

Alma sent an accusatory glance at Peterson. "It's *his* fault. But for him you would not be placing your life in danger with these night rides."

"If not for Peterson we wouldn't have survived this long," Olivia protested. "Papa left us nothing. He died under less than honorable circumstances and left a mountain of debt and scandal behind. By the time his bills were paid there was nothing left."

"You should have told Neville instead of letting him believe there was money for his education."

"I couldn't do that to him. Papa promised Neville he could study at Oxford, and I hadn't the heart to disappoint him. Bringing him home now would break his heart."

"What about your heart?" Alma asked. "You'll never

find a husband if you continue to risk your life for the sake of your family."

"Have you a better suggestion?" Olivia asked. "Perhaps you could take in wash. I could always become a governess, but the money wouldn't be enough to keep up this house and pay Neville's tuition."

Alma flushed. "You needn't be so flippant about it. Taking in wash would be better than what you're doing. This has got to stop, Livvy. One day your luck will run out—then what?"

"I can't stop, Auntie, not yet," Olivia argued. "Last night wasn't as profitable as I had hoped."

Alma's shoulders sagged. "Livvy, dear, please reconsider. Robbing coaches could be the death of you."

Seized by inspiration, Olivia grew thoughtful. "Maybe there's another way to get the money we need to survive."

"What precisely does that mean?"

"Didn't we just receive an invitation to the dowager Dutchess Stanhope's ball? She's the wealthy widow who tried to rope Papa into marriage, if you recall. It wouldn't be difficult to slip up to her chambers and . . ."

"Absolutely not! I forbid it. You are not going to steal from people we know."

"You know as well as I that the countess is a nasty old harridan. She probably invited me to her ball to humiliate me. She has never forgiven Papa for turning her down. The only sensible thing he's ever done, in my opinion."

"We rarely attend society functions," Alma reminded her.

"With good reason. We can't afford it. We will need new ball gowns, and we'll have to rent a hackney to carry us there."

"You're actually thinking of going, Miss Livvy?" Peterson asked.

" 'Tis too good an opportunity to miss. Can you find a fence for the studs and ring we lifted last night?"

"I always do, Miss Livvy."

"Oh, dear, this is terrible," Aunt Alma lamented after Peterson quit the room. "I haven't been to a ball in ages. Go without me, Livvy, and save the expense of a gown for me."

"You know I can't, Auntie. Neville isn't here to escort me, and I'll need a proper chaperone even though I have been on the shelf for several years."

"Hardly on the shelf, dear," Alma protested. "You're only four and twenty."

"Nearly five and twenty and on the shelf," Olivia repeated. "It's all right, Auntie, I've adjusted to my lack of prospects. Without a dowry there's little hope of my marrying."

"What about Lord Palmerson? He'd marry you without a dowry if you'd but agree."

"Viscount Palmerson is a toad," Olivia asserted.

Alma shrugged. "I'm inclined to agree. There's some nasty gossip circulating about him."

"I despise him. He got a merchant's daughter with child, and she threw herself off London Bridge when he refused to wed her. Besides, he drinks too much and gambles too deeply. And don't forget, he led my father into debt and dissolution," she added bitterly. "Rumor has it his pockets are as empty as ours, which makes me wonder why he wants to wed an earl's penniless daughter."

"There is nothing to substantiate the rumor that Palmerson got the girl with child. Any man could have led your father astray; it just happened to be Palmerson."

"Honestly, Auntie, you don't like Palmerson any better than I do."

"I know, dear, but I worry so about you each time you attempt something dangerous or foolish. I have horrible nightmares about you swinging from the gallows." Her voice shook. " 'Tis terrible, just terrible."

Olivia placed her arms around the diminutive woman and gave her a reassuring hug. She loved Alma dearly. She was the only mother she and Neville had known since their true mother died bringing Neville into the world eighteen years ago. Their father had withdrawn from his family after his wife's death and spent the remainder of his life pursuing worldly pleasure. He had died four years ago, defending the honor of a prostitute in a duel, leaving behind a mountain of debts.

"Don't worry, Auntie, I'll be careful. Peterson would never let anything happen to me."

"Things have a way of going wrong," Alma wailed. "I rue the day Peterson talked you into the folly you now pursue."

"It was my idea, not Peterson's," Olivia reminded her. "He joined me because I was determined to travel the course no matter what." Her chin rose stubbornly. "Besides, I feel no guilt for what I do. The people I steal from are the same ones who fed my father's appetite for debauchery. His so-called good friends made no effort to stop his slide into ruin, even though they were aware that he could ill afford to keep up with them. Fairfax House on Grosvenor Square went to repay Father's gambling debts. If he hadn't bought this run-down townhouse, we would have nowhere to live."

"Is there nothing I can say to stop you?" Alma ventured.

"Nothing. If things work out at the ball, perhaps I may put an end to my night rides."

"I can only hope," Alma sighed.

"Go get your bonnet and shawl, Auntie. We'll visit the dressmaker as soon as I eat something."

Olivia munched on toasted bread and sipped tea as her mind returned to the man who had been riding in the coach last night. He looked like the kind of man she'd sworn to avoid at all costs. A rake if she ever saw one, on his way home from an amorous assignation. How many innocents had he ruined? she wondered in a fit of pique.

Handsome beyond reason, the man had a look of dissipation about him despite the solid length of his body and broad shoulders. She judged him to be a jaded nobleman with a penchant for debauchery. He was just like Lord Palmerson, who had led her father to ruination and an early grave.

Olivia could not help wondering about the man's identity. His coach carried no crest, but he reeked of money and breeding. And that sardonic smile of his had raised the hairs on the back of her neck.

Olivia shrugged off a sudden premonition of doom and finished her breakfast. She had better things to do than fantasize about a man she was unlikely to meet again.

Gabriel paced before his grandmother, the dowager marchioness of Bathurst, hands clasped behind his back, a scowl etched across his brow.

"No need for dramatics, Bathurst," Lady Patrice admonished. "You know how I feel about your providing an heir to inherit the ancestral title and lands. Had your brother lived, I'm sure he would have done his duty."

"Damnation, Grandmama, must you constantly carp about my unmarried state? I'm only thirty. Papa didn't wed until he was five and thirty."

"Leave your dear departed father out of this," Lady Patrice said crisply. "I'm getting on in years and wish to see an heir before I turn up my toes. If you'd stop your carousing you might find a young lady to your liking. I understand the crop of debs entering the marriage mart this year is exceptional."

"Exceptional for what reason, Grandmama?" Gabriel groused. "Exceptionally young? Exceptionally bland and docile? Exceptionally empty-headed? I have no interest in those kinds of women."

Lady Patrice pounded her silver-headed cane on the polished parquet floor with enough force to command Gabriel's attention. "The dowager Countess Stanhope is giving a ball this evening. Everyone who is anyone will be there. I assume you received an invitation."

Gabriel shrugged. "I suppose. Grimsley takes care of those things."

"I expect you to attend," Lady Patrice said in a voice that brooked no argument. "You can look over the young ladies while you're there."

Gabriel loved his grandmother dearly, but she was a bit of a tyrant when it came to ordering his life. Still and all, he wouldn't think of disappointing her. He'd attend the ball, but he had no interest in furthering his matrimonial prospects. Grandmama could lead him to water but she couldn't make him drink.

Gabriel bent and kissed the paper-thin skin of Lady Patrice's cheek. "Very well, Grandmama, I shall attend Lady Stanhope's ball, but don't expect me to find the love of my life there. I'm enjoying myself far too much to let myself be leg-shackled any time soon."

Lady Patrice's dark blue eyes, so like her grandson's, glittered with satisfaction. "You're a good lad, Bathurst. I knew you'd see things my way. By the by," she said, giving him an innocent stare, "have you replaced your last mistress? That actress was hardly up to your usual standards."

Gabriel gave a bark of laughter. "You never cease to amaze me, Grandmama. I am no longer seeing Colette, nor have I found anyone to replace her."

"Don't," Lady Patrice said. "I have a good feeling about tonight. You will stay for tea, won't you?"

"Of course, but I can't stay long. If I'm to attend Lady Stanhope's ball, I should like to bring reinforcements."

"Are you by chance referring to those disreputable cronies of yours? High time they found themselves brides, and long past the time to disband the Rogues of London. Let tongues wag about someone else for a change. I'm heartily sick of hearing about my grandson's escapades. Now sit down while I ring for tea— your constant pacing wearies me."

Gabriel left his grandmother's house an hour later. Climbing into his curricle, he took up the reins and aimed his pair of high-stepping grays toward White's. Braxton and Westmore didn't know it yet, but they were going to a ball.

# Chapter Two

Accompanied by his two friends, Gabriel strolled into the throng of people attending the dowager Countess Stanhope's ball and felt a crushing dread when he noted the overabundance of young women dressed in virginal white, the color worn by every young lady newly come out.

"I don't know why I let you talk me into this," Ramsey complained in an aside to Gabriel. "Look at all the attention we've garnered. This room holds more eager mamas anxious to wed their daughters to titles than I've seen in a long time."

"I'm not looking for a wife," Luc drawled, "and fortunately, no one is goading me to wed. My title isn't important enough to warrant the attention you two get."

"Grandmama means well," Gabriel replied. "She simply cannot understand why I refuse to take a wife."

Ramsey gave a bark of laughter. "Does your grandmother know that you're too busy wenching, to wed? You, Westmore and I are unrepentant rogues. I wouldn't be surprised if we all ended up in perdition when we cock up our toes."

"Then so be it," Gabriel responded. "I'm going to greet Grandmama, then get roaring drunk."

"Isn't that your grandmother talking to the dowager countess?" Luc pointed out.

Gabriel blew out a long-suffering sigh. "Indeed it is. Excuse me, gentlemen, duty calls."

"Oh-oh, here comes Lady Hayworth with her two dowdy daughters in tow," Luc warned before Gabriel had time to escape, "and the indomitable lady has *that* look in her eyes. It's time for me to leave. I'll catch up with you later."

"Coward," Gabriel hissed as Luc beat a hasty retreat, leaving Ram and Gabriel to face Lady Hayworth and her two marriageable daughters.

"Lord Bathurst, Lord Braxton," Lady Hayworth greeted with great gusto. "Was that Lord Westmore I saw hurrying off?"

"Indeed it was," Gabriel replied. "He recalled a previous engagement."

"You remember my daughters, don't you? Honoria, Lucinda, make your curtsey to the marquis and earl."

Gabriel pasted on a pleasant smile. While both ladies were known to him, neither appealed. Honoria was a bit long in the tooth and somewhat plump, while Lucinda, younger and prettier, was as empty-headed as a butterfly. Her fluttering eyelashes and flapping hands utterly exhausted him.

After exchanging a few inane pleasantries, Gabriel took his leave. "Excuse me, ladies, Grandmama requires my attention."

Connie Mason

"I will accompany you, Bathurst," Ram said, "for I have yet to greet our hostess."

"Phew, that was a close one," Gabriel said. "After I speak to Grandmama, I intend to leave. I've made an appearance and fulfilled my commitment. Shall we collect Westmore and head over to Brooks's? There's little here to . . ." His words halted in mid-sentence. "Bloody hell, who is that?"

Gabriel could not help staring at the lady who stood poised in the doorway. Why hadn't he seen her before? Where had she been keeping herself? It was obvious she wasn't new on the marriage mart, for her poise and maturity marked her as a woman well past the first bloom of youth. But her age detracted not at all from her glowing beauty.

Ram followed the direction of Gabriel's gaze. "Well, I'll be damned. Imagine finding Lady Olivia Fairfax here. She's really something, isn't she?"

An understatement, Gabriel thought. Not only was the lady exceptional in every way, but she was also an original with dark red hair and a flawless complexion. Most redheads had pasty complexions and freckles, but Lady Olivia was the exception.

"Is she married? I don't see a husband hovering over her. Is she amenable to taking a lover?"

"Keep your cock in your breeches, Gabriel," Ram advised. "Lady Olivia Fairfax is unmarried. She's the daughter of the late Earl of Sefton."

"I've heard the name but I'm not familiar with him."

"He died rather dishonorably while you were with Wellington on the Peninsula."

"Dishonorably?"

"He dueled over a prostitute working Covent Garden. Rather stupid of him, but the man's sense deserted

20

him after the death of his wife. Unfortunately, certain of his friends took advantage of him. 'Tis said he left a mountain of debt for his young son and daughter to resolve."

"They must have done well by themselves. Lady Fairfax and her companion are decked out in the latest fashion."

"Her companion is Lady Alma Fairfax, spinster sister to the deceased Lord Sefton, her brother. She stepped in and raised Sefton's children after their mother's death."

"Why hasn't Lady Olivia wed? It's beyond imagining that a woman of her great beauty should remain unmarried this long."

"No dowry," Ramsey said, shrugging. "I understand Doncaster went through the family fortune, including his daughter's dowry. After his debts were paid, there was barely enough left to keep them in genteel poverty and send the young heir to Oxford. This is all hearsay, you understand, for no one knows the exact state of the family's finances. The lady rarely attends society functions."

"Do you know her?"

"I've met her."

"Introduce me. If she needs a protector, I'm her man."

Ram grinned. "Thinking with your cock again, are you? Virgins are off limits to men like us. You don't want to end up leg-shackled, do you?"

"You're assuming the lady is virginal, Ram," Gabriel said. "Just because there's been no gossip about her doesn't mean she hasn't taken lovers. Look. Isn't that Lord Palmerson sniffing around her? They appear to know one another quite well. If she's acquainted with that odious bastard, she can't be as pure as you think. Didn't he get some merchant's daughter with child and refuse to marry her? Killed herself, didn't she?"

"That's the rumor."

"Despite her obvious friendship with Palmerson, I want to meet her. Introduce me."

Trying to keep the contempt from her expression, Olivia let her gaze range over the crush of people in Her Grace's elegant ballroom. "This is going to be easy," she said in an aside to her aunt. "There are so many people milling about that when the time comes, my short disappearance is unlikely to rouse suspicion."

"I wish you wouldn't do this, dear. What if you're caught? What if—"

"Don't worry, Auntie, I'll be careful. We need the money, and this is the only way. Let's go greet our hostess."

"Olivia, my dear, what a pleasant surprise."

Olivia suppressed a groan. Palmerson was the last person she wanted to see. He made her skin crawl. "Lord Palmerson," she said curtly.

"I've been thinking about you, Olivia. When are you going to accept my proposal? I still have the special license I procured when I first proposed. Your refusals grow tiresome."

"I haven't changed my mind, my lord. I have no intention of marrying you."

Palmerson raked a slim hand through his slick hair and regarded Olivia coldly. "That surprises me. I know Sefton squandered your dowry. I'm your only hope of having a husband and family."

"You could have stopped my father's decline had you wanted to," Olivia replied with icy disdain.

"Why do you continue to blame me for your father's death? He brought about his own downfall. There was nothing I could do to stop him."

"So you say. But you were his friend; you should have helped him."

"That's water under the bridge, Olivia. There's a quadrille beginning—shall we dance?"

"No, I—"

Palmerson gave her no opportunity to decline, hooking her arm beneath his and literally dragging her onto the crowded dance floor. She glanced back at her aunt, saw her swaying dizzily and tried to break away from Palmerson to go to her aid, but he swept her off into the dance. From the corner of her eye, she saw a man place a steadying hand against her aunt's waist.

That one brief glimpse was enough to freeze the blood in Olivia's veins. It was *him*, the man whose coach she had robbed! Damnation! What rotten luck. Then calm prevailed once more as she recalled that he had no reason to suspect her.

"Relax, Olivia, I'm not going to bite you."

"Lady Olivia to you," she reprimanded. "Familiarity breeds contempt, my lord."

"We are old friends, Olivia. We've known one another for many years." He leaned close. "We would be more than friends should you agree to be my wife."

Mercifully, the dance ended. "Shall we step outside for a breath of air?" Palmerson said.

"No, thank you," Olivia replied. "My aunt needs me. She doesn't look at all well."

She walked swiftly toward her aunt, stopping abruptly when she saw Alma chatting with *that* man. A second man she vaguely recognized was with him. Olivia wanted to turn and run, but a glance over her

23

shoulder provided her with a view of Palmerson advancing toward her. She had no choice but to seek out her aunt if she wished to avoid further contact with Palmerson. She would just have to make sure she gave the disturbing man from the coach no reason to suspect she was the thief who had robbed him.

When she arrived at her aunt's side, both men turned to her with expectant looks, but only one commanded her attention. In the light of hundreds of candles, his ruggedly handsome face showed none of the dissipation she'd noted on the night of the robbery. His broad shoulders strained at the seams of his superfine dark blue coat, and his tight buff breeches left nothing of his anatomy to the imagination. His midnight-black hair was several shades darker than his dark blue eyes, and his brows had an unmistakable aristocratic arch to them.

He reeked of arrogance and debauchery; he was the kind of man she neither liked nor trusted. His friend was as handsome and appeared as jaded as he. Though he looked familiar, she couldn't recall his name.

"Olivia, dear," Aunt Alma began, "you remember Lord Braxton, don't you? We met him a year ago at the Eggerlys' rout. And the gentleman with him is Lord Gabriel Wellsby, the Marquis of Bathurst. Lord Bathurst, my niece, Lady Olivia Fairfax."

She had robbed a marquis, Olivia thought, gulping back a lump of dismay as she offered a slightly shaking hand to Lord Bathurst. In the manner of a perfect gentleman, he took her hand and bowed over it, but the way he teased her palm with his fingertips was beyond unsettling. Olivia felt the heat of his breath through the thin material of her glove and snatched her hand away before her trembling undid her.

"They're playing a waltz, Lady Olivia; would you honor me with a dance?"

Olivia was surprised that the very proper dowager dutchess would allow the controversial waltz to be played at her ball. It was still considered risqué, and she hadn't bothered to learn the steps.

"I'm sorry, my lord, I'm not familiar with the steps," Olivia demurred.

"They're simple really, just follow me."

Without so much as a by your leave, he placed an arm about her waist and swept her onto the dance floor. He held her close—much too close for Olivia's peace of mind.

"You have the most unusual green eyes," Gabriel said as he whirled her into a turn that caused her to stumble.

She clutched his shoulder more tightly as his strong arm steadied her. "Don't fret, a little misstep isn't a catastrophe. Follow me. One, two, three—turn. One, two, three—turn. That's it," he said when she fell into the rhythm. "You have a natural feel for dancing."

Nearly breathless and caught up in the music, Olivia did not reply.

"Have we met before, Lady Olivia?" Gabriel asked, staring intently into her eyes.

"I attend few society events," Olivia said, finally finding her voice. "I doubt we have met before."

"Strange," he mused. "I could have sworn—"

"You are mistaken," Olivia said curtly.

His arm tightened around her waist, and she felt the alarming brush of his leg between her thighs as he executed a smooth turn. Though his move was not overtly sexual and in accordance with the dance, Olivia felt a tug in forbidden regions of her body. When she'd danced with Palmerson she'd felt nothing but revulsion, but Bathurst was not Palmerson and revulsion was definitely not what she was experiencing. The pressure of his hard male body against hers was disconcerting.

"Do you know Palmerson well?" Gabriel asked.

Olivia blinked. "What? What did you say?" What was Bathurst implying?

"Palmerson—is he an intimate friend?"

Olivia tripped over his foot, but Bathurst's strong arms remained firm and steady about her. Anger soared and she tried to pull away, but his implacable grip on her waist held her firmly in place. She had naught but words with which to flay him. "How dare you! If you're implying what I think you are, you couldn't be more wrong."

"Forgive me, my lady, I didn't mean to be impertinent."

Olivia gazed up into the rakish marquis's face and saw not one particle of remorse. The man was impossibly arrogant. He deserved to be robbed. During the rest of the waltz she remained stubbornly mute, holding her body stiff and refusing to look at him.

"Are you angry with me?" Gabriel asked with a hint of amusement.

"Not at all," Olivia lied. "I'm not some emptyheaded young chit who can't tell an unrepentant rake from a gentleman."

"How many unrepentant rakes besides Palmerson do you know, Lady Olivia?"

"Only one, Lord Bathurst," Olivia replied, looking directly into his eyes.

To her mortification, the handsome marquis threw back his head and laughed. "Touché, my lady. Well done."

Before Olivia had time to congratulate herself on her glibness, Bathurst swept her out the open French doors onto the balcony. She came to rest against the railing in a dark corner, hemmed in by Bathurst's impeccably attired form.

"You looked as if you needed a breath of air," Gabriel said with aplomb.

"You're mistaken," Olivia replied coolly. "Return me to the ballroom immediately. My aunt will worry if I am missing."

She tried to duck around him, but he trapped her against the railing with his arms braced on either side of her. "I'll let you go if you answer one simple question, Lady Olivia."

Olivia had no choice but to accede. She could only hope his question had nothing to do with the robbery. It didn't.

"Are you as innocent as you claim?"

"How dare you!" she cried as she swung her hand back and delivered a well-aimed blow to his face. He reeled backward but did not release her.

"What have I done to deserve this kind of cavalier treatment from you?" Olivia demanded. "Why would you ask such an insulting question?"

"I want to be your lover," Gabriel returned, "and I avoid virgins like a plague. I saw you talking to Palmerson. His unsavory reputation surpasses even mine." He shrugged. "I just assumed—"

"You assume too much," Olivia protested.

Gabriel stared into Olivia's angry green eyes and felt a strange sense of familiarity. Something tugged at his memory, but the sensation was too vague to retrieve. He had gazed into those same emerald-hued eyes before, he was sure of it. Where? When? Gabriel knew he

27

was acting like an unprincipled ass, but he couldn't seem to help himself. There was something about Olivia Fairfax that brought out the worst in him.

Her smooth shoulders gleamed enticingly in the moonlight, and the empire waist of her green and gold muslin gown served to enhance the firm contours of her perfect breasts. If she was following the dictates of current fashion, she would be wearing nothing but a single petticoat beneath the low-necked gown. The heady thought of how few layers of clothing separated them sent a surge of hot blood to his loins.

Gabriel wanted her. Why did this woman seem so familiar? Damn and blast! Why did she have to be an innocent? Or was she? She'd never really given him an answer. With marked reluctance, he removed his arms from the railing and stepped away.

"Once again, I beg your forgiveness, Lady Olivia. I've never encountered a woman who fires my blood as you do. You're a lady, and I've treated you with disrespect, but you cannot truly blame me. You're exceptionally beautiful and even more intriguing, Lady Olivia."

"Surely you jest, my lord. I had a Season several years ago and am considered on the shelf. Turn your dubious attentions on one of the young things looking for a husband. I have no dowry and no prospects, and am quite satisfied with my life."

"And no lovers," a perverse devil made Gabriel add. "Too bad. I understand you're in financial straits. I could help if you were looking for a protector."

"I can protect myself, thank you," Olivia huffed as she moved cautiously away. If she wasn't mistaken, the marquis had just asked her to be his mistress. The man's insolence knew no bounds.

With a sniff of disdain, Olivia sidled around him and

all but ran through the French doors into the crowded ballroom. She had a mission and no one was going to stop her, especially not a presumptuous rogue like Bathurst.

Olivia found Aunt Alma sitting on the sidelines with a group of matrons looking over the husband material for their daughters. Alma rose at once and pulled Olivia into an alcove.

"Where did you get off to, Livvy? I saw you dancing with Lord Bathurst, but then you disappeared. I was beginning to worry, especially after what I learned about the marquis."

Olivia's attention sharpened. "What did you learn, Auntie?"

"The man is an insensitive rogue, a gambler and womanizer. He came into his title when his older brother drowned in a boating accident. Bathurst was with Wellington on the Peninsula. He's a war hero, I'm told. He had intended to make the army his career until he was called home following the death of his brother. Rumor has it that Bathurst didn't want the title, but he had no choice. His brother left a wife but no heir."

"It doesn't take a seer to recognize Bathurst for what he is," Olivia observed.

"I spoke briefly with his grandmother, the dowager marchioness. She's worried about him and his unwillingness to provide an heir for the title. Do be careful, dear. I fear he's set his lustful sights on you. Since he seems unwilling to wed, his attentions cannot be honorable."

"Don't worry, Auntie, I can take care of myself."

"That's not all," Alma whispered. "They say he won't wed because he's in love with his brother's wife. That he joined the army because the woman he loved spurned him and wed his brother. Bathurst hasn't vis-

29

ited the ancestral estate in Derbyshire or his sister-in-law since he returned home three years ago."

"Bathurst doesn't seem the type to pine over a lost love," Olivia scoffed.

"I'm inclined to agree, dear, but people will talk." She leaned closer. "The marquis is one of the infamous Rogues of London, those scandalous men we've read about in the broadsheets."

"My observation is that the marquis is a natural-born hell-raiser, probably incapable of telling right from wrong. I seriously doubt he's in love with his brother's widow. I think he has no heart, and even fewer scruples."

Alma gave her a strange look. "Did the marquis insult you, dear Livvy?"

"You may as well know, Auntie. It was the marquis's coach Peterson and I robbed."

Alma swayed and hissed out a breath, her eyes wide with panic.

"Steady, Auntie, Bathurst didn't recognize me. He has no reason to believe I am anything but what I appear to be."

"His presence here changes everything," Alma said in a quavering voice. "We must leave immediately."

"It changes nothing, Auntie. Neville's quarterly fees to the university are due, and the roof won't fix itself. I have to do this."

"Are you sure there's no other way?"

"We've exhausted that subject, Auntie. Go back to the ladies and enjoy yourself."

"What are you going to do?"

The question answered itself when a young man approached Olivia, requesting a dance. She graciously accepted and was led out onto the dance floor. While going through the steps with her partner, she felt a prickling sensation at the back of her neck and saw Bathurst standing on the sidelines, staring at her with a puzzled look on his face. She danced several more dances with different partners, then suddenly found herself facing Bathurst again. He sent the young men hanging about her a lowering look, and they scattered like leaves before the wind.

"I've requested another waltz and can think of no one I would rather share it with than you," he said, bowing before her.

"I've decided to sit out the next dance," Olivia snapped. She turned to leave and found the dowager Dutchess Stanhope blocking her way.

"Olivia, my dear, how delightful that you came," the dowager said with barbed enthusiasm. "We rarely see you out and about these days. Tell me," she said, leaning forward, her eyes avid with curiosity, "where did you find the funds to purchase those lovely gowns you and your aunt are wearing? Did you rob a bank? Or better yet, find a wealthy protector? Is Palmerson still panting after you?"

Olivia wanted to fall through the floor. If the dowager's purpose was to insult her before the marquis, she had succeeded. "Aunt Alma and I manage quite nicely with what Papa left us, but thank you for your concern," Olivia answered sweetly. "Excuse me, I simply must rest my feet," she added as she beat a hasty retreat.

Gabriel watched Olivia hurry away, an amused look on his face.

"She's hopelessly on the shelf, you know," the dowager said with a hint of malice. "Her father's unsavory reputation and her lack of dowry make her quite unsuitable."

"I was away from England during the war years and am not familiar with Lady Olivia's family."

"Lord Sefton could have wed me after his wife died, but he chose a life of debauchery instead. I understand he left his family quite penniless but for a small yearly stipend. I don't know how Olivia manages to keep the family solvent."

Gabriel recognized malicious intent when he heard it; obviously, the dowager was taking out her frustrations with the father on the daughter. Why had Olivia Fairfax attended the ball if she was so reviled by the hostess? he wondered. How many potential husbands had the dowager scared off with gossip about Olivia's father and financial affairs?

"Lady Olivia and her aunt are dressed in the height of fashion," Gabriel remarked. "Perhaps you are mistaken about her lack of funds."

"Humph! 'Tis unlikely, my lord. I am up on all the current gossip. As for you, Bathurst, your unsavory reputation is hurting your chances to wed. Your grandmama is most distressed over the situation."

A flash of anger darkened Gabriel's eyes. "I am aware of my grandmother's sentiments. As you probably guessed, I'm here only because she asked me to attend." He inclined his head. "If you'll excuse me—"

Without waiting for a reply, he strode off. Pausing in the doorway, he scanned the crowd for Olivia and failed to find her. She wasn't on the dance floor or with her aunt. He didn't see Palmerson either, and wondered if they were together. For some reason, the thought of Olivia and Palmerson together made him angry.

Was Palmerson Olivia's lover? If she was, Gabriel would have no qualms about pursuing the lady. He wanted the redheaded hellion in his bed and would stop at nothing to get her there. Since he had no intention of marrying and wasn't looking for a wife, her lack of dowry was of no concern.

Not even Gabriel's best friends were aware of his reasons for remaining unwed. They thought, along with everyone who knew him, that he was in love with his brother's widow, but that wasn't the case at all. As long as it suited his purposes, he let the story stand. He did care for Cissy, but only as a sister-in-law. He allowed her to live at Bathurst Park because he didn't have the heart to turn her out. His reasons for avoiding marriage were far more complex.

Unable to locate Olivia in the crowd, Gabriel decided to bid his grandmother farewell before he departed. Then he spotted Olivia leaving the ballroom, and everything else fled from his mind. She appeared nervous, looking over her shoulder and moving quickly. Gabriel was suddenly sure she was meeting Palmerson at a previously designated location for an intimate tryst.

Gabriel didn't want to believe it of her. She had turned down his proposal—why would she accept Palmerson's? One good reason came to mind. Palmerson was willing to marry her, while his own intentions were less honorable.

The moment Olivia disappeared out the door, Gabriel pursued her. He saw her ascending the staircase and hung back until she reached the top landing. Surprised at his own curiosity, Gabriel followed. He saw her enter a chamber and stopped abruptly, wondering if he really wanted to know what was going on inside.

He wanted to know.

# Connie Mason

Gabriel made no attempt at stealth as he rattled the doorknob before opening the door. He saw her immediately, and the look on her face when she saw him was priceless. Surprise. Shock. Incredulity. Anger.

He remembered to breathe again when he saw she was alone, standing before an ornate chest in what appeared to be a lady's bedchamber.

Her eyes were wide with alarm as she rounded on him. "What are you doing here?"

Gabriel leaned negligently against the doorjamb, his arms folded over his chest. "I might ask the same of you. Hasn't he shown up yet?"

"*He?* Who, pray tell, are you talking about?"

"You're meeting Palmerson here, aren't you?"

Her stunned expression told him he was way off the mark. But what other reason could she have for slipping off alone?

"You're despicable!" Olivia charged. "What made you think I was meeting a man?"

Gabriel shrugged. "What else was I to think?"

"That I was looking for the ladies' retiring room. My feet hurt, and I wanted to rest."

Gabriel made a slow perusal of the ornately furnished bedchamber, his disbelief clearly evidenced by the elegant arch of one dark brow. "If I were to hazard a guess, I'd say this is Lady Stanhope's bedchamber."

Though Olivia appeared flustered, Gabriel thought she recovered with admirable aplomb. "I lost my way. This is a large house, and the directions to the ladies' retiring room were unclear. I'd best leave and find someone who can direct me."

Instead of allowing her to brush past him, he snagged her about the waist and dragged her into his arms. Her sweet, flowery scent, the pressure of her lightly clad

34

body, her lush mouth so close to his, sent common sense fleeing. Pressing her against the solid length of his hardening body, he lowered his mouth and kissed her, using his tongue to prod her lips open so he could taste her.

Her soft breasts seemed to beg for his touch, but when he slid a hand around to caress a pouting nipple, she twisted away, staring at him as if he were the embodiment of sin.

"Why did you do that?"

Gabriel shrugged. "I couldn't resist."

Green eyes flashed. "Because you're a rogue and a debaucher of women."

Gabriel stared into those angry green orbs and experienced another strong tug of familiarity. "Are you sure we've never met before?"

Olivia stifled a cry with the back of her hand and fled.

# Chapter Three

Nothing was going right, Olivia silently groused as she reentered the ballroom and sought out her aunt. It was time to leave; nothing more could be gained from tonight's debacle. Olivia rued the day Lord Bathurst had stepped from the coach and into her life. Though she was sure he didn't associate her with the highwayman Ollie, she couldn't explain his uncanny ability to recognize something familiar about her.

Olivia found Alma and suggested it was time to leave. Her aunt sensed Olivia's distress and quickly agreed.

"I'll make our excuses to the duchess while you get our wraps and summon the hackney," Alma said. "Are you all right, dear? You look shaken. Did something go wrong?"

"Everything went wrong, Auntie. I'll explain later. Go find Her Grace; I'll meet you in the foyer."

Olivia hurried off, anxious to leave before Bathurst

intercepted her. She hated to think of the consequences if he should recognize Ollie in her.

Lord Ramsey Braxton spied Gabriel striding into the ballroom with a determined expression on his face. Now what was he up to? Ram wondered. He had no reason to connect Lady Olivia's sudden departure with his friend's dour countenance as Gabriel spied him and hurried over.

"Have you seen Lady Olivia?" Gabriel asked tersely.

"She and her aunt just left," Ram replied.

"Damn," Gabriel muttered as he hurried off, leaving his friend with his mouth gaping open.

Gabriel ran down the long flight of stairs and out the door just as the coach carrying the woman he sought pulled away from the curb.

"What in blazes is the matter with you?" Ram asked from behind him. "What did you say to Lady Olivia to make her flee in such haste?"

"What makes you think I said anything?"

"You both went missing at the same time, then returned to the ballroom from the same direction. I know you, Bathurst. We've been friends a long time. Lady Olivia is not your type."

"Are you ready to leave?" Gabriel asked, ignoring Ram's rebuke.

"I thought you'd never ask," Ram said with a sigh of relief. "Luc already left. He said he'd meet us at Brooks's."

"Let's go, then. You can tell me all you know about Lady Olivia in the coach."

"You're beginning to worry me, Bathurst," Ram said. "Lady Olivia is off limits to men like us."

"You don't understand, Ram, and to tell the truth, neither do I. There's something . . . something about her that reminds me of someone. Until I learn who, I can't let it rest."

"What did Lord Bathurst say to you?" Aunt Alma asked once she and Olivia had safely returned home. "Did he recognize you? Oh, my dear child, whatever will we do?"

Olivia knew she had been deliberately uncommunicative during the ride home but she'd needed to think. Meeting Lord Bathurst at the ball had thoroughly unsettled her. The marquis was an unconscionable rake; he had brazenly asked her to become his mistress without one whit of shame. Shock had rendered her nearly speechless when he'd asked if she was an innocent. A gentleman wouldn't speak so disrespectfully to a lady, but obviously, Bathurst was no gentleman.

Should he recognize her as the highwayman, Olivia was reasonably certain he would turn her over to the law, and that frightened her. Never had she felt so vulnerable. Discovery would ruin her family.

Olivia sought to reassure her aunt despite her own bleak view of their future.

"It's not as bad as you think, Auntie. I'll admit meeting Bathurst was a shock, but I'm positive he didn't recognize me. There will be no more balls or public outings for the time being, however. I cannot let him see me again."

"Oh, dear, however will we survive?"

"Pete and Ollie will ride again," Olivia said. "Only next time we'll pick our marks more carefully. Go to bed, Auntie. I'll be up directly."

Muttering to herself about sin and perdition, Alma

took one of the two candlesticks from the hall table and slowly ascended the stairs. Olivia picked up the other candlestick and walked into the kitchen. She wasn't surprised to find Peterson waiting for her.

"It didn't go as I expected," Olivia said.

He sent her a sharp look. "What happened?"

Olivia plopped into a chair and dropped her head into her hands. "Nothing went right. The whole evening was a disaster from beginning to end. All that money spent on gowns for Auntie and myself, and for what? We could have used the cash to repair the roof. I fear we don't have enough pots to place under the leaks the next time it rains."

More trusted friend than servant, Peterson patted Olivia on the shoulder in an awkward attempt to comfort her. "Tell me, Miss Livvy."

"*He* was there."

"He? Who?"

"He's a marquis. Lord Bathurst, the man from the coach we robbed."

"That shouldn't worry you," Peterson scoffed. "There's no way he could associate you with Ollie. You're an earl's daughter with an unsullied reputation."

"I'm not sure about that," Olivia replied.

Olivia recalled Bathurst's reaction to Palmerson and his mistaken conclusion about their relationship, and fervently wished she had stayed home.

"Shall Pete and Ollie ride again, Miss Livvy?"

"I see no help for it," Olivia answered. "You've been with us a long time, Peterson; I think of you as family. Placing your life in danger was never my intention. I won't ask this of you, it has to be your decision."

Peterson's sagging chin firmed. "When do we ride?"

"Soon. If we're lucky, we'll find a rich lord and his

wife returning from a social event at one of the grand manor houses on the outskirts of London."

"Did you receive Lord and Lady Barrow's invitation to a party at their country manor Saturday next, Bathurst?" Luc asked over lunch with Gabriel and Ram at White's several days later.

"Grimsley called my attention to it just this morning."

"You're going, aren't you?" Ram asked. "Lady Barrow would be disappointed if her favorite cocksman didn't show up."

Gabriel's dark eyes crinkled with amusement. "I thought you held that title."

"We've all tupped the lady at one time or another," Luc observed, "but you're still her favorite."

"I suppose I should put in an appearance," Gabriel said. "What about you two?"

"I'm going," Ram returned.

"Oh, well, as long as you two are going, I'll just tag along," Luc said. "Shall we share a coach?"

"Let's take mine," Ram suggested. "Just purchased a pair of high-stepping bays at Tattersall's and want to try them out on the turnpike."

They agreed on a time and parted. Gabriel's grandmother had sent a note asking that he call on her, and he tooled his curricle around the park in a misty rain to her elegant townhouse in Mayfair. Huntly, Lady Patrice's ancient butler, directed Gabriel to the drawing room, where the elderly lady sat before the fire, a lap rug spread across her legs and a book propped against her chest.

"So good of you to come, Bathurst," she said. "Such nasty weather we're having."

"You didn't bring me here to talk about the weather, Grandmama. What have I done now?"

"Did any of the young ladies at the dowager's ball capture your attention?"

"There were many lovely young ladies present," Gabriel said cautiously.

"But none who appealed," she guessed.

"You know my views on marriage, Grandmama. Why do you continue to press me?"

Lady Patrice shook her perfectly coifed white head with sad resignation. "My dear boy, what can I say to change your mind? You had loving parents, so you cannot blame them for your aversion to marriage. What is the difficulty?"

"I don't wish to wed," Gabriel said through clenched teeth.

"I don't like your tone of voice, Bathurst."

"Forgive me, Grandmama, but I find all this talk of marriage tiresome."

"I saw you dancing with Lady Olivia Fairfax," she remarked. "I hope you have no aspirations in that direction. She's a nice enough gel, I suppose, but too old, and her lack of dowry put her on the shelf years ago."

For some reason, those words rubbed Gabriel the wrong way. "If Lady Olivia interested me, her lack of dowry wouldn't matter. Neither would her age, which seems just about right to me."

"Really?" his grandmother said with a definite sparkle in her voice. "How interesting."

"If I *were* interested, which I'm not. Is there anything else you wanted, Grandmama?"

"I understand the Barrows are giving a lavish house party at their country estate Saturday next. I suppose you and your dissolute friends will attend, since you are all on such intimate terms with Lady Barrow." She wagged her head. "Lord Barrow's failure to curtail his wife's extramarital affairs is appalling."

"Grandmama—"

"No, dear boy, I won't chide you for your involvement with the lady, for I wouldn't dream of dictating to you."

Gabriel rolled his eyes. "Of course you wouldn't, Grandmama." He kissed her wrinkled cheek. "Take good care of yourself. You and Cissy are all I have left."

"Ah, yes, Cissy. Now I recall why I asked you to attend me. I received a letter from her just yesterday. You have woefully neglected her and Bathurst Park since your return to England. You haven't answered her letters, and she asked me to convey a message. She wants you to visit her."

"Did she say why?"

"No, but I'm aware of your fondness for Cissy and cannot understand your reluctance to return to the family estate. I do wish you would set aside your aversion to Bathurst Park and pay Cissy a visit."

Gabriel lowered his gaze. "I have no desire to return to the ancestral estate."

"Is the gossip true, then? Is Cissy the reason you refuse to wed? Are you in love with your brother's widow?"

"Do I look like I'm pining for want of love, Grandmama?"

Lady Patrice regarded him through myopic eyes. "Something is eating at you, dear boy. If it's not Cissy, what is it? Something or someone has turned you against marriage."

"I have to leave, Grandmama. Don't worry about me. I like my life just the way it is."

So Cissy wished to see him, Gabriel mused as he left his grandmother's townhouse. He should have visited her after his return from France but he couldn't bring himself to return to his boyhood home. He had a good steward in Winthorpe and received reports regularly, so he saw no reason to leave London. The excitement of city life suited him; he was never bored, never lacked for companionship, male or female. London was where he belonged.

Gabriel was far from bored as his thoughts turned to the Lady Olivia, the redheaded hellion who had haunted his dreams since Lady Stanhope's ball. Though he had racked his brain, he still couldn't recall where he had met her before—and he *had* met her, he'd stake his life on it. Yet every time he tried to retrieve her image from some buried memory, it eluded him. One day, he promised himself; one day it would come to him.

"The Barrows are having a grand party Saturday next at their country estate, Miss Livvy," Peterson said. "It came direct from their Town housekeeper, who told the Presleys' butler, who told Mrs. Hamilton."

"Our cook?"

"Aye, Miss Livvy. Mrs. Hamilton told me herself. There should be some easy pickings on the road after the party."

The way things were going lately, nothing would be easy, Olivia reflected sourly. But she had no alternative.

"Very well, Peterson, let's do it."

"I'll take care of everything, Miss Livvy. You can depend on me."

\* \* \*

43

Gabriel strolled into the Barrows' library to get away from the other guests and examined the shelves of books lining the wall. He had arrived at the Barrow country estate yesterday afternoon with Luc and Ram and was already bored. A decanter of brandy and glasses sat on a sideboard, and he helped himself. He shouldn't have come, he reflected. He wasn't in the mood for Leslie's shenanigans, nor did he feel comfortable with her cuckold of a husband keeping tabs on her.

Gabriel grimaced with distaste as he recalled how Leslie had draped herself around him when he'd found himself alone with her in the upstairs gallery. Tupping the sensuous Leslie while her husband was away was one thing, but cuckolding the earl while he was in residence went beyond even Gabriel's morals.

Besides, Gabriel thought grumpily, he couldn't banish Lady Olivia from his mind long enough to let Leslie in. There was something eerily familiar about the green-eyed hellion. But close observation of her face and figure revealed nothing concrete upon which to base his theory. He felt as if he were going mad—mad with wanting a woman who should be off limits to him. He blew out an exasperated breath and took another long swallow of Lord Barrow's excellent brandy.

"Bathurst, what in the world are you doing in here alone? I've been looking all over for you." Lady Leslie Barrow turned a contemptuous look at the shelves of books, then bestowed a provocative smile on Gabriel. "Can't you find anything more exciting to do than read?"

"I needed a moment alone," Gabriel replied.

Leslie locked the library door and sidled up to him. Gabriel watched her through shuttered eyes. Should she exhale too deeply, her ample breasts would fall out of her low-necked bodice. While the gown was fashioned in the latest style, it had been dampened, along with her chemise, to reveal the curvaceous figure beneath.

Leslie wound her arms around Gabriel's neck and pressed her body against his in blatant invitation. "Edmond has taken some of the guests to view the lake and swans—we are finally alone."

"This isn't a good idea, Leslie," Gabriel replied, carefully removing her arms and stepping away. "Not with Edmond so close at hand."

"Good God, Gabriel, don't tell me you've suddenly developed scruples and a conscience."

*What I developed was a yen for green-eyed redheads.* "You know me better than that, Leslie, but this is neither the time nor place to indulge ourselves. You have a house filled with guests who demand your attention, and besides, my friends are doubtless looking for me as we speak."

"Another time, then," Leslie said, somewhat mollified. "I'm returning to Town soon. Edmond wants to take the waters at Bath, and I convinced him to go alone. I'll let you know when it's safe to call upon me."

"Do that," Gabriel said with a lack of enthusiasm that Leslie appeared not to notice.

Damn Lady Olivia Fairfax! Nothing Leslie had to offer interested him, and it was all Olivia's fault.

Gabriel suffered through the rest of the day and the next, alleviating his boredom with hunting in the morning and talking business with his peers during the afternoon preceding the grand ball Leslie had planned for that evening. Gabriel suggested, and Luc and Ram agreed, that they should leave immediately following the midnight supper instead of remaining at Barrow

Manor another night, as some of the guests were doing.

"What's wrong with you, Bathurst?" Ram asked. "Why aren't you off somewhere with Lady Barrow? Or losing heavily at cards? Or drinking with your usual gusto? Are you ill?"

Gabriel frowned. He must be acting completely out of character. "I'm fine, Braxton. Perhaps I've become too jaded to enjoy these tame amusements."

"They don't have to be tame," Ram observed. "Lady Barrow has been eyeing you all evening. I'm sure you two could meet clandestinely before the midnight supper. Go make her happy."

"Not tonight," Gabriel muttered. "I'm not in the mood."

Ram's brow furrowed. "Now I *am* worried."

Gabriel laughed. "Am I so depraved that my lack of desire for clandestine sex rouses your suspicion?"

Ram shrugged. "What else am I to think? Unless . . . have you set your sights on another woman? Are you still panting after Lady Olivia?"

"I never pant," Gabriel said, offended. "I'll admit Lady Olivia is enticing, but you of all people should know I'm not looking for a wife. Dallying with Lady Olivia would seal my fate."

"I am in complete agreement with you about holy matrimony," Ram allowed. "I know you have your reasons, just as I have mine. Would you care to share them?"

"Would you be willing to share yours?"

His lips clamped together tightly, Ram shook his head. Gabriel wasn't surprised at Ram's reaction; he felt much the same. The demons that drove him were private, to be shared with no one. He'd told no one his reasons for remaining unwed, not even Grandmama.

"I thought not," Gabriel said smugly. "Lady Leslie is sending me signals again. I may as well dance with her. I wouldn't want to burn my bridges when I have nothing waiting for me on the other side."

"You should take another mistress, Bathurst. You've had a dry spell since you gave that actress her congé."

"I'm considering it, Ram. If you see anyone you think would suit, let me know. Excuse me, the next set is forming and Leslie is without a partner."

Gabriel and Ram were nearly asleep as their coach rocketed down the turnpike to Town. Gabriel's head lolled against the squabs while Ram sprawled out beside him. After the midnight supper they had taken leave of their host and hostess and headed back to London. Luc had made an assignation with the promiscuous Lady Barbara Silvers and decided to spend the night in her bed, and had remained behind.

Ram's high-stepping bays were eating up the road despite the rain and fog and quarter moon that scudded behind the clouds, leaving a night as black as the inside of hell. Neither Gabriel nor Ram was worried about highwaymen, for only hardy souls would venture out on so dismal a night.

A shot roused Gabriel from a light doze; then the coach ground to a halt. "Bloody hell, not again," Gabriel cursed, shaking himself awake. This time he was ready.

Ram was slower to awaken. "Why have we stopped?"

"Highwaymen," Gabriel hissed. "Do you have a weapon? After my last encounter with them I always load and prime my pistol before venturing out."

"I have my pistol right here," Ram said, reaching into

47

a hidden space between the squabs. "Never leave home without it. It will only take a moment to load and—"

The moment escaped him as the door banged open and two highwaymen appeared in the opening. "Outside, both of you."

Gabriel recognized that voice despite the muffler pulled up over the highwayman's nose and mouth. What bloody rotten luck!

The highwayman spied Ram's pistol and barked, "Toss your weapon out the door."

"Do it," Gabriel hissed in an aside to Ram. Ram obeyed, albeit grudgingly.

"Get out!" the highwayman ordered.

Ram exited first, followed by Gabriel. As Gabriel stepped through the door onto the wet ground, he heard a sudden intake of breath and stared into the highwayman's shocked face.

"You!" the highwayman gasped.

"I didn't think we'd meet again so soon," Gabriel drawled as he took advantage of the highwayman's distraction and slid his pistol into his hand.

"Do you have a weapon concealed on your person?" the highwayman asked.

"Not this time, Ollie."

"Search him, Pete," Ollie said.

Gabriel raised his arms, concealing the small pistol in his palm while Pete searched his pockets.

"He's unarmed, Ollie."

Ram appeared startled by Gabriel's use of the highwaymen's names. "Are these the same highwaymen who robbed you several weeks ago?"

"The very same," Gabriel said.

"Where's my driver?" Ram asked.

48

"Right here, milord," the driver called out. "All tied up right and proper, I am."

"No one will get hurt if you do as we say." The highwayman shoved a cloth sack beneath their noses. "Empty your pockets and place your valuables in the sack."

Cursing bitterly, Ram tossed his purse into the sack.

"Your jewelry, too. Rings, watches, shirt studs, everything."

Gabriel obeyed the gruff order as he divested himself of his valuables with his left hand while keeping the pistol concealed in his right. He watched both highwaymen closely, waiting for the opportunity to discharge his pistol without endangering himself or Braxton. Getting killed for a paltry sum of money and a few baubles was a senseless waste of life. But he wanted the highwaymen . . . wanted them bad, especially the younger one.

Ollie tossed the sack of loot to Pete. "Get out of here, Pete. I'll stay behind and keep these two covered."

"Not on your life, Ollie. We leave together."

Ollie shot a glance at Pete, then started backing away toward a waiting horse. Gabriel's hand tightened on his pistol, ready to aim and fire the moment the highwaymen turned their backs. The opportunity arrived when the robbers mounted their horses. With remarkable speed, Gabriel took aim at Pete and fired.

As luck would have it, Pete's horse moved forward and it was Ollie, not Pete, who appeared in Gabriel's sights. A high-pitched cry, not at all what one would expect from a rough thief, sent chills racing down Gabriel's back. Ollie slumped over the saddle, and Gabriel spit out a curse. He didn't feel good about this, not at all.

49

"You got him, Bathurst!" Ram shouted.

Gabriel started to sprint toward the wounded highwayman, but Pete brought his pistol around, stopping Gabriel in his tracks.

"Stop right there! Are you all right, Ollie?" Pete called. "Can you ride?"

Ollie's voice was strained, and Gabriel could tell the thief was hanging on to consciousness by a slim thread. Gabriel's instinct was to go to the outlaw's aid, but common sense told him it was no more than the culprit deserved.

Ollie merely grunted as Pete grasped the wounded highwayman's reins and galloped off down the road.

Olivia hung on to the horse's mane for dear life. The burning in her shoulder had turned into excruciating pain, and the buzzing in her head threatened to submerge her in blackness. But she couldn't faint, wouldn't faint. She had to get home. Home to Aunt Alma.

*Think*, Olivia told herself. Think of anything but the agony tearing at her shoulder. Bathurst, yes; thinking of Bathurst was good. Anger could banish the pain. And she *was* angry. Cruel fate had placed Bathurst in her path tonight. Was she being punished for robbing rich noblemen of their baubles? How unfair that she should find the marquis in the coach after establishing that the horses pulling the conveyance did not belong to someone they had previously robbed.

Olivia had thought of the marquis often since the dowager's ball. She remembered his arrogance, the heat of his body as they danced, and his disturbing ability to undress her with his eyes.

Why couldn't she forget him?

Peterson slowed the horses and moved up beside her.

"Are you all right, Miss Livvy? Where did the bastard's bullet hit you? Your aunt is going to kill me."

"My shoulder," Olivia gasped. "I think the bullet went in and out, but it hurts like the very devil."

"Hang on," Peterson pleaded. "We'll be home soon."

"Are we being followed?"

"No, but we'd best hurry. Fortunately, the rain will aid us."

Suddenly a black pit seemed to open beneath Olivia and she swayed in the saddle. "I don't think . . ."

She was barely conscious as Pete pulled her off her horse and onto his own mount. He cradled her in his arms as his sturdy horse carried them both home.

Alma was waiting for them in the kitchen when they arrived. "I've brewed a fresh pot of tea," she said at the sound of the door opening. "You must be wet to the core and half frozen."

When she turned to welcome them, the cup fell from her hand and shattered on the floor. "Livvy! Dear God, never tell me she's dead."

"No, my lady, not dead, just wounded. Best put some water on to boil."

"Take her to her room," Alma ordered once her wits returned. Though some might call her flighty, she always came through in a crisis. "I'll put water on to boil and bring up the medicine chest."

After setting the teakettle on the tripod over the flames, Alma gathered up her medicinal supplies and hurried after Peterson. "What happened?"

"It was *him*, the bloody marquis," Peterson spat as he stood back so Alma could tend her wounded niece.

Alma removed Olivia's muffler and carefully peeled off her coat.

"What marquis?"

"Bathurst."

"You can tell me about it later," Alma said crisply. "I'll be needing that hot water now."

When Peterson left, Alma removed Olivia's bloody shirt and quickly located the places where the bullet had entered and exited her flesh. Making a compress of clean cloths, she pressed it hard against the wound to stop the bleeding, relieved to learn she wouldn't have to dig out a bullet.

Olivia remained unconscious as Alma cleaned the wound with the hot water Peterson brought, slathered it with salve and bound it with a bandage. Then she finished undressing Olivia and put her into a night-gown.

She had done all she could. Should a fever develop, she would be forced to call a physician, and that could prove disastrous. Alma had no idea how she would explain a bullet hole in a gently bred earl's daughter.

# Chapter Four

The tormented cry of the wounded highwayman had lodged in Gabriel's brain and he couldn't escape it no matter how hard he tried. Three days after the holdup, he sat in his study trying to concentrate on business issues, but his mind refused to cooperate. He had even tried to banish his thoughts by exploring more pleasurable pursuits, such as gaming at Crocker's and sampling the women at Madame Bella's, but neither helped.

Since shooting the highwayman, Gabriel had tossed and turned in his bed, his mind playing the highwayman's ungodly scream over and over. He shouldn't regret shooting a criminal, but strangely, he did. He must be getting soft in his old age, Gabriel decided. He had shot men before, but only during times of war, when a soldier's life depended upon his good aim.

With a will born of determination, Gabriel shook his head to clear it of the unfortunate incident and tried to concentrate on the report from Winthorpe, the steward of Bathurst Park. Unbidden, his thoughts wandered along a more pleasant path.

Olivia Fairfax.

For reasons beyond his comprehension, his curiosity about the lady ran rampant. Where did she live? Who were her friends? Did she have enemies? Apparently, she was something of a recluse, for she was seldom seen out and about in society. Did she have admirers besides Palmerson? Unable to concentrate on the report, he rose and moved to the window. Rain pelted against the pane; solid sheets of water splashed into the street in front of the house, obscuring the occasional brave soul who dared to venture out on this bleak and blustery day.

Gabriel turned away from the window and pulled the cord to summon Grimsley. Moments later a tall, slim man of indeterminate age entered the study. Grimsley, though impeccably dressed, was rougher around the edges than most gentlemen's gentlemen, and knowledgeable in areas slightly outside the law. He had served as Gabriel's batman during the war and had saved his hide on more than one occasion. Gabriel had depended upon Grimsley then and the man served him well now, in more than one capacity.

"You look peckish this morning, milord," Grimsley observed. "Are you ill? Is there something I can do for you?"

"I'm not ill, but there *is* something you can do for me. I know it's a devilish day outside, but this is important. I need some information, and since you are so good at obtaining it . . ."

Grimsley smiled. "I'm your man, milord. What do you want to know?"

"Lady Olivia Fairfax, daughter of the deceased Earl

of Sefton. I want to know everything about her."

One of Grimsley's gray-tinged brows rose in question. "Anything in particular you wish to know?"

"I want to know where she lives, if her father left her money, and the names of her suitors. I understand she lives with her aunt. Does she have any other relatives? Anything you can tell me about the household will be helpful."

"I'll do my best," Grimsley promised. He turned to leave.

"I apologize again for sending you out in this beastly weather," Gabriel said.

"Think nothing of it, milord. We experienced worse than this on the Peninsula."

"Take the coach, Grimsley."

Gabriel returned to his report. With Grimsley in charge, the information he needed would soon be forthcoming.

Lady Alma wrung her hands worriedly as she fussed over her niece, lying so pale and still in her bed. Since Olivia's run-in with Lord Bathurst's pistol three days ago, her recovery had been too slow to suit Alma. Olivia had become feverish the day after the dreadful incident, and none of Alma's remedies seemed to help.

"Aunt Alma, are you still here? I feel so hot."

Alma regarded Olivia with tender concern. "You're still feverish, dear. It's been three days. I think it's time to call a doctor."

"No!" Olivia cried, struggling to sit up. "You can't, Auntie, you know you can't."

Gently, Alma patted Olivia's shoulder and urged her to lie down. "You're becoming upset, my dear, and it's not good for you. I won't do anything you don't want me to. Rest while I fetch you a nourishing broth."

Once Alma was certain Olivia was comfortably settled back in bed, she quietly left the room. Stepping around puddles of water collecting beneath the numerous leaks in the roof, she hurried to the kitchen.

"How is she?" Peterson asked as he banged a pot on the scarred table.

"Still feverish. I threatened to call a doctor, but she would have none of it." She sniffed and wiped a tear from the corner of her eye. "I'm worried."

"I doubt a doctor would come out in this weather anyway," Peterson said.

"What are you doing?" Alma asked.

"Looking for more pots to put under the leaks."

Alma went into the pantry and came out empty-handed, her eyes filled with panic. "We don't have a soup bone. Whatever are we going to do?"

Peterson grabbed his slicker from a hook. "Don't worry, Lady Alma, I'll get you a soup bone."

Gabriel prowled his study, pausing from time to time to peer through the window at the street outside. Grimsley had been gone for hours and it was growing dark. He shouldn't have sent his trusted man out on a day like this when tomorrow would have sufficed. Grimsley was due an increase in salary, and Gabriel decided to make it a substantial one.

He was turning away from the window when he saw his coach rambling up the street. He proceeded to the foyer and waited impatiently for the coachman to drop Grimsley off at the front entrance. The door opened on a gust of wind that nearly blew him off his feet.

"Get into some dry clothes before you report your

findings," Gabriel ordered. "Would you prefer tea or brandy?"

Grimsley flashed a grin. "Brandy, milord."

Gabriel returned his smile. "I thought as much. The brandy and I will be waiting in my study."

Grimsley presented himself in the study a short time later. Gabriel handed him a snifter of brandy.

"My information about Lady Olivia is sketchy, but it may be of some value to you, milord," Grimsley began as he settled in a chair opposite Gabriel. "The lady and her aunt are a reclusive pair."

"What did you learn? Can you tell me where she lives?"

"Indeed I can, milord. I found her house. She lives south of Mayfair, in Chelsea." He pushed a piece of paper forward. "I wrote down the house number. It's not an impressive place."

Gabriel glanced at the address and slipped the paper into his pocket. "What else?"

"As you already know, Lady Olivia's maiden aunt lives with her. She has a younger brother but no other close relatives in England. According to neighbors, they have two servants, a combination cook/housekeeper who comes in daily, and a man of all trades who lives on the premises. My guess is that they exist on the edge of poverty."

"I understand the brother is away at school. How do they manage to pay his expenses?"

" 'Tis somewhat of a mystery. The lad is eighteen. Some say the Earl of Sefton left enough blunt to keep his son in school. No one seems to know for sure. Those who knew the earl say he went into a decline after his wife died. He got involved with a fellow named Palmerson and all sorts of debauchery."

"Palmerson!" Gabriel repeated. "The man is a menace to society. Go on, Grimsley."

"The Earl of Sefton was killed in a duel over a doxy from Covent Garden. 'Twas quite a scandal. 'Tis said he was goaded into dueling by Palmerson. Don't know what Palmerson had to gain by it, but it sounds suspicious to me, especially when I learned he has proposed marriage to Lady Olivia."

Gabriel went still. "Has she accepted?"

"Not that I heard. And that's the sum of it, milord. The lady and her aunt rarely attend social functions, though some old family friends still invite them. Peterson, the man of all trades, looks after them as if they were his own kin."

"You've done well, Grimsley," Gabriel said. "But then, you've yet to fail me. You've earned a nice bonus for your work, and a substantial raise come the first of the month."

"Thank you, milord, you're more than generous."

"Take the rest of the day off; you deserve it. One of the footman can let me in when I return tonight."

"You're going out, milord? In this weather?"

"Lord Braxton sent a note around. He and Westmore invited me to meet them at Brooks's for a late supper."

Grimsley rose stiffly. "Very good, milord. I wish you a pleasant evening."

"Good night, Grimsley."

Gabriel left his study and asked a footman to have his coach brought around. Then he repaired to his chamber to dress for the evening. Throckmorton, his valet, helped him don a spotless linen shirt and evening clothes, settled his coat around his shoulders, and handed him his top hat and cane. Looking every bit the elegant marquis, Gabriel left the house.

When he gave the coachman directions, however, he could think of only one place he wanted to go. "Chelsea, Jenkins. And after that, Brooks's."

Jenkins climbed into the driver's box and the coach rattled off down the rain-swept street toward Chelsea. When they arrived at the formerly fashionable but now seedy residential district, Gabriel located the address Grimsley had provided and rapped on the roof. The coach halted before a narrow townhouse that might have been grand once but was now in desperate need of refurbishing.

Why hadn't Lady Olivia used part of her monthly stipend for repairs? Gabriel wondered. The mystery deepened, along with Gabriel's determination to solve it. If not tonight, then one day soon. One didn't make calls on ladies who were barely acquaintances at this time of night. Though he might not be a gentleman in the strict sense of the word, he did adhere to some of the restrictions dictated by society.

Gabriel thumped on the roof and the coach jerked forward. He was deep in thought when the coach rolled to a stop and Jenkins opened the door.

"Brooks's, milord." Holding an umbrella aloft over Gabriel's head, Jenkins kept pace with him until they reached the entrance.

The door opened and Gabriel ducked inside. He spied Braxton and Westmore immediately. They were standing near the fireplace, deep in conversation with Lord Paxton. Gabriel strode over to join them.

"Bathurst," Ram greeted. "You're late. My stomach is touching my backbone. What kept you?"

"There was something I had to do first. Hello, Paxton, I thought you were abroad."

"Just returned, old chap. Got myself leg-shackled, don't you know."

"Congratulations."

"Aye, well, her dowry was worth it. I must go now; the little woman is waiting for me."

Ram chuckled as Paxton ambled off. "There's a prime example of what marriage will do to a man."

"Let's find a table and order dinner," Luc suggested. "Bathurst can tell us what kept him over our meal."

After placing their orders, Ram and Luc glanced expectantly at Gabriel. "Who is the woman who delayed you?" Luc asked without preamble.

"What makes you think it was a woman?"

"Never say it wasn't," Luc guffawed.

"Perhaps our friend has kept himself busy trying to learn the identity of our highwaymen," Ram ventured.

"I doubt it," Luc retorted. "The nasty weather hasn't let up since the robbery. I'm sure Bathurst has been holed up in his townhouse, same as we have. Nothing like a warm drink and a cozy fire in one's hearth when the weather turns beastly."

"I *have* been thinking about the robbery," Gabriel admitted. "I plan to send Grimsley around to hospitals and doctors known to treat criminals to inquire if anyone was brought in recently with a bullet wound."

"You did what you had to do," Ram maintained. "Think no more about it. 'Twas but a paltry sum they stole. You can afford it."

"That's beside the point, Braxton. Being robbed twice by the same highwaymen is a bit galling."

"Let us know what happens," Ram said, digging into his plate of lamb chops and potatoes. "I'm eager to sit down to cards. I feel lucky."

"I think I'll pass tonight," Gabriel said. "There's something I need to do."

Ram set his fork down and stared at Gabriel. "I know! You've found a new mistress. Who is she? She must be something to have you in such a dither."

Gabriel's dark brow arched. "As a matter of fact, there is no mistress." He set down his fork and patted his mouth with his napkin. "Now, if you'll excuse me, I must be off."

Luc and Ram looked at one another as Gabriel strode off, their faces creased with worry.

"What do you suppose has gotten into Bathurst?" Ram said. "He's not himself lately. I've never seen anything consume him like those highwaymen. It sounds almost as if he regrets shooting one of the bastards."

"Lud, Braxton," Luc chided, "Bathurst wouldn't let a robbery affect him like this. It's a woman, mark my words."

"I haven't noticed him with any particular woman," Ram mused.

"Nor have I . . . unless . . . gads, you don't think he's gone soft on Lady Olivia, do you?"

"She's on the shelf, don't you know. I doubt Bathurst would waste his time on a woman with no dowry, no matter how lovely she is. Besides, dallying with an unwed lady isn't Bathurst's style. Eventually she would demand marriage, and our friend has no intention of getting leg-shackled."

Gabriel had no idea his friends were speculating about his love life as his coach rocked along the road through the wet night. He had given Jenkins a direction that brought him once again to Chelsea. He rapped on the roof, and the coach pulled up to the curb before Olivia's townhouse. Though Gabriel had no intention of intruding tonight, he sat against the squabs and stared at the flickering light visible through the windows.

Realizing that lingering outside Olivia's home was a waste of time, Gabriel was about to signal Jenkins to continue on when he noticed a hunched figure approaching the house. The person carried a package beneath one arm, wore a slicker and was definitely male. When the man entered the house without knocking, Gabriel's eyes narrowed. Obviously, Grimsley hadn't learned everything about Lady Olivia Fairfax.

Gabriel rose before noon the following day, having slept little the night before. He dressed, ate a light breakfast and left the house. Since the day had turned unusually fine after nearly a week of rain, Gabriel decided to drive his curricle to Chelsea. Perhaps he would invite Lady Olivia for a ride through Hyde Park. Given sufficient time in her company, he might recall where they had met before.

Chelsea looked depressingly dreary in the daylight. Rows of aging townhouses that had seen better days lined the streets, and even the people out and about looked downright seedy.

Gabriel parked in front of Olivia's house and leaped lightly to the ground. He adjusted his jacket, reached for his cane and walked jauntily up to the front door. The knocker was missing, so he used his cane to announce his presence. Long moments passed before the door opened, revealing an elderly man with graying hair and a long nose, wearing what passed for livery—a pair of dark breeches and a rusty black coat over rumpled linen.

Was this Olivia's man of all trades? He seemed somewhat startled to see Gabriel but quickly recovered.

"How may I help you, milord?"

"Please inform Lady Olivia that Lord Bathurst has come to call on her. Is she receiving?"

"I . . . er . . . this is not a good time, milord."

The man appeared thoroughly rattled, and Gabriel wondered why. "I suggest you announce my presence to Lady Olivia and let her decide."

"I'm sorry, milord, I cannot do that. Lady Olivia isn't . . . that is, she—"

"Who is it, Peterson?"

"His Lordship, the Marquis of Bathurst. He wishes to see Lady Olivia."

Looking past the butler, Gabriel saw Lady Alma standing near the stairs, looking every bit as rattled as Peterson.

"Oh my, oh my," Alma repeated. "He can't. I mean, 'tis not possible."

Without waiting to be invited, Gabriel stepped past Peterson into the foyer, removed his hat . . . and stopped so fast he almost skidded into one of the buckets filled to overflowing with last night's rain. A drop of water plopped from the ceiling onto his head, and when he looked up, another drop splashed into his eye. He dashed it away and suddenly became aware of several more buckets placed strategically around the foyer and beyond.

Gabriel rounded on Peterson. "What is all this?"

"The roof, milord; it leaks," Peterson intoned dryly.

"I can see that. Why hasn't it been repaired?"

"Because not everyone has your great wealth," Alma answered, stepping forward to defend Peterson.

"Where's Lady Olivia?" Gabriel asked, ignoring Alma's gibe.

Alma cast a worried glance toward the stairs. "She's . . . unavailable."

Gabriel had had outside of enough. "What's wrong with her?"

"My niece is a bit under the weather and not up to receiving, my lord."

"Have you summoned a doctor?"

Lady Alma paled. "That's not necessary. I'm perfectly capable of handling minor illnesses."

Grimacing, Gabriel cast a discerning glance at the slimy walls and wet floor. "The living conditions here are appalling. 'Tis no wonder Lady Olivia is ill."

Lady Alma's hands fluttered helplessly. "I assure you, Olivia will be right as rain very soon."

Neither Lady Alma's frown nor Peterson's furrowed brow was reassuring. "I will judge Lady Olivia condition myself," he said, striding toward the stairs.

Alma placed herself in front of him. "Lord Bathurst, you cannot! It isn't done. You and my niece are barely acquainted."

He stepped around her. "Be that as it may, I'm going up. You may come along, but you cannot stop me."

"Peterson, do something," Alma pleaded.

"What would you have me do?" Peterson asked, eyeing Gabriel's height and bulk. "He is a marquis while I"—he shrugged—"I am a servant."

Gabriel ascended the staircase, noting as he went that the banister wobbled and the stair treads gave beneath his weight. Alma tripped up the stairs after him, wringing her hands and muttering to herself.

"Show me the way," Gabriel said, letting Alma precede him.

Alma scooted past him and flattened herself against a closed door at the top of the stairs. One dark brow

64

cocked upward, Gabriel placed his hands around Alma's waist and lifted her aside. Then he rapped once on the door and called Olivia's name. When he received no answer, he rapped again.

"Lady Olivia, 'tis Bathurst. Your aunt said you're unwell. May I be of some help?"

This time he heard a weak, "Bathurst? Oh no, go away."

"See?" Alma said, glaring at him. "Olivia doesn't wish to see you. It just isn't done, my lord."

Gabriel knew he was breaking rules, but something was wrong, very wrong. If Olivia needed a doctor, he was going to make bloody sure she got the care she required. Perhaps she couldn't pay a doctor, but he could.

"I'm coming in," Gabriel called.

He gave her a moment to prepare herself, then opened the door and stepped inside. His gaze flew to the bed, where Olivia's slight figure was barely discernable beneath the quilt that covered her. A wealth of russet hair was spread out over the pillow, framing a face that was deathly pale but for two red spots warming her cheekbones.

"What are you doing here?" Olivia gasped.

Gabriel approached the bed. "You *are* ill. I'll send Jenkins for my personal physician immediately."

"No!" Alma protested. "Please leave, my lord. I promise to send for my own doctor."

Gabriel stared at Olivia, his brow furrowed in concern. "You're feverish. How long have you been like this?"

"A day or two," Olivia said feebly. "Go away, I don't want you to see me like this."

"What have you done for her?" Gabriel asked,

rounding on Alma. "I'm not a doctor, but I have sufficient knowledge of fevers to know you should be forcing liquids down her."

Olivia tried to sit up, but Gabriel grasped her shoulders and gently pushed her back down. He felt the heat of her flesh through her linen nightgown and cursed beneath his breath. Apparently, Lady Alma's homemade concoctions had done little to ease Olivia's fever. He knelt beside the bed and took Olivia's hand.

"Lady Olivia, I know why your aunt hasn't summoned a doctor. Perhaps you can't afford medical care, but I can."

"It . . . isn't that," Olivia croaked. "Don't worry, I'll be fine. Aunt Alma is taking good care of me. I don't need your help. Goodbye, Bathurst."

Gabriel rose but didn't leave as Olivia ordered. His expression was dark with disapproval as he directed his gaze around the sparsely furnished bedroom. "You don't belong here. The roof leaks and the plaster is crumbling."

"We are quite aware of the situation," Alma replied, biting her bottom lip to keep it from trembling.

"How dare you come uninvited into our home and insult us," Olivia charged. "Nor can you dictate our lives. How we conduct our affairs is no concern of yours."

Olivia was right, Gabriel reflected. He hardly knew Olivia Fairfax and her aunt and had no business interfering in their lives, but a doctor was needed, and for reasons that eluded him, he felt compelled to help.

"I shall send Jenkins for my physician."

"Since I won't let him examine me," Olivia replied, "you'll be wasting your time and his."

Exasperated, Gabriel dragged a hand through his

dark hair. "Why are you refusing my help?"

"We don't accept charity. Besides, I'm sure your help comes with a price I'm not willing to pay. A man of your unsavory reputation always wants something in return."

Gabriel gave a snort of indignation. "I've asked nothing of you."

Closing her eyes, Olivia recalled the night of the ball. Not only had Lord Bathurst made an improper proposal, he had taken liberties and asked questions of a very personal nature. Furthermore, if he should learn she was the highwayman who had robbed him of his valuables, her goose was cooked. She could not allow a doctor to attend her wound without inviting suspicion.

"I promise to summon my own doctor if you will but leave me alone," Olivia assured him. She'd pledge anything to get rid of Bathurst. Her shoulder hurt like the very devil, and she felt as if she were baking in the fires of hell.

Gabriel seemed to weave back and forth before Olivia's fading vision. Staring into his far too handsome face, she wondered what had brought him to her bedside. He was the last person in the world she'd expected to see. She could tell by the look in his eyes that he thought her pathetic, and she didn't want his pity. She wanted nothing from the Marquis of Bathurst.

"Why are you here, my lord?"

"Are your suitors so few that you fail to recognize one when he comes calling? I thought you might enjoy a ride in the park."

"Another time, perhaps," Alma cut in. "Olivia should rest now."

"Please go, Bathurst," Olivia agreed. "Auntie is right, I *am* tired."

"What about the doctor?" Gabriel pressed.

"I'll send Peterson directly," Alma replied, crowding him toward the door. "I'll show you out."

"Very well, but you won't get rid of me that easily. I'll return tomorrow."

Olivia couldn't relax until Alma returned to say that Bathurst was gone.

"Why did he come?" Olivia said.

Alma patted Olivia's shoulder reassuringly. "Bathurst is interested in you, Livvy. I could see it in his eyes."

"Bathurst's interests lie in one direction," Olivia scoffed. "South of his belt. He wants but one thing from a woman, and obviously he thinks I'm available and willing to give it to him. I'm sure he believes a woman on the shelf is desperate for a man."

"Perhaps you can bring him up to scratch," Alma speculated. "He needs an heir, and your bloodlines are impeccable."

"Bathurst is an unrepentant rogue and uninterested in marriage. I doubt there's a woman alive capable of bringing him up to scratch. Besides," she said wearily, "I wouldn't have him on a silver platter."

"You're tired, dear," Alma observed. "Take a nap while I warm some broth for you. Bathurst is right about forcing liquids down you. He's also correct about summoning a doctor. Your persistent fever worries me."

"Wait one more day, Auntie," Olivia urged. "If the fever doesn't subside by then, you can send Peterson for Dr. Drayton. We can sell the last diamond stud to pay his fees and buy his silence."

Alma sent her a skeptical look. "Very well. One more day, Livvy, but no longer."

Olivia's pale face remained in Gabriel's thoughts long after he returned home. Why he should care about Olivia's welfare escaped him, but he did care, and it occurred to him that he should do something about it.

"Grimsley!"

Grimsley must have been standing outside the door, for he appeared almost instantly. "You called, milord?"

"Please summon my physician and direct him to Lady Olivia's home. You know the address."

"At once, milord."

"And Grimsley . . ."

"Aye."

"Instruct Dr. Barnsworth to attend me immediately after he's seen his patient. And make sure he knows a bonus will be included in his fee."

"Very good, milord."

Gabriel knew Olivia wouldn't appreciate his interference, but for the life of him he couldn't imagine why she and her aunt were so adamantly opposed to seeking medical help. Was there something they didn't want anyone to know?

What secrets were they harboring?

Something about her intrigued him, beckoned him, made him want to unravel the mystery surrounding Lady Olivia Fairfax.

A knock on the door jerked him from his reverie. Grimsley entered at his command.

"Dr. Barnsworth is on his way to Chelsea, milord. He promised to call upon you before he returns to his office."

"Thank you, Grimsley. Show him into my study the

moment he arrives. And, Grimsley, have you learned anything about the two highwaymen that robbed me and Braxton?"

"No, milord, they seem to appear and disappear quite mysteriously. I've put the word out on the street and hired Bow Street Runners to keep an eye out in all the disreputable places that thieves gather. Sooner or later they're bound to make a mistake, and when they do, you'll be the first to know.

"I did, however, locate your ring at a pawn shop and took the liberty of purchasing it for you."

Gabriel took the ring from Grimsley and placed it on his finger. "You're a gem, Grimsley. Whatever would I do without you? As for the outlaws, I prefer to keep the law out of it until I learn their identities. Something tells me I know them, or at least one of them."

# Chapter Five

Olivia knew something had happened the moment her aunt entered the bedroom. Had Bathurst returned? What did he want now?

"What is it, Auntie?"

"Bathurst has sent his physician," Alma wailed. "Whatever will we do now?"

Olivia tried to sit up, but pain sent her reeling back against the mattress. "Damn that man! Why can't he mind his own business? Send the doctor away."

"You know that will make Bathurst more suspicious than he already is."

Concentrating on the problem at hand, Olivia sought a way to avoid the physician without bringing Bathurst back with more questions. Inspiration brought a weak smile to her lips. "Show the doctor in, Auntie. He doesn't have to examine me closely. You said yourself my wound wasn't infected. We'll just tell him I developed a fever for no apparent reason."

"Are you sure, Livvy?"

Olivia's mouth flattened. "Very sure. When the doctor reports back to Bathurst, and I'm sure he will, there will be little to report."

Prowling his study in a foul mood, Gabriel cursed Olivia for making him care about her. He had his reputation as a rogue and profligate to uphold. A man driven by dark secrets had no business succumbing to tender feelings. No, not tender feelings. What he felt for Olivia was definitely sexual in nature. There was only one thing he wanted from her.

Two hours later, Grimsley ushered the good doctor into Gabriel's study. "How did you find Lady Olivia, Doctor?" Gabriel asked before the man had time to settle into a chair.

"I had no idea Lord Sefton had left his family destitute. Their living conditions are appalling, and hardly conducive to good health."

"I agree wholeheartedly," Gabriel said.

Barnsworth eyed Gabriel with curiosity. "How well do you know the family?"

"I just recently became acquainted with Lady Olivia and her aunt. Why do you ask?"

"I found Lady Olivia to be . . . how shall I put it? Stubborn and uncooperative, but I did my best to reach a diagnosis."

Gabriel stifled a smile. *Stubborn* was putting it mildly. Olivia had been without proper guidance too long and placed too much value on her independence. She pretended cool reserve, but intuition told Gabriel she was every bit as hot-blooded as he was. Suddenly aware that Barnsworth was waiting for him to continue, Gabriel brought his erotic musings under control.

"Have you reached a diagnosis, Doctor? Will Lady Olivia make a full recovery?"

Speaking through pursed lips, Barnsworth said, "I found the entire visit disconcerting. The only examination the lady would allow was cursory at best. She said she'd been feverish for several days but had no other symptoms. I was allowed to listen to her heart, and it sounded strong. Her lack of other symptoms was strange, but not out of the ordinary."

Growing impatient, Gabriel cut the doctor off. "Did you reach a diagnosis and prescribe medication?"

"Medical science has yet to discover why fevers occur without other symptoms. According to Lady Alma, your young lady has a strong constitution and is rarely ill, so I predict her fever will abate when it runs its course. I left an elixir to bring her temperature down, and prescribed a few days of bed rest and fresh air once the fever leaves her."

Not good enough, Gabriel thought skeptically. "Is that all? Could Lady Olivia be consumptive?"

"No, definitely not. I ruled that out immediately. Trust me, Bathurst, Lady Olivia will be right as rain in a few days."

Gabriel had no choice but to trust the doctor. "Very well. Send your bill to my solicitor. I'll see that a bonus is included for your prompt attention."

"Good of you, Bathurst," Barnsworth blustered. "I'll be on my way."

"Grimsley will see you out."

Barnsworth had his hand on the doorknob when Gabriel said, "One more question, Doctor. Is Lady Olivia up to receiving visitors?"

"Give her a few days, Bathurst. You know how ladies hate to be seen when they're not at their best."

Barnsworth's parting words brought a wry grin to Gabriel's lips. The type of women Gabriel visited could only be described as ladies in the broadest sense, and were always at their best when a male was present. He supposed Olivia, like all women, was vain, and he should wait until she was sufficiently recovered before he visited.

A week after Dr. Barnsworth's visit, Olivia was sitting in the parlor, still pale but recovered enough to resume normal activities. Her wound was healing and her fever had long since departed. Her appetite had returned, and she felt herself growing stronger every day. Fortunately, Bathurst hadn't returned, but his absence didn't solve the problems plaguing her.

She'd had to let Mrs. Hamilton go, leaving Aunt Alma and Peterson in charge of the household, but their finances were still critical. Peterson had offered to hire himself out, but Olivia had decided against it. There was but one diamond stud left to sell, and after that, nothing. The workhouse loomed in their future, large and frightening.

Seeking help from relatives was out of the question. Olivia's father had gone through his own fortune and her mother's dowry. Upon the death of her maternal grandparents at sea several years ago, a distant cousin had inherited the title. Olivia had appealed to him for help after her father's death, but he had ignored her plea. If her maternal grandparents had still been alive, Olivia knew they would have helped her, but unfortunately, they were beyond helping anyone.

Olivia's musings were interrupted by Peterson's hasty entrance. "Miss Livvy, come quickly! The strangest thing is happening."

Olivia started to question Peterson, but her words halted abruptly when she heard pounding and scraping noises from somewhere above her. "Good heavens! What is that?"

"That's what I've been trying to tell you, Miss Livvy. Workmen have arrived to replace the roof. They're working even as we speak."

"That can't be!" Olivia cried. "Tell them to stop immediately. Surely they have the wrong address. I didn't order a new roof."

"I ordered them away, but they insisted they had the right address. Lady Alma is at the market, but I doubt she would order a new roof without your consent. When I told them we couldn't pay, they said they had already been compensated."

"There must be some mistake."

The pounding continued, only this time it came from the front door. Peterson hurried off to answer the summons. "If that's one of the workmen, I'll have a word with him," Olivia called after him.

Olivia settled back in her chair, certain she could clear this up in a matter of minutes.

"Lord Bathurst, my lady," Peterson announced in a formal tone.

*Drat!* Olivia thought as Gabriel appeared in the doorway looking suave and distinguished in a coat of gray superfine that displayed the breadth of his shoulders to perfection. His pristine white cravat was tied with casual elegance, and his buff breeches clung to hard thighs and the long legs of a man who must surely be the envy of those lacking Bathurst's blatant masculinity.

His hard-edged forehead, noble nose and strong jaw spoke eloquently of his aristocratic lineage. His cheeks appeared sculpted of granite. His lips were full and sensual with just a hint of dissipation, and there was innate intelligence and, yes, wickedness lighting his eyes. Though she tried not to, Olivia couldn't help noticing the way the long muscles of his legs flexed as he strolled gracefully toward her.

"I see the roofers have arrived," Gabriel remarked.

Olivia stared at him with dawning comprehension. "It was *you!* You ordered the workmen."

"Guilty," Gabriel said.

"How dare you!"

"I dare many things," Gabriel drawled.

"You know I can't pay for a new roof. You must order the workers to stop what they're doing immediately."

"Never say you don't need a new roof, for I know better."

"That's not the point."

"What *is* the point?"

"I hardly know you and therefore cannot allow you to do this. First you sent your physician against my express wishes, then you employed roofers on my behalf without my knowledge. It just isn't done. Repairs to my home will be made when I can afford them. Your charity is unacceptable."

"Who said anything about charity? I can think of several ways you may repay the debt. Some of them quite pleasant."

Heat warmed Olivia's cheeks. His words left little doubt as to his intentions where she was concerned. Rogues don't change their wicked ways, a little voice inside her warned.

"Take yourself and your roofers away, Bathurst. I know what you're after, and it won't work. You're a rake with all the instincts of a rutting stallion."

76

Gabriel threw his head back and laughed. "What do you know about rutting stallions, Lady Olivia?"

"Enough to know one when I see one. I'm sure there are women who enjoy being insulted, but I'm not one of them."

Her words seemed to run off him like rainwater during a storm. "I've brought my curricle. It's such a fine day, I thought you might enjoy a ride through the park." His silver gaze made a leisurely journey over her features. "You're too pale. Fresh air and sunshine will do you a world of good."

"You're probably right, and I would enjoy a ride . . . with anyone but you."

"What's this about a ride?" Alma asked as she bustled into the room. She saw Gabriel and her eyes widened. "Lord Bathurst, good day to you."

"Good afternoon, Lady Alma," Gabriel said politely. "I've come to take Lady Olivia for a ride in my curricle."

Alma peered into Olivia's pale face. "You *could* use the air, Livvy."

"Auntie!"

"Oh, dear, did I say the wrong thing again?"

"It's all right, Auntie, I'll handle it."

"I almost forgot, dear. Did you order repairs on the roof?"

"I most definitely did not!" Olivia huffed, sending Gabriel an aggrieved look. "The roofers are another of Lord Bathurst's *charitable* acts. He's just full of them."

"He is, isn't he?" Alma said. "Be sure to take a wrap and bonnet, dear," she said in parting. "Wouldn't want you to catch a chill after your recent . . . illness."

"Auntie, where are you going?" Was her aunt going to leave her alone with Bathurst? Didn't she realize how dangerous Bathurst was to them, or how badly he could hurt them if his prying unearthed the truth about her?

"I'm off to the kitchen, dear. I talked the butcher into parting with a prime piece of beef for the price of a lesser cut," Alma said enthusiastically. "Peterson and I are going to prepare a special meal tonight."

Embarrassment brought a flush to Olivia's cheeks. Now Bathurst really would think they were destitute.

She could feel Gabriel's hard gaze lance into her and glared up at him. "Why are you staring at me like that?"

"Olivia—"

"Lady Olivia to you."

"If you insist, my lady," Gabriel mocked. He held out his hand. "I don't think you'll need that wrap, but perhaps you should fetch one anyway. As your aunt says, we don't want to tempt fate after your illness."

Mesmerized by the sensual promise in his eyes, Olivia almost grasped his hand, but at the last minute, good sense prevailed. Just being alone with Bathurst tempted fate.

"I don't think—"

"Peterson!" Gabriel shouted.

Peterson appeared instantly. "You called, my lord?"

"Fetch Lady Olivia's wrap and bonnet."

Peterson sent a worried look at Olivia, then hurried off to do Gabriel's bidding.

"I can't go with you," Olivia protested. "Lady Alma is too busy to act as chaperone."

"For a lady who's on the shelf—your words, not mine—you seem overly concerned about your reputation. If I'm not mistaken, your age allows you more latitude than a newly come out miss."

78

Peterson reappeared. "Your spencer, bonnet and gloves, Miss Livvy."

Gabriel held out his hand. Peterson handed the articles of clothing to Gabriel and discreetly withdrew.

Olivia realized that Bathurst wasn't going to take no for an answer. The man was as unmovable as granite once his mind was made up. She could protest till doomsday and he would still be standing there, challenging her with his wicked smile. Cursing herself for a fool, she grasped his outstretched hand and rose to her feet, letting him tie the bonnet under her chin and help her into her spencer without a murmur of protest. To her everlasting shame, she found the Marquis of Bathurst physically attractive, intellectually stimulating and dangerously intriguing. Her very life, however, depended on resisting those attributes she found most appealing.

"I knew you'd see it my way," Gabriel drawled as he took her elbow and guided her out the door. An awkward moment occurred when he lifted her onto the high-sprung seat of his curricle. The sudden movement sent pain coursing through her healing wound, and she turned her face away so Bathurst wouldn't see her wince.

"Are you comfortable?"

"I'm fine," Olivia answered through clenched teeth.

"I thought we'd ride through Hyde Park," Gabriel remarked, setting his high-stepping team into motion.

Though she fought against it, Olivia began to enjoy the outing. It had been many years since she'd ridden in such a fine carriage. The scenery along Park Lane was breathtaking in the bright summer afternoon. The granite and marble facades of the houses gleamed with polished luster, and the pristine glass of the windows flashed in the sun as they passed by.

Hyde Park was a bustling place at this time of day. People strolled along a paved promenade in a setting of lush hedges, flowers, trees and stone benches, while horses and carriages vied for space along the thoroughfare. The towering three- and four-story houses that formed the square surrounding the park, however, served to remind Olivia of her own state of poverty.

"The park is crowded today," Gabriel remarked as he drove the curricle through one of the exits.

"Where are we going?" Olivia asked as they rolled past costermongers, hurdy-gurdies, street peddlers and itinerate musicians.

Gabriel sent her a mischievous grin. "You'll see."

When they left the city via London Bridge and headed into the countryside of Surrey, a frisson of wariness slid down Olivia's spine. Being alone with Bathurst wasn't a good idea for several reasons, not the least of which was the attraction that simmered between them.

"Take me home, Bathurst," Olivia ordered in her haughtiest voice. "I've just recently recovered from an illness, and this is my first day abroad."

"Are you unwell?" Gabriel asked sharply.

"Not really, but—"

"We won't go far," Gabriel assured her.

Moments later he veered off the road onto a crooked lane boxed in on both sides by hedgerows. When the lane opened, revealing a small lake inhabited by four graceful swans, Olivia clapped her hands delightedly.

"How lovely. I didn't know something this peaceful existed so close to the City."

"I thought you'd like it," Gabriel said as he set the brake and leaped to the ground.

Olivia watched in trepidation as Gabriel removed a blanket from beneath the seat and spread it out on the lush grass beside the lake. Then he lifted her out of the curricle as if she weighed nothing and carried her to the blanket.

Olivia's first thought was that Bathurst had done this before, many times before, with a variety of women. If he had seduction in mind, he was going to be disappointed. She had no intention of falling victim to his predatory ways. If he thought she would offer her body in payment for the new roof, he didn't know her very well.

"I am perfectly capable of walking, my lord," Olivia said as he carefully lowered her to the blanket and sprawled out beside her.

"You may call me Gabriel."

He searched her face, his intense gaze settling on her eyes. She lowered her lids and studied her hands. He stared at her so long, Olivia feared he recognized something in her features. Did he suddenly realize she was Ollie, the highwayman? Her fears grew when he said, "Did anyone ever tell you that you have beautiful green eyes? I know I've met you before but I can't seem to recall where. I'm sure it will come to me."

"We'd never met before the dowager Dutchess of Stanhope's ball," Olivia asserted. "You've known so many women, perhaps I resemble one of your . . . paramours."

"No woman of my acquaintance looks like you," Gabriel maintained.

Olivia felt her lips heat beneath his gaze and licked moisture over them with her tongue, unaware of the effect this simple act might have upon him.

"Are you teasing me, Livvy?"

Olivia's eyes widened. She had no idea what he meant, but she did object to his using a name only permitted to family members.

"No one calls me Livvy except those close to me, my lord."

A wicked smile curved his lips. "I intend to get close, *very* close to you, Livvy."

His gaze returned to her lips. He leaned close. So close that the scent of leather, tobacco and pure maleness enveloped her, soaked into her pores. Her senses reeled. Closing her eyes, she inhaled deeply. She felt his breath brush her cheek and began to tremble. Damn the man! Why was she letting a notorious womanizer and rake do this to her?

His hard body was close, close enough for her to feel his heat. It stoked a corresponding fire in her. She opened her eyes and saw him watching her. She tried to put distance between them but was held in place by invisible bonds.

"Don't," she said breathlessly.

"Don't what?"

"Look at me like I'm a tasty morsel you wish to devour. Your manners are despicable, Lord Bathurst."

His lips kicked up at the ends. "Why," he murmured, his head bending to hers, "do you think I'm called a rogue?"

Had she not been so shocked, she would have slapped him. Instead, she remained frozen in place, head tilted up to look at him, her lips slightly open.

What happened next was inevitable. His mouth took hers. The kiss was pure heat. It spread through her, warming every part of her. The kiss teased and titillated. Without conscious volition, she moved closer, drawn to him, needing to feel the solid weight of his chest against her aching breasts. Nothing in her limited experience of men had prepared her for this moment.

The only thing that kept her from sliding her hands beneath his shirt and touching him was a tiny spark of reason that remained. Sanity fled when his tongue slipped between her teeth, boldly tasting her. Trembling, she drank in the subtle taste of him. Pressing her palms against his chest, she intended to push him away. Instead, her hands crept up to his shoulders and circled around his neck.

She heard him groan; then he dragged her closer, until she was half-reclining in his arms. His thighs felt like granite columns holding her in place. The kiss went on and on until Olivia suddenly became aware of his rampant sex pushing against her belly. A wanton urge to shift her hips closer to that mysterious hardness gripped her, but she tamped it down.

When Olivia felt her bonnet fall away, she knew she was headed for trouble. Bathurst was too experienced, too sure of himself, too masculine. She realized that he had already unfastened her spencer and cupped her breast through her gown. Her breath ceased.

"You fit my hand perfectly," he murmured against her lips. "I like it that you don't wear a corset. You're slim enough to get away with it."

Gabriel's words released Olivia's breath. "Don't!" Pushing herself from his arms, she quickly fastened her spencer. "How dare you take liberties with my person."

He grinned at her. "You seemed to enjoy what I was doing."

Heat crawled up her cheeks. She should have made a greater effort to resist. She should have demanded to be taken home. Instead, she had lain complacent against him and let him work his magic on her.

"You took advantage of my inexperience," Olivia charged.

Gabriel stared at her, one elegant brow cocked upward. "Are you saying Palmerson hasn't had you?"

"How dare you! Your audacity appalls me." She pushed herself to her feet. Using her right arm was still painful, but she wasn't about to let the contemptible rake help her get up.

"Will you forgive me if I apologize, Livvy?"

"Apology not accepted," Olivia huffed. "You may take me home, Lord Bathurst. You will, of course, present me with a complete accounting for the cost of my new roof, and I shall endeavor to repay you down to the last farthing."

"I don't want your money."

"Nevertheless, you shall have it. 'Tis less costly than what you want from me."

"What, pray tell, is that?"

*My heart, my soul, everything that I am.* She walked to the curricle and hoisted herself up. "This conversation is ended, my lord."

"My name is Gabriel. We're not leaving until you say it."

*Arrogant toad.* "Very well. I wish to leave . . . Gabriel."

His smile was almost worth the anguish he was causing her, but she'd bite her tongue before she'd admit it. She watched through lowered lids as he bounded into the curricle and took up the reins. If not for the impossible man beside her, she could almost regret leaving the peaceful glen behind for the stench and filth of the City.

"Your cheeks are beginning to show some color," Gabriel observed as they crossed London Bridge. "The outing has been good for you, just as I knew it would be. If it doesn't rain tomorrow morning, I'll come for you around ten. We'll have a picnic luncheon."

"Rather tame fare for you, isn't it?" Olivia ventured. "Men of your ilk rarely leave the gaming hells and bordellos before dawn and sleep until midday."

"Perhaps I'd rather be with you than sleep," Gabriel drawled.

"And perhaps pigs fly," Olivia scoffed. "I have no idea why you are determined to seduce me, Lord Bathurst, unless courting an aging spinster amuses you."

"Have you looked at yourself recently, Livvy? I'd challenge anyone who described you as an aging spinster. As for courting you, forget that pretty sentiment. I'm not interested in marriage."

"Am I your entertainment for the week, or month? I see no point in establishing a relationship with you, no matter how platonic."

"I'm not interested in a platonic relationship, Livvy." His eyes darkened to smoky gray. "I want to be your lover. I can afford to keep you and your family in comfort. You won't have to pinch pennies to keep your brother in school, and your aunt won't need to argue with the butcher for a better cut of meat than you can afford."

While his words sent fury charging through her, Olivia had to admit that for one brief moment she was tempted. She was astute enough to know that her lack of dowry and her advanced age made her unacceptable as a bride, but she had always wondered what it was like to feel passion, to know a man's intimate touch. She'd had a taste of it this afternoon and was ashamed to admit she wanted more. But not from Lord Bathurst. He was the kind of man who took and took and gave nothing of himself in return. Though she might receive material things from Bathurst, she would always yearn for something more.

"I'd accept Lord Palmerson's marriage proposal before I'd let you keep me," Olivia returned. "At least his offer is honest and my reputation would remain intact."

A carriage was parked outside Olivia's house when Gabriel pulled up. He reined in behind it and stepped down onto the street. "Looks like you have company, Livvy."

A frown pulled down the corners of Olivia's mouth. The carriage belonged to Palmerson, the last man on earth besides Bathurst she wished to see.

"Probably one of Aunt Alma's friends," she lied. Gabriel handed Olivia down. "Thank you for the ride, my lord—"

"Gabriel."

"Of course . . . Gabriel."

"I'll see you tomorrow."

"Why? We both know nothing can be gained from our association. Goodbye, Lord Bathurst."

Gabriel saluted her. "*Adieu*, Livvy. Ten o'clock. Be ready."

Gabriel chuckled to himself as he watched Livvy disappear into the house. What an invigorating afternoon! He couldn't recall when he'd felt so alive this early in the day. The boredom he'd experienced of late gave way to euphoria. There was nothing boring about Lady Olivia Fairfax. This afternoon he'd had a brief taste of the smoldering passions lurking beneath her prickly exterior. He'd had her breast in his hand, kissed her and felt her excitement.

He could picture her now, draped in the finest silk

and wearing the jewels he planned to lavish upon her. Immediately that vision was replaced with another. He saw her in his bed, her vibrant hair spread out over the pillow, her naked body splayed wantonly, inviting his touch. And her face . . . he imagined her dreamy expression, for him alone, and grew instantly hard.

The vision dissolved when another man entered the picture. Palmerson. Why would a man with empty pockets want a woman with no dowry? It didn't make sense. Gabriel's jaw firmed with determination.

*Palmerson couldn't have Livvy.*

Gabriel headed down Pall Mall to Brooks's. He was in such a good mood, he wanted to share it with his friends. He spied Ram sitting in a deep leather chair perusing a newspaper and joined him. Ram greeted him and set the paper aside.

"I stopped by your townhouse but you were already gone," Ram said. "Grimsley said you left early this morning. Couldn't sleep?"

"You might say that," Gabriel replied. "It was such a glorious day, I decided to go for a drive."

"Alone? Come on, Bathurst. I know you better than that. Who is she?"

"You don't know her," Gabriel hedged.

"Surely you jest. No woman escapes my attention." He snapped his fingers. "I know! That new actress at the opera house. Was she good? Maybe I'll try her after you tire of her."

Gabriel sent Ram a smoldering look. "I was with a lady, not an actress."

"A lady? How boring."

"I was anything but bored. In fact, I feel more energetic than I have in a long time. The game of pursuit and conquer always did excite me."

"Are you referring to new game in Town? An unwed lady, perhaps?"

Gabriel remained stubbornly mute.

"Bloody hell, Bathurst, you're inviting disaster. Mark my words, dallying with ladies can lead to trouble. Have you forgotten our vow so soon?"

"How could I forget? Don't trifle with ladies of good birth if you want to avoid the parson's trap. Fear not, Braxton. My intentions toward this lady will most definitely *not* lead to the altar."

# Chapter Six

Palmerson was waiting for Olivia when she entered the parlor. Aunt Alma, looking more harried than usual, was pouring tea. Palmerson rose immediately, his face set in stern lines.

"What were you doing with Bathurst, Olivia? He's a scoundrel and a libertine. I won't have my future wife associating with his kind. The only proposal you'll get from him is an indecent one."

Olivia felt the ragged edges of her temper fraying. Palmerson had no right to dictate to her. "I am most definitely not your future wife, my lord, nor am I likely to be. Furthermore, I expect nothing from Bathurst."

Palmerson sent her a patronizing smile. "I'm your only hope for marriage and a family of your own, my dear. If I'm not mistaken, you will soon turn twenty-five. You're completely on the shelf."

"My age has nothing to do with how I feel about you," Olivia retorted.

Palmerson leaned against the crumbling mantel and smiled benignly. "Unless I miss my guess, you're just a breath away from the workhouse. There's nothing for your precious brother to inherit but an empty title. You are alone; you need me."

"Have you suddenly come into a fortune, Palmerson?" Olivia asked sweetly.

The subtle shift of Palmerson's expression told Olivia she had hit a nerve.

"I expect to come into a substantial sum of money very soon," Palmerson stated. "We can be married tomorrow, or next week, if you prefer. It's what your father wanted."

"You may have fooled my father, but not me. You're the one who led Papa to ruin."

"Your father was an adult, Olivia," Palmerson replied. "He knew what he was doing. You cannot blame me for his downfall."

Olivia's eyes narrowed thoughtfully. "Why do you want to marry me, Palmerson? I'm penniless. Do you love me? Am I so beautiful you cannot resist me? What is it? I don't understand. Why aren't you pursuing a woman of wealth?"

Alma made a gurgling sound in her throat. "Livvy's tongue tends to run wild, my lord."

"I'm very fond of you," Palmerson averred. "Your father wanted us to wed; we discussed the details before his death. I am but fulfilling a dead man's wish. And you *are* lovely, Olivia, never doubt it." He pushed himself away from the mantel and reached out to stroke her cheek. She moved sharply away. "I find you desirable, Olivia; is that so hard to believe?"

"Behave yourself, my lord," Alma warned.

"Peterson will show you to the door," Olivia said.

Peterson appeared almost immediately. "This way, my lord."

Palmerson shot Olivia a disgruntled look. "Very well, my dear, but I'll be back. You *will* marry me; you can count on it. Meanwhile, keep away from Bathurst."

"Oh, dear," Alma said after Palmerson strode off. "That man just won't give up. Why do you suppose he is so adamant about marrying you when there is nothing to be gained from the union?"

"That's precisely what I'd like to know," Olivia mused. "Forget Palmerson, Auntie, I'm not going to marry him."

"He expects to come into money; maybe you should rethink your position. We *are* in rather desperate straits, Livvy. Perhaps we should call Neville home from the university."

"No! I couldn't do that to him. He's too close to finishing his education. I'll think of something, Auntie."

Alma pursed her lips in thought. "What about Bathurst? He seemed interested, and Lord knows he has more than enough blunt to provide for a wife."

Olivia gave an unladylike snort. "Bathurst isn't looking for a wife. Palmerson was right when he said Bathurst would offer nothing but an indecent proposal."

Alma frowned. "Are you saying he . . . Oh, dear, and to think I encouraged you to go riding with him. Did he insult you, Livvy?"

"Forget Bathurst, Auntie. Nothing happened that I couldn't handle."

Alma wrung her hands, her distress palpable. "Whatever are we going to do?"

"Pete and Ollie will do what they have done in the past."

"No! I won't allow it! It's much too dangerous. Look

what happened the last time Pete and Ollie took to the road."

"It won't happen again, Auntie, I promise."

"You don't know that! No, Livvy, I absolutely forbid it."

Olivia hated to worry Alma, but there was no other way. All she could do was hope and pray that fate didn't place Bathurst in Pete and Ollie's path when they chose their next victim.

"We'll discuss this later, when you're not so upset," Olivia hedged. "I'm going up to my room now to rest."

"I'll call you when dinner is ready, dear," Alma said as she wandered off to the kitchen.

Olivia's mind whirled with dark thoughts as she climbed the stairs. Bathurst wanted her in his bed and Palmerson wanted her for his wife. Of the two men, it was Bathurst who intrigued her, who called forth something she barely recognized in herself. His touch had roused wantonness in her, and his kisses created a need that still plagued her.


Seated in his favorite chair, a snifter of brandy in his hand, Gabriel smiled as he recalled the pleasurable hours he had spent with Olivia. He was already looking forward to tomorrow. He wondered how long it would take to seduce her to his bed. Seduction, after all, was his specialty, and Olivia was the woman upon whom he had set his sights.

Admittedly, Olivia was different from most of the other women he'd bedded, but that was what made her so compelling. Her refreshing originality appealed to his jaded tastes. Oh, yes, he would have Olivia Fairfax, and soon.

A discreet knock at the door caught Gabriel's attention. "Enter."

Grimsley appeared in the doorway. "Lords Braxton and Westmore, milord."

Luc and Ram strode into the room. "Are you hibernating?" Ram asked, one elegant brow raised in question.

"We waited for you all evening," Luc said. "When you failed to show up, we assumed you were detained by a woman." He sent Gabriel a sharp look. "Are you still pursuing Lady Olivia? It's a lost cause, you know."

"Bathurst is smarter than that," Ram snorted.

Gabriel chafed beneath his friends' gentle chiding. "What makes you so sure she's a lost cause?"

Ram paled visibly. "Never say you've bedded her! That's not like you, Bathurst, not like you at all. Next thing, you'll be announcing your engagement."

"Now, *that* will never happen," Gabriel asserted. "I do find Lady Olivia fascinating, however. There is an air of mystery about her that intrigues me."

"Forget Lady Olivia," Luc advised. "Braxton and I thought you might like to join us."

"What mischief are you two up to tonight?"

"Madame Bella is holding a special viewing of her newest acquisitions. Only her best customers are invited," Luc revealed. "The women are advertised to be virgins new to the profession, and will go to the highest bidders."

"Interesting," Gabriel murmured. "I suppose you and Braxton intend to participate in the bidding."

"Virgins are usually off limits to us," Ram said, "but this is different. These women have willingly offered themselves, so the rules no longer apply. You'll join us, won't you, Bathurst?"

Gabriel regarded his friends thoughtfully. Somehow, bidding for the privilege of deflowering a virgin didn't appeal, but his friends would think it odd if he didn't attend.

"Well, Bathurst, are you coming with us or not?" Luc asked.

"What time does the bidding start?"

"Eleven sharp."

"I'll be there."

Madame Bella's establishment for the entertainment of discerning men was packed when Gabriel entered the drawing room shortly before eleven that night. The auction was about to begin. Gabriel looked over the two scantily clad women prancing about the room with a jaundiced eye. One was plump and blond and the other buxom and brunette. Though both women were young and lovely, neither possessed the lissome grace or mature beauty that Olivia Fairfax had in abundance.

"What do you think?" Ram asked as he and Luc joined Gabriel.

"They'll do," Gabriel said tersely.

"I'm bidding on the blonde," Luc said, "though the brunette has two very fine points in her favor."

Ram grinned. "Those fine points are precisely why I'm bidding on the brunette. What about you, Bathurst?"

"I think I'll pass. It wouldn't be right to outbid my two best friends."

Gabriel would never admit that neither woman appealed to him.

A moment later the auction began. At first the bidding was spirited, but as the prices climbed, only a handful of Madame Bella's wealthiest clients were left.

Gabriel watched in silence as Westmore made a substantial bid for the plump blonde.

"Not bidding, Bathurst?" a female voice purred into his ear.

Gabriel smiled down at Bella, eyeing her full-bosomed figure with familiarity. Though she was no longer young, the madam's face and figure were still exquisite. Gabriel recalled with fondness the numerous times he had sported in the madam's bed, and wondered why she suddenly seemed too overblown for his tastes.

"Not tonight," Gabriel said.

Bella entwined her arm with his and smiled up at him. "Perhaps you'd like someone a bit more experienced, a woman who knows how to please a man. I'm always available to *you*, Bathurst."

Gabriel gave her a lighthearted pat on the bottom and gently removed her arm. "Not tonight, Bella. There's somewhere else I need to be."

She arched an elegant brow at him. "What's the lucky lady's name, Bathurst? Do I know her?"

"I doubt it."

"Very well, I'll forgive you this time, but the invitation still stands."

Gabriel was more than a little relieved when she blew him a kiss and sauntered off. Turning his attention once more to the auction, he saw Luc and the blonde climbing the staircase together, while the bidding continued for the brunette. He watched for several minutes and was gratified to see that Ram won out against the other bidders.

"Bathurst, what a coincidence."

Gabriel whirled to find Palmerson standing at his elbow. "Palmerson, why am I not surprised to find you here? Couldn't you top Braxton's bid?"

"I have no need to bid on a doxy," Palmerson said smoothly. "None can compare with my future bride."

"Your future bride? To whom are you referring? I didn't know you were engaged."

"Not officially, of course, but Lady Olivia Fairfax will soon be my bride."

"Really?" Gabriel pulled out his pocket watch and snapped it open. "Forgive me, I've somewhere to go."

"A moment of your time is all I ask. In a few words, keep away from Olivia. I'm well aware of your reputation with women, and I don't approve of you seducing my fiancée. I've already had her, and I don't share what's mine."

Gabriel stiffened. "You've had her?" Instead of feeling betrayed, he should have been jubilant. Seducing an experienced woman was more his style than wooing a virgin.

"I can't make it any plainer, Bathurst. Olivia Fairfax and I are lovers, and I wasn't the first. I've already proposed, but she's making me cool my heels. She's too stubborn and independent for her own good. She'll come around when she realizes I'm her only hope for marriage."

Gabriel regarded Palmerson as he would a worm that had just crawled out of the woodwork. "If you cared about the lady, you would be more careful of her reputation. Indulge me by explaining your reasons for wanting to wed Olivia. I should think you'd be looking for an heiress to bail you out of debt."

"I expect to come into a fortune soon, not that it's any of your concern. Heed my words, Bathurst. Stay away from Olivia Fairfax."

"I'll take your words under consideration," Gabriel said with a dismissive nod. "Excuse me, I must be off."

As Gabriel drove his phaeton through London's deserted streets, he mulled over everything Palmerson had told him. For some reason, the thought of intimacy between Olivia and Palmerson disgusted him, but that didn't make him want her any less. As for Palmerson's warning, it would go unheeded. Gabriel feared neither Palmerson nor his threats.

Sydney Germaine, Viscount Palmerson, brooded over his conversation with Bathurst long after the bidding had ceased and most of Madame Bella's clients were above stairs with the women of their choice. Palmerson sat in a corner, nursing a drink while he formulated a plan to force Olivia to marry him before it was too late. If Olivia didn't wed him soon, all would be lost. He needed this marriage, had planned it for years, right down to orchestrating Sefton's untimely death. Unfortunately, Olivia hadn't fallen in with his plans.

Olivia blamed him for her father's slide into debauchery and stubbornly refused to be persuaded otherwise. Once they were wed, he would beat the stubbornness out of her, but until she was his, he had to tread carefully. Unfortunately, time was running out. Olivia had to be his wife before her twenty-fifth birthday.

Drumming his fingers against the table, Palmerson racked his brain for a solution to his problem. It came to him slowly, but it was so ingenious that he couldn't help smiling. It would take some prior planning and a good deal of preparation, but with so much at stake, the trouble would be worth it.

\*　　\*　　\*

Olivia hardly expected Bathurst to call after she had told him there was no point in continuing their association, but here he was, standing before her as handsome and confident as ever.

"Another fine day, Lady Olivia," Bathurst said when Peterson ushered him into the parlor. "Are you ready?"

"I thought after yesterday—"

"You thought wrong." He glanced at Alma, who had just entered the room. "Good day, Lady Alma, you're looking exceptionally well this morning. I've come to take your niece on a picnic."

"I'm not going," Olivia replied.

"You'll need your bonnet and spencer," Gabriel said, ignoring her.

"I'll get them," Alma offered.

"Auntie!"

"Oh, dear, I've spoken out of turn again, haven't I?" She squared her shoulders. "My niece doesn't wish to go with you, my lord."

"Of course she does."

Olivia felt her cheeks heating. Did Bathurst actually believe she would fall into his arms like all his other women? Who did he think he was, to order her about like one of his lackeys? She didn't need a man in her life, especially not Bathurst. Being with him was too risky. She didn't fancy the gallows, which was where she would end up if he learned the truth.

"I'm sorry, my lord, but—"

He threaded her arm in his and led her toward the door. "You don't really need a wrap, Olivia. If you get chilled, I'll lend you my coat."

Disgruntled, Olivia realized that Bathurst wasn't going to take no for an answer. "Would you please fetch my bonnet and spencer, Auntie?"

"I knew you'd see things my way," Gabriel said as Alma hurried off.

Alma returned a few minutes later. Olivia fumed in impotent rage as Gabriel helped her on with her spencer and tied the bonnet strings beneath her chin.

"It's a shame to cover all that glorious hair," Gabriel murmured.

"Most people think red hair is hideous."

"I'm not most people."

"So I've discovered. Very well," she said crisply. "Let's get this over with."

An uneasy silence ensued as Gabriel handed Olivia into the curricle and bounded up beside her. The horses were prancing down the road when Olivia deigned to speak. "I don't understand you, my lord."

"Call me Gabriel. What don't you understand?"

"Your persistence. Why are you pursuing me?"

"Because it pleases me."

"You're wasting your time. I have nothing to offer a man of your rank."

"Don't you? Palmerson hinted otherwise."

"Palmerson? I can't believe you'd take anything Palmerson told you seriously."

Gabriel's brows shot upward. "Really? He said he was your lover."

Angry color crept up Olivia's neck. "He what? How dare he! Is there no end to that man's effrontery?"

"Are you denying it?"

"Take me home, Bathurst. I refuse to remain in the company of a man who thinks ill of me."

Gabriel drove over London Bridge and into the country as if he hadn't heard her. "Blame your lover, not me. He's the one maligning your reputation. You

99

haven't answered my question. Are you and Palmerson lovers?"

"Your question doesn't deserve an answer. Where are you taking me?"

"You enjoyed the lake so much yesterday, I thought we'd return."

"That's not a good idea."

A wicked grin kicked up the corners of his lips. "Afraid to be alone with me?"

"Any woman in her right mind would be afraid to be alone with one of the Rogues of London."

He turned the horses down the narrow lane to the lake. "But you're different, aren't you, Olivia?"

"I should hope so. I'm perfectly capable of putting rogues in their places."

"I admire your spunk." He studied her features through narrowed eyes. "I wish I could remember where we've met before."

Olivia went still. "How many times must I tell you we've not met before the night of Dutchess Stanhope's ball?"

Gabriel sent her an oblique look. "I'll believe it when my mind tells me it's so. Ah, here we are."

"It looks like rain," Olivia observed. "Perhaps we shouldn't linger."

Gabriel scowled up at the sky. "It was clear when we left, but this is England, after all. Nevertheless, it doesn't appear threatening yet. You can tell me about Palmerson while we set out our picnic lunch."

"I'm not leaving the curricle, and I don't wish to discuss Palmerson."

"Do you deny that he's your lover?"

"Why do you care?"

"Because *I* want to be your lover. You're too good

for Palmerson. If you loved him, you'd marry him."

"I wouldn't marry Palmerson if he were the last man on earth," Olivia huffed. "Does that answer your question?"

"Not really. Are you sure you want to sit here?" She nodded her head. "Very well, if you're not going to leave the curricle, let's discuss you. You fascinate me, Olivia. I admire your independence and feisty spirit. You deserve a lot of credit for managing to stay afloat financially after your father's death, but I can help you if you'd let me. Palmerson is in dun territory; he can offer you nothing but his name."

"What can *you* offer me, Bathurst?"

His silver eyes glowing with dark fire, Gabriel said, "Whatever your heart desires. Money to keep your brother in school, servants, jewels, gowns for you and your aunt, everything a woman in your position could want."

Olivia's mouth flattened. "*My position?* I'm an earl's daughter. Why shouldn't I hold out for marriage? I would be ruined if I accepted your scandalous offer. Just because I lack a dowry and am on the shelf, that doesn't mean I should sacrifice my reputation."

"According to Palmerson, he has already ruined you. How many men besides myself do you suppose he's regaled with your amorous escapades?"

"The swine!" Olivia spat. "You can't deny, however, that he has offered me his name. Can you say the same?"

"No, Olivia, I can't and won't offer you my name. For reasons of my own, I've sworn never to marry."

"A rogue to the very end, Bathurst?"

"I wouldn't have it any other way. But you can't claim you're not attracted to me, Olivia."

*Not attracted to him?* A shiver coursed down her spine. She could only thank God the rogue didn't realize how his nearness disturbed her.

"You're shivering. Are you cold?" His arm came around her. "Let me warm you."

Her trembling increased.

"Dare I hope your trembling has something to do with me?"

"One can always hope," Olivia replied tartly. "Kindly remove your arm."

"I don't think so. I'm going to kiss you, Olivia."

Olivia's senses froze as he slid her onto his lap. She felt the heat of his body through the layers of their clothing, and her mouth went dry as he stared at her lips. Then those sensuous lips were covering hers, and he was taking his time to learn the shape of her mouth with the tip of his tongue. Holding her mouth tightly shut, she tried to withhold a response, but her inexperience was her undoing.

His tongue prodded against the seam of her lips and they opened to the heat and taste of him, and when his tongue slid confidently into her mouth, she felt as if her world were spinning out of control. A muffled protest rose in her throat, exiting in a sigh when she felt his hand slide beneath her skirt and skim up her legs, finally coming to rest on her thigh. She was still adjusting to the sensation of his large, hot hand on her bare flesh when his fingers began to move. His kisses grew harder, more demanding, and all she could do was wind her arms around his neck and hang on. Bathurst was like no other man she'd ever known.

Rogue was his name, seduction was his game, and she was his victim. When he cupped her between her legs, she stiffened, all her senses centered on the warmth of his touch and the unfamiliar sensations soaring within her.

His fingers moved upon tender, swollen flesh. "Relax," Gabriel whispered against her lips. "I'm not going to hurt you."

"Stop," Olivia panted. "I . . . this is . . . Do you seduce every woman you meet?" The subtle movement of his fingers against her drove coherent thought from her mind.

"Of course," he murmured. Then he kissed her again, deeply, his tongue moving in and out of her mouth in a rhythm that held no meaning for sexually inexperienced Olivia.

He tore his mouth from hers to ravenously kiss the pink shell of her ear, the softness of her neck, the tender hollow at the base of her throat. Olivia cried out in sudden and unexpected need when one of his fingers pushed inside her. She arched against him, sending his finger deeper. Then his thumb rubbed against a place so sensitive, her body began to vibrate in spontaneous reaction.

She was so caught up in the moment that she didn't realize Gabriel had unfastened her clothing and bared her breasts until she felt the wet heat of his mouth on her swollen nipple. With so many sensations battering her at once, her body seemed to work independently of her mind. She couldn't think, could only feel. Her body was all liquid heat and softness, her bones melting.

An ache was building inside her, and her arms locked around him as his finger sank deeper into her, filling her, arousing her. In and out his finger slid as his lips and tongue suckled and licked her breasts. Instead of stopping him, she pressed herself closer, pressing against the hard ridge of his sex. Her breath caught; she dragged in desperate sips of air, her body suddenly gone rigid and her blood pounding.

Incapable of moving or thinking, all she could do was reach for the elusive ecstasy taunting her. When she grasped it she cried out, a cry of surprise and wonder.

Shocked, Gabriel realized he wanted Olivia with a need that was staggering, a hunger so consuming he feared he'd burst into flame. His body was hard, his sex thick and turgid. He couldn't recall when a woman had challenged his jaded senses like Olivia did.

More than anything, Gabriel wanted to flip up her skirts and drag her beneath him, but a curricle was too confining for that sort of activity and the skies were too threatening to linger. Soon, he promised himself; soon he'd have her naked and panting for him. Soon he'd bury himself deep inside her, feel her tightness wrap around him, hear her cry out his name in ecstasy. No matter what prior claim Palmerson had on her, she *would* be his. There was a connection between them that defied explanation, and he knew Olivia was aware of it.

Olivia stiffened and pulled away. She looked dazed, and a smile stretched his lips. The radiant face of a sated woman was the most beautiful sight in the world. Not only did it please him, but it stroked his ego as well. Did Palmerson make her face glow and her body throb?

"What just happened?" Olivia asked in bewilderment.

"You experienced pleasure."

The confused look on her face gave him pause for thought. "Palmerson must be an inept lover if he failed to satisfy you."

His words seemed to bring her out of her trance. "Blast you! What you just did is unforgivable." She fumbled with the fastenings of her clothing, her expression mutinous. "Take me home."

"There's something compelling between us, Olivia," he said with a hint of puzzlement. "You sense it too, I know you do."

Sheer panic seized her. "There's nothing, do you hear, nothing!" She had to put distance between her and Bathurst.

Grasping the sides of the curricle, she half rose, preparing to leap to the ground. A muscular arm curved around her waist, pulling her back into the seat.

"Where are you going?"

"Anywhere. Far away from you."

Gabriel's brow furrowed in consternation. "I told you I wouldn't hurt you. Why do you fear me?"

"You don't understand! You're dangerous." *Oh, God, had she said too much?*

"Relax, Olivia, I'll take you home. The weather is too threatening for our picnic anyway. But this isn't finished between us. Nothing will be settled until you're beneath me and I'm buried deep inside you. Don't fight it, Livvy, it's meant to be. From the moment I saw those green eyes of yours . . ." He paused, his expression thoughtful.

Olivia bit her lip as tremors of fear coursed through her. Gabriel's seductive words didn't frighten her as much as his sharp intellect. She waited with bated breath for him to continue.

"Sorry, I had a momentary lapse. I know I saw you at the dowager's ball, but my mind refuses to accept that as our first encounter."

Nearly sick with relief, Olivia vowed to avoid the far-too-handsome, much-too-sensual, roguish Lord Bathurst in the near and distant future.

# Chapter Seven

Olivia hadn't slept well the past few nights. After her last encounter with Bathurst, nothing in her world was as it should be. Confused emotions warred inside her. She enjoyed being with Bathurst too much, even though she knew his intentions were dishonorable. It wasn't difficult to see how he had earned his reputation. No decent woman was safe in his company. At least he was truthful about what he wanted from a woman. He offered no false promises, no lies.

Dimly she wondered what had set him against marriage. Most men wanted heirs to inherit their lands. Bathurst was a marquis; he had a great deal to lose should he fail to provide heirs.

Reluctantly she tore her thoughts away from the disturbing marquis and concentrated on her desperate straits. Not only did she owe Bathurst for the roof he'd financed, but she was also behind on her brother's quarterly tuition at the university. There was nothing left to sell, and their larder was nearly bare. Something had to be done, and soon.

Aunt Alma had removed Olivia's bandage before her last outing with Bathurst, and her wound appeared to be healing nicely. It occurred to her that Bathurst might have seen the puckered scar when he'd bared her breasts, but since he hadn't mentioned it, she supposed he had been too carried away to notice.

There was no help for it. Pete and Ollie would have to ride again.

A knock on her door roused Olivia from her silent musings.

"Are you awake, Livvy?"

"Come in, Auntie."

Olivia turned away from the window and smiled at Alma. "Good morning, Auntie. Is something wrong?"

"No, dear, everything is as usual. I just wanted to tell you I'm off to do the marketing. Is it all right if I take Peterson with me? I feel safer on the streets with him along."

"By all means, take Peterson with you," Olivia said distractedly.

"Are you all right, dear? You seem distraught."

"I'm fine, Auntie, truly. Run along."

"Is it Bathurst? He hasn't come around lately."

"That's exactly how I want it. I hate being indebted to him for our new roof. I hope I never see him again."

Alma rolled her eyes. "If you say so, dear. Well, then, I'm off. I'll try not to be too long."

Olivia lingered a few minutes longer, then went downstairs to fix her breakfast. She found a hunk of bread and a piece of cheese to go with her tea and sat down to enjoy the meager meal. Unfortunately, her mind was too preoccupied to taste what she was eating.

The moon was on the wane; tonight would be a perfect night for Pete and Ollie to don their disguises and take to the road. If Olivia had had any other choice, she wouldn't be a highwayman, but fate and her father's indulgences had turned her into an outlaw. She prayed that tonight's caper would prove lucrative enough to pay their bills and feed them for a long time to come. The oftener Pete and Ollie rode, the more dangerous it became. Her greatest fear was that somewhere at the end of the road, the gallows was waiting for them.

After finishing her breakfast, Olivia proceeded to tidy the house. It was good having a roof that didn't leak, but being indebted to Bathurst bothered her. He wanted things from her she wasn't willing to part with: her virginity and her good name. But perhaps he had given up on her. He hadn't been around since the day he'd attempted to seduce her in his curricle.

Immersed in her thoughts, Olivia didn't hear the commotion at the door right away. When it finally occurred to her that someone was banging on the front portal with great impatience, she hurried to answer the summons. She nearly slammed the door in his face when she saw Palmerson standing on the doorstep.

"Good day, Olivia, may I come in?"

"I'm alone, Lord Palmerson. You may return when Aunt Alma is here, but I wouldn't advise it."

"I know you're alone. I saw your aunt and butler leave."

A chill snaked down Olivia's spine. "Were you watching the house?"

"Why would you think that?" He stepped around her and closed the door, leaning against it as he regarded her through slumberous eyes.

"You *were* watching the house," she charged. "What do you want, Lord Palmerson? State your business and kindly leave."

"Draw in your claws, Olivia. I merely came to invite you to Lady Filmore's musicale tonight. A diva from Italy will perform. It should prove quite entertaining."

Olivia's mind whirled with possibilities. What was to stop her from slipping above stairs at the musicale and pinching some of Lady Filmore's jewels? It would certainly be less hazardous than conducting another robbery on the highway. She'd never forgive herself if Peterson was made to suffer for her folly.

"Very well, my lord, I'll accompany you, but don't read too much in my acceptance."

"Splendid, my dear! I'll call for you at nine sharp."

Olivia returned to the kitchen and drank another cup of tea while she deliberated the pros and cons of her venture. Bathurst wasn't the type to attend anything as tame as a musicale, so she wouldn't have to worry about eluding the sharp-witted marquis. Palmerson could be fooled, but not Bathurst. She would simply slip away while the diva was performing and pinch a few of Lady Filmore's baubles.

Olivia was washing her teacup when Alma and Peterson returned from the market.

"We found some good bargains today," Alma trilled.

"Your cloak is damp, Auntie. Is it raining?"

"It is a bit damp outside."

"Perhaps you should go upstairs and change before you catch a chill. I'll put your purchases away."

"Thank you, dear," Alma said. "The past few days have been so lovely, I forgot how quickly the weather could turn."

She hurried off, leaving Olivia and Peterson alone.

"We need to talk," Olivia began.

"That we do, Miss Livvy. There's a waning moon tonight. Shall Pete and Ollie ride?"

"No. I've discovered another way to solve our financial difficulties, at least for the time being. Palmerson called while you and Auntie were gone. He invited me to Lady Filmore's musicale tonight. As you well know, Lord and Lady Filmore are wealthy patrons of the arts. They're currently sponsoring opera and have invited an Italian diva to perform at their musicale. There should be quite a crush of people in attendance; I shan't be missed for the few minutes it will take to pinch a few baubles Lady Filmore will scarcely miss."

"I don't like it, Miss Livvy," Peterson argued. "Palmerson is not to be trusted, and you'll be alone with him."

"I can't continue to endanger your life, Peterson. I don't know what we would have done without you after Papa died. I'm thinking it's time Pete and Ollie retired."

"That's the best news I've heard in a long time," Alma said delightedly.

"Auntie, how long have you been standing there?"

"Long enough to hear you renounce your life as an outlaw."

Olivia and Peterson exchanged glances over Alma's petite head. Olivia hoped he understood that he wasn't to mention her caper tonight to Alma. The less she knew, the better off she'd be.

"Yes, well, outlaws lead precarious lives. We'll find another way to support ourselves."

"Just so, my dear," Alma said, beaming. "I know you'll think of something."

"I've accepted Lord Palmerson's invitation to attend

a musicale at the Filmore's tonight," Olivia continued.

"Palmerson!" Alma gasped. "I thought you couldn't stand the man."

"I've decided a little socializing will do me good."

"But with Palmerson? I know you're old enough to make your own decisions, dear, but why would you accept Palmerson's invitation when you can't abide the man? Lord Bathurst—"

"Forget Bathurst. He can offer me nothing."

"He put a new roof on our house. He can't be all bad."

"Bathurst does nothing without a reason," Olivia said. "Enough about the marquis. I'm going with Palmerson, and that's final. Don't wait up for me."

"You look quite dazzling tonight," Alma said as Olivia descended the stairs that evening.

"I hope no one remembers my gown as the same one I wore to the dowager's ball."

"Why should you care? It looks lovely on you."

"Here's your wrap, Miss Livvy," Peterson said, handing Olivia a richly fringed and embroidered shawl that had once belonged to her mother. It was the one item she hadn't been able to part with.

Palmerson arrived precisely at nine. A delighted smile stretched his lips when he saw her. "I'll be the envy of every man attending the musicale."

Something in his tone of voice made Olivia uneasy, but she had no choice but to carry out her plan. She tried not to flinch when Palmerson gripped her elbow and escorted her out the door.

Alma stared at the closed door a long moment, then turned to Peterson, a frown wrinkling her brow. "I don't like this, Peterson. Whatever could Olivia be thinking? I thought she detested Palmerson. I do wish I had gone with her."

"Would it make you feel better if I went to the Filmore mansion to keep an eye on things?"

"Would you, Peterson? I know I can depend on you."

"Of course, my lady, if it will ease your mind," Peterson said.

Olivia sat as far away from Palmerson as possible in his closed coach. Unfortunately, he kept sliding closer, until she was scrunched into the far corner.

"You're sitting too close, my lord," she complained.

"Am I, my dear?" he said, displaying no remorse for his boldness.

"Please move away. I can scarcely breathe with you crowding me. What's taking so long? I don't recall the Filmore mansion being this far."

"Look out the window, Olivia."

A tremor of fear coursed down Olivia's spine when she pulled aside the leather curtain and saw that they had left the City and were headed into the countryside.

"We're leaving Town!"

"I'm well aware of that, Olivia."

She tried to disguise her panic. "Where are you taking me?"

"Before I tell you, will you marry me?"

"No, thank you. I don't wish to marry you, Palmerson. You know I have valid reasons to reject you, so why do you persist?"

"Then you leave me no recourse."

Color drained from her cheeks. "Whatever are you talking about?"

No answer was forthcoming as Palmerson pulled a small vial from his pocket, sprinkled several drops of the clear liquid onto his handkerchief and shoved it against her face.

The sweet, pungent odor shocked her senses, almost as much as Palmerson's surprising move. She tried to fight, tried to hold her breath, but the wind left her lungs and she was forced to inhale. The moment the fumes entered her air passages, the fight went out of her. She felt herself floating, as if her mind was no longer attached to her body. Blackness teased the edges of her consciousness; then she fell into a deep void from which there was no escape.

Olivia remained unconscious as Palmerson carried her into the Hare and Hound, a seedy inn on the outskirts of London, where he had arranged for a room earlier that day. The innkeeper barely glanced at Olivia when Palmerson approached him. The room was paid for, and the gentleman's affairs were none of his business.

"I expect friends to arrive later tonight," Palmerson said. "When they ask for me, direct them to my room."

"Er . . . are ye certain that's wise, milord?" He gave Palmerson a sly wink. "They might show up at the wrong time, if ye get my meaning."

"That's exactly what I'm hoping for," Palmerson murmured.

Scratching his head, the innkeeper shrugged and turned away as Palmerson mounted the stairs with Olivia in his arms.

Palmerson carried Olivia into the room, placed her on the bed and removed all her clothing except her chemise. He wanted his friends to find him and Olivia in a compromising position, but he didn't want them to see too much of her. Once they were "discovered" together, Olivia would be ruined and forced to accept his proposal.

Peterson rushed into the parlor, out of breath and shaking, his face pale.

"What is it, Peterson? Is it Olivia? Has something happened to her? Oh, please, don't keep me in suspense," Alma begged.

Struggling to catch his breath, Peterson wobbled to a chair, where he collapsed. "There is no musicale at the Filmores' tonight," he gasped.

Alma's hand flew to her chest. "What! You must be mistaken."

"No mistake, my lady. The house was dark when I arrived. At first I thought I had the wrong address and went up to the door to inquire. A servant answered my knock and told me the Filmores were abroad and not expected to return any time soon. I nearly expired on the spot. What has Palmerson done with Miss Livvy?"

Alma's legs began to crumple beneath her. Peterson leaped from his chair to steady her. "We must try to remain calm, Lady Alma. We shall put our minds to the problem and—"

"And what, Peterson? How will we rescue our Livvy from that monster? No telling what he'll do to her."

"He won't hurt her, my lady; he doesn't dare."

"Knowing Palmerson, he would dare anything to get what he wants, and for some obscure reason he wants Livvy. What if someone finds out she's alone with him? It would ruin her. Livvy considered herself on the shelf, but I did so hope that one day she would find a man she could love, one who would love her despite her lack of dowry. But if Palmerson has her, all is lost. She's ruined, whether or not Palmerson . . . whether he . . . oh, dear, I can't even say it."

"We'll find them, Lady Alma."

"How? What are we going to do?" She began sobbing quietly into her handkerchief.

Peterson looked confused, as if he wasn't sure himself what to do.

"Where do we start? Who can we trust to help us?" Alma wailed.

Peterson's brow furrowed. Suddenly he looked up, the tension easing from his body.

"Bathurst."

"The marquis? Oh, dear, are you sure?"

"I can't think of another. He seemed interested in Miss Livvy; what have we got to lose?"

"Hurry, then, Peterson. Lord only knows what the viscount has in mind for our Livvy."

Gabriel shifted impatiently while Throckmorton tied his cravat.

"Hold still, milord, else we'll be at this all night."

"Do hurry, Throckmorton. Braxton and Westmore are waiting for me at White's. We're to attend the opera tonight and Lady Symore's rout afterward."

"Then you'll want to look your best, milord," Throckmorton sniffed. "There." He stepped away to view his handiwork. "Perfect. I'll get your—"

The door opened, cutting Throckmorton off in midsentence. It was Grimsley, his face twisted into a grimace. "There's a 'person' below insisting that he speak with you, milord. He says it's urgent."

"A person, Grimsley? Surely you can do better than that. Does this person have a name?"

"Peterson, milord."

Gabriel whirled so fast he nearly knocked Throckmorton off his feet. "Peterson, you say? Is he alone?"

"So it would seem, milord."

"Show him to the library. I'll join him directly."

Grimsley left. Gabriel shoved his arms into the coat Throckmorton held out for him and strode out the door. "Don't wait up, Throckmorton. I'll probably be late."

Gabriel took the stairs two at a time. Peterson was Olivia's servant; there was no reason for the man to be here unless . . . No, that didn't bear thinking about.

Peterson was pacing the library when Gabriel burst into the room. He turned at Gabriel's entrance. The servant's face was ashen and drawn; his eyes were wide and filled with panic, as if he carried the weight of the world on his stooped shoulders.

"What is it, man?" Gabriel asked tersely.

"We had no one else to turn to, milord," Peterson said. "Lady Alma and I are frantic with worry."

His patience wearing thin, Gabriel shouted, "Get to the point, man! Has something happened to Lady Olivia?"

Peterson looked so miserable, Gabriel feared the worst. He'd tried not to think of Olivia these past few days. She'd told him quite emphatically that she wanted nothing to do with him, and he'd decided to honor her wishes . . . for the time being. But he hadn't given up on her, not by a long shot. Olivia Fairfax wasn't the kind of woman one forgot easily. He wanted her, and he always got what he wanted.

"Miss Livvy is gone, milord. She was abducted by a man who is up to no good, I'm sure."

"Abducted? What do you mean?" He stepped to the sideboard, poured two fingers of brandy into a snifter and handed it to Peterson. "You look like you could use this. Now sit down and start from the beginning. I can't help if I don't know all the details."

Peterson took a large gulp of brandy, shuddered, then perched on the edge of a chair. "You're our only hope, milord. We are in desperate need of your help."

"Tell me," Gabriel said, forcing a calm he didn't feel.

Peterson sucked in an unsteady breath. "Lord Palmerson invited Miss Livvy to a musicale at the Filmores' tonight."

Gabriel frowned. "The Filmores are out of town."

"Exactly," Peterson rasped. "Lady Alma was worried about Miss Livvy, her going off with Palmerson and all, so I offered to go to the Filmores' and keep an eye on things. That's when I discovered Palmerson's duplicity."

"How do you know Olivia didn't go willingly with Palmerson? What makes you think he abducted her? She did agree to accompany him, didn't she?"

Peterson's thin lips flattened. "I know Miss Livvy and she wouldn't do such a thing. She doesn't even like Palmerson." He hesitated a moment, then said, "She had a reason for accepting Palmerson's invitation."

"What reason?"

Peterson drew himself up to his full height. "I'd never betray a confidence."

A tightness developed in Gabriel's chest and spread throughout his body. If Palmerson harmed one hair of Olivia's head, he'd call out the bastard and take great pleasure in skewering him.

"Can you tell me anything else? Something that will assist me in my search?"

"You're going to help us? Oh, milord, I don't know what to say, except offer my gratitude."

Gabriel gripped Peterson's shoulders. In another min-

ute the man would be blubbering. "Pull yourself together. I'll get to the bottom of this. If Olivia is indeed
missing, I'll find her."

"What can I do to help?"

"Return home and keep Lady Alma calm. I'll send
word around when I learn something. Are you afoot?"

"Aye, milord."

"I'll drive you home," Gabriel said as he strode out
the door.

After Gabriel delivered Peterson home, he drove his
carriage to St. James's Square. He hadn't the foggiest
idea where to begin looking for Olivia, or even if she
wanted to be found, but starting at the clubs seemed a
good idea. Palmerson had cronies among the *ton*. Perhaps one of them would reveal something helpful.

Gabriel's first stop was Brooks's. None of Palmerson's cronies were about, so he left. Boodle's proved
just as fruitless. He encountered Braxton and Westmore
at White's, and without telling them why, he begged off
accompanying them to the opera. His search for Palmerson's friends proved as futile at White's as it had at
the other clubs. His last hope was Crocker's gambling
hall.

Luck was with him. He found three of Palmerson's
cronies at Crocker's. Lords Dearborn, Sanford and
Fordham were engaged in a high-stakes game of whist.
Gabriel watched from the sidelines as the men finished
a hand. All three men were second or third sons of noblemen with no hope of inheriting either title or fortune,
and were as deeply in dun territory as Palmerson. Gabriel knew them to be wild, unprincipled rakes with
little to commend them. While Gabriel might be a
rogue, he would never stoop to kidnapping or rapine.
His association with women was subtler, and he used

neither ruthless means nor brutality in his seduction of them.

Gabriel's patience was rewarded when he heard Lord Sanford remark, "Too bad Palmerson isn't around to see us winning for a change."

"He's enjoying himself with his ladybird at the Hare and Hound," Fordham reminded him.

"Maybe he'll share with us," Dearborn said.

"Not likely," Fordham guffawed. "He intends to marry the girl. Told me so himself."

The fourth player at the table, Lord Hollingsworth, an acquaintance of Gabriel's, glanced up at him and waved a greeting. "Bathurst. Didn't see you, old man. Care to join the game?"

"No, thanks," Gabriel replied. "I'm on my way out. Good night, gentlemen."

"The Hare and Hound," Gabriel repeated as he beat a hasty retreat.

Head spinning, Olivia opened her eyes and had no idea where she was or why. A sweet, cloying smell lingered in the air, and she blinked repeatedly to bring her scattered wits into focus. She recognized nothing, neither the room in which she found herself nor the bed upon which she was lying.

She turned her head and saw Palmerson sitting in a chair, staring at her with a gleam in his eyes that did not bode well for her. Fear clawing at her, she tried to rise, and suddenly realized that her hands had been tied to the bedpost.

"It's about time you awakened. I was beginning to think I'd given you too much chloroform."

"Untie me. What have you done, Palmerson?"

"Made sure you will marry me. You're ruined, my

dear, utterly and irrevocably ruined. After we're found together, you will have no choice but to become my bride."

"Where are we?"

"At an inn—that's all you need to know. I've been waiting for you to awaken so we can begin. You can't imagine how hard it was to keep my hands off you. Your breasts are beautiful—I've been admiring them for hours. The curve of your hips, the length of your legs—you are perfection. I could have taken you while you slept, but I want you awake and responsive when I make love to you."

Glancing down, Olivia became aware that her clothing had been removed down to her shift, rendering her vulnerable and exposed to Palmerson's vile intentions.

She pulled at her bindings. "You're despicable! How could you do such a thing to me? Release me this minute!"

"Not a chance, Olivia." He stretched and got to his feet. "I'm going to make it impossible for you to refuse my proposal."

Olivia watched in stunned silence as Palmerson removed his neckcloth, jacket and vest. When he started to unbutton his breeches, she opened her mouth to scream.

"Go ahead and scream," Palmerson taunted. "No one will come. I've planned this carefully and paid well not to be disturbed. Once our romantic tryst becomes fodder for the gossip mill, you'll have no choice but to marry me."

Angry breath whooshed from Olivia's lungs. "Toad! Monster! Why do you want me? I have nothing to offer you. No matter what you do to me, I'll never agree to marry you."

"You will once you consider how the scandal will affect your aunt and brother. You want Neville to be able to take his place in society, don't you?"

"I always thought you were a bastard, Palmerson; now I know it. Threaten anything you want, I still won't marry you."

He released the final button on his breeches and kicked them off. The bulge in his drawers sent fingers of fear sliding down Olivia's spine. She decided to scream despite Palmerson's warning that no one would interfere.

"I warned you," Palmerson snarled as he snatched a silk scarf from the nightstand, grasped her chin and stuffed the fabric into her mouth, effectively stifling her cry. "As you can see, I left nothing to chance."

Olivia kicked out wildly, but it did her little good. Palmerson fell on top of her, pinning her beneath him. Avoiding her flailing legs, he raised her shift above her hips and slammed his loins down on hers. She felt his rampant sex prodding against her and twisted her body to avoid what she feared was inevitable. She wasn't going to make it easy for him.

Gabriel entered the Hare and Hound in a towering rage. He had spotted Palmerson's coach in the courtyard, and the urge to kill was a roaring inferno inside him. He had felt this way before, but it was on the battlefield, after seeing his regiment cut down by Napoleon's forces. Briefly the thought occurred that Olivia had willingly accompanied Palmerson, but it didn't ease the terrible blackness raging through him.

Teeth clenched, hands fisted, Gabriel approached the innkeeper. "I'm looking for a . . . friend," he said, nearly choking on the word. "Lord Palmerson. Kindly direct me to his room."

Gabriel was prepared to use force, maybe even wave his pistol in order to get the information he wanted, but such measures proved unnecessary.

The innkeeper shrugged. "Upstairs. Second door on the left. You toffs are strange, but as long as I get my money, it's none of my affair."

Gabriel dashed up the staircase, stumbling through the dimly lit hallway until he found the room. Had the door been locked, Gabriel would have broken through, but the doorknob turned easily beneath his hand. A muffled sound coming from behind the door sent panic racing through him, and he flung the door open. It crashed into the wall with a loud bang.

If Gabriel thought it strange that Palmerson didn't react to his forced entrance, he didn't have time to think about it. The alarming sight of Olivia struggling beneath Palmerson, a gag stuffed in her mouth, her arms restrained and her bare legs flailing wildly, sent all thought fleeing.

"Get away from her!" he roared.

Apparently startled by a voice he hadn't expected to hear, Palmerson lifted his head and glared at Gabriel. "What in blazes are you doing here? This is none of your business."

Gabriel glanced at Olivia, his heart pounding erratically when her pleading gaze met his. "I'm making it my business. Move away from Olivia."

"Dammit, Bathurst, I'm going to marry Olivia. Go away—you're not wanted here."

Gabriel's gaze shifted again to Olivia; she was shaking her head in vigorous denial. "It seems I am wanted—to rescue the lady."

"I don't care what the lady wants!"

"I do," Gabriel growled as he pulled Palmerson off of Olivia and flung him to the floor. "Put on your clothes and get out of here."

Palmerson started to rise, saw the pistol in Gabriel's hand, and blanched. "Damn you for interfering! You'll not get away with this."

"I already have. Get dressed before I toss you out on your arse without a stitch of clothing."

Palmerson pulled on his breeches first, then reached for the rest of his clothing. A small sound from Olivia momentarily distracted Gabriel. Palmerson took advantage of the brief lapse and lunged at Gabriel. Though Gabriel wasn't expecting the move, his years in the army had honed his senses to a fine edge and he easily avoided Palmerson's attack. He brought the butt of his pistol down on Palmerson's head, watching dispassionately as Olivia's abductor collapsed at his feet.

Turning back to Olivia, he removed her gag.

# Chapter Eight

Olivia feared she was hallucinating. Bathurst couldn't be here. Yet he was, bigger than life.

"How . . . how did you know where to find me?" Olivia asked in a shaky voice. "Aunt Alma and Peterson thought I was attending a musicale. For that matter, so did I." She buried her face in her hands. "How could I have been so stupid?"

"This is not the time for recriminations, Olivia," Gabriel said as he quickly released her arms from their bindings.

"What are you going to do?"

"Dress the bastard and get him out of here before he regains consciousness."

Once her mind began functioning again, Olivia's thoughts returned to the vile thing Palmerson had almost accomplished, and anger replaced shock. But she needed more than anger to reassure her. She needed to feel Gabriel's arms around her, holding her, comforting her. She wanted his strength, his—

Her thoughts splintered when Gabriel hoisted Palmerson over his shoulder.

"Where are you going?"

"I'll be right back."

"Gabriel . . ."

The door opened and closed; then he was gone. Olivia's thoughts spun off in all directions as she huddled on the bed, her arms curled around her knees. Gaining a modicum of control, she knew she had nothing to fear with Bathurst in control and chided herself for doubting his ability to handle any situation fate threw in his path.

The door opened, and the object of her thoughts stepped into the room. Gabriel went to her immediately and perched on the edge of the bed. "Are you all right?"

His nearness reassured her, though tears were still very close to spilling down her cheeks. Unable to speak, she nodded.

"He didn't hurt you?"

She shook her head. "He tried to . . . he wanted to . . ."

Gabriel's expression hardened. "I know what he wanted to do."

"What did you do with him?"

"I wanted to kill him."

"I'm glad you didn't. He's not worth it."

"I put him in his coach and instructed his coachman to take him home."

"Wasn't the innkeeper suspicious?"

"I told him Palmerson was deep in his cups and gave him enough blunt to curb his curiosity."

Her eyes shimmering with gratitude, Olivia reached

125

out to him, unaware how deeply the gesture aroused his masculinity, and suddenly she was in his arms. He murmured soothing words in her ear, but the words weren't as comforting as his arms. She felt his heart beating against her cheek, felt the heat of his body through the thin material of her chemise, and didn't have the willpower to refuse his comfort.

"I wish I *had* killed him," Gabriel muttered, nuzzling her neck. "I let him off too easy. Even if you were lovers, he had no right to take you against your will."

Shuddering, she raised her head and gazed into his eyes. "Help me forget it ever happened."

"Tell me what you want," Gabriel said.

She lifted her chin, her invitation unmistakable. Then he kissed her. The kiss did exactly what she hoped it would. Thoughts of Palmerson dissolved in the heat generated by the meeting of their lips. The kiss went on and on, robbing her of breath and will and replacing them with desire. His mouth on hers was like a healing balm, shoving the memory of Palmerson's attack to the far reaches of her mind. She didn't want to remember; she wanted to feel. She wanted Gabriel to erase what had almost happened tonight. She wanted . . .

Gabriel groaned against her lips and swore—dark, incoherent oaths of passion that she found wildly exciting. When his tongue prodded against her lips, she opened to him, savoring his taste and scent. His hands came up to cup her breasts, stroking her nipples with the pads of his fingers, sending shards of need shooting through her.

She arched against him, her arms curving around his neck to bring him closer. A strangled groan slipped past his lips, and suddenly he broke off the kiss.

"This is going too fast, Livvy. You know what's going to happen if we keep this up, don't you?"

Olivia didn't care, as long as his delicious kisses continued. She couldn't seem to get enough of them. "Don't stop, Gabriel, please don't stop. You're the only one who can take the awful memory of Palmerson away."

"Are you sure, Livvy? You know I can't marry—"

"Shhh, don't spoil this."

He dragged her onto his lap. She could feel the heat expanding between them and the hardness of his erection pressing against her bottom. Driven by instinct, she moved against him, rocking gently.

"Damnation, Livvy! If you don't stop that, this will end too soon. I've wanted you for so bloody long, I'm randy as a goat."

Olivia knew she should call a halt, but being in Gabriel's arms, his hands stroking her, felt too good to stop now. *This is wrong*, she told herself. Nothing good would come of surrendering to Bathurst.

"Maybe this isn't a good idea," she said feebly, ignoring the demands of her aroused body.

Gabriel's hand stilled beneath her chemise. She felt his shoulders tense and his fingers tighten against her thigh.

"Shall I stop?" he rasped. "I will, but it won't be easy."

His hand began to move in impatient circles over her hip and bottom. Hot, heavy tension built in her lower body with each heady stroke. When he eased her thighs apart to touch her, she stiffened and clung to him. He moved his fingers between her legs, touching her dewy center, teasing her sensitive nub with the pad of his thumb until she felt wet and swollen.

His finger pushed inside her. "Tell me, Livvy. Do you want me to stop?"

"Stop?" Could she bear it? What she really wanted was to bring this unnamed torment to a satisfying conclusion, to savor the delicious sensations that Gabriel's hands and mouth had aroused. A moan of pleasure escaped her lips as his talented fingers played inside her. If he stopped now she would surely die. "No, don't stop."

Anticipation thrummed through her as he laid her down on the mattress and removed her chemise.

Gazing at her with glittering eyes, he smiled his appreciation of all he saw. "You're even more beautiful than I imagined."

Olivia started to cover her private parts, but Gabriel wouldn't allow it. "No, don't hide yourself from me. I want to see all of you."

She held herself still, her breath coming in rapid little pants as she stared pointedly at his clothed body. "That's hardly fair when you're still fully dressed."

Had she said that? Had Bathurst managed to turn her into a wanton with a few kisses and caresses?

"Anything to oblige a lady," Gabriel drawled.

Olivia didn't know whether to watch or close her eyes as Gabriel rose and began to strip. She was no young chit prone to faint at the sight of a man's bare chest, but despite her advanced age she had never seen a grown man's unclothed body. And with the haste Gabriel was shedding clothing, she was about to see more than she had bargained for.

He glanced at her and grinned, then sat on the edge of the bed and removed his shoes and hose. When he rose to take off his breeches, Olivia averted her eyes.

"Look at me, Livvy. You're too brave to act the coward."

Olivia's gaze lifted. No one had ever accused her of being a coward. Her eyes widened slightly when he slid his breeches and drawers down over his hips, but she didn't look away. She couldn't have even if she'd wanted to. His body was magnificent. Her first look at a man in full arousal was a potent reminder of what she was about to do. Her breath caught as he settled on the bed and placed his hand on her hip.

He pressed her against him, the blunt edge of his erection probing between her thighs as he kissed her. He seemed so large, so threatening, she feared he would split her in two. She knew she wanted this but wasn't sure she was ready. She had no experience of this kind of activity, and Gabriel had too much.

Would he laugh at her clumsy efforts? There were so many things to consider and so little time before he . . .

As he lifted himself over her, his tongue began a leisurely journey from her lips to her breasts. When he gently nipped and suckled one of her nipples, the blood flowing through her veins became a raging river of flame. He didn't linger long at his tender feast, but quickly moved down the creamy flat of her stomach, coming to rest at the burnished silkiness between her thighs.

A shocked cry escaped Olivia's mouth when he flicked his tongue up and down her cleft, grazing the swollen petals hidden there. "You can't . . . you mustn't."

Gabriel lifted his head. "Relax, Livvy, I'm not going to hurt you." Sliding his hands beneath her bottom, he spread her with his thumbs and lifted her into his mouth, feasting on her as if he were starving for the taste of her.

So intense were the feelings pouring through her that Olivia felt as if she were being consumed by the exquisite, earth-shattering sensations. Without conscious thought, she opened herself wider to him, watching his dark head as he lapped at her. Secret, forbidden thrills built within as his ravenous mouth devoured her.

Balanced precariously on the brink of a great discovery, Olivia cried out when Gabriel left his succulent feast and levered himself upward. Squirming uncomfortably, she felt a tremendous pressure as he pushed inside her.

The pressure eased and he went still, staring down at her. "Before I continue, I need to know if you've done this before. Was I wrong in assuming that Palmerson was your lover? Tell me now, before I take this all the way."

Dimly, Olivia wondered if he would stop if she told him she'd never known a man before. She didn't want him to stop. She'd come this far; she wanted to know the rest. "Would it make a difference, Bathurst?"

"Not as long as you understand there will be no offer of marriage. It's not you, Livvy. It's me. For reasons I can't explain, I will never marry."

"Don't worry, Bathurst, I expect no commitment from you. I came to terms with being unmarriageable long ago. I want this to happen, I want you to love me. I want to experience this at least once in my life, to solve the mystery of becoming a woman, and I want you to be the one to reveal it to me. But I won't become your mistress. Once we leave this room, we must go our separate ways."

"Will I take your virginity if I continue?" Gabriel persisted.

The muscles in his arms bulged, as if he were under a great strain, and the planes of his face were stark with a raw hunger that both thrilled and frightened her. But she wasn't going to back down now. She might never get another chance to become a woman.

"Don't you want me, Gabriel?"

Baring his teeth, he flexed his hips and broke through her maidenhead in one swift thrust, burying himself deep inside her. Olivia was expecting some discomfort, but she wasn't prepared for the pain. It roiled through her in turbulent waves as she fought for breath.

"Bloody hell," Gabriel muttered. "You *were* a virgin. Too late now, love, the deed is done and the worst is over. Try to relax; the pain will go away soon."

Olivia wasn't so sure. She felt stretched and filled and sore. Where was the blinding pleasure she'd hoped for? Was this all there was to it? She didn't realize she'd given voice to her fears until Gabriel said, "Don't worry, I'll make this good for you."

Lifting her legs, he shifted her position to ease the pressure. Then he stroked her and kissed her, running his fingers along the soft skin of her inner thigh, easing the tension from her muscles. She inhaled sharply as he rocked against her, creating a friction that brought a subtle return of the sensations she'd experienced before Gabriel came inside her.

"I'm all the way in, Livvy. Can you feel it? Let the feeling carry you away."

Carry her away? Where? Obviously, her inexperience was showing.

Suddenly she felt the need to move her hips back and forth, to meet his strokes and meld their bodies closer.

Her subtle response brought a groan from Gabriel's throat. He thrust faster, deeper; she rose up to meet his stokes, surprised to find the pain easing, and to her great surprise, the act became much more enjoyable. His breath rasped loudly in her ear; her own speeded up to match her heartbeat. Something was happening, something strange and wild and exhilarating.

Gasping for air, she began to enjoy the ride, relishing the way he felt deep inside her. Miraculously, he no longer seemed too large, but exactly right. Her fingers biting into the muscles of his back, she locked herself against him, holding him tight within the cradle of her thighs. The pressure intensified, became too exquisite to bear, and all thought fled except for this, for him, for *Gabriel*. Buffeted by a blinding rush of pure rapture, she called out his name as waves of incredible pleasure picked her up and carried her beyond the realm of reality.

Gabriel felt himself shattering and pulled out, shouting her name as he poured his seed onto the bedding. Then he covered her mouth with his and drank deeply of her pleasure.

Breathing hard, he collapsed beside her and pulled her into his arms. She was so silent, so still, he wondered what she was thinking. Until he had broken through her maidenhead, he hadn't believed she was untouched. Did she blame him for thinking her impure? Did she regret what they had done? Then a horrible thought occurred. Did she expect him to offer marriage even though he'd told her he could never wed?

When he felt warm droplets falling against his chest, he tilted Olivia's chin up, regarding her with concern.

"What is it, Olivia? Did I hurt you? The first time is always uncomfortable."

"It hurt, but the pain passed quickly. You're very good at this, Gabriel. I'm sorry if I disappointed you."

"Whatever gave you that idea?" He kissed the tip of her nose. "You were wonderful. It pleased me to know I was the first."

She winced and looked away. "You almost weren't. Thank you again for being here when I needed you. I'm not helpless, you know. I'm strong. I wasn't making it easy for Palmerson."

"Forget Palmerson. Why are you crying?"

"I'm sad because this will be the last time we'll be together like this. You averted a tragedy tonight, but I can't risk damaging Neville's place in society by causing a scandal. This is goodbye, Gabriel."

Gabriel wasn't at all convinced this was farewell. One taste of Olivia wasn't enough for him.

"We should leave, Livvy. We've lingered too long as it is."

He pulled on his breeches, then found her chemise and handed it to her while he gathered the rest of her things. When he turned back, Olivia had pulled the garment over her head and was sitting on the edge of the bed. She looked small and vulnerable and beautifully disheveled. He wanted to pull her back into bed and make love to her again. Gathering his scattered wits, he finished dressing.

When Gabriel glanced at Olivia and saw that she was having trouble fastening her gown, he moved behind her to help. Touching her was a mistake. The urgent need to kiss her overwhelmed him. Turning her to face him, he lifted her chin and covered her mouth with his.

Losing himself in the taste and scent of her, in the softness of her body pressed intimately against his, he nearly succumbed to his lustful desires again. But before he could be so foolish as to push her back on the bed, Olivia had the good sense to break off the kiss. She was still resting in his arms, looking like a woman who had just been thoroughly loved, when the door burst open and three men tumbled inside.

"I say, Sanford, you've gotten this all wrong. That isn't Palmerson."

Crying out in alarm, Olivia dove under the covers, but it was too late; the trio had already seen her face.

"Bathurst!" Fordham gasped. "So sorry, old man. Didn't mean to interrupt. We thought . . . that is, we were led to believe that Palmerson would be here with Lady Olivia."

Dearborn was too busy staring at Olivia to speak.

"So that was his game," Gabriel muttered darkly. Having three notorious gossips find him in a room with Olivia would have sealed her fate whether he had raped her or not. But it hadn't happened that way. Now there would be the devil to pay, and it would be up to him to make things right. Unfortunately, doing the "right thing" didn't include a proposal.

"Get out!" Gabriel shouted. "If any of you repeat what you've seen here tonight, I'll make your lives miserable."

Gabriel could tell by the avid looks on the men's faces that his threat wouldn't silence them. By tomorrow, everyone in London and beyond would know that he had thoroughly compromised Olivia. He was willing to bet that the London *Times* would carry a distorted account of the story. Olivia would be ruined socially, and he couldn't do a bloody thing about it.

"Our mouths are sealed," Sanford said, his eyes sparkling with amusement. "Come along, lads, let's see if we can find Palmerson."

The three men withdrew and Gabriel slammed the door behind them. Olivia peeked out from beneath the blanket, her face ashen. "How did they know?"

"Apparently, Palmerson arranged for London's three most notorious gossips to find you here with him. I should have seen it coming. I'm sorry, Livvy. Lingering in the room was a mistake."

"You're sorry!" Olivia cried, nearly frantic with grief and anger. "I've just made my family the object of the nastiest bit of gossip since my father's duel, and all you can say is you're sorry?"

"I'll do all in my power to protect you. I'll take the full blame. I'll say I forced you."

"Fat lot of good that will do. It's not just my reputation that will suffer, but Auntie's and Neville's as well. They'll be cut from society. Neville could be sent down from school if they hear of this fiasco.

"Take me home," she said, adjusting her shawl around her shoulders. "What's done is done; there's no help for it. The family has lived with scandal before."

"Olivia, I didn't intend for it to happen this way. I followed you here to help you, not ruin you."

"Better to be ruined by you than Palmerson," Olivia said honestly. "I haven't asked you to compromise your principles, Bathurst, and rest assured I won't demand a marriage proposal. I made a choice tonight and have no regrets."

Gabriel followed Olivia out the door and down the stairs. The innkeeper was sleeping on a stool in a corner, and only two uninterested customers were in the common room. Gabriel hustled Olivia through the door and handed her into his carriage. After giving Jenkins directions, he climbed in beside her.

Gabriel thought Olivia was displaying admirable

Connie Mason

composure, and he felt a twinge of remorse. Seducing her had always been his goal, but he had to admit the time and place had been all wrong. He hadn't meant it to happen like this, but their passions had gotten out of control. Olivia had needed him and he had obliged, thoroughly enjoying every minute of it. There was nothing jaded about his response to Olivia, and he hadn't felt that way in a very long time. She was fresh, innocent, and whether she realized it or not, made for loving.

Marriage was the usual solution in a situation like this, but proposing to Olivia was not an option for him. He could never wed, and if she knew why, she would agree. He could, however, help her financially.

"I'm going to open a bank account in your name and deposit a substantial amount in it, Livvy," he began. "It's the least I can do for you."

Jerking her head around, Olivia glared at him. "Absolutely not! I refuse to accept a farthing from you. I need neither your guilt nor your help."

Gabriel heaved a weary sigh. Olivia was making this difficult. Why couldn't she give him the satisfaction of providing financial help? Pride and independence were admirable traits, but Olivia took them too far. Or did she? Didn't he admire her for those very qualities? Blast it all! Why was he so confused?

"You're being stubborn, Livvy. Please let me do this for you."

She shook her head. "No."

"Very well. Do as you please. I will, however, instruct my solicitor to deposit a sum of money in the bank for your use, whether or not you choose to accept it."

"You're wasting your time, Bathurst," Olivia bit out.

"Paying me for services rendered will not endear you to me."

Long minutes of silence ensued; then Gabriel said, "When shall I see you again? Will you attend the opera with me Saturday night?"

"We won't be seeing each other again, Gabriel. I thought I made that clear."

"I suppose you hate me now. I wanted you in my bed, but I didn't want you to hate me afterward."

"Hate you? No, I don't hate you. How could I? You rescued me from Palmerson. Marriage to him would be unthinkable. I wish I knew why he's pressuring me to marry him."

"I'll have Grimsley look into it for you. If Palmerson has a motive, my man will find it."

"That offer I will accept. Thank you, Gabriel," Olivia said, turning to stare out the window. What had happened tonight between her and Bathurst had been so extraordinary, she could compare it to nothing in her life thus far. Staring into the darkness, she allowed her thoughts to return to that dingy little room where she had lost her virginity.

She had never guessed that making love could be so sublimely pleasurable or so rewarding, and she suspected it wouldn't be that way with anyone but Bathurst.

"Are you all right?" Gabriel asked when the silence between them grew lengthy. "You've been through a lot tonight."

Olivia almost laughed. She'd gone through a lot the night he had shot her, too. Yet she had survived.

"I meant to ask you something before Palmerson's friends burst in on us," Gabriel said. "I noticed a scar on your left shoulder. I didn't get a good look at it in the dim light, but it appeared fairly new."

Oh, God, he *had* noticed. She'd been too caught up in their lovemaking to think about it.

"The scar isn't a new one," she lied. "It happened last summer when Neville was home from the university. He was practicing with our father's pistol and I got in the way."

Gabriel gave her a startled look. "What a ghastly accident. I hope you both learned a lesson. Firearms are dangerous to those who don't know how to use them."

Olivia shrugged. "It was a minor wound. Neville was horrified, but no real harm was done."

Olivia returned her gaze out the window, and Gabriel sank back against the squabs in contemplative silence. When they neared her house, he asked, "Shall I come in with you?"

"That's not necessary. I'll explain to Aunt Alma and Peterson myself."

"Will you tell them about us . . . about what happened tonight? If you don't, they'll learn about it in the newspapers. I'm afraid my threats won't stop Palmerson's friends from making the most of this."

"I'll tell them what I want them to know," Olivia said. "They needn't know what really happened between us at the inn. Palmerson's friends didn't actually catch us doing . . . you know. They just suspect that something took place."

"That's for you to decide, Livvy. I'll see you tomorrow."

"No! Please, Gabriel, my way is best. You're not ruined, I am. Men are held blameless in these situations. They can go about their usual business without recrimination, while women are cut by society. I prefer to face this on my own terms. You have no intention of offering for me, so I wish to make the break a clean one."

"You could become my mistress and let me handle the gossips. You wouldn't be sorry, Livvy, I promise."

"I'm already sorry . . . for having met you." She meant it. Had she never met Bathurst, she would have never known what was lacking in her life.

When the coach stopped in front of her house, she turned to gaze at him. Once they parted tonight, they might meet again as polite acquaintances but never as lovers. She searched his handsome features, desperately wanting to memorize everything about him. She tried to say something memorable, but nothing came to mind. Lacking words, she simply walked out of his life.

Two very concerned people met Olivia at the door. Aunt Alma was nearly beside herself with worry, and Peterson seemed to have aged in the space of a few hours. Alma gathered Olivia into her arms and refused to let go until Olivia gently freed herself.

"I'm fine, Auntie, truly."

"I saw you drive up in Bathurst's coach. I'm so relieved he found you. Peterson said we should trust him, but I was so afraid Palmerson would hurt you before the marquis found you."

"Palmerson lied to me about the musicale, then he used chloroform to render me unconscious," Olivia began. "He took me to an inn on the outskirts of the City and—"

"Oh, dear, I'm not sure I want to hear this," Alma said, fanning herself with her handkerchief.

"It's all right, Auntie, Bathurst arrived in time and sent Palmerson on his way."

"Bully for him," Peterson cheered. "I knew asking Bathurst to help was the right thing to do."

"There's more," Olivia whispered.

"It can wait, dear," Alma murmured.

"No, Auntie, I need to talk about it. Then I'm going to forget this ever happened. Neither Bathurst nor I knew that Palmerson had enlisted his friends' help to further his vile plan. They were supposed to burst into the room and find Palmerson and me together in a compromising position. Bathurst and I lingered in the room too long, and you can guess the rest. Naturally, they thought the worst. It should be all over Town by morning. The newspapers will probably carry an account the day after that."

Peterson spit out a curse, and Alma staggered into a chair, her face ashen. "You're ruined, Livvy! Dear God, the whole family is ruined. There's no help for it now. Bathurst will have to offer for you."

# Chapter Nine

Gabriel slept late the following morning. After a leisurely bath, he ate and retired to his study. What an ass he'd been to take Olivia's virginity in that mean little inn. Had he not tarried to indulge his lust, he would have gotten Olivia home without anyone being the wiser. As far as seductions went, this one had been a disaster.

He had made love to Olivia while she was in a state of shock, and that had been reprehensible behavior, even though it was what she had wanted. He had planned to take her the first time on silk sheets, with all the time in the world to savor her. What had actually happened defied imagination.

For one thing, Olivia had been an innocent. To make matters worse, they had been discovered by a trio of notorious gossips. Worse yet, he hadn't planned the events that happened last night. What in bloody hell was he going to do? Once the *ton* learned what had happened, life would become unbearable for Olivia and her family.

What was he to do? he wondered bleakly. His reason for remaining unwed remained valid, and because Olivia wouldn't let him take care of her financially, he could do nothing to ease her troubles. If he could nip the scandal in the bud, he would, but it was probably already too late. And once his grandmother heard, all hell would break loose. She was aware of his reputation as a womanizer and a rogue, but by ruining a woman of good breeding and refusing to do the "right thing" he would most certainly earn her wrath.

He had never wanted to hurt Olivia, but loving her had been an extraordinary experience. He lapsed into a contemplative mood as he recalled every sweet moment he'd spent with Olivia. A surge of heat flooded his body and pooled in his loins. With Olivia, once would never be enough.

*With Olivia, once would have to be enough.*

Gabriel couldn't trust his control where she was concerned. Losing himself inside her could result in disaster. With other women, control had not been a problem. Withdrawing at the moment of ejaculation came naturally to him after doing it for so many years. But with Olivia, withdrawing had been almost impossible. The urge to give her his seed had been a compelling need that had nearly been his undoing.

He wanted to be inside her now, wanted his mouth on her breasts and his hands on her delectable backside. Lord, what was wrong with him? Stifling a groan, he went to the sideboard, filled a glass with brandy and carried it and the full bottle back to his chair.

At lunchtime Grimsley brought him a tray, but Gabriel preferred the bottle. He sat brooding for hours, rising occasionally to prowl the room, then returning to his chair and his bottle. Daylight turned to dusk, and a very worried Grimsley returned to ask if his lordship intended to step out tonight and should he care to bathe and dress before he left. Gabriel dismissed him with a wave of his hand, informing the concerned servant that he intended to spend the night at home.

Grimsley blinked. "At home, milord?"

"At home," Gabriel repeated. "And bring another bottle; this one is empty."

Sometime during the long night, Gabriel fell asleep with the glass dangling from his hand and the empty bottles lying on the floor at his feet. He awoke to sunshine streaming through the window and the sound of the door banging open. Bleary-eyed, he shook his head to clear it as Ram burst through, followed closely by Luc. Thrusting a newspaper beneath Gabriel's nose, Ram asked, "What in bloody hell is wrong with you, Bathurst? Your goose is cooked now."

Gabriel raised bloodshot eyes to his friends and tried to summon a smile, but a grimace was all he could manage. "Good morning to you, too. To what do I owe the pleasure of this early visit?"

"Have you seen the morning paper?" Luc asked.

Gabriel tried to focus on the newsprint at the end of his nose but was too foxed to make out the words. "I'm afraid I'm not in the best of shape this morning. What's so bloody important?"

"Listen while I read you an item from the gossip column," Ram said, clearing his throat.

"*It has come to the attention of this writer that one of the Rogues of London was seen at the Hare and Hound with a lady of previously impeccable reputation. The Marquis of B and Lady O seemed to have found*

143

*common ground together, in a horizontal position, according to those who saw them in a state of dishabille. Does this mean a wedding is imminent?"*

"Blast and damn!" Gabriel snarled. "Palmerson's cronies couldn't wait to tell the world what they saw at the Hare and Hound."

"Exactly what *did* they see?" Luc asked. "Naturally, Lady O is Olivia Fairfax. And by the way, Bathurst, you look like hell."

"You really went off the deep end this time, old boy," Ram added. "Why did you have to go after an innocent when there are plenty of other women around to satisfy your needs?"

"How do you know she was innocent?" Gabriel growled.

"Never say she wasn't," Ram replied. "The lady has shunned society since her father's death. There hasn't been a scrap of gossip attached to her."

"Go away," Gabriel ground out.

"Are you going to offer for her?" Luc asked, undeterred by Gabriel's surliness.

Gabriel kicked at the empty bottles he'd suddenly discovered at his feet. "You both know that's not an option for me."

"Lady Olivia is ruined," Ram added unnecessarily.

"Don't you think I know that?" Gabriel barked.

"What happened?" Ram asked. "I know you well, my friend. To my knowledge, this is the first time you've compromised an innocent. We warned you, but you refused to listen."

Gabriel studied his fingernails. "I won't deny I wanted Olivia, and asked her to be my mistress. She refused, of course. The family is in desperate straits; she needs a protector. There is little I can do now to stop this malicious gossip."

"So you're not going to marry her," Luc surmised.

"Didn't I just say so?" Gabriel said irritably.

"You're not yourself, Bathurst," Luc observed. "Perhaps we should leave and return when you're in better spirits."

When no answer was forthcoming, Ram and Luc let themselves out of the room. Grimsley arrived a few minutes later with breakfast and a freshly pressed newspaper. Gabriel snatched the paper off the tray and turned immediately to the gossip column. He read it through twice before he let the paper fall from his hands.

"Is something wrong, milord?" Grimsley asked worriedly. "You don't seem yourself."

"Have you read the morning news, Grimsley?"

"Not yet, milord. I usually peruse it after you're finished."

Gabriel retrieved the paper and handed it to Grimsley, pointing out the gossip column with one blunt finger. "You may as well read this. I suspect the entire staff will be talking about it now that it's become public knowledge."

Grimsley read the article in question, his eyebrows rising higher with each word. "Is this true, milord?"

"I'm afraid so, Grimsley."

"Then I suspect congratulations are in order. You'll require a special license, of course, but that can be arranged easily enough. I'll see to it immediately."

"I'm not getting married, Grimsley. There is something you can do for me, however."

If Grimsley was shocked at Gabriel's refusal to wed

the woman he had ruined, he didn't show it. "I am at your service, milord."

"I want to know more about Lord Palmerson and his reasons for attempting to ruin the woman he planned to wed. The woman in question has no dowry, so there would be no monetary gain for him. I refuse to believe he loves her."

"I will do my best to obtain the information, milord," Grimsley promised, "but I need to know the lady's name before I can begin an investigation."

"Since I know you are discreet, I will tell you. 'Tis Lady Olivia Fairfax. Palmerson is eager to marry her, and I want to know why."

"Very good, milord. I hope my contacts will provide something of value."

Gabriel sat in contemplative silence long after Grimsley left. He stirred himself to pick at his breakfast, then took himself to his chamber to bathe and dress for the day. He couldn't hide himself away, nor could he pretend the gossip didn't exist. The best thing he could do was to go about his normal business and frequent his usual haunts.

A note arrived as Gabriel was preparing to leave the house. As soon as the footman handed it to him, Gabriel knew who had sent it. His grandmother had wasted no time in summoning him. He had hoped for a ride in the park first, but Grandmama's note had taken that option from him. Girding himself for the confrontation, Gabriel set off on his favorite mount.

A boy ran up to take the reins as Gabriel dismounted before his grandmother's townhouse. "Don't unsaddle him," Gabriel instructed. "I won't be long."

Lady Patrice was waiting for Gabriel in the morning

room, her lined face drawn and her lips pursed in disapproval.

"How are you, Grandmama?" Gabriel asked as he bent and kissed her sagging cheek.

"I'll tell you after we discuss your wedding plans."

"I see you've read the morning paper."

"Is it true? Are you the Lord B who compromised Lady O at the Hare and Hound?"

It was on the tip of Gabriel's tongue to deny it, but he wisely decided against it. He had yet to lie to his grandmother without being caught. She knew him too well.

After a painful pause, he said, "It's true, Grandmama, but there are extenuating circumstances."

"Forget the circumstances, they hardly matter. I assume Lady O is Olivia Fairfax."

"I'd prefer to keep the lady's name out of it."

"It's too late for that, my boy. All of London is buzzing with your latest escapade. This time you've gone too far. You've compromised an unwed lady, and there is only one thing for it. I might have wished you'd ruined someone with a sizable dowry, and one not so long in the tooth, but the gel has good bloodlines." She tapped her chin. "We'll have a quiet wedding and a small reception."

Gabriel listened to his grandmother with growing apprehension. The old girl was really off on a tear. There would be no wedding, and he had to let her know before this went too far.

"Stop, Grandmama! There will be no wedding. I'll do anything short of marriage to put down the gossip, but that's all I can promise."

Lady Patrice pounded her cane on the floor, her determination implacable. "No grandson of mine will

Connie Mason

shirk his duty. You *will* marry Lady Olivia and provide the heir you should have produced years ago." She sent Gabriel a hard look. "Perhaps she's already increasing."

"No, Grandmama, that's not possible."

"Are you saying nothing happened at the Hare and Hound?"

"I won't lie to you, Grandmama. All I'll say is that I took precautions."

"Ha! I know all about precautions, and they don't always work. That's beside the point, however. You've ruined a woman whose reputation was above reproach, and you'll marry her."

"Grandmama," Gabriel said with waning patience, "I simply cannot—"

"And I say you will. This conversation is over. You'll be married here, of course. I'll make the arrangements. All that is required of you is to obtain the special license and show up at the appointed time."

His thoughts in turmoil, Gabriel took his leave a short time later. His grandmother was so set on a wedding that nothing he said had swayed her. And because he loved his grandmother, he would bow to her wishes. She was old and frail and unaware of his reasons for remaining unwed. When all was said and done, he found, he could not deny his grandmother the pleasure of seeing him settled.

But though Grandmama might force him to marry, she couldn't force him to produce heirs. His line would die out with him.

Two days after her narrow escape from Palmerson at the Hare and Hound, Olivia ate her lunch without tasting the food. She felt as if her world was slowly disintegrating.

148

As she picked at her food, she suddenly became aware that the morning paper was missing. It was usually sitting on the kitchen table when she came down to breakfast and here it was lunchtime and she still hadn't seen it.

"Auntie, have you seen the morning paper?" Olivia asked.

Alma's fork paused midway to her mouth. "The paper, dear? Uh, I . . . um . . . you'll have to ask Peterson. Perhaps he forgot it this morning."

A chill slid down Olivia's spine. "Peterson never forgets. Something's wrong. You may as well tell me."

"Oh, dear, this is terrible, simply terrible," Alma dithered. "I was hoping it wouldn't come to this."

"Auntie—"

"Oh, very well. Peterson and I didn't want you to read the newspaper this morning. There's an article in the gossip column we knew would upset you."

"I appreciate your trying to protect me, but I want to know what is being said about me. May I see the paper, please?"

Her lips formed into a thin line, Alma rose and retrieved the newspaper from a drawer where she had placed it earlier. Olivia turned to the gossip column and silently read the damning words—words that ripped her reputation to shreds.

Though she hadn't been a part of polite society for a long time, having the family name dragged through the mud again hurt. She had worked so hard to rise above the embarrassment her father had caused, and now she had created an even bigger scandal. Neville would never be accepted by society, and Aunt Alma would share in her disgrace.

"It's not so bad," Alma ventured after Olivia had

read the offending article. "The gossip will disappear once you and Bathurst are wed. Some good will come of it. All our financial problems will disappear. Perhaps it's for the best, Livvy."

Olivia ground her teeth in frustration. "There's not going to be a wedding, Auntie. Bathurst won't offer for me. If he did, I wouldn't accept."

Alma's mouth formed an O of surprise. "Why would you say that? Obviously, the marquis is interested in you. Why else would he have come to your rescue?"

"Because he's a decent human being," Olivia said. *And an amazing lover.*

Bathurst had made his position perfectly clear before they'd made love. She recalled how she'd all but begged him to make love to her, and how he'd obliged beyond her wildest dreams. Bathurst's vow to remain unwed was puzzling, and she could only assume that hedonistic pleasure and debauchery meant more to him than a wife and family.

"I'm going upstairs, Auntie," Olivia said, ending their conversation before Alma could question her further. "Send Peterson up when he returns from the market."

"Oh, no," Alma lamented. "Don't tell me you and Peterson are going to . . . to—"

"We may have to. There's nothing left but Father's watch, and I'm saving it for Neville."

She rose and left the kitchen before the conversation returned to Bathurst.

His grandmother's stern admonition still ringing in his ears, Gabriel dismounted before Olivia's run-down townhouse. No one ran up to take the reins, so he tethered his horse to a bush and forced himself up the front steps. His hand was on the brass knocker when he realized he couldn't go through with this. He had started to turn away when the door suddenly opened.

"Lord Bathurst!" Alma said, apparently as startled as he. "I didn't hear you knock."

Gabriel summoned a smile. "Lady Alma, good day to you. How did you know I was here?"

"I didn't. I came out to sweep the stoop and there you were. It's about time you showed up, my lord. I assume you've read the morning paper."

"Indeed," Gabriel acknowledged.

"I'm glad you decided to offer for my niece. You've placed her in a terrible position."

Gabriel stiffened. "If you recall, madam," he said coolly, "it was Palmerson, not I, who abducted your niece."

"I know that, my lord, but society doesn't. Besides, I wasn't born yesterday. Had you and Livvy left the inn immediately, her reputation would still be intact."

"What did Olivia tell you?"

"Enough to show you aren't as innocent as you pretend. Your reputation precedes you, my lord. No young woman is safe in your company."

"Your man Peterson must have thought otherwise, else he wouldn't have enlisted my help."

"There was no one else," Alma said, shrugging.

"Auntie, who are you talking to?"

Gabriel's eyes lifted and warmed when he spied Olivia descending the staircase. His gaze slid over her slowly, as if he could see beneath the worn gown that hid her ripe curves. He remembered how her naked body looked, flushed with passion and swollen with desire, and felt the stirrings of arousal.

"I expect you to do your duty by my niece," Alma

reminded him as he strode to the staircase to await Olivia.

"Bathurst, what are you doing here?" Olivia asked when she reached the bottom landing.

"It's good to see you, too," Gabriel said dryly. "We need to talk," he added before Olivia could reply. "In private."

"I can't imagine what more we have to say to one another."

"Take Lord Bathurst into the parlor, dear," Alma said. "I'm sure you two have much to discuss. I've some errands to run, and I'm taking Peterson with me."

"Auntie," Olivia began, but it was already too late to call Alma back.

Olivia stormed into the parlor. "Is this necessary, my lord?"

"My grandmother and your aunt seem to think so."

Olivia turned on him, her expression fierce. "If this is about what I think it is, you may as well leave now."

Gabriel stared at her, thinking how beautiful she looked when roused by anger. Her eyes sparkled and her face was becomingly flushed. It was all he could do to keep from pulling her into his arms and kissing her pouting mouth.

Gathering his straying wits, Gabriel said, "Sit down, Olivia."

Scowling, Olivia stood her ground. "I'll stand, thank you. What is it you wish to say to me?"

Hands behind his back, Gabriel began to pace back and forth before her. "We'll be married as soon as arrangements can be made. The notice of our engagement will appear in tomorrow's newspaper. That should stop the gossips."

Olivia's eyes narrowed. "When did you change your mind about marriage, Bathurst?"

"I didn't. My grandmother read the gossip column in today's *Times* and gave me a thorough dressing-down. Grandmama may be old and fragile, but she still considers herself the head of the family. She abhors scandal and ordered me to offer for you. Since I love her dearly, I shall bow to her wishes, albeit reluctantly. There is one thing, however, I wish to make clear: There will be no children from our union."

Olivia's chin went up. "I respectfully refuse your marriage proposal and take full responsibility for what happened at the Hare and Hound."

"You're refusing my offer?" Gabriel asked, stunned. "Perhaps you haven't seen this morning's newspaper."

"I've seen it. It's no worse than I expected. I'm grateful it was you and not Palmerson. What Palmerson intended was rape, what we did was . . ."

"Pleasurable, I hope," Gabriel offered.

Olivia flushed and looked away. *Pleasure* was putting it mildly. "I don't hold you accountable for . . . for what happened that night. We did nothing I didn't want to happen."

"Nevertheless, we were intimate and caught in the act."

"I don't understand you, Bathurst. You had every intention of seducing me and making me your mistress. From what you said, I thought marriage was never in your plans."

"That's true," Gabriel admitted. "Were you my mistress, I could have protected you. You would have wanted for nothing. That, however, is a moot point now. Our being caught together changes everything."

"That's ridiculous," Olivia snorted. "How like a man

153

to twist things to serve his own selfish purposes. Nothing has changed. I will become neither your mistress nor your wife. Tell your grandmother I won't be pressured into marrying a man who doesn't want a wife or family."

"My name will protect you, Livvy," Gabriel cajoled. "The scandal to your family could be avoided."

"My father already saw to the ruination of our family name. Society has finally begun to forget what he did, and one day my indiscretion will be forgotten, too, or replaced by another more interesting piece of gossip."

"No one will offer for you," Gabriel reminded her.

"My marriage hopes died with my father. I've reconciled myself to life without a husband and family." She met his gaze unflinchingly. "I'm not ashamed of what we did. I'll always have the memories we created that night."

A mixture of relief and incredulity robbed Gabriel of speech. It was true he didn't want to marry Olivia, but it wasn't because he didn't have feelings for her. What he truly feared was losing control when inside her and bringing a child into the world. Yet, incredibly, she had turned him down. He was a marquis, for God's sake, and rich. What was Olivia thinking?

It occurred to Gabriel to wonder why he was upset. He should be pleased with Olivia's decision. He could truthfully tell his grandmother that Olivia had refused him and then return to his decadent ways.

"Is that your final word, Olivia?"

"It is."

His lips thinned. "Very well. I won't bother you again." He turned to leave.

"Gabriel, wait!"

Gabriel turned slowly, one elegant brow raised in

question. "Have you changed your mind?"

"No. I . . . I just wanted to . . . thank you again."

Shock shuddered through Gabriel. He had ruined Olivia and she was thanking him? Suddenly something snapped inside him and he reached for her, bringing her into his arms. He stared into the glittering green depths of her eyes and was lost. Nothing short of death could have stopped him from kissing her.

A warm, sluggish wanting settled in his belly and inflamed his soul. He waited for her to tell him to stop, and when she didn't, he slid his tongue into her mouth and drank deeply of her sweet essence. He felt the tentative probing of her tongue against his and groaned her name into her mouth.

"Stop me," he growled.

"I . . . can't."

Olivia tasted him with her tongue and felt a hollow ache deep inside her. She knew it was too late to stop him when he opened her bodice and lowered his mouth to her breasts. Arching into his caress, she felt her heart thump wildly as he sucked her nipple into his mouth and rolled his tongue around the pebbled nub.

"Not here," Olivia gasped.

"Where?" The sound was low and tortured; she barely recognized it as his voice.

"Upstairs."

Scooping her into his arms, Gabriel flew with her up the stairs. He remembered the location of her room and carried her through the open door, slamming it shut behind him. Then he lowered her to the bed and followed her down. "I want you, Livvy. I don't know what you've done to me and I don't care as long as you let me love you."

Olivia barely registered his words as he undressed her

155

with a swiftness that spoke volumes about his knowledge of women's clothing. Then he stood back and stared at her, his glittering gaze traveling over her nude body with a desire he couldn't conceal.

Her body thrumming with need, Olivia watched Gabriel remove his clothing. Everything about him pleased her: his broad shoulders, his slim waist and sculpted chest. His hips were narrow and his legs muscular, but it was the weapon he wielded between his legs that robbed her of breath. Thick and long, it rose upward against his flat belly from a nest of black curls. Then her thoughts scattered as he lowered himself onto the bed.

Pressing his lips to the soft skin beneath her breasts, he kissed down each rib and dipped his tongue into her navel, then sucked her belly, making a love mark there.

"I want to taste you everywhere," he murmured as his lips traced the line of her hips.

Apparently, her sigh of pleasure was all the encouragement he needed as he kissed down one leg, then licked upward slowly along the inside of the other, drawing damp circles with his tongue. When he reached the tender place where she throbbed and ached, he blew a hot breath on the swollen center, and Olivia's body went taut as a bowstring.

This wasn't supposed to be happening, she vaguely thought. But how could she resist one more chance to be in Gabriel's arms? She wanted him and he wanted her; nothing else mattered.

Then Gabriel placed his mouth against her aching core, and she stiffened and murmured a protest. "I'm not going to hurt you, Livvy," he soothed. Grasping her buttocks in his hands, he deepened his kiss, using his lips and breath and tongue to stroke and suckle her, until she was shaking like a leaf and close to shattering.

One more flick of his tongue and she cried out. She felt herself pulsing violently against his mouth and pressed herself into his intimate caress, offering him more of herself. She was breathing hard, dying. Finally the convulsions stopped and her breath eased. She lay there in total confusion as he shifted and crawled back up her body, drawing her legs up and thrusting his swollen staff inside her. He began to move, urging her to follow with erotic words. Matching his rhythm, she rubbed herself against him and let her instincts guide her.

Her body throbbing, her heart pounding, she waited in eager anticipation as he kissed and caressed her. His body continued to thrust and shift, and his kisses grew hotter and more intense.

"You taste so good," he whispered against her lips. "You're so wet and tight inside; I love the way your muscles squeeze me. Can you come again?"

No answer was forthcoming. She couldn't breathe, much less speak. When he kissed her, she lost all sense of reality. Buffeted by new sensations, she opened her mouth to his probing tongue. She tasted herself on his tongue, smelled the passion surrounding them and felt him moving against her, becoming a part of her, moving in her, kissing her, his hands all over her, touching all those places that gave her pleasure. Each time he thrust inside her he shifted, creating a new sensation, making her feel him in different ways.

"I'm nearly there, Livvy—don't make me wait too long."

He pushed upward, moving faster and harder until something gave inside her. She caught her breath, certain she would die from pleasure; then she exploded.

From somewhere far away she heard him call her name, felt him shudder and withdraw, spilling his seed onto her stomach.

Shifting, he collapsed beside her, his chest heaving and his breath rushing from his mouth in loud gasps.

"We'll be married tomorrow," Gabriel said when his breathing slowed.

"I haven't changed my mind, Gabriel. I won't marry a man who feels nothing but lust for me and refuses to sire children. You should leave before Aunt Alma returns."

Gabriel shot to his feet, his expression hard, implacable. "You're making a mistake, Olivia, but I'm not going to beg you to marry me. The only reason I offered marriage was because Grandmama demanded it of me."

His harsh words convinced Olivia that she had made the right decision. Gabriel didn't want a wife. Besides, she had a more compelling reason to refuse Gabriel. The highwayman named Ollie still stood between them.

Deflated, Olivia watched as Gabriel dressed and strode to the door. Pausing with his hand on the knob, he looked back at her as if expecting her to stop him. When she remained stubbornly mute, he stormed out, slamming the door behind him.

# Chapter Ten

Gabriel left the house in a huff. He hadn't intended to make love to Olivia in her own home, but he should have anticipated the explosive passion between them. With Olivia, once would never be enough.

It had never occurred to him that Olivia would refuse his offer. Now he could tell Grandmama that he had done his duty. The sooner she knew there would be no wedding, the sooner she would stop pestering him.

Huntly opened the door at Gabriel's knock. "Is Grandmama in?" Gabriel asked.

"You'll find her in her sitting room, milord."

Gabriel took his time mounting the stairs and entered the sitting room after a brief knock.

"Bathurst, back so soon? When is the wedding to be?"

"There will be no wedding, Grandmama. Lady Olivia refused me."

"Balderdash! No one refuses a marquis."

"You don't know Olivia. She's stubborn and independent, and has some outlandish notion about marrying for love."

"The chit is ruined. Doesn't she know you're her last hope for marriage and a normal life?"

"I'm afraid not, Grandmama. I did my best to convince her, but obviously it wasn't good enough. Now, I have an appointment to keep, so I must be off."

"You're pleased," Grandmama remarked. "You really do intend to remain single, don't you?"

"I do, indeed." He kissed her fragile cheek. "Goodbye, Grandmama."

"Is it because of Cissy?" Grandmama persisted.

Gabriel paused. "Cissy has nothing to do with it, Grandmama. Marriage isn't for me."

"Don't be too smug, my boy," Lady Patrice muttered as Gabriel strode away. "I'll see you married, and soon."

Olivia washed, dressed and was in the kitchen fixing a cup of tea when Alma and Peterson returned. After Gabriel had left, she couldn't seem to put her thoughts in order. Once again she had responded to the marquis with wanton abandon. He held her in thrall, coaxing her into his arms with a simple look and kissing her into compliance. What a fool she'd been. There was no future for her and Bathurst, and the sooner she realized it, the better off she'd be.

"Did I give you and Bathurst enough time, Livvy?" Alma asked when she returned from the market. "Have you set a date?"

Olivia didn't want to discuss the marquis, but she knew Alma wouldn't be put off. "I refused Bathurst's offer."

"You didn't! Do you know what that means?"

Forcing a calm she didn't feel, Olivia said, "I know exactly what that means. I'm doing Bathurst a favor by not marrying him. His heart isn't in it. He was forced into proposing by his grandmother, and I refuse to wed a man for any reason but love. Besides, Auntie, what if, after we married, Bathurst recognized me as the highwayman who robbed him on the turnpike? He would most likely expose me and seek an annulment, which would be an even bigger scandal than we've already created."

"Oh, dear, whatever are we going to do now? I had so hoped Bathurst would provide the answer to our financial problems. The butcher refused to extend our credit, and I came away empty-handed."

"There's still Papa's watch."

"That belongs to Neville. And speaking of Neville, he'll be sent down from the university if his fees aren't paid soon."

Determination stiffened Olivia's jaw. "I'll take care of it, Auntie." She excused herself and went in search of Peterson. She found him in the parlor, dusting the furniture.

"You shouldn't have to perform maid's work," Olivia said.

"I don't mind, Miss Livvy. After you wed the marquis, you'll have more servants than you can handle. I hear he's exceedingly wealthy."

"I'm not marrying Bathurst," Olivia declared in a voice that brooked no argument. "It's time for Pete and Ollie to ride again. The sky is overcast today, and most likely the moon will be obscured by clouds. Bring the horses around after dark."

Peterson frowned. "Lady Alma isn't going to like this."

"Can you think of another way to provide food for the table? Pinching a purse here and there will ease our problems without causing undue hardship to the wealthy lords and ladies we rob."

Peterson heaved a heavy sigh. "Very well, Miss Livvy, but I don't like it. Seeing you wounded and bleeding put a damper on my enthusiasm for our escapades."

"It won't happen again, Peterson, I promise."

Gabriel was at White's Club, engaged in a game of cards, when he learned about the daring holdup by the highwaymen known as Pete and Ollie. Lord Prestley, a rotund earl famous for his wealth and debauchery, spread the word about the dastardly outlaws who'd stopped his coach and robbed him and his current mistress of their purses and jewels.

"They pinched all our valuables," Prestley blustered. "Scared poor Lily half to death."

"They didn't seem too dangerous to me," Gabriel drawled. "The same Pete and Ollie held up my coach a while back, and then again when I hitched a ride from a house party with Braxton. That time I shot and wounded one of them. Apparently, the shooting didn't scare them off."

"Too bad you didn't kill the bugger," Prestley complained. He sent Gabriel a sly look. "What's the latest on you and Lady O?"

As luck would have it, Lord Sanford strolled up to join the group at that moment. "Have you set a date for the wedding, Bathurst? You really should be more careful where you and Lady Olivia meet for your assignations." Sanford no longer tried to hide his mirth.

"You should have seen your face when Dearborn, Fordham and I burst into your little love nest."

Gabriel sent Sanford a look that would have peeled varnish from furniture. "Ah, Sanford, I've been looking for you so you could correct an error in judgment. You were mistaken. It wasn't Lady Olivia you saw with me at the Hare and Hound."

Sanford must have been too dense to take the warning, for he said, "I don't make mistakes like that. It was indeed Lady Olivia Fairfax I saw with you at the Hare and Hound, though you weren't the man I thought I would find with her."

"Enough!" Gabriel warned. "If you prefer, we can settle this on the dueling field. Or you can apologize for your mistake."

Sanford realized at once that he was treading on dangerous ground. It would take a man braver than he to meet Bathurst on a dueling field. Not only was Bathurst an expert marksman with pistol and a superior swordsman, but he was also known to excel at fisticuffs.

"I say, old boy, perhaps I *was* mistaken."

"Indeed you were. By the way, have you seen Palmerson lately? There's something I wish to discuss with him."

"I'll give him your message should I see him," Sanford said, edging away.

A week after that conversation, another coach was stopped by Pete and Ollie and its occupants robbed. Gabriel knew it wouldn't be long before the highway men were caught and hanged, and for some strange reason, that thought caused an uncomfortable feeling in the pit of his stomach.

The following day, Gabriel encountered Palmerson at Brooks's. The viscount flew into a rage when Gabriel strong-armed him into an alcove for a private conversation.

"What you had planned for Lady Olivia was too low even for a snake like you Palmerson," Gabriel charged.

"I did nothing. You're the one who compromised her," Palmerson raged, "but I won't allow you to marry her. Olivia's mine, do you hear? Her father gave her to me before he died."

"If Lady Olivia belongs to you, why did you wait so long to claim her?" Gabriel growled. "Were she yours, you would have no need for a forced seduction."

"She wouldn't have me!" Palmerson cried. "Do you think I would have planned her seduction if she had agreed to marry me?"

"I don't know; you tell me."

"You're a bastard, Bathurst, a bloody bastard. You have no business sticking your nose where it doesn't belong. Olivia would be my wife now if you hadn't interfered."

"You have a strange way of showing affection, Palmerson," Gabriel sneered. "Since when was rape considered seduction? The lady wasn't willing."

"The lady doesn't know what she wants. She needed a little persuasion; I was merely helping her make up her mind to accept my proposal."

Gabriel pinned Palmerson with his steely gaze. "Make me understand why you want to marry Olivia Fairfax. She isn't wealthy, and I know for a fact that your pockets are empty. You can't love her if you were willing to ruin her. Come clean, Palmerson. What do you *really* want from Olivia?"

"None of your bloody business. Just keep out of my way." He touched his fingers to the back of his head and winced. "I owe you for the lump on the head you gave me at the Hare and Hound. My friends said you bedded Olivia. I can't believe she would let you have her and not me."

"Perhaps your friends lied."

"And perhaps they didn't. It doesn't matter," he snarled. "I still want her. Everyone knows you'll never wed Olivia. She should be eager now to accept my proposal and put a stop to the gossip."

"You don't know Olivia if you think that," Gabriel muttered. "Furthermore, if you attempt to hurt her again, I'll be forced to retaliate."

Palmerson's eyes narrowed. "What is your interest in Olivia?"

Gabriel wished he knew the answer to that question. His interest in Olivia was puzzling, even to a man like him, who usually wanted only one thing from a woman. Olivia, however, was different from the other women he knew. Vibrant, independent, obstinate, she was an entity unto herself. He could think of a dozen more adjectives, but none would do her justice. Mostly he wanted her. Wanted to be inside her, around her, over her, beneath her, loving her in every way a man loved a woman.

"My interest, Palmerson, doesn't concern you. I advise you to ponder long and hard on my words. Hurt Olivia and you'll answer to me."

Inclining his head, Gabriel strode off.

Olivia sat at the kitchen table counting the money the fence had given Peterson for the goods he'd brought in from the last two robberies. Alma and Peterson sat with her, waiting for the results.

"Along with the cash, there should be enough to pay Neville's tuition and fill our larder," Olivia said. "If we're careful, we can scrape by for a few weeks."

"Thank God," Alma said fervently. "I'm afraid my poor heart won't stand much more of this. Why couldn't you have married Bathurst?"

"We've already discussed my reasons," Olivia said dismissively. "Peterson can take Neville's tuition up to the university."

"Shall I leave immediately, Miss Livvy?"

"That won't be necessary, Peterson."

Three pairs of eyes turned toward the speaker. Olivia let out a squeal and ran to embrace her brother. "Neville! What are you doing home?"

Neville, tall for his eighteen years but still wearing the immaturity of youth upon his face and form, resembled Olivia in the color of his hair and eyes. While he lacked her prettiness, he was a handsome lad who would one day set ladies' hearts aflutter. His one fault was his hot temper, and Olivia's greatest fear was that it would get him in trouble.

The subtle change in Neville's expression warned Olivia that all was not well. "What is it, Neville? What brought you home? We weren't expecting you."

"You would know the answer better than I, Livvy," Neville said. "Gossip has a way of reaching even the remotest corners of England. The headmaster called me into his office to question me, and I hadn't the foggiest notion what he was talking about. I was aghast when he showed me the gossip column about you and Lord Bathurst. Since you didn't see fit to invite me, I thought I'd come home for the wedding. It's my right as head of the family to give away the bride."

"I'm sorry, Neville, I didn't think it important enough to call you home from school. It was all a terrible misunderstanding. There will be no wedding."

"Misunderstanding? How could that be? Were you or were you not at the Hare and Hound Inn with Lord Bathurst?"

"Nothing happened. You'll return to the university tomorrow, and that's final."

"I'll do no such thing," Neville huffed. "Not until I get to the bottom of this. As your brother, it's my responsibility to see that the gossip is laid to rest. Perhaps you should begin by telling me exactly what did happen."

"Don't pester your sister," Alma scolded. "She has enough to deal with right now."

"That's why I'm here. Did Bathurst start the scandal?"

"Definitely not!" Olivia maintained. "Bathurst rescued me from a dangerous situation involving Lord Palmerson."

"Palmerson! That bastard! Then it wasn't Bathurst who took advantage of you."

"Dear me, no. Lord Sanford and his friends were the ones who started the gossip about Olivia and Bathurst," Alma said.

"Auntie, please," Olivia admonished.

"Really, Livvy, I'm not a child," Neville said firmly. "I will not return to school until I find out what's going on. I've been kept in the dark long enough. I don't even know where you're getting the blunt to pay my university fees."

Neville was growing up, Olivia thought. No longer was he the child who trusted his sister to provide for him. He was a young man broaching maturity and ready to spread his wings. He was curious, hotheaded and prideful. She had to send him back to school before trouble found him.

"You can't neglect your studies, Neville. You're too close to finishing your education. As for Palmerson, thanks to Bathurst, he didn't hurt me."

"I'm not going back to the university until I settle things with Palmerson."

"You'll do nothing of the kind," Olivia confronted. "Let me handle things as I see fit."

Clamping his lips together, Neville said nothing, but she could tell by his closed expression that she hadn't convinced him.

"I'll help you unpack and get settled in, my lord," Peterson said, much to Olivia's relief.

"When did you get so formal, Peterson? I've always been Master Neville to you."

"You're a man now. You deserve to be addressed formally. Follow me—your room is just as you left it."

"That bad, eh?" Neville joked. "I shouldn't be attending the university while my family is scraping to get by." He glanced around him, wrinkling his nose in distaste. "Why didn't you tell me how bad things were?"

"We're getting along just fine, Neville," Olivia assured him. "Go with Palmerson; we'll talk later."

After Neville left, Olivia collapsed into a chair. "I hadn't counted on Neville coming home. He's going to complicate things for us."

"I'm sure you can calm him down, dear," Alma soothed. "You know how impetuous lads his age can be."

"I hope you're right, Auntie," Olivia said. "I hope you're right."

Neville waited until everyone was asleep that night before dressing in his best suit and venturing out. As head of the family, he knew what had to be done to reclaim his sister's honor, and he wasn't afraid to act accordingly. Hailing a hackney, he directed the driver to Brooks's, determined to confront Olivia's nemesis at one of the gentlemen's clubs.

The man Neville sought wasn't at Brooks's, so he continued on to White's. He wasn't there either. Neville finally located Lord Palmerson at Crocker's.

Cornering the viscount near the refreshment table, Neville asked, "Lord Palmerson, do you remember me?"

"I don't believe I do," Palmerson said, looking down his nose at Neville. "Should I?"

"I'm Neville Fairfax, Earl of Sefton. Surely you remember my father. And if I'm not mistaken, you're acquainted with my sister."

"Sefton! My God, man, you've grown up."

"Children have a way of doing that," Neville said dryly. "Is there somewhere we can talk without being interrupted?"

Palmerson's eyes narrowed. "What is this about, Sefton? I haven't time for childish games."

Neville stiffened. "I don't play games, Palmerson. I know what you did to my sister, and I'm prepared to defend her honor."

Palmerson chortled. "You? You've no experience at this sort of thing. Besides, I did nothing to your sister. Bathurst is the man you should challenge, but if I were you, I would think twice about it. He's too experienced for a green lad like you."

"I know the truth, Palmerson."

Their angry confrontation had begun to attract attention, and several men sidled close to eavesdrop.

"Be careful what you say, Sefton," Palmerson

warned, "else you'll find yourself in a great deal of trouble."

"My sister's name has been sullied, my lord," Neville charged, "and you, not Bathurst, are to blame. Therefore I must challenge you."

"Surely you jest."

"I do not jest. The choice of weapons is yours."

A buzz of excitement rose up around them. Neville paid the onlookers little heed as he waited for Palmerson to accept his challenge and name his weapon.

"Are you sure this is what you want, Sefton? I don't like killing children, but if you insist—"

"Are you too cowardly to accept my challenge?"

Palmerson loosed a gale of laughter. "Afraid of you? Hardly, dear boy. Very well, I accept. Pistols."

Lord Sanford shoved through the crowd to stand at Palmerson's side. "I'll act as your second, Palmerson."

"Do you have a second, Sefton?" Palmerson asked.

Neville glanced about, saw no one he knew, and shrugged. He could always enlist Peterson, but he wanted to keep the family out of this.

Then a man stepped forward. "If you won't be talked out of this folly, then I'll be your second." He held out his hand. "I'm Ramsey Dunsford, Earl of Braxton."

"Thank you, Lord Braxton," Neville said, grasping Braxton's hand.

"Meet with my second, Braxton, to set up a time and place," Palmerson instructed.

"Are you sure this is what you want, Sefton?" Ram asked.

"Positive," Neville replied.

"And you, Palmerson. Are you sure you want to duel a man young enough to be your son?"

"I'm not Palmerson's son," Neville bit out.

"I don't relish murdering children," Palmerson replied. "Perhaps the young puppy will change his mind before the duel."

"I won't change my mind, Palmerson," Neville said as he sketched a bow. "Good night, my lord."

Neville made a hasty exit, unaware that Ram had followed him outside. "Are you afoot?" Ram asked.

"My hired hackney left," Neville answered. "It's not far, I'll walk home."

"Let me give you a lift. My carriage is parked just down the street."

"Thank you."

"Can I change your mind about the duel?" Ram asked.

"No. My grudge against Palmerson is twofold. He insulted my sister and had a hand in my father's death."

"You're Lady Olivia's brother, are you not?"

"I am," Neville allowed. "If you know that much, you've heard the gossip about my sister and Bathurst."

"Indeed I have. I read about the affair in the paper. Shouldn't you be challenging Bathurst?"

"I know the truth," Neville replied.

"So do I," Ram mumbled. "May I offer you my dueling pistols?"

Neville nodded. "I haven't seen my father's pistols recently, so I'm not sure they're still available."

"I'll be in touch with you after I've spoken with Palmerson's second."

"Don't come to the house," Neville cautioned. "I don't want my family to worry."

"Very well. I'll send a note around tomorrow."

Olivia knew something was amiss with Neville but couldn't put her finger on it. He had slept late and then

171

prowled about the house like a caged animal. When she spoke to him about returning to school, he flatly refused. When she suggested that he go out for a bit of air, he muttered something about waiting for a note from a friend.

When the note finally arrived, Neville was so secretive about it that Olivia wondered if it was from a girl. A handsome young man like Neville probably had countless females fawning over him.

When she questioned Neville about the note and sender, he told her it was nothing that concerned her. Olivia took the rebuff in stride but still couldn't help worrying about her young brother.

When Neville left the house later that afternoon, Olivia decided to clean his room. She was making up the bed when she saw a crumpled piece of paper lying on the floor and picked it up. Curious, she smoothed it out and read the message. It was from Lord Braxton, stating that Neville was to meet Palmerson at six o'clock the following morning in a secluded section of Hyde Park.

Olivia staggered under the weight of what she had just learned. Neville was going to duel with Palmerson! How could this have happened? *When* could this have happened? Neville had been home but a short time. Palmerson would kill Neville. She had to stop it, but how?

Racing down the stairs, Olivia grabbed her wrap and bonnet and flew out the door.

Praying she'd find Palmerson at home, she hailed a hackney and directed the driver to Palmerson's address. "Wait for me," she threw over her shoulder to the driver as she stepped down from the hackney and hurried off.

Grasping the brass knocker, Olivia pounded on the

door. A few minutes later, Palmerson's butler appeared in the entry. "May I help you, madam?"

"Is Lord Palmerson at home?"

"I'm not sure, madam. If I find him in, whom shall I say is calling?"

"Please tell him Lady Olivia would like to speak with him," Olivia said in her haughtiest tone. "It's a matter of utmost importance."

"Step into the drawing room, my lady, and I'll see if the viscount is in."

Teeth clenched, Olivia tapped her foot impatiently while the butler went for Palmerson. She knew Palmerson was in or the butler would have said immediately that he wasn't home.

"The viscount will see you," the butler said from the doorway. "Follow me, madam."

Olivia was shown into Palmerson's study and told to wait. After a short time, Palmerson appeared.

"Olivia, you're the last person I expected to see here. To what do I owe this pleasure?"

"You know very well why I'm here," Olivia blasted. "There will be no duel. How dare you challenge my brother! He's only eighteen."

"For your information, your brother challenged me. I gave him every opportunity to back out. If you didn't want him to challenge me, you should have told him it was Bathurst who bedded you at the Hare and Hound."

"Neville is dueling no one! You will write a note telling him you've changed your mind, and I will deliver it."

He laughed. "You jest. Do you want me to appear a coward?"

"I don't care how you appear to your cronies. I only care about my brother."

"Perhaps I can oblige you after all," Palmerson said with sly innuendo. "Marry me, and I'll call off the duel."

Olivia recoiled as if struck. There had to be some other way to save her impetuous brother. "And if I refuse?"

"I'm an expert marksman, you know. Your brother doesn't stand a chance. I may have to leave the country for a while if I kill him, but it won't be for long."

"Go to hell, Palmerson!" Olivia spat. "I'll find another way to stop you."

Spinning on her heel, Olivia fled. Once she had settled inside the waiting hackney, she burst into tears. What had she done? Had her refusal to marry Palmerson become her brother's death sentence? Perhaps she should go back and agree to Palmerson's terms.

No, not yet. First she had to speak to Neville and try to talk him out of this folly.

Neville was home when she returned, and she lit into him without preamble. "What have you done? Are you out of your mind? I refuse to allow you to duel with Palmerson."

Neville blanched. "How did you know?"

"I found the note from Lord Braxton. You're to write an apology immediately."

"Neville challenged Palmerson?" Alma asked from the doorway. "Oh, dear, how could you?"

"Well, Neville?" Olivia said from between clenched teeth.

"I'm sorry, Livvy, I won't back down. Our family honor is at stake."

"Our father destroyed our honor years ago."

"Then it's up to me to restore it. There's nothing you can say to change my mind. Don't worry, Livvy, I'm a pretty good shot and don't intend to die."

"Oh, you fool!" Olivia cried, bursting into tears. "Palmerson intends to kill you. I just spoke with him, and he is as stubborn as you are. He refused to cry off."

"You went to see Palmerson? After what he did to you?"

"You left me no choice."

Olivia decided to keep Palmerson's conditions for stopping the duel to herself, for if all else failed, she would be forced to marry him to save Neville's life.

"I'm going upstairs, Livvy," Neville said. "Try not to worry. Unlike our father, I'm dueling for an honorable cause."

"Young fool," Olivia lamented after Neville left the room. "Oh, Auntie, what am I to do? I can't let Neville die, and he surely will if he duels with Palmerson."

"There is but one thing you can do, Livvy," Alma said in a no-nonsense tone.

"What? If you know how to save Neville, please tell me."

"Bathurst. He's the only one that can stop this farce. This is not the time for pride, dear. Beg him to help us if you have to."

Olivia thought long and hard, then gave her aunt a squeeze and rushed out the door.

# Chapter Eleven

It took Olivia fifteen minutes to find a hackney and another twenty to reach Gabriel's townhouse. She had never been to his home before but knew he lived on the most fashionable street in Town. The driver seemed to know exactly where it was located and delivered her promptly to Gabriel's mansion in Park Lane. Olivia leaped to the ground, rushed past the marble columns, raced up the stairs and banged the brass doorknocker.

"Please, God, let him be home, please, God, let him be home," Olivia prayed over and over.

A footman opened the door. If he was startled to see a wild-eyed woman at the door, he gave no hint of it. "May I help you, madam?"

"Lord Bathurst—I must see him," Olivia gasped. "Is he in?"

"Who is it, Thomas?" Gabriel called from the top of the stairs. "Tell whoever it is to leave a card. I'm on my way out."

176

Olivia nearly collapsed in relief at the sound of Gabriel's voice. Pushing Thomas aside, she ran to the foot of the stairs and called out, "It's Olivia, my lord. I must speak with you. It's of vital importance."

"Olivia?"

Olivia feasted hungrily on Gabriel as he descended the stairs. He was resplendent in fitted black waistcoat, linen shirt embellished with snowy white lace, and tight buff breeches that molded his thighs and calves. She let her gaze follow the breadth of his shoulders to his narrow waist and hips, then down the length of his strong legs to his highly polished boots. He was so breathtakingly handsome, she almost forgot why she had come.

Gabriel appeared stunned to see her, and Olivia couldn't blame him. If anyone had seen her entering Gabriel's house, it was bound to be remarked upon, and gossip about her and the marquis would accelerate. But it didn't matter. Nothing mattered but saving her brother's life.

Gabriel reached the bottom landing and placed an arm around her quaking shoulders. "You're shaking, Livvy." He turned to the footman. "Thomas, fetch Grimsley. Tell him to bring tea to my study." His arm still around her, he guided Olivia down the hall to his study, a magnificent room furnished in leather and heavy dark wood—a room that perfectly matched Gabriel's personality.

He led her to a chair and seated her. "What happened, Livvy? Has Palmerson been bothering you again? By God, I'll have his hide if he's touched you."

"It's not me, it's Neville," Olivia managed to gasp out.

"Neville? Your brother? Isn't he away at school?"

"He heard the gossip about us and came home."

"I hope you reassured him. Is that what has you so upset? You shouldn't be here, you know. If you were seen, the gossips would have a field day."

Grimsley appeared with the teacart, and Olivia held her tongue while he poured, then silently retreated. Gabriel picked up her cup, carried it to the sideboard and poured a generous dollop of brandy into the tea.

"Drink up," Gabriel ordered. "You look like you need it."

Olivia took a sip, felt the burning liquid slide down her throat and fill her stomach with satisfying warmth. She took another swallow, then set the cup down and cleared her throat.

"Now, then," Gabriel began, "tell me what has you upset?"

"Neville knows the truth about Palmerson and what he tried to do to me and challenged him to a duel," she blurted out.

"And Palmerson accepted?" Gabriel asked with a note of disbelief.

"They're to meet at dawn tomorrow in a secluded part of Hyde Park. If Palmerson kills Neville, and I'm sure he will, it will be murder. Neville is but eighteen and unskilled in weaponry." She gazed up into Gabriel's distinctive midnight blue eyes, her own eyes pleading. "I didn't know who else to turn to, my lord."

"My name is Gabriel, Livvy. You came to the right person." He knelt at her feet. "Do you trust me?"

Olivia nodded.

"Then trust me to help your brother. Who is his second?"

"Lord Braxton."

"Braxton! At least he's in good hands. Your young brother is discovering, perhaps for the first time, that honor is worth fighting for. He's the head of the family now and feels compelled to defend your honor."

Olivia leaped to her feet. "You sound as if you agree with him. I came to you for help, not to hear you expound upon a man's sense of duty."

Gabriel rose and gently pulled her toward him. "I'm only explaining Neville's rationale, Livvy. He's too young to duel, however, and Palmerson shouldn't have agreed to meet him."

Olivia gazed up at the man she'd come to love. "Can you help?"

The heat from his body surrounded her. His lips hovered over hers, so close she could see the fine lines radiating out from his mouth. "There is always something one can do."

His tone was grimly determined, his conviction clear. Olivia felt as if an onerous weight had been lifted from her shoulders.

"I've already called on Palmerson. He offered a deal I couldn't accept."

Gabriel's eyebrows lifted in surprise, then lowered in anger. "You went to Palmerson? What did he do? Did he touch you? Hurt you?"

Olivia shook her head. "No, nothing like that. He said he'd call off the duel if I agreed to marry him."

Olivia could feel Gabriel's body stiffening. "The bastard! How long ago did you call on him?"

"An hour, two hours—what does it matter?"

"Let me handle this, Olivia. Wait here for me."

"No, I want to go with you!"

"Olivia," Gabriel said sternly, "this is the only way I'll agree to help. Promise you'll stay put until I return. I won't be long. Grimsley will furnish whatever you need in my absence."

"My lord . . . Gabriel, there must be something I can do."

Cradling her chin, he lifted her face to his and kissed her. He tasted wonderful—warm, wet, seductive. The scent, the feel and taste of him, the evocative thrust of his tongue intoxicated her as he lashed the inside of her mouth with almost desperate need. It was a kiss of fiery intensity, of raw, untamed passion. But as quickly as the kiss began, it ended. He held her at arm's length, his breath coming in harsh gasps.

"I won't be long, Livvy."

Then he was gone. In a daze, Olivia stared at his departing back, loving him so much it hurt.

Grim purpose darkened Gabriel's eyes as he spoke to Grimsley on his way out.

"The young lady appeared distraught, milord," Grimsley ventured.

"I want you to keep Lady Olivia here until I return," Gabriel instructed. "Show her to the library and see that she is made comfortable. Have Cook fix her something tempting to eat. Whatever you do, don't let her leave the house."

"Trouble, milord?"

"Everything connected with Olivia spells trouble," Gabriel drawled. "Have my carriage brought around."

Minutes later, Gabriel directed his carriage toward Palmerson's West End home on Oxford Street, a respectable but somewhat less fashionable neighborhood than Mayfair. He hoped to find the viscount at home but was prepared to seek him at his clubs if necessary. Gabriel stopped his rig at the curb outside Palmerson's townhouse and set the brake, more than a little surprised to see Braxton's carriage parked nearby.

Leaping to the ground, Gabriel marched up to the door and rapped briskly. The door opened and he stepped inside. "Please inform the viscount that Lord Bathurst wishes to see him," he told the footman.

"Lord Palmerson has a visitor, my lord. Kindly wait here while I inform him of your presence."

Gabriel would have none of it. He wanted Palmerson and he wanted him now. Stepping deeper into the foyer, he shouted, "Palmerson, show yourself." He waited a moment, then repeated his demand, this time louder.

Palmerson appeared in the doorway, wearing a disgruntled expression. "Are you looking for me, Bathurst?"

"Damn right."

"Bathurst!" Braxton said from behind Palmerson. "I wondered what you'd do when you heard."

"Why didn't you tell me what was going on?"

"I was going to if I failed to talk some sense into Palmerson and that young hothead Lady Olivia calls brother."

"Have you made any headway?"

"Unfortunately, no," Braxton said regretfully.

"Then it's time for me to take over," Gabriel declared.

"May I ask how you learned about the duel?" Palmerson inquired.

"No, you may not," Gabriel returned. "But I intend to put a stop to it."

Palmerson laughed. "Just how do you propose to do that? If young Sefton refuses to back down, why should I?"

"Because I say so," Gabriel said in a low growl.

"Sorry, old boy, there's nothing you can do."

With slow deliberation, Gabriel removed his right

181

glove and slapped it against Palmerson's cheek.

Palmerson sucked in a startled breath. "You're challenging me? On what grounds?"

"On general principles. Braxton is my witness. If you refuse, it will be all over Town in less time than it takes to say your name."

Gabriel was pleased to note that Palmerson's face went bloodless.

"You give me no choice, Bathurst. I accept your challenge."

"I'll act as your second," Braxton offered.

"I'll notify Sanford," Palmerson said. "He and Braxton can arrange a time and place."

"There's no need for a meeting of seconds, Palmerson. I already know the time and place. Six o'clock tonight, beneath the oak tree by the statue of the wood nymph in Green Park. Since you claim to be proficient with a pistol, let's make that the weapon of choice." He turned to leave.

"Wait! That's unacceptable. Choose another time."

"Either agree to my terms or cry off with young Sefton. I'll wait while you write a note of apology. I'll arrange to have it delivered myself."

"And be laughed at by my peers? Not on your life."

"Very well, I'll see you on the dueling field."

"You're a merciless bastard, Bathurst," Palmerson raged. "She's not worth it, you know. The bitch has eluded me for years, ever since her father's death. I offered her my name; can you say the same? You had no right to steal what rightfully belonged to me. It isn't done. I hope you're prepared to die."

Gabriel didn't dignify Palmerson's words with an answer. Turning on his heel, he stalked off.

"Bathurst, wait!" Ram cried. "I'll leave with you."

A footman held the door open, and Gabriel and Ram walked out together.

"I dare say Palmerson is shaking in his boots," Ram laughed. "That was brilliant of you, Bathurst. Will you kill him?"

"Probably not," Gabriel said, "though I should. I just want to make sure he's in no condition to meet young Sefton tomorrow."

"What if he gets lucky? Palmerson is good. You could be killed."

"That's a chance I'm willing to take."

"You really do care for her, don't you?"

"If you're referring to Lady Olivia, of course I care for her. I proposed to her, didn't I?"

"Because of your grandmother, or so you said, but I wonder . . . What *really* happened between you and Lady Olivia at the Hare and Hound?"

"We've been friends a long time, Braxton. You should know better than to ask a question like that."

"Forgive me," Ram said. "It's because I'm your friend that I ask. You're risking your life for Lady Olivia and her brother, and that reveals a great deal about your feelings for the lady."

"Forget my feelings and concentrate on the duel. I'll pick you up in my curricle at five-thirty."

Gabriel climbed onto the driver's bench and took up the ribbons. He didn't hear Ram mutter as the carriage rattled off down the street, "Poor besotted fool."

Olivia had followed Grimsley from the study to the library, where she had been instructed to make herself comfortable while a meal was prepared for her. Awed by her opulent surroundings, Olivia stared at the thousands of leather-bound books lining the shelves.

She had known the marquis was wealthy, but it was hard to imagine such abundance after living in near poverty the past several years.

Though impatient for Gabriel to return, Olivia nevertheless enjoyed examining the books and savoring the light but delicious repast Grimsley brought to her. She had just pulled *Gulliver's Travels* from the shelf when the door opened and Gabriel stepped into the room.

"I'm glad you found something to occupy your time," Gabriel drawled.

The book fell from Olivia's hand. "Gabriel, you're back! What happened? Did Palmerson cry off?"

"I took care of it, Livvy. You're not to worry about a thing."

Olivia felt a tremendous weight drop from her shoulders. She was so relieved, she launched herself at Gabriel. He caught her against him and held her close. It seemed like the most natural thing in the world to rise up on her toes and kiss him. What started out as simple gratitude soon escalated, and passion took over where gratitude left off.

The heat between them burst into flame. His arms tightened around her, and she felt his body harden. She gasped against his throat as his hand covered her breast and his hips rocked against hers.

Olivia made a stab at sanity. "Gabriel, we shouldn't . . ."

"Shhh, love. There's not much time left. Let me love you."

His words barely registered as she concentrated on his hands and what they were doing. He had unbuttoned her dress and pushed it down along with her chemise, baring her breasts. His fingertips brushed back

and forth over her nipples, making them pucker into taut buds. Then his talented mouth covered one sensitive tip and he stroked it with his tongue. The wet heat of his mouth was unbearably erotic against her swollen flesh, and a yearning sound came from her throat at the startling pleasure of it. A multitude of sensations overwhelmed her. She arched and pressed forward, begging for more, her fingers clawing at his shoulders, her head arched back.

"Shall I stop, Livvy?" Gabriel whispered against her damp skin.

She wanted to say yes, but the word died in her throat. She couldn't bear for Gabriel to stop. Mutely she shook her head. Grinning, Gabriel slowly lowered her to the thick carpet.

He removed her shoes with one hand while the other searched beneath her skirts for the tapes of her petticoat. Deftly he untied them and pulled it off. Her dress was the next to go, followed swiftly by her shift. When she lay naked but for her stockings held up by dainty garters, he spread her thighs apart, knelt between them and looked up the length of her legs to the very core of her.

"You're so beautiful." His eyes glittered as he gazed at the fiery curls between her thighs.

Olivia sucked in a startled breath when he touched the soft skin of her stomach, his thumb brushing lightly over her navel. Then his fingers slid downward, parting the petals of her sex, teasing and rubbing her exquisitely sensitive center. He slipped a finger inside her, pressing it deep, drawing it out, then sliding over her swollen nub.

Her knees began to shiver and shake. He removed his finger and kissed his way up the inside of her leg. Never had Olivia felt so vulnerable, so exposed. It wasn't fair. Grasping his lapels, she tried to tug his coat over his shoulders.

He raised his head. "Not yet, Livvy. I need to taste you now. The rest can come later."

When he placed his mouth at that place where his fingers held her open, a pleading moan escaped her lips. She wanted him, desperately needed him inside her, but he seemed disinclined to oblige her.

"Patience," he growled.

He blew on her and pressed his mouth on her until she was ready to beg for his fingers, his tongue, his shaft. Then he gave her what she wanted as his lips and tongue created a suction that brought a keening wail from her lips. Her breath caught sharply when his fingers traveled into the crease of her buttocks, stroking a place outrageously impermissible yet boldly arousing. Her mind went blank with confusion. She tried to protest, but somehow her body yielded without her permission. Pounding pleasure strummed through her. She pulsed again and again, arching against him as his mouth and hands sent her spiraling into oblivion.

When her breathing eased into frantic bursts, he moved away and unfastened his breeches. Flexing his hips, he came hard and deep inside her. Still caught in the delicious aftermath of her climax, she wrapped her legs around him and rode him to an even higher peak. She heard Gabriel's harsh breathing, felt his muscles tense and his staff jerk inside her. Then, at the last possible moment, he pulled out and released his seed onto the carpet.

"You still have your clothes on," Olivia murmured.

"Not for long," Gabriel whispered huskily.

Rising on his elbow, he removed his coat and shirt

and used his linen to wipe the damp spot on the rug. Then he hoisted himself to his feet and pulled Olivia up with him. When he lifted her into his arms and started toward the door, she let out a squeal of protest.

"My clothes! I'm naked. What will your servants think?"

"I pay them well not to think."

"Nevertheless, I'm not leaving this room unless I'm fully dressed."

Her determined tone must have gotten through to Gabriel, for he set her on her feet and folded his arms across his bare chest.

"Very well, but make it fast. The hour grows late, and I want to make love to you again before . . ."

"Before what?"

Gabriel's gaze slid away from hers. A chill of apprehension snaked down Olivia's spine, but she shook it off.

"I have an appointment later—one I must keep."

Olivia hurried into her clothing. "I should go home. Do you think Palmerson has sent a note of apology to Neville yet?" When Gabriel frowned, Olivia said, "That *is* what's going to happen, isn't it? An apology is the only way Neville can save face."

"I've taken care of it," Gabriel said evasively. "Palmerson won't be available to duel with Neville, that's all you need to know."

Olivia went still. "What did you do, Gabriel? How did you get Palmerson to cry off?"

"That's not important. You said you trusted me. Leave the details to me."

Gabriel opened the door and ushered her into the hall. Then he offered her his arm, and together they ascended the marble staircase to his room. To Olivia's vast relief, all the servants were elsewhere except for Thomas, who was stationed at the front door; and if Thomas saw them, he gave no hint of it.

But once the door to Gabriel's bedroom was closed, there could be no prying eyes. Clothing was hastily discarded, flying hither and yon. Gabriel snatched her to him with a suddenness that ripped the breath from her lungs, and moments later Olivia found herself lying on a very large, very comfortable bed with hunter-green velvet hangings and a matching counterpane.

He stretched out beside her, his hands moving expertly over her body, and all the sensations she'd experienced on the library floor began anew. "I'd like to drape you in silks and satins and adorn you with jewels the color of your eyes," Gabriel murmured. His gaze turned dark and intense. "I know I've seen green eyes like yours somewhere. Help me to remember, Livvy."

Olivia reached up and stroked his cheek. "We've never met before, I swear it. Many women have green eyes."

Gabriel groaned and grasped her hand, bringing it down to his groin. "We'll debate that later. Touch me, Livvy. Touch me where I ache for you."

Olivia flexed her fingers, then curled them around his erection. He was hard as marble yet hot to the touch; the tip was velvety smooth and crowned with a drop of pearly moisture. She moved her hand experimentally and was rewarded with an extended groan that seemed to begin deep in Gabriel's chest.

Startled, Olivia tried to remove her hand, but Gabriel stopped her. "Did I hurt you?" she asked.

"God, no! Don't stop."

Emboldened by Gabriel's response, she moved her hand up and down his length, astounded when his sex seemed to grow within her closed fist. A devil inside her compelled her to lower her head and touch the tip of her tongue to the pulsing head. The unexpected intimacy sent Gabriel arching violently upward. Then abruptly his hands were on her waist, lifting her and settling her astride him.

"Ride me, Livvy."

Guided by his hands on her hips, Olivia pounded against him, flesh slapping against flesh. She was so hot she was melting. Head thrown back, eyes closed, breathless and panting, she rode him mercilessly, until a thundering roared in her head and her body began to vibrate. She came in a rush of pleasure so exquisite she thought she'd died and gone to heaven.

"Livvy, get off me! Now!" Gabriel pleaded. "I'm going to . . . oh, God, oh, God . . . too late . . ."

Clamping her legs tightly around him, she refused to let go. Then she felt the hot spurt of his seed against her womb, felt him shudder and heard him call her name. She settled more closely against him and listened to the frantic beat of his heart.

Gabriel cursed violently. "That shouldn't have happened. I've never released my seed inside a woman before. I can't believe I let it happen. You felt so damn good, I couldn't pull out in time."

"And I couldn't let go. I know how women get pregnant, Gabriel, but I don't think this one time will make a baby. I know you don't want a wife and children, and I'd never trap you that way. I don't know what got into me."

Gabriel grinned. "*I* did, twice."

Olivia's cheeks reddened. "You know what I mean. This can't happen again, Gabriel. We seem to explode whenever we're together."

189

"That's not a bad thing," Gabriel said, glancing distractedly at the clock resting on the mantel.

Olivia noticed the direction of his gaze and made a move to leave the bed. "You have an appointment to keep. I should leave."

"Rest a moment while I speak to Grimsley. There's no great hurry."

Olivia stifled a yawn. She *was* exhausted, and a few more minutes wouldn't hurt anything. "Very well, a few minutes, but no longer."

Gabriel bent and kissed her full on the lips before hoisting himself out of bed and disappearing through a door that Olivia assumed led to his dressing room. She yawned again and stretched, watching the door for Gabriel's return.

Olivia awoke with a start, dismayed to find she had been asleep. She glanced out the window and was surprised to see the sun falling below the horizon. Why hadn't Gabriel awakened her? Had he left yet for his appointment? He'd been so secretive about it, she wondered if he was keeping something from her. But that was nonsense, she scoffed. She had no right to interfere in his affairs.

Olivia rose from bed and discovered that someone had left a pitcher of hot water on the washstand. She washed, dressed and prepared herself for the embarrassment of being seen leaving Gabriel's bedroom.

But that wasn't her only worry. Gabriel was close to identifying her as Ollie the highwayman, and she couldn't allow that to happen. How many times could she placate him with denials? How long could she lie about her unlawful activities? While her mind told her to forget Gabriel, her body and heart wanted more of him.

It couldn't be, and she knew it.

Inhaling a sustaining breath, Olivia opened the door to Gabriel's bedroom, stepped into the hall and looked around. Had they come up one flight of stairs or two? Should she turn right or left? She'd been so absorbed in Gabriel, she hadn't paid attention to their direction. Completely lost, Olivia merely stood there, waiting for inspiration to strike. Grimsley arrived instead.

"Milady, Lord Bathurst's carriage awaits you. If you're ready, I'll escort you to the door."

Olivia turned several shades of red. "Thank you, I'm ready now."

"How long ago did Lord Bathurst leave?" Olivia asked as she followed Grimsley along a corridor.

A long pause ensued. "I'm not quite sure," Grimsley murmured with a reluctance that disturbed Olivia.

Had she missed something? "Did Lord Bathurst leave a message for me?"

"No, milady."

Olivia didn't believe him. Grimsley knew more than he was telling her. Did Gabriel's appointment concern Palmerson? Intuition told her it did. "I'm worried about Bathurst. Do you think he'll be all right?"

Grimsley turned abruptly, his expression wary. "You know? I thought . . . that is"—he shrugged—"I didn't think he'd told you. His Lordship should be at Green Park now, but there's no cause for alarm. He's an excellent marksman. Lord Palmerson doesn't stand a chance."

Olivia's face went bloodless. "They're dueling?"

"You didn't know? Dear Lord, what have I done? His Lordship will have my hide for this."

"Thank you, Grimsley," Olivia cried as she raced past him.

"Milady, wait! What are you going to do?"

"I'm going to Green Park," she threw over her shoulder.

"You can't go alone. I'll go with you."

Olivia didn't bother to answer as she rushed past a startled Thomas, who opened the door just in time to prevent a collision. Relief surged through her when she spied Gabriel's carriage at the curb. At least she would not have to waste time hailing a hackney. Olivia had no idea what she was going to do once she arrived at Green Park; she just knew she had to be there. Damn Gabriel for not telling her! Did he intend to kill Palmerson? Was that how he was taking care of things?

Grimsley caught up with her, gave directions to the driver and piled into the carriage beside her. "His Lordship isn't going to like this," he warned.

"His Lordship isn't God," Olivia replied. "I hoped Bathurst would convince Palmerson to cry off. I never wanted him to settle the matter with bloodshed."

"I don't think His Lordship intends to kill Palmerson," Grimsley offered.

"What if Palmerson gets lucky and wounds or kills Bathurst?"

Grimsley gave an undignified snort. "That's highly unlikely, milady."

"Can't this carriage go any faster?"

"We're going as fast as we dare," Grimsley replied.

They rode down Regent Street and turned right on Piccadilly. The late afternoon crowds were beginning to thin as they neared Green Park.

"Do you know where the duel is being held?" Olivia

asked as they turned into the park's entrance.

"I do indeed, milady," Grimsley said. He leaned out the window and shouted instructions to the driver. "It won't be long now."

"Do you think we'll be in time?"

"I sincerely hope not, milady," Grimsley said.

As luck would have it, they reached the dueling field too late. With Lord Braxton's help, Gabriel was in the process of donning his discarded jacket while the surgeon and Lord Sanford assisted a wounded Palmerson. No one else was present. Calling out his name, Olivia leaped from the carriage before it came to a full stop and launched herself toward Gabriel.

Gabriel whirled about, his shock apparent when he saw Olivia running toward him with Grimsley hard on her heels.

"What are you doing here?" he asked harshly. "I told you I would take care of Palmerson." He turned to Grimsley, a scowl darkening his brow. "You shouldn't have brought her here."

Grimsley looked stricken. "Forgive me, milord."

"Don't blame Grimsley," Olivia charged. "I tricked him into telling me. I would have come alone had he not insisted on accompanying me. Is killing Palmerson how you intended to help me? How badly is he wounded? Will he live?"

Gabriel sent her an inscrutable look. "I didn't think you cared about Palmerson. Killing the bastard wasn't my intention. I planned to wound him so he couldn't meet your brother tomorrow. You may go home and tell the young fool he's off the hook. And a 'thank you' wouldn't be amiss."

Olivia didn't know why she was so angry, except that

Gabriel could have been killed, and it would have been her fault.

A voice drifting through the encroaching darkness splintered her thoughts. "Damn you, Bathurst! You and your whore haven't heard the last from me!"

# Chapter Twelve

Seething with anger, Gabriel handed Olivia into his carriage and took up the reins. He hadn't wanted Olivia here and was grateful she hadn't witnessed the actual duel. It had been over within minutes. Palmerson's hand had been shaking so badly that he'd missed Gabriel, but only by a hair breadth. Gabriel's bullet, however, had gone exactly where he had aimed. The bright bloom on Palmerson's right shoulder assured Gabriel that Palmerson wouldn't be using his arm for a while.

Gabriel glanced at Olivia. Her mouth was compressed and her eyes were dark and stormy. Well, he could be just as obstinate. He hadn't told her about the duel with good reason. She wouldn't have approved his method of handling the situation.

Why couldn't she understand that violence was the only thing Palmerson understood? Trying to reason with him had failed. Strangely, Palmerson had seemed pleased at the prospect of killing young Sefton, forcing

Gabriel to resort to unscrupulous methods.

"Where are you taking me?" Olivia asked through gritted teeth.

"Home. It's where you wanted to go, isn't it?"

"You needn't bother. I could hire a hackney."

"Why are you so angry? I did what I set out to do. Your brother is in no danger of getting killed or wounded. Besides," he growled, "I owed that bastard for what he tried to do to you."

Olivia rounded on him. "Don't you understand anything? What if you had been wounded, or worse? It would have been my fault. I never meant for you to place yourself in danger. Why are you so careless with your life?"

"My life was never in danger, Livvy. Give me some credit. I knew exactly what I was doing."

"Did you?" A tense silence ensued.

"We've arrived," Gabriel said, reining in before Olivia's house. "I will accompany you inside."

"That's not necessary, my lord."

"Don't argue, Livvy."

Grasping her elbow, he handed her down and escorted her up the steps. Neville flung open the door before they reached it, his expression fierce.

"What gave you the right to interfere, Livvy? I'm no child. I can take care of myself. Aunt Alma told me you'd gone to Bathurst for help. I don't need help. There's nothing either of you can do to stop the duel."

The young puppy really was feeling his oats, Gabriel thought as he extended his hand to Neville. "You're Lord Sefton, I assume. I'm Bathurst."

His manner less than cordial, Neville shook hands with Bathurst.

"You've no reason to berate your sister, Sefton," Gabriel chided as he ushered Olivia through the door. "She loves you and feared for your life."

Neville glared at Gabriel. "Just what is your involvement with my sister, Bathurst? She said you rescued her from Palmerson, but I believe there's more to it than that. Is any of the gossip true? Have you compromised Olivia?"

"Neville!" Olivia gasped. "What *is* the matter with you? You should be grateful to Bathurst."

"Indeed you should," Alma piped up. "Why, if not for Bathurst, we'd be knee deep in rainwater. He had our roof repaired and refused to accept repayment."

Neville digested that bit of news, then asked, "Is Bathurst providing the blunt to keep me in school?"

"Of course not!" Olivia denied. "Do you know what you're suggesting, Neville?"

Gabriel had heard above enough. "If I may intervene, Olivia, perhaps I can ease young Sefton's mind. He may feel better when he's made aware that we're to be married."

Neville's gaze flew back to Olivia. "You told me there would be no wedding. I want answers, Livvy. I may be young, but I'm not stupid."

"Please, children," Alma said, wringing her hands. "I do so hate confrontations."

"I didn't lie to you, Neville," Olivia said. "Bathurst proposed and I turned him down."

Neville's eyes widened. "I don't understand. At your advanced age, you ought to jump at the chance to marry a marquis. It's not as though you have that many men to choose from. Our father saw to that when he squandered your dowry."

Gabriel clamped a hand on Neville's shoulder. "Enough! Apologize to your sister."

"That's not necessary, my lord. Neville but spoke the truth," Olivia pointed out.

Gabriel's grip tightened on Neville's shoulder. "Nevertheless, you *will* apologize, Lord Sefton. Your sister has denied her own needs to provide for her family."

Neville's bravado crumbled beneath Gabriel's harsh words. "I'm sorry, Livvy. I shouldn't have said what I did. I do appreciate what you've done for me, but you can't stop me from meeting Palmerson tomorrow."

"I beg to differ with you, Sefton," Gabriel said coolly. "There will be no duel. Palmerson has suffered an injury and is temporarily incapacitated. I suspect you'll be receiving a note to that effect very soon."

"How dare you!" Neville blasted. "It's my right to defend my sister's honor. What did you do to him?"

"Please, Neville, calm yourself," Olivia pleaded. "Apologize to Lord Bathurst."

"I'm sorry, Livvy, I can't do that. I've done all the apologizing I'm going to do today." Whirling on his heel, he stalked away.

"I'll talk to him," Alma said, hurrying after her nephew. "He's not always so disrespectful, my lord."

"I knew he would be angry, but I hoped he'd understand," Olivia lamented.

"He's young," Gabriel replied. "This is the first time he's been in a position to assert himself as an adult. If he didn't love you, he wouldn't be so adamant about defending your honor. You should send him back to Oxford as soon as possible."

"Thank you, my lord. Knowing that Neville won't have to meet Palmerson on the dueling field is a great relief to me. I'm sorry if I sounded less than grateful, but trading your life for Neville's wasn't acceptable to me."

"I told you, Livvy, I was in no danger. I'm glad you cared enough to worry about me." He tipped her chin up and lightly brushed her lips with his. "Does that mean you've changed your mind about accepting my proposal?"

"I won't marry you, Bathurst."

"Then I'll be on my way, Olivia. You know where to find me should you change your mind."

Peterson appeared at his elbow. "I'll show you out, milord."

"Goodbye, Bathurst, and thank you again," Olivia said, offering her hand.

Gabriel stared at her fingers—so long, so white, so delicate—and recalled how they felt on his body. His gaze slid up her arm, past her shoulder to her mouth, remembering the way her tongue had lapped him. He felt himself harden and stifled a groan.

Grasping her hand, he turned it palm up and placed a kiss in the center. "Goodbye, my lady. Until we meet again."

Olivia snatched her hand away and all but ran up the staircase. Gabriel grinned and strode out the door Peterson held open for him. Despite Olivia's reluctance and his reservations, they *would* see one another again. It was inevitable. Their passion was like a drug. Seductive. Persuasive. Addictive.

Later that evening, Gabriel called Grimsley into his study. The servant spoke before Gabriel could state his reason for the summons.

"I'll pack my bags immediately, milord, and I won't blame you if you dismiss me without a letter of recommendation."

Gabriel's head shot up. "What the devil are you talking about?"

"I failed you, milord. I should be dismissed."

"Rubbish! That's not why I summoned you. You're a highly valued member of my household. It would be wrong to blame you for Olivia's curiosity."

Grimsley appeared vastly relieved. "Then you'll be wanting to know what I found out about Lady Olivia's family."

"I do indeed."

"The family is poverty-stricken, milord, with no visible means of support. I found no evidence that the deceased Lord Sefton left his children anything but the house they are living in. While his wife lived, they resided in a fine house on Grosvenor Square. He sold it after his wife's death, bought the inferior abode in which the family now resides and squandered the profit. The legacy of his debauchery still haunts them."

"If that's true, how does Olivia manage to keep her brother at Oxford?" Gabriel mused.

"I have no idea, milord."

"What of Palmerson? Did you learn anything of value about him?"

"No more than we already know. He's in dire straits. His creditors are hounding him, and he's very close to being thrown into debtors' prison. The consensus of the *ton* is that he needs to marry money."

"The mystery deepens," Gabriel muttered. "Thank you, Grimsley. If you learn something new, let me know. You may go."

"Thank you, milord. Shall you be eating in tonight?"

"No, I'm eating out. I need to make the rounds tonight. I'm anxious to know how much the *ton* knows about my duel with Palmerson. I hardly think it will remain secret for long."

During the following days Olivia tried to convince Neville to return to Oxford, but he refused. Furthermore, he was demanding answers. He wanted to know where his tuition money was coming from, and he continued to quiz Olivia about her relationship with Bathurst. Neville might be young but he was astute beyond his years. Olivia feared for her brother's future; without funds he would have no standing in society and would be severely limited in choosing a bride.

In order to provide for Neville's future, Olivia decided that Pete and Ollie would have to commit more robberies and demand a larger percentage from the fence.

She encountered Peterson in the kitchen and broached the subject. "We need to talk, Peterson."

"Indeed we do, Miss Livvy. What are we going to do about His Lordship?"

"His Lordship? Bathurst?"

"No, Master Neville. I fear he's going to cause trouble."

"He's going back to Oxford, Peterson. I've been thinking long and hard about his future. His education is nearly complete. He'll return home for good at the end of the term, and he'll need money. It's up to Ollie to find the funds to launch him in society."

"The danger of being caught increases each time we ride," Peterson warned.

"I know, but it can't be helped. Find someplace new to keep the horses. We don't want them traced back to us should someone ask questions."

"When do we ride again?"

"As soon as Neville returns to Oxford."

"Very good, Miss Livvy. Leave everything to me."

"I hate to ask you to place your life in danger again, Peterson, and if you'd rather not ride with me, I'll understand."

"Pete and Ollie are a team, Miss Olivia. I have no intention of letting you go it alone."

"Thank you, Peterson. I don't know what I'd do without you. Neville deserves the kind of life our father denied him."

Neither Olivia nor Peterson heard the telltale click as someone softly closed the kitchen door.

Several days had passed since Gabriel's duel with Palmerson. After a night out on the town, Gabriel returned home well after midnight, his pockets heavier than when he'd left. Thus far he'd heard no gossip about the duel. But with Sanford involved, Gabriel knew that word *would* leak out. Embroiling Olivia in more gossip had never been his intention, but there was little he could do to stop it.

Despite the late hour, Grimsley met Gabriel at the door. "You have a visitor, milord. I told him he should go home and return on the morrow, but he insisted that he see you the moment you arrived home. I put him in the study."

"Damnation! Nothing can be that important. Did he give his name?"

"Lord Sefton, milord."

Gabriel blanched. "Sefton! Good God! Something must have happened to Livvy. I'll see him immediately."

Striding to his study, Gabriel burst through the door and spied Neville sitting in a leather chair beside the fireplace. Neville leaped to his feet when Gabriel entered the room.

"Is it Olivia?" Gabriel demanded. "What's happened to her? Tell me."

Neville plunged his fingers through his mussed hair, his agitation apparent. "Nothing has happened to Livvy, but my visit does concern her. I know we parted on less than friendly terms, Bathurst, but apparently you are the person Livvy turns to for help. She trusts you; I can do no less."

"Sit down, Sefton. You look in need of a drink. Will brandy do?"

Neville nodded distractedly.

Gabriel poured two fingers of brandy in a snifter and waited until Neville took a healthy swallow before speaking. "Now then, Sefton. What matter of importance brings you here at this time of night?"

"What I am about to tell you must be kept in strict confidence," Neville warned. "How much do you know about a pair of highwaymen known as Pete and Ollie?"

"Not much, though I became one of their victims on the turnpike one moonless night. I also had the pleasure of wounding Ollie the next time we met."

"What! You shot Ollie? Bloody hell, do you know what you did?"

"Of course. Why should it upset you?"

"You shot Olivia! You hurt my sister!"

Gabriel went still—very, very still. Then he exploded in fury. "What in God's name are you talking about? Of course I didn't shoot your sister. The only way that could have happened is if she were . . ." He made a gurgling sound in his throat and went deathly pale.

"Exactly," Neville said. "I didn't know until I overheard a conversation between Olivia and Peterson tonight. After I return to Oxford, Peterson and Olivia intend to resume their unlawful activities.

"I was stunned. I had no idea. I didn't know what to do. Then I thought of you. If you proposed to Livvy, you must care about her. Will you help me keep her safe, Bathurst? I'll beg if I have to."

"Let me think." Gabriel began pacing. Olivia and Peterson. Pete and Ollie. Why hadn't he seen the connection before? Green eyes staring at him from beneath the shadow of a hat brim. Livvy's eyes. No wonder she seemed so familiar.

Livvy's illness coincided with the shooting. The reason she wouldn't let his physician examine her closely was because she feared he'd discover the bullet wound. The knowledge that he had grievously hurt Olivia nearly brought him to his knees. Damn her! Damn her to hell!

"Bathurst, please," Neville pleaded. "I implore you. Olivia will hang if she's caught."

"Of course I'll help you, Sefton. Was there ever any doubt? Tell me everything you know. Then I'll decide what I must do to keep your sister safe.

Neville recounted nearly word for word the conversation he'd overheard between Olivia and Peterson.

"The pieces are beginning to fit together," Gabriel mused, "except for one thing. Why does Palmerson want to marry Olivia, and why was he so eager to accept your challenge?"

"I haven't a clue. I've been away at school for the past several years and knew little of what was happening with my family. I wasn't even told the nature of Father's duel until after he was buried. Olivia must have been desperate for money to do what she did. She's sacrificing her life for me. Do you know how that makes me feel?"

"I can well imagine," Gabriel muttered. "If I'm to help, you must do exactly as I say."

"Anything. I'll do anything to help Livvy."

"Very well. You're to return to Oxford tomorrow."

"Bedamned! How can you ask that of me?"

"It's the best for all concerned. Let me handle Olivia."

Neville's eyes narrowed. "You're not going to turn her over to the law, are you?"

"Don't be impertinent! I know what I'm doing. By the way, you might offer your congratulations on the occasion of my marriage to your sister."

"I thought Livvy refused your suit."

"None of that matters now. Go home, Sefton. Trust me to take care of your family. Pete and Ollie are going to drop out of sight forever, and your family will have a sudden turn in fortune. As for Peterson, without Ollie, I predict he'll die in his bed of old age."

Neville looked unconvinced. "Will you let me know if you encounter problems?"

Gabriel sent him an aggrieved look. "There will be no problems. Leave everything to me."

"Very well," Neville agreed. "Anything is better than what Livvy is doing with her life." He rose, stifled a yawn and started toward the door. "Good night, my lord. I'm indebted to you."

"Wait, Sefton. One more thing. I'd like permission to sell your home. I hope you're not sentimental about the place."

"I have no fond memories of the townhouse. What do you intend for Aunt Alma?"

"I shall place her with my grandmother, for the time being, at least."

"I can always rent lodgings when my education is complete," Neville mused. "Perhaps I'll buy a commission in the army."

"I'll have my solicitor deposit the money from the sale of your house into the bank in your name."

"Very well, you have my permission to proceed. Now I really must leave."

"You're unlikely to find a conveyance this time of night. You may borrow one of my horses. Grimsley will show you to the stables and make arrangements to have the horse returned tomorrow. I'm sure he's hovering nearby to show you out."

Sure enough, Grimsley was standing guard outside the study. Gabriel spoke to him briefly; then both Neville and the servant left. Gabriel lingered over his brandy another half hour, mulling over his plans for Olivia and the future they would share.

Gabriel was out of bed early the following morning despite having retired in the wee hours. There was much to do and too little time in which to complete everything. He discussed his plans with Grimsley while he ate breakfast.

"I'm moving temporarily to my country estate," Gabriel said. "I want you and Throckmorton to pack my belongings and follow within the week."

"How soon will you leave, milord?"

"Today."

Grimsley appeared shaken. "So soon? Is there trouble over your duel with Palmerson?"

"No, nothing like that. There's trouble, but it involves Lady Olivia."

"How may I help?"

Gabriel trusted Grimsley with his life and felt no qualms about telling him the reason for his hasty departure. As concisely as possible, Gabriel explained about Pete and Ollie and why he had to remove Olivia from London.

"My word!" Grimsley gasped. " 'Tis hard to believe."

"My sentiments exactly, but the facts are irrefutable. Everything I know about Olivia fits with what her young brother told me. I can't let her be caught, Grimsley."

"Of course you can't, milord. 'Tis unthinkable. How do you propose to keep her at Bathurst Park?"

"I'm going to marry her, even if I have to blackmail her to do it. It's the only way I know to save her life. Fortunately, I still have the special license I purchased a few weeks ago, so that won't be a problem."

He tossed down his napkin. "I'd best get going. There's much to accomplish before I depart. I'll speak to Jenkins myself about readying the coach for the journey to Bathurst Park."

"Very good, milord. All will be done according to your wishes."

Gabriel went immediately to his grandmother's townhouse. Though the hour was early, he found Lady Patrice in her sunny breakfast room sipping coffee and perusing the London *Times*.

"Bathurst, what brings you around so bright and early? How glad I am to see you, dear boy. I've been feeling shamefully neglected of late. Will you join me? I'll ring for breakfast."

Gabriel gave his feisty grandmother a peck on the

cheek and sat down opposite her. "I've already eaten, Grandmama, but I'll have coffee."

Lady Patrice raised a hand, and a footman immediately brought a cup and poured from a silver urn.

"What brings you out this time of day?" Grandmama asked.

Unaccountably nervous, Gabriel cleared his throat. He knew his announcement would make his grandmother happy, and was startled to realize it would also make him happy, though it shouldn't. Marrying Olivia would gain her nothing but heartache and disillusionment. It would, however, protect her, and that was what he must concentrate on.

"Don't keep me in suspense, dear boy," Grandmama chided. "Obviously, you've come to impart news of great importance."

Gabriel grinned. "I'm getting married, Grandmama."

Grandmama clapped her hands excitedly. "Oh, dear boy, how simply marvelous. You couldn't have made me happier. How did you convince Lady Olivia to accept your proposal?"

"It's a long story, one I don't have time for right now."

"We'll hold the wedding here, of course. I'll arrange everything. All that will be required of you is to produce the bride and the license."

"I'm getting married at Bathurst Park, Grandmama. Olivia and I are leaving immediately for the country."

Lady Patrice's eyebrows shot upward. "Is that wise? What about Cissy? She lives there, you know. Won't that be rather awkward?"

"I don't see why it should. My involvement with Cissy ended when she wed my brother. I harbored no hard feelings for either her or Ned, and I'm certainly not pining for her. Bathurst Park is large enough for all of us if Cissy should choose to remain after I marry, but I suspect she'll prefer to move into her own dwelling. Ned left her well provided for. I let her remain at Bathurst Park because I had no intention of marrying or returning there."

"Nevertheless, you're not getting married without family in attendance," Grandmama argued. "I'll bestir myself and come to the country. I can be packed and ready to leave within the week. You must postpone your wedding until I arrive. It would mean a great deal to me, Bathurst."

As usual, Gabriel didn't have the heart to deny his grandmother's request. "Very well, Grandmama, I'll wait until you arrive. But there is something you can do for me in return."

"Anything, dear boy, anything."

"I'd like you to invite Lady Alma, Olivia's aunt, to move in with you as your companion. Olivia will balk at leaving her aunt behind, and I'd like to have my bride to myself for the first few weeks. You can bring her along with you to Bathurst Park for the wedding. And I'd like you to find a place in your household for Peterson, the family retainer."

"A companion," Lady Patrice mused. "A capital idea, Bathurst. I know Lady Alma, and we should rub along quite well together. Say no more, dear boy. I'll send my carriage around with a note instructing Lady Alma and Peterson to attend me later today."

"Thank you, Grandmama. I knew I could count on you. Olivia will be gratified to learn that her family will be taken care of. Goodbye, Grandmama. I'll see you at Bathurst Park."

"Indeed you will, dear boy, indeed you will."

Connie Mason

Gabriel's next stop was White's. As long as his grandmother and Lady Alma planned to attend his wedding, he decided to invite his two best friends. He found them engaged in a lively conversation in a private alcove.

"Bathurst, join us," Luc greeted. "We were just discussing a financial venture. Will you lend us your opinion?"

"Another time, perhaps. I have something of importance to tell you."

"We're all ears," Ram said.

"You're both invited to a wedding. It's to be held at Bathurst Park. I'll need a best man."

"You're serious!" Luc said. "By God, Bathurst, Lady Olivia must be a miracle worker. Is she with child?"

"God, no! Well, what do you say?"

"I'd be honored to be your best man, Bathurst, but I'll defer to Braxton. He's known you longer than I have. Who will attend Lady Olivia?"

"Perhaps Cissy will do the honors."

"Your brother's wife? I thought you and Cissy ... well, you know. I thought she was the reason you never visited your Derbyshire estate. 'Tis common knowledge you were courting her until she threw you over for your brother."

"That was years ago. There was nothing of consequence between Cissy and me after she married Ned. I was disappointed when she chose Ned but held no grudge against either of them."

"So," Ram inquired, "how did you convince Lady Olivia to marry you? Was the gossip finally getting to her? Word of your duel with Palmerson has begun to surface, which has revitalized the gossip about you and Olivia."

"I should have known Sanford couldn't keep his

mouth shut," Gabriel said. "Have either of you seen or heard from Palmerson?"

"He seems to have disappeared. Licking his wounds, I suppose," Luc ventured. "Have you set a date for the wedding?"

"No. Actually, Olivia doesn't know about it yet."

"What?" Luc and Ram cried in unison.

"A minor problem. Grandmama will leave for Bathurst Park in a few days, and I shall expect you both within the week. The wedding will be held as soon as everyone arrives."

"We'll be there with bells on," Luc assured Gabriel. "And good luck convincing your bride you'll make her an excellent husband."

He did indeed need luck, Gabriel thought as he left White's. Olivia was not one to be coerced into anything. He knew now why she had refused his proposal. She had feared he would identify her as the highwayman. But surely she didn't believe he'd expose her, did she? Her opinion of him must be low indeed for her to fear reprisal. It was bad enough that he had shot and wounded her.

The thought that he had nearly killed Olivia fueled his temper. He could wring Olivia's graceful neck for placing herself in danger. Well, he would marry her to put an end to her illegal activities. She would be safe as his wife.

Unfortunately, there was a serious downside to their marriage. In order to protect Olivia from disappointment and grief when his life fell apart, he would have to deny the passion he felt for her. He couldn't afford to lose himself inside her as he had the last time they made love.

He couldn't give Olivia a child.

# Chapter Thirteen

Olivia was feeling pleased with herself. Neville had abruptly changed his mind about returning to the university, and she had sent him off by coach early this morning with funds to pay his quarterly tuition and provide a generous allowance.

Now she was back where she had started—desperately searching for funds. The only answer was Pete and Ollie. They would ride tonight, she decided.

Peterson was marketing this morning, and Olivia waited patiently for him to return to lay Pete and Ollie's plans. A loud pounding on the door brought her down from her room, but Alma reached the foyer before she did.

"Lord Bathurst, do come in," she heard Alma saying. "I'll tell Olivia you're here."

"I'm right here, Auntie," Olivia called from the doorway. "You're out early, my lord."

"We need to talk, Olivia," Gabriel said. He glanced

at Alma. "I'd like a moment alone with Olivia, if you don't mind."

"Not at all," Alma replied. "There's something that needs doing in the kitchen."

"To what do I owe the pleasure of your visit?" Olivia asked as she led the way into the parlor.

"My duel with Palmerson has become public knowledge," Gabriel revealed. "The gossips are having a field day with it, which means the talk and innuendos about us won't go away any time soon."

"I hope you're not here out of some misplaced sense of duty. I will not marry you for any reason, Bathurst."

*Unless you said you loved me and meant it*, Olivia thought.

"You're wrong," Gabriel said in a low growl that sent warning signals down her spine. "You and I are leaving immediately for my country estate in Derbyshire."

"You're mad, Bathurst. What makes you think I'd go anywhere with you?"

"Because you value your life and care about what happens to Peterson."

"You're not making sense."

"You'll understand in a moment. Has your brother returned to the university?"

Olivia frowned. "I saw him off this morning. Why should that matter to you?"

"Excellent. I was hoping he'd keep his word."

"What *are* you talking about?"

"Look at me, Livvy."

She stared into his dark eyes and was immediately reminded of the last time they were together. Their loving had been wild, frantic, and his eyes held the same unyielding glint now as they had then.

Connie Mason

"After we speak to your aunt, you're going to pack a small bag, fetch your cloak and bonnet and accompany me to my coach. Then we're going to travel together to Bathurst Park. We'll be married there as soon as Grandmama and your aunt arrive. Pack only enough to get you by until a wardrobe befitting the wife of a marquis can be completed."

"You're insane!" Olivia exclaimed.

"Am I? I'm doing what I must to protect you . . . Ollie."

"I don't need pro . . . what did you call me?"

"I know, Livvy. *I know.* Your days of robbing people are over. How long did you expect to get away with your illegal activities?" His voice rose angrily. "I shot you, for godsake! I could have killed you!"

This couldn't be happening. Being recognized by Bathurst had been her worst nightmare. Olivia pretended not to understand. "I don't know what you're talking about. If you're accusing me of doing something illegal, of course I deny it."

Simmering rage gave Gabriel's features a hard edge. "Neville overheard you and Peterson talking and came to me for help. You can't begin to imagine how I felt when I realized I had shot you. When I noted your wound, I accepted your explanation because I didn't believe you would lie to me. Not only have you been risking your own life but also that of a servant you obviously care about. You don't have the sense God gave you."

Gabriel grasped her arm, preventing her from retreating from the heated blast of his temper. She had finally been exposed and could no longer deny Gabriel's accusations.

"Neville had no right to involve you. He should have

214

come to me first. Why do you care what happens to me?"

"God only knows why I feel responsible for you. Perhaps it's guilt. Or perhaps it's because you have no one but an untried boy to look after you and your aunt." He gave her a look that sent hot blood rushing through her veins. "Or maybe I want to keep you as a bed partner and am not ready to break off the alliance."

Olivia didn't believe a word of it. "Liar. You didn't wed all the other women you've bedded. Why me?"

His eyes grew hot, then turned the color of smoke. "Damned if I know. But right now you're the only woman I want."

Olivia's chin went up. "For how long? Do you want children with me? Can you promise you'll never look upon another woman with desire?"

"Damnation! There will be no children. And I can't say I'll be with you forever. Forces over which I have no control dictate my life span. As for other women—"

"Wait—go back to that last sentence. What are you talking about? What kind of forces dictate your life?"

Gabriel's long fingers stabbed through his hair. "Forget I said that. It's not important."

"Why don't you want children? I can't marry a man who doesn't want children. It's unnatural."

"Dammit, Livvy, don't question me!"

Alma poked her head through the door. "I heard shouting. Is everything all right in here?"

"Come in, Lady Alma. You need to hear this."

Alma walked into the room, her worried gaze darting between Olivia and Gabriel. "What has Livvy done now, my lord?"

"Nothing. In fact, everything is fine. Olivia has

agreed to become my wife. The ceremony will be held at my ancestral home in Derbyshire."

Alma's eyes glowed with pleasure. "That's the best news I've heard in a long time. Just think, Livvy, you and Peterson won't have to—" She clapped a hand over her mouth. "Oh, dear."

"It's all right, Lady Alma," Gabriel said. "I know all about Pete and Ollie, and you can rest assured that those two outlaws will never ride again."

Impulsively Alma clasped Gabriel's hand between her own. "You don't know how relieved I feel. I've been so worried about my dear niece and Peterson. Why, Livvy could have been killed when you . . . that is . . ."

Olivia rolled her eyes, as if asking for divine intervention. "Bathurst knows everything, Auntie."

"However did he find out?"

"He learned about Pete and Ollie from Neville. Apparently, Neville overheard Peterson and me talking."

"I don't care how he found out. I'm just glad it's over." Alma's brow furrowed. "You're not going to expose Livvy, are you, Lord Bathurst?"

"And have my marchioness revealed as a highwayman?" Gabriel asked dryly. "I'm taking Olivia away from London and temptation. You'll no longer have to worry about finances. Your family is my responsibility now."

"Responsibility or burden?" Olivia asked. "I won't have it, Bathurst."

"Neville gave me permission to sell this house and place the proceeds in the bank in his name. I've turned the matter over to my solicitor. You won't be living in poverty any longer."

Olivia's temper exploded. "How dare you arrange my life without consulting me! Neville had no right to

216

appoint you his agent. This is the only home we have. What is Aunt Alma to do? Where will Neville live when he finishes his education?"

"I'm working on Neville's problem. As for Lady Alma, my grandmother has need of a companion and I think she and your aunt will do famously together. Grandmama will be sending a carriage around for your aunt and Peterson later.

"You might want to pack your belongings, Lady Alma, and inform Peterson that he will serve in my grandmother's household until other arrangements are made."

Alma hurried off in a flurry of skirts. Olivia waited until she was gone, then asked, "What other arrangements, Bathurst?"

"In the fullness of time, both your aunt and Peterson will be living with us."

"Are they to become hostages to force my compliance? What will happen to them should I refuse to marry you?"

"Dammit, Livvy, you're trying my patience! You're going to marry me and that's final. I don't need hostages to force your compliance. I have all the ammunition at my disposal that I need."

Hands on hips, Olivia faced him squarely. "What ammunition, my lord?"

"The identities of Pete and Ollie."

Olivia's lips compressed. "So you *do* intend to expose me and Peterson."

"Not at all. But I suggest you think twice about refusing my proposal."

Gabriel realized he was being unnecessarily harsh, but he couldn't allow Olivia to return to the kind of life she'd led since her father's death. Besides, he'd promised Neville he'd put a stop to his sister's illegal activities, and so he would.

Prodded by a healthy dose of guilt, he intended to assume full responsibility for Olivia and her family. He had desired her and had taken her without a thought for her reputation; now he must pay the consequences. He couldn't give Olivia children, but he could see that she was taken care of for the remainder of his life and beyond. Once there was no longer any danger of Olivia being caught, he would bring her back to London.

She would need friends after he . . . well, hopefully, that wouldn't be any time soon. Thus far he'd seen no signs of . . . what he feared most.

Olivia whirled around and gave Gabriel her back. "You win, Bathurst."

Gabriel stared at the graceful curve of her spine, at her neck, stiff with indignation, at the proud tilt of her head, and felt something unbearably tender and protective rise up inside him. He had lusted after Olivia from the very first moment he'd laid eyes on her. But once he'd had her, he'd only wanted more. Not even his favorite mistress had pleased him as well as Olivia, whose innocence and unworldly demeanor kept him in a constant state of arousal. He must be getting old, he reflected. Though he knew he shouldn't, the thought of settling down with Olivia was enormously appealing. What he couldn't afford was losing control during their intimate moments. He wouldn't hurt Olivia by giving her children.

Grasping her shoulders, Gabriel turned her to face him and tilted her chin up to him. There were tears in her eyes, and he smoothed them away with the pad of his thumb. "Livvy, trust me to keep you safe and provide for your family. You won't be unhappy, I promise."

When no reply was forthcoming, Gabriel lowered his head and brushed a kiss across her lips, but one taste wasn't enough. His tongue traced the outline of her mouth, a silent demand that she open to him. At first her lips remained taut, unyielding, but finally they parted beneath his gentle persuasion. The kiss started out slow and indolent, then erupted with insatiable passion.

Gabriel couldn't help himself. The nature of his kiss turned starkly sensual, blatantly bold as he dragged her against him and tightened his hold.

Olivia whimpered in protest. He felt so stunningly aroused, so brazenly hard, that it stole her breath. What had begun as a simple kiss had quickly escalated into something wildly passionate, and she mustn't let that happen. Gabriel lusted, not loved; he took without permission, and his idea of a happy marriage was not hers. What kind of man refused his wife children?

She broke away, panting from the effort to control her response to Gabriel's stirring assault. She glanced into his eyes, stunned at the smoldering pits of sensuality staring back at her.

"Please, Gabriel, not here, not now."

His arms fell to his sides. "Forgive me. I become totally unbalanced when I'm with you. Fetch your things and tell your aunt we're leaving."

Olivia wanted to refuse, but how could she? She didn't believe Gabriel would expose Peterson, but she couldn't take that chance. A kernel of common sense told her that Gabriel was right to curtail her activities, that her luck couldn't hold forever and one day the law would catch up with her. But his domineering ways still rankled.

Being on the shelf for so many years had given Olivia the kind of independence few women enjoyed, and surrendering her freedom to an arrogant rogue like Bathurst wasn't going to be easy. A thought occurred to her, and she smiled. She wouldn't have to surrender her hard-won independence. The unrepentant rake would probably take a mistress and leave her to her own devices soon after the wedding.

"You win this time, Bathurst," Olivia bit out. She turned to leave. "I'll only be a moment."

"Olivia," Gabriel offered as he followed her to the foot of the stairs. "You must understand why I feel obliged to do this. Guilt is killing me. I put a bullet in you. I compromised you. That makes me responsible for you."

Olivia spun around on her heel. "Guilt? Responsibility? Your reasons for offering marriage are unacceptable to me."

A lazy smile lifted his lips. "How about lust? That sounds like a good reason to me."

"Damn impossible rogue," Olivia muttered as she stomped up the stairs.

Watching from below, Gabriel admired the pert swaying of her hips and the shapely turn of her ankles. "Pack only the essentials," he called after her. "I meant what I said about a new wardrobe."

Gabriel cooled his heels a good thirty minutes before Olivia reappeared carrying a small satchel. Both Lady Alma and Peterson were with her.

"Shouldn't Livvy have a chaperone?" Alma asked. "Perhaps I should go with you."

"No need. My brother's widow resides at Bathurst

Park. I expect to see you and Grandmama in a few days. I promised Grandmama that I wouldn't set the date until she arrived. You can help with the details."

"How exciting!" Alma exclaimed, apparently placated by Gabriel's promise. "I've always dreamed of planning Livvy's wedding."

Peterson cleared his throat. "If I may be so bold, milord . . ."

"Go ahead, Peterson, you may as well have your say."

"Miss Livvy told me you were aware of our . . . er . . . activities, and I want to say that I only agreed to her scheme because she would have gone alone had I not accompanied her. I wouldn't endanger her life for anything in the world."

"It's rather late for those sentiments," Gabriel observed. "Are you ready, Olivia?"

Olivia hugged both her aunt and Peterson, then turned to Gabriel. "I'm ready, my lord. Your blackmail has worked. Your silence has bought a bride."

Gabriel sighed in frustration. It was not a very auspicious beginning, but it was more than he had hoped for. That he was getting married at all was a miracle in itself. He had sworn he would have no part of matrimony after he'd heard his mother's last words to his brother. Those words had changed his life. His brother's too, though Ned hadn't lived long enough to experience the results of their mother's confession.

Banishing his unpleasant memories, Gabriel placed Olivia's hand in the crook of his arm and escorted her out the front door and into his coach.

"Will we reach your estate today?" Olivia asked as the coach rattled off.

"No. We'll spend the night at a respectable inn along

the way. You'll find the King George to your liking, I believe. The inn caters to titled travelers."

Olivia fell silent, and Gabriel wondered what she was thinking. He didn't have long to wonder.

"You said your brother's widow lives at Bathurst Park. I take it she hasn't remarried?"

Gabriel shifted uncomfortably. "I suppose Cissy has had many opportunities to wed, but hasn't found a man to her liking."

"How old is she?"

"About your age."

"Will she stay on at Bathurst Park after we're wed?"

"If she wants to, but I suspect she'll move to her own small estate. Blythe House was part of her dowry."

When Olivia's gaze drifted back to the passing scenery, Gabriel's thoughts turned inward. He remembered how Cissy looked the day she had told him she was going to marry his brother. She was so beautiful, so ethereal with her delicate features and silvery blond hair. She had apologized prettily for choosing Ned, explaining that her parents had urged her to accept the heir instead of the spare, and so she had.

Gabriel could recall a moment of burning anger, but it hadn't lasted long. They were all so damn young. He and Ned had been close, and he harbored no ill will toward his brother and Cissy after they wed. Then his mother, in one of her lucid moments, told Ned something that had irrevocably changed his life.

Glancing out the window, Gabriel noted that it had begun to rain. It had been threatening all day, but he had hoped it would hold off until they stopped for the night. He lowered the leather window curtains when wind and rain began to blow into the coach, unfolded a blanket and spread it across Olivia's knees.

Lightning streaked across the sky and thunder rumbled. When the coach began to flounder in the mud, Gabriel realized they couldn't go much further for fear of becoming stranded on a deserted stretch of road. Rapping on the roof, he instructed Jenkins to stop at the next inn they came to. A short time later, the coach turned into the yard of a dismal-looking inn that Gabriel was certain offered little more than the meanest accommodations. Nevertheless, it was a welcome port in the storm.

Jenkins jerked open the door and pulled down the steps. Water dripped off his nose and he was soaking wet. Gabriel stepped down first, grimacing when mud squished around his boots. He held out his arms for Olivia, and when she would have stepped down into a swirling puddle, Gabriel swept her up and carried her beneath the sign of the Cock and Crow and into the boozy warmth of the inn. Jenkins hurried after them, holding an umbrella over their heads.

Gabriel set her on her feet inside the door and turned to address the coachman. "See to the horses, Jenkins, then warm yourself by the fire. I'll arrange for accommodations and a hot meal."

The innkeeper hurried up to greet them. "Good evening, milord. Be ye wanting a hot meal and a room?"

"Indeed. Two rooms. The best you have. And a place for my coachman to bed down."

"The meals be no trouble, milord, but I've no rooms to let." He gestured expansively to the crowded common room. "As ye can see, we're nigh to bursting tonight."

Gabriel looked for Olivia and saw that she had wandered over to the huge hearth in the common room. Her shivering form convinced him that even the mean-

223

est accommodations were better than none at all. "There must be something available." He extracted a gold crown from his pocket and offered it to the innkeeper. "My . . . wife is chilled and exhausted. Anything with a bed and fireplace will do."

The innkeeper stared at the gold piece for a heartbeat, then plucked it from Gabriel's fingers. "There be one room ye can have, milord, but it ain't fancy. The Cock and Crow ain't the kind of place what attracts wealthy travelers."

"I told you, we'll take whatever is available."

"There be a small room that belongs to me daughter. She can bunk in with me and me wife tonight, and ye can have her room. The bed is clean and there's a small hearth in the room. If that be all right, I'll send a boy up to stoke the fire while ye eat. Me wife's a tolerable cook. She prepared a hearty meat pie tonight."

"Excellent," Gabriel said. He removed another coin from his purse. "I'd like a tub and hot water delivered to the room. Be sure my coachman is taken care of."

The innkeeper snagged the coin and it disappeared into his pocket. "I'll arrange for the tub, milord, but all I can offer yer coachman is a bench by the fire and a hot meal."

"That will do. My . . . wife and I will wait in the common room for our dinner."

Gabriel collected Olivia and steered her toward an empty table. Jenkins entered the inn a moment later, carrying their bags. He gave them over to the innkeeper and headed for the warmth of the fire.

"I need to speak to Jenkins, Livvy," Gabriel said as he seated her at the table. "The innkeeper has offered us his daughter's room. He's having it prepared while we eat. Our food should arrive soon."

"My lord," Olivia said when he would have walked away. "Are we to share a room?"

His eyes darkened. "There were no accommodations available. I had to bribe the innkeeper for his daughter's room. I wasn't eager to sleep on a bench in the common room and assumed you would share my feelings." Inclining his head, he strode away.

Restraining her anger, Olivia stared at his departing form. Having her life arranged and her opinions ignored did not sit well with her. She didn't want a man telling her where to go and what to do. She was certain Gabriel thought of her as just another woman to warm his bed. Common sense told her that he wouldn't remain faithful to their wedding vows. He had proposed for reasons unacceptable to her. Duty and guilt were poor substitutes for love and respect. He had put a bullet into her, and his masculine pride demanded that he wed her, but her feminine pride rebelled.

Their food arrived, and Gabriel returned to the table. "Smells good," he said, placing a generous serving of flaky meat pie on Olivia's plate before filling his own.

Olivia ate in silence. She was hungry, but the smell of unwashed bodies and stale ale sent her stomach into spasms. She sipped ale cautiously until her stomach settled, then began to eat. When the fruit tart smothered in Devonshire cream arrived, she merely looked at it and pushed it away.

"I can't eat another bite."

"You're exhausted," Gabriel said. He pushed back his chair. "Shall we retire?"

"Good night, milord, milady," the innkeeper called as they mounted the stairs. "Sleep well."

The room proved to be a cozy haven beneath the eaves. A fire danced merrily in the hearth, and a tub of steaming water awaited them. A small but adequate bed was pushed snugly beneath the single window, which was being battered by driving rain.

"It looks clean enough," Gabriel said after a cursory inspection. "We're lucky to have it." He plucked her cloak from her shoulders and untied her bonnet strings. "Off with your clothes and into the tub with you."

"Where are you going while I bathe?" Olivia challenged. She didn't belong to him yet and wanted him to know it.

"Livvy, I've seen you before."

Her chin rose defiantly. "You've never seen me bathe before. Something that personal should be reserved for married couples."

"You sorely try my patience, Livvy. Very well, if you prefer to bathe in private, I'll go down to the common room and share a bottle with Jenkins."

Olivia smiled in satisfaction as Gabriel let himself out of the room. What really counted was that she had won a round in her battle for survival as Gabriel's wife. She was convinced that once they were married he would return to London to indulge his sensual nature, leaving her alone, without even the comfort of children to fill her empty days.

Olivia stripped and stepped into the tub. The hot water felt wonderful and she sank down into the welcoming warmth. After a short soak, she took up soap and cloth and scrubbed herself from top to bottom. When she finished, she rested her head back against the rim and closed her eyes, her long auburn tresses spilling like a bright cloak over the edge.

Gabriel decided it was time to leave when men began bedding down on benches in the common room. He finished his ale and took his leave of Jenkins. He wasn't drunk, but the ale had created a glow that spread throughout his body and pooled in his loins. He thought of Livvy lying snug and warm in bed and couldn't wait to join her. He visualized her body flushed from her bath, her long legs splayed in sensual abandon and her arms reaching for him.

He felt his cock thicken, felt it throbbing, and lust for his green-eyed little thief propelled him up the stairs. Light leaked from beneath the door, and he eased it open. His gaze went to the bed. It was empty. Fear rose in his throat. Knowing his Livvy, he supposed she'd probably sneaked down the back stairs and run off.

*Damn her!* He advanced into the room, glanced at the tub and froze. She appeared to be sleeping; her head was propped against the rim of the tub, and her long hair tumbled down to the floor. Relief speared through him.

Shedding his coat and long-sleeved shirt, Gabriel reached for her and carefully lifted her out of the tub, wrapping the towel around her dripping body. She murmured and stirred but didn't awaken as he carried her to the bed and dried her rosy skin with the towel. Then he stripped off his clothes and joined her.

Driven by the need to kiss her sweet lips, to taste her scented flesh and place his tongue in her fragrant center, he turned her into his arms. If he didn't feel her tight sheath cradling his cock and hear her moaning gasps while he pleasured her, he would surely perish.

"I want you, Livvy," he whispered against her mouth.

"Ummm."

The moment his mouth claimed hers, she awakened.

"Gabriel, what are you doing?"

"Making love to you."

"No, I don't want—"

A flare of amusement mingled with the heat in his eyes as he lowered his head and kissed a fiery path to her navel. His warm tongue slid around and inside the tiny hollow.

"Are you sure about that?"

"Yes . . . no . . . I don't know. You confuse me."

"I can make you want me."

His fingertip parted the curls between her thighs, easily finding the sensitive nub between them. She made a helpless noise at the touch, a protest that he ignored. His mouth descended, and she felt his fingers spreading her. His lips parted and his tongue darted out, investigating her with stabbing strokes. She felt ecstasy pull in every part of her body; her nerves screamed for more. Coherent thought shattered at the sight of his head between her thighs.

"Gabriel, please!"

He grinned up at her. "I always aim to please, love." Then he bent his head again and placed his mouth over her, his tongue probing and stroking with delicate skill.

As he settled more firmly between her legs, Olivia gave a sigh of surrender and arched up against him. Sensation unfurled inside her. Trembling, she strained toward the elusive pleasure that seemed just out of reach.

Her lips parted, but no sound emerged. He was utterly remorseless. His ability to wring so powerful a response from her was awesome, but she couldn't help herself. He touched something in her heart, something that no other man had exposed, and it frightened her.

Then he shattered her with an artful flick of his tongue. She was still shuddering with tremors of bliss when his mouth closed over hers, feeding her the sweet essence of her own desire. When he flexed his hips and slid deep inside her, she welcomed him into her body with a cry of gladness, returning his kiss and arching against him as he began to move forcefully upon her.

A spark caught fire inside her. She felt possessed. Consumed. Engulfed in a raging inferno, she twisted her fingers in his dark hair and moved in rhythm to the churning thrust of his hips. Her body reverberated with raw sensation and her mind shut down.

"Livvy, look at me."

His voice came to her as if from a great distance. Her gaze lifted to his. His face wavered into focus, his eyes two glittering orbs of desire.

"Let yourself go. I've got you, love. Give yourself to me."

His words brought a measure of sanity. How could she give herself to him when he would never completely belong to her? Men like Bathurst possessed. They held on to their possessions, demanding complete surrender and offering nothing of themselves in return. But no matter how desperately she wanted to withhold a response, his expert lovemaking brought her to a shuddering climax.

Gabriel groaned as tremors ripped through him. The feel of her contractions squeezing him, her in-drawn breath at each plunge of his body into hers—it was too much. A storm was building inside him. He drove into her relentlessly, penetrating deeper and deeper with every wild thrust. Her climax sent him spinning over the edge. He pulled out just in time, spilling his seed onto her stomach.

Rolling away, he found the towel on the floor and gently wiped away the puddle of semen. Olivia turned away from him, but he gathered her in his arms and brought her against him. He was nearly asleep when he felt her tears dampening his chest. Rising on his elbow, he turned her face toward the dying light of the fire.

"Why are you crying?"

"Why don't you want children?"

He sighed. "Go to sleep, Livvy. One day you'll thank me for taking precautions."

# Chapter Fourteen

Never had Olivia seen anything as majestic as Bathurst Park. Surrounded by forests, orchards and formal gardens, the spacious manor sat like a jewel in the center of nature's splendor, its reflection mirrored in the sparkling lake behind it. It glittered in the sunlight like a grand lady attired in her elegant best—a matriarch that resided in quiet grace in a bucolic setting.

Derbyshire, situated in the Midlands, was renowned for its rolling hills, verdant farmland and hedgerows of hawthorn, brier roses and holly. It was the center of fox hunting, drawing members of the *ton* to the area during the hunting season.

"Your home is magnificent," Olivia said as they passed through the gate and continued on to the manor down a broad lane lined with hedgerows.

"Yes, it is, isn't it?" Gabriel said. "Though I've tried not to, I've missed it."

231

"How long has it been since you visited your ancestral estate?"

"Too long, I suppose. I left after my mother's death and never returned. Ned inherited the title shortly after he married Cissy, and there was no reason to remain. I bought a commission in the army and served on the Peninsula with Wellington. Ned died three years ago, while I was abroad. I never found the time to visit Derbyshire after my return. Fortunately, I have an excellent steward in Winthorpe."

Olivia couldn't imagine what had kept Gabriel away from his family estate for so many years, but he was a man with many secrets.

The coach pulled up before the front steps and Olivia stared out the window, her gaze wandering appreciatively over the ivy-covered facade of weathered pink stone topped by turrets and battlements. It was too new to be described as a medieval castle and too old to be called a modern structure.

Gabriel stepped down first and extended his hand. Olivia tore her gaze away from the manor house and put her hand in his. "You didn't prepare me for such grandeur, Gabriel. Is your brother's widow expecting us?"

"There wasn't time to send a messenger ahead. I imagine she'll be surprised but gracious."

Olivia certainly hoped so. Something about Lady Cissy Wellsby bothered her despite the fact that she'd never met Gabriel's sister-in-law. But the impression that she had missed something important about Cissy persisted.

An elderly servant opened the door, his face wreathed with smiles when he saw Gabriel. "Milord, welcome home. We didn't expect you. How wonderful to have you home again."

Gabriel returned the man's exuberant welcome. "Briggs, you haven't aged a year since I left. Still spry as ever, I see. Believe it or not, it's good to be home."

"I hope your stay will be a lengthy one, milord."

"Time will tell, Briggs. My household is a day or two behind me. And Grandmama will arrive soon with her companion. Please see that rooms are prepared for my fiancée. The suite next to mine will do."

Briggs's gaze turned to Olivia, as if he was startled by Gabriel's revelation. But being a good servant, he merely bowed and said, "Welcome, milady. If you'll excuse me, I'll summon Lady Cissy to greet you properly."

"Do we have guests, Briggs?"

The voice startled Olivia. The sweet, dulcet tones were softly rendered and melodic. When Lady Cissy walked into the foyer, Olivia immediately stepped behind Gabriel. She felt dowdy and awkward compared to Gabriel's lovely sister-in-law. Cissy was so beautiful, it hurt to look at her. She was petite, blond and fragile, the pale oval of her face as perfect as her shapely body. She was so exquisite, she seemed to glow in her pale pink ruffled dimity gown. She looked like a child playing grown-up and appeared years younger than Olivia, though Gabriel had said they were of an age.

Calling out Gabriel's name, Cissy clutched her throat and began to sway. Gabriel caught her in his arms. She immediately melted against him, clinging to his broad shoulders and whispering his name in a breathy little sigh. The contrived performance disgusted Olivia, and intuition told her there was more between Cissy and Gabriel than he had told her.

After a few minutes of clinging, Cissy spied Olivia

over Gabriel's shoulder and stiffened in his arms. Gabriel unwound her arms from around his neck and set her away from him.

"Forgive me for not letting you know I was coming, but there wasn't time," Gabriel apologized. "I left London rather suddenly."

Ignoring Gabriel's words, Cissy eyed Olivia with hostile curiosity. "Who is that woman, Bathurst? Briggs should have directed her to the servants' entrance."

"Olivia isn't a servant, Cissy, she's—"

"Never tell me she's your mistress, Bathurst, for I refuse to believe you'd bring your doxy into my home. She looks like a beggar," Cissy said, wrinkling her nose. "Did you pick her up in the gutter? She's not even young. I didn't know women of her ilk appealed to you."

Bristling with indignation, Olivia stiffened her shoulders, appalled at Cissy's lack of manners. A scathing retort gathered in her throat, but Gabriel forestalled her.

His lips compressed into a thin line of disapproval, he placed a protective arm around Olivia. "You've just insulted my bride-to-be, Cissy. Meet Lady Olivia Fairfax, my intended bride. Olivia, this is Lady Cissy Wellsby, my brother's widow."

The color drained from Cissy's face. "You're getting married? I was led to believe you would never wed. I thought it was because of me. I . . . I can't believe it. I thought you and I . . . I've been waiting for you to come home to tell you—"

"Cissy," Gabriel warned, "you've said enough. Olivia is exhausted and would like to freshen up in her room. We'll talk later. Come along, Livvy, I'll show you to your suite. It's next to mine in the west wing."

234

"You're giving her the suite next to yours?" Cissy gasped.

"Why not? It's where she belongs."

"When is the wedding to be?"

"As soon as Grandmama arrives. She and Olivia's aunt will be in charge of the arrangements. I'm counting on you to act as chaperone while Olivia is in my home."

"Why the hurry, Bathurst?" Cissy asked snidely. "Is your intended already increasing?"

Gabriel's tone was gently chiding. "Cissy! What has gotten into you? You've always been so well-mannered."

Cissy's blue eyes brimmed with tears, but Olivia was not impressed. A fool could see that Cissy hated her, and Olivia was no fool.

Cissy wanted Gabriel.

"Forgive me, Bathurst," Cissy pleaded. "I've been so lonely since Ned died. I'll wait for you in the study. We can talk after you get your bride-to-be settled."

"She doesn't like me," Olivia whispered as Gabriel steered her toward the stairs.

"You must forgive Cissy," Gabriel explained. "She's angry with me for not visiting her since I resigned my commission and returned to England."

"Why *didn't* you return?"

"I was too late for Ned's funeral and saw no reason to leave London."

Olivia thought there was more to it than that but did not press the issue. Cissy and Gabriel shared a past that was something of a mystery, but it was obvious that Cissy didn't like the idea of Gabriel taking a wife.

They reached the top landing and Gabriel turned down a lengthy corridor, then another. "This wing has traditionally belonged to the lord and his lady," Gabriel said. "The suites are adjoining, each with a separate sitting room. There's also a bathing room with modern plumbing between the two suites. I had the manor modernized after I inherited the title."

"Why would you do that if you were never here?" Olivia queried.

"Cissy lived here, and I wanted the estate in good repair should I ever decide to return. Ah, here we are," Gabriel said, opening a door and ushering her inside.

Olivia stepped into the sitting room and stopped abruptly, the grandeur of her surroundings momentarily blinding her. Plush carpet covered the floor, and cream silk adorned with tiny pink roses decorated the walls. A pink satin sofa and matching chairs arranged near a fireplace and a delicately carved lady's writing table and chair were among the furnishings.

"Does it meet with your approval?" Gabriel said. "This was my mother's suite until . . . well, that doesn't matter."

"Am I displacing Cissy?"

"No. Ned never occupied these rooms after he inherited the title. He preferred the east wing. Though these rooms have been kept in readiness for my return, they have not been occupied. Would you like to see the bedroom?"

"Shouldn't you wait until we're wed to give me these rooms?"

Gabriel's brows lifted. "Livvy, we're as good as wed." He opened the door and stood aside while she entered.

Olivia's gaze was drawn immediately to the floor-to-ceiling windows draped in deep rose satin to complement the cream and pink silk wall covering. Then her gaze settled on the huge bed hung with curtains the same color as the drapery. Placed strategically around the room were an ornate dressing table complete with mirror and an assortment of brushes, a fainting couch covered in rose damask, and a chest of drawers. The mantel above the fireplace held a clock and an assortment of pictures that must have belonged to Gabriel's mother.

"My rooms are beyond the dressing room," Gabriel said, indicating a door opposite the one they'd entered by. "The bathing room can be reached through the dressing room."

"There are no locks on the doors," Olivia observed. "What's to keep you from entering my room whenever you please?"

"Nothing. Once we're wed, you'll sleep in my bed."

"Until you tire of me," Olivia pointed out.

Gabriel drew his finger along her jaw and down the pulsing vein in her neck. "What makes you think I'll tire of you?"

Olivia shrugged. "It's what rogues do. We both know why you're marrying me."

Gabriel's dark brows shot upward. "We do?"

"Of course. Guilt. You shot me and feel obligated to accept responsibility for me and my family. But you don't have to do this, Bathurst. I can take care of myself."

"Can you? Let's see," Gabriel mused, counting off on his fingers. "You are without funds, you were shot, kidnapped and nearly raped. You dress in men's clothing and rob unsuspecting travelers, and you're just begging to be hanged. I'm saving you from yourself, Olivia. Your family will be much better off with me looking after them."

Connie Mason

Indignant, Olivia stiffened. "I was doing just fine until you came along."

He stepped closer and dragged her into his arms. "*Were* you doing fine, Livvy? It would be intolerable to me if something happened to you because I failed to protect you," he said honestly. "Why must you question my motives?"

"Because your motives are suspect!" Olivia shot back. "You never wanted to marry, and I'll never be the kind of wife who can ignore her husband's affairs while conducting liaisons of her own. What do you say to that, Bathurst?"

His eyes glittering wickedly, he lifted her chin and claimed her lips.

*Little ninny*, Gabriel thought as he slid his tongue between Olivia's sweet lips and deepened the kiss. He had no idea how long Olivia would please him, but it made him feel good to know she intended to honor her wedding vows.

Gabriel fought to control his raging desire with little success. His muscles grew taut, his cock rigid and insistent, and his control was stretched almost to the breaking point. He'd told himself he wouldn't make love to Olivia again until they were wed. It was a test of sorts. He wanted to prove that he could restrain his ardor where Olivia was concerned, but all his good intentions flew out the window as their bodies meshed and her lips clung sweetly to his.

Gabriel's hands were working feverishly at the buttons on the back of her dress before he realized how close he was to surrendering to lust. He broke off the kiss. In another moment he'd have her stretched out on the bed with her skirts hiked up around her waist and his cock buried deep inside her.

238

She looked confused when he set her away from him, and the breath left his lungs in a great whoosh. Her eyes were glazed with passion and her lips dewy and swollen from his kisses. When she looked like this, she was dangerous. He couldn't afford to let his guard down; he didn't dare give her his child.

Above all, he did not want her to fall in love with him. That would be cruel, for when his time was up . . . So far there were no signs, but that could change tomorrow, or the next day, or the day after that. With a will born of necessity, Gabriel put distance between himself and Olivia. He would make love to her, but not now, when his raging desire made controlling himself impossible.

"There's plenty of time to rest before dinner," Gabriel said coolly. "I'll send up a maid to help you bathe. While you're resting, I shall speak to Cissy about hiring seamstresses to fashion a wardrobe for you."

Beating a hasty retreat, Gabriel paused in the hallway and inhaled deeply, willing his erection away. Cissy awaited him in the study, and it wouldn't do for her to see how weak he was where Olivia was concerned. Once control returned, he strode briskly to his meeting with his brother's widow.

"I thought you'd never get here," Cissy complained when Gabriel entered the room. "Whatever are you thinking, Bathurst? I don't know what you see in that woman. One has but to look at her to know she brings nothing to the marriage."

"I don't need anything from Olivia," Gabriel replied.

"Is she increasing?"

"There will be no Bathurst heirs."

"I'll never forgive Ned for not giving me children," Cissy lamented. "He kept putting me off, insisting that we had plenty of time to make babies. Because of his stubbornness, he died without issue."

Gabriel applauded Ned's decision but withheld his opinion from Cissy. "Before I leave instructions concerning Olivia, I want to know about Ned's death. I was told he drowned, but I know for a fact that Ned was a strong swimmer. How could he have drowned?"

"I don't know. What I do know is that Ned was never the same after that conversation with your mother shortly before she threw herself out the window. You were here at Bathurst Park; you must have noticed. Sometimes I wonder what your mother said to change him."

Gabriel knew precisely what had troubled Ned. "How did Ned seem the day he drowned?"

"The same as usual. He wanted to go fishing before the approaching storm broke."

"Tell me truthfully, Cissy. Do you think Ned took his own life?"

Cissy's blue eyes widened. "Why would he do that?"

*Because he couldn't live with what he had learned from our mother*, Gabriel thought. "You're right, Cissy—forget I asked." Then he abruptly changed the subject. "I want you to help make Olivia feel welcome."

"How can you ask that of me?" Cissy cried. "I waited years for you to return home. You know I preferred you to Ned. I loved you, Gabriel. Ned was my parents' choice, not mine."

"Nevertheless, you *did* wed Ned. I vowed on your wedding day to move on with my life. We were both young. What we had together no longer exists. You were Ned's wife, and I had no right to think of you as anything but my sister. There can never be anything between us, Cissy."

Cissy launched herself at Gabriel, her arms twining about his neck in desperate appeal. "You don't mean that, Gabriel. You loved me, I know you did. I realize we can never marry, but we can be lovers."

"Cissy," Gabriel warned, removing her arms from around his neck, "I'm marrying Olivia. I no longer feel that way about you."

Hands on hips, Cissy stomped her foot like a spoiled child. "I don't believe you! Admit it, Gabriel. I'm the reason you've never married."

"I'm sorry, Cissy. Grandmama and some of my close friends might believe that, but it's simply not true."

"Don't lie, Gabriel. You can't possibly love Olivia."

"I'm under no obligation to explain my feelings for Olivia to you."

"I knew it!" Cissy crowed. "You don't love her. Deny it all you want, but it's me you love, me you want."

Gabriel heaved an exasperated sigh. "You're wrong, Cissy, but you're going to think what you want no matter how vehemently I deny it. All I require of you right now is your help. I wish to see my bride properly dressed, even if it means employing every seamstress in the village.

"Can you have the seamstresses and their helpers here tomorrow morning at ten o'clock?" Gabriel continued. "I want Olivia outfitted with fashionable gowns, lingerie and hats ... and a wedding dress, don't forget that. I'll contact the cobbler myself."

"Because you ask it of me, I'll do as you wish, but I don't have to like it," Cissy said, pouting.

"I knew I could count on you," Gabriel replied. "I leave everything in your capable hands. I want the first gown finished by the day after tomorrow and will pay a bonus when it's delivered."

If looks could kill, Gabriel would be dead. Her lips compressed into a straight line, Cissy spun on her heel and stomped off.

An uneasy feeling warned Gabriel that Cissy was going to prove troublesome. He suspected he had made things worse by asking her to help with Olivia's wardrobe. But he had never dreamed that Cissy expected to take up where they'd left off before she wed Ned. Cissy wanted more from him than he was willing to give. He could only hope that once he and Olivia were wed, Cissy would return to her family or establish her own household. If she decided to remain, the situation could turn hellish.

The lady's maid Cissy assigned to Olivia looked down her nose at her new mistress and said, "I am Annette, your lady's maid, milady. Where have they put your trunks? Lady Cissy instructed me to unpack and see that you are made comfortable."

Olivia returned Annette's haughty look. She refused to be intimidated by a servant. "I had to leave my belongings behind."

Annette's eyebrows lifted. "I see. If you remove your dress, I'll see that it is pressed and made presentable for dinner tonight."

"I'd prefer a tray in my room," Olivia said. "Can that be arranged?"

"Of course, milady. Is there anything else you wish?"

"Not right now. I'm going to take a nap. See that I'm not disturbed. I'll bathe when I awaken."

"Very good, milady."

No wonder the maid held her in disdain, Olivia thought. Her green velvet gown was travel-worn and dusty. The hem was frayed and the once elegant lace trim torn. She looked like a poor relative instead of the intended bride of a marquis. She didn't belong here. She wanted Gabriel's love, not his guilt.

Olivia peeled down to her shift and stretched out on the bed. Her eyelids drooped, and she was asleep within minutes. She awakened an hour later, stretched to loosen her muscles and arose. Annette was nowhere in sight, so she decided to prepare her own bath. She opened the dressing room door, found the connecting door to the bathing room and was pleasantly surprised to find the tub already filled with steaming water. She shed her shift and, sighing gratefully, sank into the tub.

Gabriel returned to his room, stripped off his clothes and donned his dressing robe. If his instructions had been followed, the tub should be filled and awaiting him in the bathing room. A leisurely soak was just what he needed to release the tension building inside him.

In a short time his life was going to change forever. He was about to take on a wife and responsibilities, something he had hoped to avoid. As long as Olivia continued to please him, he would not need a mistress, but he couldn't predict how long lust for his wife would keep him faithful. Before he'd met Olivia, his life had been filled with hedonistic pleasures, and a lengthy string of lovers had littered his days and nights.

Gabriel walked through the dressing room into the bathing room and stopped abruptly, his body reacting spontaneously to the sight of Olivia, her coral-tipped breasts bobbing above the water and her eyes closed as she soaped her hair.

"Hand me the towel, Annette," Olivia said, extending a hand. "I've gotten soap in my eyes."

Somehow Gabriel found the strength to move,

though his gaze did not waver from Olivia's pert breasts bobbing in the water. Reaching for the towel, he placed it in her outstretched hand.

"Thank you."

"My pleasure," Gabriel said.

Olivia's eyes shot open. "You! What are you doing here?"

"I believe that's my bathwater you're using."

"Oh, I thought . . . I'm sorry."

"No need to apologize, Livvy. The tub is large enough for two." He peeled off his robe and tossed it aside.

Olivia started to rise. "You may have the tub."

Gabriel pushed her back down into the water. "Your hair is still soapy." He grabbed a pitcher of clear water from the washstand and held it above her head. "Tilt your head back."

When Olivia complied without protest, he poured a stream of water over her russet tresses. While she squeezed the water from her hair, Gabriel stepped into the tub and lowered himself into the water.

"I'm getting out." Water splashed onto the floor as she tried to leave the tub.

Grasping her wrist, he tugged her down. She fell against him, her breasts brushing against his chest. "You have lovely breasts, Livvy."

Lowering his head, he tugged a ripe nipple into his mouth and began to suckle her. He wanted to taste her, to touch her, to put himself inside her.

The tips of Olivia's breasts became almost painfully tight as Gabriel's mouth pulled and lapped at her nipples. Her mouth opened in a silent plea, but Gabriel seemed to know what she wanted without being told. His hands moved over her waist and hips to the taut mounds of her buttocks, kneading them with firm, deft strokes.

She possessed no will. None at all. Gabriel had stripped it from her. "Someone could come in," she whispered on a tremulous breath.

Gabriel's lips lifted in sardonic amusement. "Let them."

Why did she let Gabriel do this to her? Olivia wondered. He controlled her body like he controlled his servants. He had but to touch her and she responded. One look into his wicked, wicked eyes and she melted. She'd tried to build a wall around her heart, but he had the ability to destroy it with the fire in his eyes and a single touch.

Olivia's thoughts skidded to a halt as Gabriel lifted her, spread her legs with his knees and slid inside her. "This is where I belong," he murmured against her ear.

"Until another woman catches your eye," Olivia gasped.

"I can't predict the future, Livvy. No one can promise the forever you're asking for. Why can't you be satisfied with what we have?"

Gabriel's vague answer did little to comfort Olivia. His fatalistic approach to life confused her. "Marriage is a lifetime commitment, Gabriel, and you're not taking it seriously."

He moved inside her, thrusting deep. "I'm serious about this. Making love is one thing we do well together."

Making love and being loved were two different things, Olivia thought. How could she endure the hurt of loving and not being loved in return? Gabriel's guilt wasn't enough to build a marriage on.

Olivia's thoughts scattered as a warm feeling of wanting settled in her belly. The driving rhythm of his hips quickened. A spark flamed inside her. She felt possessed, consumed, engulfed in a raging inferno. Water splashed over the sides of the tub as his hips churned and his mouth claimed hers in a searing kiss. One sensation after another tumbled through her as she twisted her fingers in his dark hair and rubbed her sensitive nipples against his chest.

A shudder rippled through Gabriel. The feel of her fingers clutching him, her in-drawn breath at each plunge of his body, the sweetness of her kiss . . . it was too much. There was so much he wanted to give her, to tell her, but he didn't dare. As desperately as he wanted to, he dared not bare his soul to Olivia, nor burden her with family secrets.

Olivia's moan sent him spinning over the edge. His rod was rooted deep within her. He felt her inner muscles contract and heard her cry out. With strength born of determination, he waited until Olivia climaxed and grew quiescent before pulling out and allowing his own climax.

"Why did you do that? Why won't you give me your child?" Olivia cried, leaping from the tub and holding the towel like a shield before her.

Gabriel lifted himself out of the water. "It's complicated and has nothing to do with you."

"It has everything to do with me," Olivia bit out. "But if you won't share your secrets with me, I shan't share mine with you." She spun on her heel and flung open the door. Gabriel grasped her arm and pulled her against him.

"You'll not keep secrets from me, Livvy."

She stared at him in helpless frustration. "You can't control my thoughts, my lord."

"I can control your body," he retorted, a dangerous gleam in his eyes. "And I can stop you from endangering your life."

"I'll do as I please. I seriously doubt you'll linger overlong in the country after our marriage. London holds too much appeal for you. You'll be visiting your usual haunts and carousing with your friends and mistress while I am left to my own devices. What I do once you're gone is my business."

Gabriel's lips thinned. "You're wrong, Livvy. I may return to London, but you'll go with me."

Olivia's eyes widened in disbelief. "Won't a wife cramp your style, my lord?"

"Perhaps, but I'll survive."

He turned her toward the door and patted her bottom. "Get dressed. 'Tis nearly time for supper. I'll escort you to the dining room."

Olivia clung desperately to the towel; the subtle scent of their lovemaking wrapped around her like a silken noose, tempting her, teasing her. "Since I have nothing to wear, I've decided to take supper in my room."

"Can you be ready in twenty minutes?"

"Did you not hear me? I'm eating in my room."

Her words flowed over him like water over a dam. "I passed your maid in the hall. Your dress has been freshened and pressed, so your excuse won't wash." He gave her a gentle push toward the door. "Twenty minutes, Livvy."

Fuming, Olivia returned to her room. The man was stubborn as a mule. Did he listen to nothing she said? Was his way the only way? Didn't Gabriel realize she couldn't compete with the elegant Cissy?

Annette was awaiting Olivia in her room. She rolled

her eyes when she noted the tangled condition of Olivia's hair.

"Sit down, milady. I shall attempt to style your hair in a becoming manner. Shall I powder it? Red hair is not currently in vogue."

"No powder," Olivia said with as much graciousness as she could muster for the haughty maid. "I like the color of my hair. *A lie, of course.* "You may style it as long as you keep it simple."

"Lady Cissy dresses in the height of fashion," Annette sniffed. "She never appears in public with a hair out of place."

"I am not Lady Cissy," Olivia said tartly.

"Forgive me, milady," Annette replied, sounding not the least bit sorry.

Fifteen minutes later, Olivia's hair had been tamed and styled in a simple topknot with streamers of curls dangling down her neck and at her temples. She had just stepped into her gown when Gabriel appeared through the connecting door, looking handsome and elegant in black waistcoat, buff trousers, with rows of lace adorning his cuffs and shirtfront.

"Good, you're ready," Gabriel said, offering his arm. "Shall we go down? We shouldn't keep Cissy waiting on our first night."

"By all means," Olivia retorted. "Heaven forbid that we offend your Cissy."

Gabriel's dark brow lifted. "*My* Cissy? Are you inferring there is something between Cissy and me?"

After a weighted pause, Olivia remarked, "You said it, not I."

# *Chapter Fifteen*

Cissy was waiting in the dining room when Gabriel and Olivia arrived. Dressed in the latest style, she wore a gown fashioned of deep rose silk festooned with white roses and ruffles. Olivia thought the neckline scandalous, and was indignant when she caught Gabriel staring at the creamy expanse of breast bared by Cissy's low neckline.

"It's about time," Cissy huffed. "You know how I admire promptness, Bathurst."

"I'm to blame," Olivia said, sending Gabriel a veiled look. "I was delayed at my bath."

"I suppose we can blame Bathurst for that," Cissy taunted.

Olivia flushed and directed her gaze to her plate. Much to her relief, Gabriel changed the subject and the talk moved to more neutral ground. The elaborate meal progressed slowly, the variety of food endless. The oyster soup and turbot in lobster sauce would have been

249

sufficient, but a succession of dishes followed, including partridge and truffles, veal sweetbreads with walnut stuffing, candied carrots and apple pudding.

"That was an excellent meal, Cissy," Gabriel complimented as he tossed down his napkin and rose. He offered Olivia his hand. "It's a mild night, Livvy. Would you care to stroll through the gardens?"

"What a splendid idea," Cissy crowed. "A stroll before bedtime is just the thing to aid the digestion."

Tired of Cissy's snide remarks and posturing ways, Olivia begged off. "If you don't mind, my lord, I believe I'll retire early. I'm sure you and Cissy can entertain yourselves without me."

Cissy smiled up at Gabriel and tucked her arm beneath his. "Shall we, Bathurst?"

"I'll see Olivia to her room and join you in the drawing room," Gabriel hedged, taking Olivia's elbow and guiding her toward the stairs.

Cissy watched them leave, then asked a footman to summon Annette. Annette appeared shortly and dropped a curtsey.

"You wished to see me, milady?"

"Yes. You may speak truthfully, Annette, for I know you are loyal to me. What is your opinion of Lady Olivia?"

"It's not for me to say, milady."

"I give you leave to speak your mind, Annette. You know how I feel about the interloper. Lady Olivia isn't worthy of a man like Bathurst."

"Indeed she is not, milady," Annette said. "Lady Olivia may be a titled lady, but she is crude and unsophisticated and dresses with no style."

"My sentiments exactly. Do you think Lady Olivia and Bathurst are lovers?"

"I *know* they are," Annette said smugly. "One has but to observe them together to know that."

Cissy frowned, then waved Annette off. "You may go."

Pacing the library in silent rage when Gabriel failed to return, Cissy blamed Olivia for his absence. Angry and overheated, she stomped off to the garden by herself. Neither the full moon nor the sweetly scented night air relieved the tension simmering through her.

Gabriel was hers, had always been hers despite her marriage to his brother. A spiritual connection between herself and Gabriel had always existed, defying logic. She was convinced she was the reason Gabriel had never married, the reason he couldn't love another woman. She was free to become his lover now and had been waiting for him to come to her. Cissy felt that Olivia was not the woman for him, and she was determined to do whatever it took to stop the marriage. She raised her eyes to heaven and prayed for divine intervention.

A rustling noise brought Cissy up short. Her dark thoughts fled, and a smile lit her face. "Bathurst, is that you?"

No answer was forthcoming.

"I know you're there, don't tease me. You want me as much as I want you."

A shadow materialized from behind a hedge and walked toward her. Moonlight illuminated his face, and Cissy gaped at a man she'd seen before, but not in a very long time. "You're not Bathurst."

"Indeed I am not," the man said, making an elegant bow.

"I know you. We met when my husband and I spent a Season in London. Lord Palmerson, I believe. You're treading on private property, my lord. Do you have business with Bathurst?"

"I mean you no harm, my lady. All I ask is a moment of your time."

"Why are you sneaking around? Shall I fetch Bathurst?"

"Bathurst is the last person I want to see," he snarled. "I've come to stop a wedding. Olivia is mine. And if what I just heard you say is true, you have reasons of your own to keep Olivia and Bathurst apart."

Cissy stared at the man as if he were the answer to her prayer. He was handsome in a dapper way, and attractively formed. More importantly, they had the same goals.

"Tell me more. Are you and Olivia lovers?"

"Indeed we are, or were until Bathurst stole her from me," Palmerson lied. "Bathurst hates me and thought to punish me by taking Olivia from me. Surely you don't think he cares for her, do you?"

"Of course not. I knew there had to be a reason behind Bathurst's sudden wedding plans. He couldn't love someone as plain and dowdy as Olivia."

"Then you'll help me?" Palmerson asked.

"It may be too late."

Palmerson sucked in a breath. "They're not wed yet, are they?"

"No, they're waiting for Bathurst's grandmother and Olivia's aunt to arrive."

"Will you help me? Can you lure Olivia out here to the garden? I need but a few minutes to convince her to leave Bathurst."

"You're very sure of yourself, Lord Palmerson."

"I hold all the cards," Palmerson said smugly. "But

you can't let Bathurst know I was here, or even mention my name."

"You must love Olivia a great deal."

"Love? Oh, yes, of course," he quickly added. "There are things about Olivia I love very much."

"I'm sure she'd be better off with you," Cissy replied. "She isn't the type to overlook Bathurst's mistresses and his carousing."

"Exactly. You want Bathurst, and I intend for you to have him."

Cissy smiled. "Then we have the same goals. I'll bring Olivia to you, but you'll have to do the rest."

"Thank you, my lady. I am forever in your debt."

"No, Lord Palmerson, I am forever in *your* debt."

Palmerson melted back into the shadows, and Cissy returned to the house, her spirits soaring. All she needed to do to banish Olivia from Bathurst's life was to lead her to Lord Palmerson.

Olivia found a nightgown and robe lying on her bed and suspected that Annette had taken pity on her and supplied the garments. She undressed quickly and donned the gown and robe, her thoughts turning to Gabriel. He must have been eager to join Cissy, for he'd left her at her door after a fleeting kiss and a brusque good night.

It took little imagination to surmise what Gabriel and Cissy were doing in the garden. Renewing an intimate relationship, she imagined. Had Cissy cuckolded her husband with Gabriel? No, Olivia decided. Gabriel would never betray his brother like that. Whatever had happened between Gabriel and Cissy in the past had taken place before Cissy and Ned were married. Did Gabriel love Cissy? English law prevented him from marrying his brother's widow, but they could become lovers. One puzzling question remained, however. Why hadn't Gabriel taken up with Cissy after his brother's death?

Olivia walked to the window, wishing upon the brightest star in the sky. But all the wishes in the world wouldn't give her the love she craved from Gabriel. Sighing despondently, Olivia ambled toward the bed and sat on the edge. She was deep in thought when she heard someone scratching on her door. *Gabriel*. She ran to the door and flung it open.

"Oh, it's you," Olivia said, disappointed when she saw Cissy. "Is something wrong?"

"Not at all," Cissy answered. "You're wanted in the garden."

"Gabriel?" Olivia's hopes soared, then quickly plummeted. How dare he summon her like a servant! Curiosity prevailed over pique. She'd go to him, but he'd feel the sharp edge of her tongue for demanding instead of asking.

"I'm not dressed," Olivia said.

Cissy tossed a glance at Olivia over her shoulder. "I don't think he'll mind."

Olivia paused but a moment before following Cissy down the stairs and through the conservatory, stopping just short of the garden. "I'll leave you two alone," Cissy said, turning away.

"Where is he?"

"Don't worry, he'll find you."

Olivia walked into the garden and followed the path. Cloaked in moonlight, the plants and trees appeared almost ethereal as they bowed to the breeze. The scent of roses lingered in the air; the night was made for lovers.

Olivia started when a man stepped from the shadows, blocking her way. "Gabriel? Cissy said you wished to see me. I don't mind telling you I'm not thrilled by your summons."

As the man moved into a patch of moonlight, Olivia gasped and staggered backwards. "Palmerson! What are you doing here? What have you done with Bathurst?"

"Forget Bathurst. I saw him ride out a short time ago. He was in a devil of a hurry. On his way to an assignation with one of his mistresses, I suspect."

Olivia spun around. "I won't listen to this." She took no more than one step before Palmerson grasped her arm and hauled her around to face him.

"If you value your brother, you'd best listen to what I have to say."

Olivia went still, very still. "What did you say?"

"Got your attention, did I?"

"Explain yourself, Palmerson."

"I'll do better than that. You're not to marry Bathurst."

Olivia twisted free. "You have no right to tell me what I can or cannot do. How did you find me?"

"Your brother told me where you were."

A shiver of apprehension slid down Olivia's spine. "My brother is at school."

Palmerson sent her a smug smile. "Is he?"

*Don't panic,* Olivia cautioned herself. Palmerson was using fright tactics to gain his own ends. "Of course he is. I saw him off myself."

"That doesn't mean he arrived at his destination," Palmerson hinted. "I happened to see him board the coach and made arrangements to take him into my custody."

"Liar! What is this all about, Palmerson?"

"Our marriage, of course. I'll make all the arrangements and come for you when everything is in readiness. You must convince Bathurst that you prefer me to him."

"You're mad! Why would I do that?"

"Because I have your brother and you want to keep him safe."

"Do you think me a fool? Why should I believe you?"

"Because I'm telling the truth."

"What proof do you have that you're holding my brother? I want an explanation. And I want to know why you are so determined to marry me."

"Your twenty-fifth birthday is next week, is it not?"

Olivia could think of no connection between her birthday and Palmerson's insane desire to marry her. "How did you know that?"

"You forget how close your father and I were."

Olivia's lips thinned. "I've forgotten nothing concerning your friendship with my father. I hold you responsible for his moral decline and death. Explain why my birthday is important."

"I think not. You'll learn soon enough. You just tell Bathurst you're not going through with the marriage. Leave the rest to me."

"I'll do no such thing. You're lying about Neville."

Palmerson snorted. "You always were a stubborn bitch. Perhaps you'll believe me when I bring irrefutable proof. I'll need a day or two to make arrangements. Meet me in two days, same time, same place. If you tell anyone, your brother will suffer."

He melted back into the shadows, leaving Olivia puzzled, frightened and angry. Was Palmerson telling the truth? Was he holding Neville against his will? How had he accomplished it? What would make Palmerson desperate enough to resort to kidnapping, and what did her birthday have to do with anything? Nothing made sense. Lost in thought, she wandered back to the house.

"Olivia, what are you doing out here? Do you know what time it is?"

Olivia started violently. "Gabriel—you frightened me."

"Forgive me. I didn't expect to find you in the garden at this time of night. Couldn't you sleep?"

"How did you know I was out here?"

"I was returning from a ride, saw someone lurking in the shadows and came to investigate. Are you all right?"

She thought of Palmerson, and an involuntary shudder passed through her.

"You're cold," Gabriel said, removing his jacket and placing it over her shoulders. "Come along, I'll see you to your room."

"Where have you been?" Olivia asked. "Were you with a woman?"

"Don't be ridiculous," Gabriel scoffed. "I couldn't sleep and thought some exercise would help."

"A stroll through the garden with Cissy would have provided that."

"I didn't invite Cissy. Why did you refuse to accompany me, then come out here alone?"

He stopped and tipped her head up. "You were alone, weren't you, Livvy? I thought I saw two figures when I approached through the conservatory. Was I mistaken?"

The moon scudded behind a cloud, and Olivia blessed the inky darkness that shielded her lie. "I was alone."

Gabriel began to walk again, guiding her through the conservatory and into the house with an arm about her shoulders. "You appear troubled. Have you not yet resigned yourself to our marriage?"

"I'll never be resigned to marrying a man who proposed out of guilt or misplaced duty."

When they reached Olivia's suite, he said, "It's late, Livvy. Go to bed. Trust me to do what's best for you."

He bent his head and brushed her lips with his. He started to withdraw, then abruptly clutched her against him, deepening the kiss into what quickly became a bold and demanding assault on her senses. Olivia wanted to respond, but Palmerson's threats intruded. She wanted to tell Gabriel everything, but feared that doing so would endanger Neville's life.

Gabriel broke off the kiss and stepped away. "What is it, Livvy? Are you worried about Cissy? Why are you trembling? Tell me what's troubling you."

"Nothing, Gabriel. I'm tired. It's been a long day."

"You're right. Go to bed. We'll talk tomorrow."

Lying in bed after Gabriel left her, Olivia was unable to sleep. Though she didn't want to believe Palmerson held Neville captive, she had to take him seriously. What if he *did* have Neville? Could she marry him to save her brother's life? Would Gabriel let her go?

When Olivia appeared at breakfast the following morning, her lack of sleep was apparent in her drawn features and the shadows beneath her green eyes. If Gabriel noticed, he said nothing. While Cissy refrained from commenting, her expression spoke louder than words. Olivia, however, had a few words of her own to say to Cissy.

"Perhaps Cissy will show me the rest of the house," Olivia suggested.

"A splendid idea," Gabriel said. "If you ladies will excuse me, I should call on my steward and visit my tenants. It's been a long time."

Once Gabriel left, Olivia whirled to confront Cissy. "You deliberately led me to believe that Gabriel had summoned me to the garden last night. Why? I hate Palmerson and want nothing to do with him."

"Does Gabriel know you and Palmerson are lovers? I can't imagine him offering for a woman with an unsavory past. He deserves better."

"Is that what Palmerson told you?"

"He told me many things. Did he convince you to leave Gabriel?"

"Obviously, you don't know Lord Palmerson like I do. The man is a predator. I hold him responsible for my father's death. I have no idea why he would go to such extraordinary lengths to convince me to marry him. As you well know, I have no dowry and had no prospects besides Palmerson, whom I wouldn't marry if he were the last man on earth."

Cissy shrugged. "Of course not. Why wed a mere viscount when you can have a marquis?"

"You had no right to lure me into the garden," Olivia charged. "I know you don't like me, and the feeling is mutual. Now you may show me the house."

The seamstresses arrived the following morning, eager to begin making Olivia's new wardrobe. Never had Olivia seen such a lovely array of cloths and patterns. Had she followed Cissy's advice, she would have ended up wearing ruffles and furbelows and looking ridiculously like a woman pretending to be younger than her years.

Fortunately, Gabriel was on hand to help her choose, and she ended up with twice as many gowns and accessories as she deemed necessary.

The bonus Gabriel offered for haste yielded one gown and a riding habit the day after her first fitting, as well as a pair of slippers and riding boots. Despite her pleasure at having something new and fashionable to wear, Olivia couldn't help thinking about her meeting with Palmerson. If he produced evidence that Neville was indeed his captive, she'd be forced to do whatever it took to keep her brother safe.

Something was troubling Olivia—Gabriel felt it in his bones. That was one of the reasons he hadn't made love to her these past two days. And he couldn't get over the feeling that she hadn't been alone in the garden during her midnight stroll. He could have sworn he'd seen two figures in the moonlight.

After breakfast that morning, Gabriel asked Olivia to go riding. She agreed readily enough, but he could tell her mind was elsewhere.

"Wear your new riding habit," Gabriel said. "I'll ask Cook to prepare a picnic so we won't have to hurry back for lunch." Olivia nodded and hurried off.

"I'd love to go riding," Cissy said after Olivia left the room.

"Some other time, Cissy. Excuse me, I need to speak to Cook."

Gabriel waited for Olivia in the foyer, a lunch basket angled over his arm. Watching in avid appreciation as she walked down the stairs, he thought her enchanting in her forest-green riding habit and pert hat with its jaunty feather.

"The color is perfect for you," Gabriel complimented.

"You picked it out," Olivia replied.

"I bought a horse for you in town yesterday," Gabriel remarked,

Olivia's eyes lit up. "You bought me a horse?"

"I hope you approve, since she's neither a gelding nor black like Ollie's mount."

Olivia had no reply. When they reached the stables, she saw a groom leading a beautiful white mare into the paddock.

"Ain't she a beauty, milord?" the groom said.

"Indeed she is," Olivia said enthusiastically, rushing forward for a closer inspection. "Thank you, Gabriel. I love her."

"Would you like a leg up, milady?" the groom asked.

"I'll help her, Linus, thank you."

Gabriel lifted Olivia into the saddle and handed her the reins.

"What's her name?" Olivia asked.

"I thought I'd let you name her."

Olivia bit her lip. "I'd like to think about it." She didn't want to a name a horse she might never ride again.

"Take your time," Gabriel said as he mounted his own sleek gelding. "Are you ready?"

Olivia nodded, and Gabriel trotted off down the long lane toward the open fields beyond the park. They rode together through a picturesque village, over lands tilled by tenants and through a forest. The sun was high in the sky when Gabriel called a halt before a rippling brook and dismounted.

"This looks like a good place to stop for lunch," Gabriel said. Grasping Olivia's waist, he let her slide down

Connie Mason

into his arms, but he didn't release her immediately. He caught her chin and lifted it.

"I've missed you, Livvy."

Olivia gave him a startled look. "I haven't gone anywhere, Gabriel."

"You're here in body but not in spirit. Do you want to tell me what's troubling you?"

"You're imagining things."

"I don't believe you. Are you upset because I'm forcing you to marry me?"

"Yes, there is that. I don't like being bullied into doing something I don't want to do."

"Are you *sure* you don't want to marry me?" He stared at her lips, at their lush curves and moist corners, and ached to kiss her. "Your kisses tell me otherwise. Shall I prove it to you?"

"We both know I have no will where you're concerned. You can kiss me, Gabriel, and I'll respond, but that doesn't mean I'm happy with the situation. Rogues makes notoriously bad husbands."

"Rogues can make their wives deliriously happy. We know how to please our women. Shall I demonstrate how well I can please you? I tried to give you time to come to grips with the situation, but you're more troubled than ever. Perhaps you've missed my attention."

"Perhaps not," Olivia returned.

"Shall we test my theory and see who's right?"

He grasped her hand and brought it to the front of his tight riding breeches. "Can you feel how much I want you? We'll always have this, Livvy."

A groan issued from his throat as Olivia's fingers curled around his erection. He grew even harder, thicker, and the need to thrust himself inside her nearly

262

overwhelmed him. He dropped to his knees on the soft grass, taking her with him.

"Darling, Livvy, I'm going to make love to you."

Startled, Olivia stared at him. He'd called her darling. Oh, God, why was her life so complicated? Tonight she would meet Palmerson and learn the truth about Neville. This might be the last time she'd have with Gabriel before circumstances forced them apart. How long would he mourn her leaving? Not long, she suspected.

Gabriel had removed his saddle blanket and was walking back to where he left her when a loud noise shattered the silence. Gabriel hit the ground, and Olivia started to rise to go to him.

"Stay down," Gabriel hissed. "Someone is shooting at us."

Olivia dropped to the ground. "Are you hurt?"

"No, are you?"

"Who would shoot at us?"

"I don't know but I intend to find out. Could be poachers mistook us for wild game."

Olivia nearly blurted out Palmerson's name, but prudence prevailed. She couldn't afford to place Neville's life in danger by giving voice to her suspicions.

Gabriel slid over to her and covered her with his body, but the danger seemed to have passed, for no further shots followed the first.

"Keep down," Gabriel advised as he rose up on his haunches. "I'm going to take a look around."

"Are you sure it's safe? Do you have a weapon?"

"No, but I doubt there's need for one. Whoever shot at us is probably gone. I won't be long."

"Be careful."

Gabriel returned a short time later, leading the horses.

"It's safe now, Livvy," Gabriel said. "I found the horses. They bolted when the shot was fired."

Olivia nearly collapsed in relief. "Thank God. Did the shooter leave a clue?"

"I saw nothing but a trail of trampled grass. Let's get back to the house. A picnic is out of the question now."

Gabriel helped Olivia to mount, and they rode off. "Our guests have begun to arrive," Gabriel said as they approached the manor. Two coaches were parked at the front entrance.

"That's Grandmama's coach," Gabriel remarked. "And the other is one of mine. Grandmama and your aunt have arrived, and so have Grimsley and Throckmorton." They left the horses with a groom and entered the house. Lady Patrice and Lady Alma were in the drawing room with Cissy, having tea and cakes.

Lady Patrice's face lit up when she spied Gabriel. "Bathurst, my dear boy, we are arrived! Come and introduce your intended to me. It's long past time we met."

"Livvy, how glad I am to see you safe and looking so well," Aunt Alma said. Olivia gave her a hug, then turned her attention to the elderly lady who had given her aunt succor.

"Lady Bathurst, I'm pleased to meet you. Gabriel speaks of you often and holds you in high regard."

"I should hope so," Lady Patrice retorted. "You may call me Grandmama and I shall call you Olivia. Let me have a good look at you, my dear."

Olivia stood still while the small, white-haired lady inspected her with eyes as keen as her mind appeared to be. Though Lady Patrice looked as fragile as glass, Olivia suspected she had a backbone of steel.

"You'll do," Lady Patrice said. "I suspect you can

hold your own against my grandson. Your dear aunt has regaled me with tales about your spirit and courage."

Olivia shot Alma a censuring look. "Oh, no, Livvy, not *that*!" Alma said, suddenly flustered. "I just wanted Lady Patrice to know that you were the glue that held the family together after your father's scandalous behavior and death."

Olivia flushed. "You give me too much credit, Auntie."

"Lady Alma speaks the truth," Gabriel interjected. "My bride is a remarkable woman."

"Remarkable indeed," Cissy tossed in. "I fail to see what's so remarkable about a woman who appeared at my door dressed like a beggar."

"Olivia looks perfectly respectable to me," Lady Patrice said. She returned her gaze to Gabriel. "It's about time you set up your nursery, Bathurst. I never believed all that nonsense about remaining single and without issue. I expect to see a Bathurst heir on the way before the year is out."

"Perhaps one is already on the way," Cissy speculated.

Olivia felt Gabriel stiffen and realized that his grandmother didn't believe Gabriel was serious about remaining childless.

"Olivia and I are hungry and dusty from our ride," Gabriel said. "If you'll excuse us, we need to change and eat something to tide us over until dinner."

"Very well. Dear Alma and I will retire to our rooms and rest after our long trip. We will discuss your wedding plans later."

Gabriel grasped Olivia's elbow and steered her toward the staircase. "I'm glad you said nothing about that little incident earlier today. I don't want to frighten the ladies with something that could turn out to be nothing."

Pausing before her suite, Olivia silently debated telling Gabriel about Palmerson's midnight visit, but decided against it. She would do nothing to endanger Neville's life.

"I intended to make love to you beside the brook today," Gabriel murmured in a low, sensual voice that nearly undid Olivia. "Will you invite me into your room, Livvy?"

This might be her last opportunity to make love with Gabriel. Olivia made a silent vow that even if she wed Palmerson, he would never be a true husband to her. No man would touch her intimately except the man she loved. Only Gabriel had the power to move her. Despite her belief that she and Gabriel weren't meant to be together, she would welcome no other man to her bed.

Olivia's mouth went dry. With Gabriel looking at her in that special way, his eyes glittering with desire and his lips curved in a seductive smile, she could refuse him nothing. She entered her suite and held the door open. Gabriel scooped her into his arms and bore her to the bed.

# *Chapter Sixteen*

His mouth was hot and hungry. His hands were suddenly everywhere, unfastening her dress, fumbling beneath her shirts, baring her to the hips in a wild flurry of fabric. Nearly as frenzied as he, she tore her bodice open so he could get to her breasts. She wanted him to touch her, to hold her in his arms and kiss her breathless.

He smoothed his hands over her shoulders and down her arms, pulling her dress with it and flinging it aside. Desperation and insatiable craving drove her as her fingers unfastened his breeches, reached within them and took him into her hands. He was hard and heavy against her palms, and so hot he scorched her. A strangled sound escaped him, a moan that echoed her own excitement.

Pushing aside her shift, he bent his head and closed his mouth over her nipple. She clenched her fingers on his shoulders and arched her head back, engulfed in sensation as he laved the engorged tip with his tongue. Then he bared her other breast, licking and suckling it. She felt his hand flatten on her thigh, then move to cup her weeping center, his fingers intruding between her thighs, his thumb circling her tender nub.

Writhing, moaning, she tugged on his jacket. "Please," she whispered against his lips, "take off your clothes. I want to feel your skin against mine."

Rising abruptly, he quickly stripped and rejoined her. Then he kissed her, again and again, until their breath mingled and she couldn't tell one from the other. Her pulse raced and her heartbeat thumped loudly in her ears.

Her questing fingers flew over him in mad desperation, resting on curves and planes of firm male flesh, the rise of his shoulders, the hard length of his torso, his hair-roughened chest. Her hand found his rigid male member and gently stroked.

Groaning as if in pain, he flung her hand away. With an economy of motion, he pulled her atop him and thrust deep. Arching her back, her throat working convulsively, she began to move in rhythm to his thrusts. Their loving was fast and furious. Their tumultuous climax came simultaneously, and as Gabriel pulled out, tears coursed down Olivia's cheeks.

She wept for the heirs Gabriel would never have.

The clock on the mantel chimed midnight. Olivia eased from bed and pulled on her discarded shift and dress, careful not to awaken Gabriel. The door opened silently beneath her touch, and she crept from her suite through the dark corridors, down the staircase and into the garden.

She prayed Palmerson wouldn't be there, that it had

all been a hoax, but her hopes were dashed when he stepped boldly into her path.

"You're late," he groused.

"You're lucky I'm here at all. I should have told Gabriel and let him handle this."

"Then you would never have seen your brother again."

"I want proof," Olivia demanded. "You've lied before—why should I believe you now?"

Palmerson stuck his hand in his pocket and pulled out a watch, dangling it by its chain before Olivia's eyes. Olivia snatched the watch from his fingers and examined it in the moonlight.

"This belongs to Neville. It was my father's. I gave it to Neville before he left for Oxford."

"I knew that would get your attention. Now do you believe your precious brother is in my custody?"

"I don't understand. I saw Neville onto the coach myself."

"I happened to see him when he boarded the Oxford coach and I hired men to stage a robbery. The coach was stopped before it reached Oxford, and Sefton was taken off."

"Did you hurt him? I'll see you in hell if you did."

Palmerson laughed. "Your threats don't frighten me. There's nothing you can do to hurt me. As for your brother, he'll be released after we're wed."

Olivia felt cornered. She'd do anything to keep Neville safe, even marry a toad like Palmerson. "What do you want me to do?"

"You're to tell Bathurst you can't marry him because you love me. And you'd better make it believable if you value your brother's life."

"Very well. Then what?"

Connie Mason

"Then you will walk out the front door and get into my carriage. We'll proceed directly to the village and be married by special license. The local rector has agreed to perform the ceremony. We'll consummate our vows immediately and proceed to London to spread the news of our nuptials."

"Gabriel won't believe my lies. He knows I despise you."

"That's not my problem. I'm sure you'll do whatever it takes to save your brother's life. I'll come around for you at precisely two o'clock. Don't keep me waiting."

"Why are you doing this? You've been pressuring me to marry you for years, and I can't figure out why. You don't love me, and I bring no dowry to the marriage."

"I'll explain after we're wed."

"Now," Olivia persisted.

"You grow tiresome, Olivia. You'll know when the time is right. Good night, my dear."

Turning on his heel, he melted into the darkness. Olivia stared after him, clutching the watch to her chest. Her heart breaking, she returned to the house. Gabriel was still sleeping when she undressed and slipped into bed beside him. He stirred and mumbled something in his sleep. Overcome by the need to touch him, she cupped his cheek and lowered her head, pressing a kiss to his lips.

She felt rather than saw him smile, and when she settled against the heat of his body, he surprised her by wrapping his arms around her and pulling her beneath him.

"I thought you were sleeping."

"I missed you. Where did you go?"

"I . . . grew warm and opened the window."

"I thought it was already open."

270

"No. I opened it."

She felt his staff grow hard, felt it rise against her stomach and lifted her hips in blatant invitation.

"I see we're of the same mind," Gabriel murmured. He spread her legs with his knees and touched her throbbing center. "This is the best cure for sleeplessness."

He slid inside her, and for a few glorious minutes Olivia forgot all about Palmerson and the lies she would have to invent to save her brother.

Gabriel awakened the following morning to birdsong and sunshine. He frowned when he realized he was alone in bed, then smiled when he recalled the previous night. Olivia had been so hot for him, she had awakened him in the middle of the night to make love. Did she love him? Stubborn creature that she was, she'd never admit it, but her actions spoke volumes about her feelings. Olivia was no Cyprian who knew how to pretend passion. She was a warm-blooded innocent, a woman whose passion was as genuine as she was.

Grimsley greeted Gabriel when he returned to his rooms. "Throckmorton has drawn your bath, milord," Grimsley announced in a calm voice despite the fact that his employer had come naked from his intended bride's suite.

"Thank you, Grimsley. What news do you bring from London?"

"Lord Palmerson has dropped from the social scene. He hasn't been seen since the duel."

"He'd be doing London a favor if he never showed his face again. The man should be shunned by society."

"I don't believe we've seen the last of Palmerson, milord."

271

"Unfortunately, I agree. Have you learned anything that might help me understand his reasons for wanting to marry Olivia?"

"No, milord. His pockets are still empty, and his vile reputation has removed him from the list of eligible bachelors. When that poor girl killed herself, his prospects of marrying an heiress died with her."

"As long as he stays away from Olivia, I don't care what becomes of him."

After his bath, Gabriel went out to find Olivia. She found him first. She encountered him in the corridor and asked for a moment of his time. Gabriel ushered her into his room and waited for her to speak, a curious expression furrowing his brow.

As the silence stretched between them, he brought her into his arms. "I missed you when I woke up this morning."

When Olivia remained mute, he held her away from him and stared into her troubled eyes. "Livvy, what is it? Has something happened? Did Cissy say something to upset you?"

Olivia's mouth worked a moment or two before words formed. "I've had a change of heart. I won't marry you."

Gabriel's eyes revealed his disbelief. He knew Olivia hadn't been herself lately, but he'd hoped her lingering doubts had been eased by their lovemaking last night. She had certainly been an enthusiastic lover.

"What are you saying? What happened? If Cissy said something . . ."

Olivia glanced away. "Cissy has nothing to do with my decision."

He grasped her chin and forced her to look at him. "Livvy, talk to me. Tell me what's wrong."

"You're not the man I want."

"You want . . . another?" A chuckle rumbled in his chest. He thought she was being her usual unpredictable self. "Who, pray tell, has won your heart? I know of no suitors begging for your favors."

"You're not the only man in my life. Truthfully, Bathurst, aren't you a little bit relieved that I've found another man to wed?"

A myriad emotions tumbled through Gabriel: disappointment, anger, puzzlement, disbelief. "Who is he?" Gabriel roared.

Olivia stared unflinchingly into Gabriel's eyes. "Lord Palmerson."

"Palmerson! You despise him. You haven't seen him since . . ." A flash of comprehension lit his eyes. "The night you were in the garden. You were meeting him, weren't you?"

Her gaze slid away from his. "Yes."

"How can you want the bastard after what he did to you?"

Her damning silence sent a dagger through his heart. He had been willing to wed her, protect her and support her family. How could she want a man with questionable character and empty pockets? It just didn't make sense. His eyes narrowed as he suddenly recalled her excuse for leaving their bed last night. Had she gone out to meet that bastard after they had made love, then returned and awakened him to make love again?

"You went to him last night, didn't you?"

She blinked. He thought he saw a flash of inner pain in her eyes but shrugged it aside. "You seem to have forgotten that I could ruin your family with my knowledge of your . . . illegal activities."

"You wouldn't do that, Gabriel. I know you too well

now to believe you would deliberately hurt innocent people. Should you betray me to the authorities, Neville, Aunt Alma and Peterson would suffer for my mistakes. I honestly don't think you want that."

"Damn you!" Gabriel shouted. "Next you'll be telling me you love him."

"Palmerson will give me children."

"If that's what this is about, then perhaps it's for the best." He shrugged. "I should thank you for allowing me to continue the way of life I prefer. I don't need a wife curtailing my activities. Refusing you children is not something I want to do, but something I have to do. You could have trusted me to do what was best for both of us, but no, you had to run to Palmerson."

He shoved past her to the door. "I hope he appreciates the time I took teaching you how to please a man. Goodbye, Olivia."

"Where are you going?"

"Back to London where I belong. You may explain to my grandmother and your aunt why you called off the wedding." The door slammed behind him with a finality that almost brought Olivia to her knees.

She wanted to race after him, to explain about Neville and plead with him to forgive her. She ran into the corridor, hoping to catch up with him. She stopped abruptly when his voice drifted up to her from the foyer. She heard him shouting for Grimsley; then the front door slammed, and a few minutes later, the sound of pounding hooves shattered the silence. Racing down the stairs, she called Gabriel's name, but it was too late. All she saw when she opened the door were his coattails flying out behind him as his horse carried him out of her life forever.

"Livvy, dear, what's wrong? Where did Bathurst go in such a hurry?"

Olivia dashed the tears from her eyes, girding herself for the ordeal ahead of her. Telling Aunt Alma and Lady Patrice the marriage was off was going to be the hardest thing she'd ever done. She turned slowly and forced a smile.

"Livvy, you've been crying! What happened? Did you and Bathurst have a lovers' spat? Dry your tears, dear. Pre-wedding jitters are normal."

"I'm not marrying Gabriel, Auntie. I called off the wedding. He's left for London."

A gasp from the staircase sent Olivia spinning around. Lady Patrice was poised on the bottom landing, one hand splayed over her heart. "You did what?"

"I'm sorry, my lady, I didn't mean to break it to you this way," Olivia said. "Don't blame your grandson. It's my fault."

Another voice entered the conversation. "You sent Bathurst away?"

"I didn't send him away, Cissy. He left of his own accord. Just as I intend to do. Auntie, may I have a word with you in private?"

"Of course, dear. Let's stroll in the garden, shall we? I wanted a moment alone with you anyway. Two letters arrived for you after you left London. In all the excitement, I forgot to give them to you."

Arm in arm, Olivia and Alma walked off, leaving a sputtering Cissy and a bewildered Lady Patrice behind.

"Who are the letters from, Auntie?"

"I don't know, dear." She pulled the two letters from her pocket and handed them to Olivia. "It never occurred to me to look."

How typical, Olivia thought, sending Alma a fond

smile. Absently she glanced at the handwriting on one of the letters and came to an abrupt halt. "This is from Neville. I recognize his handwriting. Do you know what this means, Auntie?"

Alma sent her a puzzled look. "I assume it means Neville reached Oxford safely."

"Exactly," Olivia cried, tearing open the envelope. "It *is* from Neville."

"What does he say, dear? He's going to be so disappointed to hear you've called off the wedding."

"Listen to this, Auntie! Highwaymen held up Neville's coach. He managed to hide his tuition money in the cushions, but they took Papa's watch. He feared the highwaymen were going to kill him when they tried to drag him onto one of their horses, but they were frightened away when another coach came along." A kernel of anger exploded inside her. "Palmerson lied to me! Damn him to hell! Had his plan actually worked, Neville would have been in grave danger."

"What has Palmerson to do with Neville? I'm so confused."

"Never mind, Auntie. Neville is where he belongs. That's all that matters."

Alma looked befuddled. "What is it you wished to tell me?"

"Nothing important."

"Livvy, you're trying my patience. Should I be worried?"

Olivia didn't know how to answer that question. Their financial difficulties hadn't evaporated, but at least Palmerson was no longer a threat. For want of a better answer, she said, "We're going to be fine, Auntie."

"What about Bathurst? Is he gone for good?"

An ache settled around Olivia's heart. The man she loved was gone from her life, and there was nothing she could do about it. She had chased him off with lies, and she doubted the truth would bring him back.

"I'm afraid so, Auntie."

Alma heaved a trembling sigh. "What about the other letter, Livvy? Do you know who it's from?"

Olivia had almost forgotten the second letter, so momentous was the first. She turned it over in her hands, noting the return address. It's from a Mr. Silas Culpepper."

"Do you know Mr. Culpepper?"

"No, do you?"

"I don't recognize the name. Open it, dear."

Olivia tore open the envelope and quickly scanned the contents. When she reached the end, she turned deathly pale and staggered to the nearest bench, clutching the letter to her heart.

"Olivia, what is it? It can't be all that bad. What more can happen to us?"

Emotion clogged Olivia's throat. "This letter, Auntie . . . I never suspected. Why did no one tell me?"

"Tell me, Livvy, I can take it. Who is Mr. Culpepper?"

"He's a solicitor, Auntie."

"A solicitor? Whatever does he want?"

"To congratulate me on becoming an heiress on the occasion of my twenty-fifth birthday."

"A . . . an heiress? He must have sent the letter to the wrong person."

"His letter sounds genuine, Auntie. He wants me to call on him at my earliest convenience. Our maternal grandparents left their fortune to Neville and me. Neville will receive his portion when he turns twenty-five."

"Why were you not told before now? What in the world was Sefton thinking?"

"I don't know, but I intend to find out. Let's return to the house. We'll leave as soon as I find transportation to London."

Lady Patrice and Cissy were waiting for them. "Do you mind telling me what happened between you and my grandson?" Lady Patrice asked. "I was so counting on this marriage to produce an heir for Bathurst."

"Obviously, Bathurst came to his senses," Cissy said with a hint of malice.

Olivia ignored her. "I'm sorry, my lady. It just didn't work out between Gabriel and me."

"I see," Lady Patrice said sagely. "All isn't lost yet, my dear. Follow Bathurst to London to mend your fences."

Olivia gave her a sad smile. "I'm afraid it's too late. Gabriel never wanted to marry me. He only offered for me because . . . well, it no longer matters. We don't suit. And I want more from marriage than Gabriel is willing to give. If you'll excuse me, I must pack and find transportation to London."

"Since there will be no wedding, I may as well return to London myself," Lady Patrice announced. "You and dear Alma will share my coach. And you'll both stay with me."

"That's very kind but—"

"No buts about it. My mind is made up. Gabriel has put your old home up for sale. I'll hear no argument. We'll leave in the morning."

When Palmerson arrived at precisely two o'clock that afternoon in his rented carriage, Olivia was too angry to confront him. She sent Peterson with a scathing note she had penned and watched from the window as Palmerson read the missive, crumbled it in his fist and flung it to the ground. She was still smiling when he leaped into the carriage and took off like a bat out of hell.

Galloping full tilt along the turnpike, Gabriel couldn't ride far enough or fast enough to escape Olivia's words. They hounded him, pounding in his brain with the fury of a violent storm. Olivia wanted him, he knew she did. But that didn't seem to matter. The hold Palmerson had on her was puzzling. The knowledge that Olivia could make love with him, then meet Palmerson in the garden, was worse than any physical pain he'd ever experienced. Had she lain with Palmerson after making love so sweetly with him?

Gabriel drove his mount until flecks of foam spraying from the horse's mouth convinced him to stop before he rode the poor animal to death. Turning into the courtyard of a respectable-looking inn, he gave instructions for the care of his horse and requested a room. He was in the common room getting gloriously drunk when he heard someone speak his name. Glancing up, he saw Braxton and Westmore striding toward him.

"What in bloody hell are you doing here?" Ram asked. "Why aren't you home preparing for your wedding?"

"The wedding's off," Gabriel mumbled. "Join me, gentleman. I'm well on my way to getting drunk."

"Looks like you've had enough," Luc said, dropping into a chair beside Gabriel. "Do you want to tell us about it?"

Gabriel motioned for the barmaid to bring drinks all around before answering. "Nothing to tell. We didn't suit."

"Hell, I could have told you that," Ram laughed.

"You're not the marrying kind. Maybe next time you have thoughts about getting leg-shackled, you'll listen to us. You don't see Westmore or me rushing to the altar."

"Shoulda listened to you," Gabriel drawled drunkenly. "Thought I was doing her a favor. I shot her, you know. Just wanted to make things right. Damn honor and all that."

"You shot Lady Olivia? By God, I should like to hear that story," Luc crowed.

"Remind me to tell it to you when I'm sober," Gabriel replied. He raised his cup. "Here's to debauchery. No matter how short my life, I intend to enjoy my freedom to the fullest."

"Amen," Ram chuckled, drinking deeply.

"Another toast, gentlemen," Gabriel said, holding his mug aloft. "To all the women I intend to love during the years left to me, and to good fortune at the gambling halls."

All three men emptied their mugs.

They returned to London the following morning. Gabriel wasn't feeling quite the thing, but he managed to stay in the saddle despite his big head. He rarely drank to excess, but the occasion had called for it. Being jilted was bad enough, but being replaced by a man like Palmerson was enough to drive any man to drink.

Olivia hated to impose upon Lady Patrice, but she had little choice. Until she spoke with Mr. Culpepper about her inheritance, she had nowhere to go and no money. They had reached London yesterday evening, and Olivia had set out early this morning for the solicitor's office. Lady Patrice had given her the use of her town carriage, and Peterson had volunteered to drive her. She had sent a messenger ahead, advising Culpepper of her imminent arrival.

When she arrived at the solicitor's, she was shown into his private office. He rose to greet her.

"Lady Olivia, I'm pleased to finally meet you. I'm Silas Culpepper."

"You'll have to forgive me, Mr. Culpepper, for appearing a bit flummoxed. You see, I had no idea my grandparents left anything to my brother and me. Your letter came as a total shock."

Culpepper frowned. "Did your father not tell you?"

"No. Do you know why he never mentioned our inheritance?"

The solicitor's frown deepened. "I don't like to disparage the dead, my lady, but your father tried to break the trust on several occasions. Fortunately, it was irrevocable. Apparently, your grandparents didn't trust your father to administer your inheritance and made ironclad provisions for you and your brother."

"My grandfather had no male heir. We were told the estate had gone to a distant relative."

"You are correct, Lady Olivia. The estate and title were entailed, but your grandparents' fortune was not. They left it to you and your brother."

"We never knew. Papa should have told us."

"I'm sorry for my own oversight in the matter. Since your father had always known about the inheritance, I assumed you and your brother had been informed as well. You didn't contact me after your father's death, and I assumed you'd get in touch before your birthday to complete arrangements for the transfer of the funds to your account. When I failed to hear from you, I grew concerned and decided to write."

"Your letter came as a complete surprise. Did anyone

besides my father know about the inheritance?"

"Let's see. I believe your father's friend Lord Palmerson knew about the inheritance," Culpepper continued. "They visited my office together a time or two. Did the viscount not mention it after your father's death?"

"No, but his knowledge of my inheritance certainly answers a lot of questions."

"I invested the bulk of the money, which has accrued considerable interest over the years. All the papers are here for your perusal. As you can see, the amount is substantial. You are a considerable heiress, and your brother's share will be even larger due to the interest his share of the funds will earn before he turns twenty-five."

Olivia riffled through the documents, her eyes wide with disbelief. "That's a great deal of money."

"I said it was substantial. It would be my pleasure to continue as your solicitor, Lady Olivia. I suggest that you withdraw, oh, say, one hundred pounds each month for pin money and send your bills to me to be paid from your account."

"Did I hear you right? One hundred pounds *a month?* For pin money?"

"Is that not enough?"

"More than enough. But our immediate needs are quite pressing and will require a more substantial sum. We have no home, nor servants to staff one, and our clothing is hopelessly out of style."

"Do you have a dwelling in mind?"

"I'd love to return to our old home on Grosvenor Square. Papa sold it to support his gambling habit. You don't suppose it's for sale, do you?"

"I would be most happy to make inquiries, my lady."

"Would you?"

"It will be my pleasure. If your old home isn't available, I shall line up others for your approval. Leave everything in my hands."

Olivia looked into Mr. Culpepper's eyes and was struck by his honesty. He had held firm against her father's attempts to claim her inheritance for himself, and she felt nothing but admiration for the solicitor. Her grandparents had trusted him, and she could do no less.

"Very well, sir, I'll leave the matter in your hands. You can contact me at the dowager Marchioness of Bathurst's residence. I'll be staying there until I find a home of my own."

"As soon as you sign these documents, you may start sending your bills to me. And sufficient funds will be placed into your account for your immediate use."

Olivia stood and offered her hand. "You've been very helpful, Mr. Culpepper. Going from poverty to wealth overnight is somewhat of a shock, but not an unwelcome one."

Culpepper sent her a stunned look. "Poverty? Dear me, had I known, I could have arranged to have interest from your inheritance transferred to you immediately. Forgive me, dear lady, for not contacting you immediately following your father's death, but I wasn't his solicitor and didn't want to intrude."

"You're forgiven, sir. Good day."

"Good day, my lady. I'll be in touch."

Olivia left in a daze. She was wealthy. She couldn't wait to tell Neville he could expect a substantial inheritance when he turned twenty-five. Financially, their troubles were over. She and her family could live in luxury the rest of their lives.

Peterson was waiting for her at the curb. "Are you

all right, Miss Livvy? You look a mite peaked. Did the lawyer give you bad news?"

"Good news, Peterson. The best. We're wealthy. I'll explain everything later."

"Where do you wish to go?"

"To Bond Street. I want to buy something nice for Aunt Alma. And for you too, Peterson. Your livery is beyond shabby."

Two hours later, Olivia had purchased so many gifts for her loved ones, they overflowed the boot. She'd hoped that spending money would fill the void in her heart left by Gabriel's departure, but her lightheartedness had been forced. What good was money if it couldn't heal the wound or lessen the pain of a lost love? There was no going back. With a few cruel words she had severed forever her relationship with Gabriel.

He would never forgive her.

Fate unkindly reinforced her dismal thoughts when she saw Gabriel strolling down the opposite side of the street with a dark-haired woman on his arm. Their heads were close together as he smiled down at her and she looked adoringly up at him.

# *Chapter Seventeen*

Gabriel had deliberately avoided his grandmother after he left Bathurst Park, but he knew he had to face her sooner or later. He wondered what Olivia had told her and if he could undo the damage she had done. Grandmama had been looking forward to his marriage, and he suspected her disappointment had been heartbreaking. Still, it would have been worse if he'd wed Olivia and failed to produce the heir Grandmama expected.

It hadn't taken Gabriel long after his return to London to revert to his old ways: carousing until the wee hours of morning, gambling as if his funds were limitless, and dallying with his former lovers. The news that he and Olivia were no longer engaged was common knowledge now, and Gabriel didn't want it said that one of the infamous rogues of London was pining over a lost love.

His short absence from London had been noticed, of course, but he had disdained an explanation, except to say he'd been called away on estate business. The insult Olivia had dealt to his ego had sent him headlong down the path to perdition. He drank, he caroused, he gambled, but he hadn't bedded a woman yet, and he blamed Olivia for his lack of desire.

What had she done to him?

Now, having finally decided to visit Grandmama, Gabriel wondered what he was going to tell her to soothe her ruffled feathers. If Olivia hadn't told Grandmama the truth about her involvement with Palmerson, and he doubted she had, he certainly wasn't going to divulge that information. The whole affair was too embarrassing for Grandmama's ears.

As he dismounted at Lady Patrice's doorstep, Gabriel wondered if Olivia and Palmerson were already wed. He supposed they were, since Palmerson wasn't the kind to let grass grow under his feet. He should send a wedding gift around to Palmerson's townhouse, he thought perversely. His thoughts returned to Olivia and his willingness to wed her. He knew now that it had been a mistake, that guilt had forced him to propose. Yes, the logic of it was simple. He had definitely acted out of guilt. After he'd learned he had shot her, his pride demanded that he take care of her.

His heart wasn't involved and never had been.

Gabriel rapped on the door and waited for a response.

"Good afternoon, milord."

"Good afternoon, Huntly. Is my grandmother in?"

"The ladies are in the drawing room, milord. I'll announce you."

"Ladies?" Gabriel shrugged. He had hoped to find Grandmama alone. "Don't bother, Huntly, I'll announce myself."

Summoning a smile, Gabriel handed Huntly his hat and strode into the drawing room. Spying his grandmother sitting in her favorite chair, he headed in her direction, ignoring the other two occupants of the room.

"Bathurst, it's about time you showed up."

"I've come to apologize for leaving Bathurst Park without an explanation."

"Where are your manners, dear boy? You haven't greeted my guests."

Still smiling, Gabriel turned to greet his grandmother's guests. The smile slipped, then disappeared when he recognized Olivia and her aunt.

"What are *they* doing here, Grandmama?"

"Don't be rude to my houseguests, Bathurst."

"Perhaps we should leave," Olivia said, rising.

"Don't go on my account," Gabriel sneered. "How did you and your aunt manage to earn Grandmama's affection?" His condemning gaze bore into Olivia. "Where is Palmerson? Has he made you his wife yet? Or does he prefer you as his whore?"

Lady Patrice pounded her cane on the floor. "Enough, Bathurst! Dear Olivia is my houseguest. How dare you insult her?"

"Houseguest! Has dear Olivia explained why she cried off our marriage, Grandmama? Did you know she and Palmerson—"

"I'm done with Palmerson," Olivia said, stopping him in mid-sentence. "Furthermore, your grandmother knows the truth, perhaps better than you. I could not have accepted her hospitality if I had lied to her."

"I doubt you'd know the truth if it hit you in the face. You certainly had me fooled. What happened? Did Palmerson suddenly realize there was nothing to be

287

gained from marrying you? Weren't your charms sufficient to entice him into your bed? They certainly were for me. Or perhaps he wanted someone with less experience."

Olivia leaped to her feet, her face pale, her body shaking with humiliation. How could Gabriel do this to her? She knew she had hurt him, but insulting her in his grandmother's presence was uncalled for.

"Desist, Bathurst!" Lady Patrice raged. "Your manners are despicable. Apologize to Lady Olivia."

"You're taking her side over mine? You believe the lies she told you?"

"Perhaps Alma and I should leave you two alone. I'm sure Olivia could enlighten you about many things."

"There's nothing left for us to say, Grandmama," Gabriel replied. "Whether or not Olivia married or intends to marry Palmerson isn't the issue."

"What *is* the issue, dear?" she asked. "Perhaps you don't know the story as I do."

"Please let it go, Lady Patrice," Olivia pleaded. "Your grandson has every right to feel as he does about me." She gazed into Gabriel's eyes, her heart breaking. "I shouldn't have accepted your grandmother's offer of shelter, but Auntie and I had nowhere to go. We'll be moving very soon to a new home on Grosvenor Square, so you can stop berating Lady Patrice for taking us in."

"Lady Alma, would you accompany me to my room?" Patrice said, rising. "I'm feeling ill."

Alma rushed to the dowager's aid. "Of course, but is it wise to leave these two alone?"

"There isn't a weapon in sight. Unless words can kill, I doubt there will be bloodshed." She leaned heavily on Alma's arm. "Shall we?"

Neither Olivia nor Gabriel was aware that the two

older ladies had left until Gabriel whirled to ask his grandmother a question. "Where in bloody hell did she go?"

Olivia made a quick survey of the room and realized they were alone. "If you'll excuse me, I'll join them."

Gabriel grasped her arm. "You're not going anywhere. You owe me an explanation. Were you using Palmerson as an excuse to avoid marrying me? And what's this about moving to Grosvenor Square? Where did you get the blunt? If I hear that Pete and Ollie are on the prowl again, I'll divulge their identities to the law myself."

His barbed words goaded Olivia to retaliate. She knew her refusal to marry him had piqued his pride, but he didn't really want a wife. She had freed him to continue his debauched way of life.

"You only proposed to salve your guilt. Get over it, Bathurst. You shot me. I recovered. You were never under any obligation to marry me."

"What should I have done? Let you and Peterson continue to endanger your lives and the lives of others? Am I supposed to do nothing while you rob unsuspecting citizens of their valuables?"

"Pete and Ollie are history, Bathurst. They won't be riding again. The need no longer exists."

"Do I have your promise on that? Can I trust you?"

Olivia turned to leave. "I think you've said enough, Bathurst. I know I have. Nothing I can say will change your opinion of me."

He grasped her shoulders and dragged her against him. "You haven't explained everything to my satisfaction. Where did you get the blunt to buy a home in Grosvenor Square?"

She tried to wrench away, to escape the heat of his

body, the sensuality of his mobile mouth, but his grip remained firm. She looked into his eyes, recalling their last night together, and realized that he was remembering too. Their lips were inches apart. Their breath mingled; she felt his fingers digging into her shoulders and wanted to scream in frustration. Her response to Gabriel had never been lukewarm. The one place they suited was in bed.

Her thoughts skittered to an abrupt halt when Gabriel's mouth came down hard on hers. She tried to push him away, but instead, her hands fisted in his jacket and pulled him closer. So much for her resistance. A moan fluttered past her lips. Her knees wobbled and her mind shut down as Gabriel licked the seam of her lips with his tongue, nudging them apart and plunging inside.

His kiss sucked the breath from her; her bones turned to water. What was he trying to prove? That she was vulnerable to his kisses? That she wanted him? True, all true, she silently lamented.

His hard hands roamed her body with the familiarity of one who knew it intimately. Her nipples swelled against his palms, and moisture pooled between her thighs. Aware of what he was doing to her, she gathered the tattered remnants of her willpower and broke free.

"No, you're not going to do this to me!"

His expression was triumphant, his grin mocking. "I already have. You want me, Livvy. Fortunately for me, I no longer want *you*. It matters not how you came into your unexpected wealth, as long as I'm not the one providing your support."

Her chin rose defiantly. "I've never asked you for anything, my lord."

"Have you not?" He thrust her aside. "Good day, my lady."

Cut to the quick, she fought to hide her breaking heart as Gabriel gave her a mocking bow and spun away. His abrupt departure left an aching void inside her, but she refused to accept defeat at the hands of an unrepentant rogue.

Gabriel couldn't believe what had just happened. He had believed he had seen the last of Olivia and had been stunned to see her at his grandmother's mansion, claiming to be wealthy enough to purchase a home in Grosvenor Square. Was there any truth to her claim? Had something happened to change the course of her life between the time he'd left her at Bathurst Park and today? In a scant few days she'd gone from pauper to heiress, or so she'd like him to believe. It made no sense.

Gabriel mulled over the turn of events as he rode to Brooks's. He'd been stunned to learn that Olivia had not wed Palmerson and had no intention of doing so. Something strange was going on, but he'd been too angry and upset to get to the bottom of it. Logic told him he didn't need a dangerous complication like Olivia in his life, but his heart told him otherwise.

Gabriel ignored the unusual buzz of excitement in the normally staid club and headed directly toward Lord Braxton, who was perusing a newspaper in a quiet corner. Ram looked up when Gabriel cleared his throat.

"What's all the commotion about?" Gabriel asked as he slumped into a comfortable leather chair. "I haven't seen this much excitement since old Northby got an heir on his fourth wife at the age of eighty-three."

"Haven't you heard?"

"Heard what?"

"Your Lady Olivia is an heiress. Apparently, she didn't learn about her good fortune until she turned twenty-five a few days ago. Her maternal grandparents had settled a substantial sum of money on her and an equal amount on her brother. I'm surprised you didn't know. It's the juiciest bit of gossip to hit London in months, save for the scandal you and Lady Olivia caused at the Hare and Hound."

"So it's true," Gabriel said, stunned. "I saw Olivia at Grandmama's house. She told me she's moving to Grosvenor Square, but I didn't believe her."

"Rumor has it, and reliable sources agree, that the inheritance was a complete surprise. Seems her father never told his children about the legacy. I heard he even tried to break the trust and divert the funds for his own use."

"Sefton really was a bastard, wasn't he?"

"I'm amazed you didn't know about Lady Olivia's sudden turn of fortune. Your own grandmother is sponsoring her at Almack's and other society events. Your former fiancée, despite being deemed unmarriageable, has become the most sought-after heiress in Town."

"I wonder what happened to Palmerson," Gabriel mused. "It's not like him to let a fortune pass through his fingers." Comprehension dawned, and with it came the knowledge of what Palmerson had been about. "Palmerson and Sefton were bosom friends, were they not?"

"They were close. The consensus is that Palmerson was responsible for Sefton's decline into debauchery after his wife's death."

Gabriel digested that bit of information, realizing immediately that Palmerson had known about Olivia's inheritance and wanted to marry her in order to gain control of her funds. It all made perfect sense now . . . except that something was missing. One vital piece of information still escaped him. Why had Olivia trysted with Palmerson in the garden? Why had she agreed to marry him, then changed her mind?

Sighing, Gabriel uncoiled his long frame from the chair and rose. "Excuse me, I just remembered an appointment."

His mind whirling, Gabriel hurried off. In a matter of days, Olivia had become the darling of the *ton*, sought after by men who coveted her inheritance. Was Olivia worldly enough to know she was being courted for her fortune?

Why should he care? Gabriel asked himself. His own reasons for avoiding marriage and producing children were still valid. Without really knowing why or how, Olivia had gotten under his skin and made him forget the tragic circumstances that made marriage and a family impossible for him. She had truly done him a favor by refusing to wed him . . . hadn't she?

Three days later, Grimsley handed Gabriel a note from his grandmother, requesting that he escort her and her guests to Almack's that night. Gabriel read the note, crumpled it in his hand and flung it to the floor.

"Is there an answer, milord?" Grimsley asked. "The messenger is waiting."

Gabriel wanted to refuse his grandmother's request. It was on the tip of his tongue to tell Grimsley to send the messenger away without a reply. But Gabriel didn't have it in him to refuse his grandmother when she asked so little of him. Swallowing his reservations, he dashed off a reply, informing Grandmama to be ready at nine o'clock, and warning that she should not expect him to dance attendance upon her houseguests. He sealed the note and handed it to Grimsley.

That same afternoon, Gabriel decided that a ride in the park was just the thing to clear his head. He rode his favorite horse to Hyde Park and headed down Rotten Row. He was galloping along at a good clip when a lady trailed by a groom approached from the opposite direction. He slowed to let her pass, but the lady drew rein and greeted Gabriel effusively.

"Bathurst, where have you been keeping yourself these days? I've missed you."

"Good day, Countess," Gabriel said, doffing his hat. "I've been meaning to call on you, but business has taken up much of my time."

Lady Leslie, Countess of Barrow, angled her horse close to Gabriel. "Why so formal, Gabriel? We are, after all, old and intimate friends."

"Indeed, Leslie. Forgive me for not calling on you upon my return from the country. Allow me to remedy that. Is your husband with you in London?"

Leslie's dark eyes sparkled mischievously. "Poor Barrow. He's been stricken with gout and remained in the country. He didn't want me to miss the season and urged me to take up residence at our townhouse until he can join me. Shall I expect you tonight?"

"I'm to provide escort to Grandmama and her guests tonight, but I can call on you later, if that meets with your approval."

"I'll be waiting, Bathurst. It will be just like old times, won't it, darling? Rumor has it you're no longer engaged. I hope that's true."

"My intended cried off," Gabriel said curtly. "I'm footloose and fancy-free."

Leslie gave him a dazzling smile. "Splendid. Until to-night," she said coyly as she rode off.

Gabriel continued on his way, wondering why he wasn't feeling elated at the prospect of bedding an enormously talented lover like the countess.

"You what!" Olivia cried, aghast. "Oh, my lady, you should not have."

"And why not?" Lady Patrice inquired. "What harm was there in asking Bathurst to escort us to Almack's? It's time you assumed your role in society. As a patroness of Almack's, I am in the perfect position to secure your place among the *ton*. The gowns you ordered for yourself and Alma have been delivered, so there's no reason to delay. You've hidden yourself too long as it is."

"I can't believe Bathurst agreed," Olivia said, shaking her head in disbelief. "He made it abundantly clear that he wanted nothing to do with me."

"I'm his grandmother, child. I asked but a simple thing of him."

Olivia hoped Lady Patrice wasn't matchmaking. There was no hope for her and Gabriel. She had seen to that when she'd backed out of their marriage and named Palmerson as her reason for doing so. Well, she wouldn't be seeing much of Gabriel once she left Lady Patrice's home.

Mr. Culpepper had worked a miracle. He'd managed to purchase the Sefton family's townhouse from the people who had bought it. The elderly Viscount Conners and his wife had been considering retiring to their estate in the country, and Culpepper's offer had arrived at a most propitious time. The deal had been completed, and Olivia and her aunt would be moving back to their old home very soon. Even more exciting was the fact that Neville, having completed his studies at the university, would be joining them.

As the time for Bathurst's arrival approached, Olivia considered crying off. The only thing that kept her from doing so was her pride. She wouldn't let Bathurst's contempt for her destroy her, nor would she let unrequited love tear her apart.

Bathurst arrived promptly at nine o'clock. Olivia paused at the top of the stairs, admiring him from afar as he greeted his grandmother. She couldn't take her eyes off him. He was magnificent in a plum-colored velvet tailcoat that molded his broad shoulders and torso and fawn-colored breeches that clung to every line of his powerful thighs. His white silk cravat was an intricate marvel, and his satin waistcoat of muted gold was fashionably embroidered down the front. Yards of lace cascaded down his shirtfront and from his sleeves.

He smiled at something Lady Patrice said, and Olivia's heart skipped a beat. Then he glanced up and saw her.

Gabriel tried not to stare at Olivia, but his eyes would not be denied the sight of her. He had always thought her beautiful, but tonight she was absolutely stunning in a dazzling silver gown studded with crystals and cut low to emphasize her magnificent bosom and shoulders. Her burnished hair, piled atop her head in loose ringlets, was adorned with crystals that sparkled in the candlelight. She looked like a goddess, and he had worshiped every glorious inch of her body.

Gabriel shook the arousing thoughts from his head and unconsciously adjusted himself to accommodate his sudden and unwelcome arousal. Olivia seemed to glide down the stairs, and when Grandmama turned to greet her lovely houseguest, Gabriel was forced to acknowledge Olivia's presence.

"Lady Olivia," he said coolly as Olivia joined the group.

"Lord Bathurst," Olivia returned.

"Where is dear Alma?" Lady Patrice asked.

"She isn't feeling well," Olivia said worriedly. "Auntie is rarely ill, so I was surprised when she complained of a dreadful headache."

"Oh, no," Grandmama said. "I've become terribly fond of your aunt. I don't feel comfortable leaving her alone while she is feeling unwell."

"I agree," Olivia said. "You go on with Bathurst. I'll stay with Auntie."

"Do not even consider it," Grandmama chided. "*I* will stay with Alma myself. Bathurst can escort you as planned."

"Grandmama, you go too far," Gabriel growled.

"Nonsense. Besides, it wouldn't do for Olivia to miss her presentation. She'd be so disappointed."

Gabriel's brows lifted sardonically. The look of absolute horror on Olivia's face told a different story. *She didn't want to be alone with him any more than he wanted to be alone with her.*

"Lord Bathurst is right, my lady," Olivia began. "He is not obligated to escort me anywhere, and furthermore, my being alone with him will start tongues wagging. There has already been enough gossip about us. Have you forgotten the engagement announcement he placed in the paper before we left London? People will think we're still a couple."

"What is so bad about that?" Lady Patrice huffed. "Since Gabriel is so eager to avoid marriage, being with you will ward off marriage-minded mamas."

"That won't fly, Grandmama," Gabriel charged. "My friends already know the engagement is off, and it's probably common knowledge by now."

Grandmama waved her hand dismissively. "It doesn't matter. Let the *ton* talk. Go along with you now and have a good time. I must go to dear Alma and make sure she's comfortable."

His jaw clenched, Gabriel watched his grandmother make her way slowly up the stairs, assisted by a footman and her cane. Why was she doing this to him? He seriously doubted that Lady Alma was ill. He suspected that this was a ploy the two ladies had hatched to throw him and Olivia together. What part had Olivia had in the nefarious plan?

"I hope you're happy," Gabriel groused.

Olivia bristled. "Are you insinuating this was my doing?"

"Isn't it? Is your aunt really ill?"

"I have no reason to doubt her. Are you begging off? It wouldn't bother me in the least if you were."

"Children, don't dawdle," Lady Patrice called from the top of the stairs. "Off with you now."

Briggs came forward with Olivia's cloak and opened the door. Gabriel ushered Olivia into the cool night air and handed her into the coach. Olivia slid to the far corner, making sure no part of him touched any part of her as Gabriel got in after her. Feeling oddly short of breath, Gabriel inhaled deeply of Olivia's scent; it filled the small space with a sensual aroma that heightened his senses. He was aware of Olivia as he had never been before.

What the devil was wrong with him?

Daring a covert glance at her, he noted that she appeared as uncomfortable as he was. Her gloved hands fidgeted in her lap as she gazed out the window at the passing traffic.

"I don't like this any more than you do," Gabriel growled.

"I'm sorry," Olivia said, sounding not at all contrite. "Blame your grandmother, not me."

"How long do you intend to take advantage of Grandmama's hospitality?"

"Fear not, Auntie and I are moving into our own home very soon. We had intended to move into temporary lodgings after we left Bathurst Park, but your grandmother wouldn't hear of it. She's rather strong-willed, as you well know. Rest assured I am *not* taking advantage of her in any way."

Clamping his mouth tightly shut, Gabriel tried to ignore the woman who had moved him as no other had. Before Olivia had left him for Palmerson, he had even convinced himself that he had deep feelings for her, that he truly *wanted* to wed her.

Dark and complex thoughts still tumbled inside his head as the coach arrived at Almack's. Wordlessly, Gabriel handed Olivia from the coach and escorted her to the door. A footman ushered them inside. Gabriel watched closely as Olivia took in the simple elegance of Almack's foyer. He escorted her up the stairs to the vestibule, flanked by card rooms on either side that were also used for suppers and banquets, then straight into the ballroom.

Olivia's delighted expression prompted Gabriel to ask, "Have you never been to Almack's before?"

"This is my first time. After Father's . . . scandalous death, no sponsor stepped forward, so I was denied admittance."

Gabriel lifted his gaze to the white ceiling that soared

thirty feet above them and imagined how it would look to someone who had never been inside Almack's before, nor viewed its pale green walls, cream moldings festooned with carvings and medallions, and enormous arched windows. Benches lined the walls, and an elevated bandstand dominated one end of the ballroom.

A hush fell over the crowd when they entered. Gabriel didn't know if it was due to the gossip circulating about them or because of Olivia's outstanding beauty. A little of both, he suspected. He introduced her to one of the patronesses, then led her to a bench.

"Would you like something to drink?"

"You don't have to pay court to me, Bathurst, I know how you feel about me."

"Do you? Do you really?"

She stared at him blankly, but her answer was forestalled when a group of potential suitors converged on them.

"You've had your chance, Bathurst, now it's ours," one of the dandies said, elbowing Gabriel aside. "Will you honor me with a dance, Lady Olivia?"

"And me," a man Gabriel recognized as a notorious spendthrift insisted.

"Where's your dance card?" asked another.

"Gentlemen, where are your manners?" Gabriel chided. "I'm sure Lady Olivia will oblige each and every one of you if you bide your time. The first dance, however, belongs to me." He held out his hand. "Shall we?"

Olivia looked uncertain, but Gabriel gave her no time to protest as he led her onto the dance floor. The band was playing a waltz, a particular favorite of his. Placing a hand on her waist, he swung her into the steps.

"So now it starts," Gabriel said coolly. "You'll not lack for suitors now that you're an heiress. Choose wisely, Livvy. Stay away from men like Palmerson and his ilk. For instance, Lord Fordham is addicted to opium. And Lord Brandon likes multiple partners but needs to wed an heiress to fill the family coffers."

"I find your advice rather amusing coming from a rogue and a womanizer," Olivia charged. "I don't plan on marrying, ever."

His sardonic look mocked her words, but the dance ended before he could reply. He escorted Olivia off the floor and left her surrounded by a bevy of admirers. Leaning against a pillar, he watched as they made fools of themselves over her. He pressed his fingertips against his temples, feeling the beginnings of a headache creeping in behind his eyes. It was painful to stand aside and watch grown men throw themselves at Olivia's feet, especially since those same men had once scorned her for her advanced age and lack of a dowry.

"You look as if you could use a friend."

Gabriel forced a smile he didn't feel. "Braxton, since when was Almack's your style?"

"Thought I'd look over the new crop of debs. Westmore's here somewhere. I talked him into joining me. There he is," Ram pointed out. "Lady Crabtree and her two daughters have him cornered. Poor bastard. What are *you* doing here?"

"Grandmama coerced me into providing escort for her and her guests tonight."

"I can't see your grandmother in this crush of people."

"She isn't here."

Ram gave him a puzzled look. "Then who . . . I say, isn't that Lady Olivia surrounded by a bevy of admirers?"

"It's amazing what money can do for one's popularity," Gabriel drawled.

"You sound jealous, old boy. Is she with Palmerson?"

Gabriel gave a snort of disgust. "Guess again. Apparently, it's over between them."

Ram's eyes widened. "Then who . . . ? Damnation, she's with *you!* Are you mad? The woman is a greater threat to your bachelorhood than I suspected."

Gabriel rolled his eyes. "You don't know the half of it."

"I'd be happy to listen to your tale of woe, my friend, but some other time. If I want to keep his friendship, I'd best rescue Westmore from the dragon and her two man-eating offspring."

Gabriel returned his attention to Olivia. She was dancing with Lord Fordham now. Gabriel cringed inwardly as Fordham held her closer than was proper.

A whiff of a familiar perfume and a sensual voice close to his ear turned his attention from Olivia to the woman who had sidled up to him while his mind was occupied elsewhere.

Sliding her arm beneath Gabriel's, Lady Leslie smiled up at him, her eyes twinkling mischievously. "Hello, darling. Surprised to see me?"

# Chapter Eighteen

Olivia smiled and made appropriate small talk with her dance partners, but her heart wasn't in it. Again and again her gaze returned to Gabriel. He appeared to be holding up a pillar at the edge of the dance floor, his shuttered eyes watching her. She frowned when she saw him rubbing his temples and wondered what he was thinking. The next time she glanced at him, he was deep in conversation with Lord Braxton.

"May I call on you tomorrow, Lady Olivia?" Lord Fordham asked as his hand tightened about her waist, bringing her closer to his perspiring body.

"I don't think—"

"Perhaps you'll honor me by letting me drive you through the park in my new phaeton," Fordham continued blitholy.

"I'm sure I'm busy tomorrow."

After a brief pause he changed the subject, startling Olivia with his candor. "Allow me to congratulate you on your good fortune. I understand you just came into a substantial inheritance."

"Thank you. My grandparents were extremely generous."

Fordham's reply, if he gave one, was lost to Olivia when she glanced at Gabriel and saw beside him a lovely woman she recognized as Lady Leslie Barrow. The smile the countess gave him was so intimate, so filled with promise, that Olivia had to look away. When she dared another look, Gabriel was leading the lady onto the dance floor.

Intuition told Olivia that Gabriel and Lady Leslie were lovers, or had been at one time. Suddenly the splendor of Almack's and all it represented faded into nothingness. Lady Leslie was a married woman. She presented no threat to Gabriel's status as a confirmed bachelor, unlike Olivia, who would be an impediment to his hedonistic way of life should he wed her. Seeing how easily Gabriel went into another woman's arms created a throbbing in her head.

"Is something wrong, my lady?" Fordham asked smoothly. "You've gone pale. Perhaps a breath of air would help."

Yes, she desperately needed air. "Thank you, my lord. Fresh air is exactly what I need."

Had Olivia noted Fordham's smug smile as he guided her toward the veranda, she would have begged off. The only person who really took notice was Gabriel.

Only two other couples were strolling the veranda when Olivia and Fordham stepped through the French doors. One couple returned to the ballroom and the other descended the steps to the garden, leaving Olivia alone with Fordham. She breathed deeply of the damp night air, wishing herself any place but here. She cared little for society and the people who had ignored her when she was a penniless spinster, and she didn't give a fig for the fortune hunters now clamoring for her attention.

Unconsciously, she shivered. "Are you cold?" Fordham asked. With subtle ease, he placed an arm around her and drew her against him. "Let me warm you, Olivia. I've heard Bathurst is an exceptional lover, but I'm not without skill." He urged her toward the steps. "There's a gazebo in the garden. No one will intrude upon us there."

"Release me, my lord," Olivia insisted. "How dare you insinuate that Bathurst and I . . . that we . . ." Her words fell off as she abruptly realized that Fordham had personal knowledge of her relationship with Gabriel, for he was one of the men who had barged in on them at the Hare and Hound.

"Don't play the coy virgin with me, Olivia. You need a husband to make you respectable, and I don't mind having an experienced woman in my bed."

"Don't you mean a rich experienced woman?" Olivia bit out. "You've said more than enough, my lord. I'd best return to the ballroom before Bathurst notices I'm missing."

"I thought you and Bathurst were through. I saw him with one of his former lovers before we stepped outside. I could have told you he wasn't the marrying kind. On the other hand, I am quite willing to leg-shackle myself to your money."

He pulled her against him and tried to kiss her, but Olivia protested. Pounding her fists against his chest, she tried to beat him off. Then he was gone, and in his place stood Gabriel. Peering around him, she saw Fordham lying at their feet.

Gabriel prodded him with his foot. "The lady is unwilling, Fordham. I suggest you find someone who welcomes your advances."

Scooting backward until he was out of range of Gabriel's booted foot, Fordham rose unsteadily. "Why didn't you say you were still interested? I would not have intruded had I known." Giving Olivia an accusatory frown, he slunk off.

"I hoped you'd be wise enough to separate the chaff from the wheat," Gabriel said. "Fordham is one of the worst. Whatever made you step outside with him?"

Olivia glared at him. "I needed air. If you don't mind, I'd like to go home."

Gabriel's dark brows edged upward. "So soon? Do you not wish to partake of the midnight buffet?"

"Send me home in your coach if you're not ready to leave," Olivia retorted. "The midnight buffet doesn't tempt me."

"Nor me," Gabriel admitted. "Almack's is notorious for serving exceptionally bad food and watered drinks. I'll see you home."

"What about Lady Leslie?"

Gabriel stiffened. "What about her?"

"Nothing. Your long list of lovers doesn't interest me. There were countless others before me, and I'm sure there will be many more after I'm long forgotten. Shall we go?"

Eager to be gone, Olivia wended her way through the crowd; Gabriel followed close behind her. She could sense eyes upon them and knew that people were curious about their relationship. She had almost reached the door when Lady Leslie stepped into her path.

"Lady Olivia, congratulations on your good fortune. I suppose it won't be long before you'll be announcing your engagement. It's amazing what an inheritance will do for a spinster with few prospects." She waved her hand dismissively. "Men are such pathetic creatures. There are exceptions, however," she added, sending Gabriel a beguiling smile.

"Please excuse me, my lady," Olivia said, stepping around her. "I'm not feeling well."

"Forgive me for keeping you. I didn't realize." Lady Leslie tapped Gabriel on the shoulder with her fan and said loud enough for Olivia to hear, "Don't keep me waiting, Bathurst. I have something special in mind for us tonight."

Gabriel caught up with Olivia. "Are you really ill, Livvy?"

In truth, Olivia was indeed feeling queasy. Her stomach roiled and her head spun, but the state of her health was none of Gabriel's business. It didn't take a genius to know that Gabriel had planned an assignation with Lady Leslie tonight.

"I am now."

A footman brought Olivia's wrap. Gabriel placed it over her shoulders and ushered her to his coach. He paused for a word with Jenkins, then handed her inside and climbed in beside her.

"You're upset," Gabriel said.

"Not at all," Olivia denied. "Should I be?"

"I thought Leslie might have upset you."

"You and I are not romantically involved, Gabriel. I know who and what you are; you can't be without a woman for very long. It's not for me to judge you or your habits."

"If I recall correctly, and I believe I do, you enjoyed certain of my habits."

Olivia's cheeks flamed. "Why are you bringing that up now?"

Lamplight inside the coach turned Gabriel's eyes luminous—warm, slumberous, seductive. For a brief moment Olivia thought she saw a tiny spark of needy vulnerability in his eyes, but it was so fleeting, she could have imagined it. But she didn't imagine her name on his lips or his hands on her when he eased her back against the leather seat and kissed her.

A rush of excitement pulsed through her veins, shattering her resistance. The familiar and beloved taste of him filled her senses, and she kissed him back. How stupid she'd been to think her will was stronger than the passion she felt for this man. Logic fled, allowing instinct to guide her. The thumping of her heart vied with the lusty sounds of their panting and the creak of leather seats as Gabriel pulled her astride him.

He unfastened her gown and pulled it down, exposing her breasts. "What are you doing?" she demanded.

"What I've been wanting to do all evening," he moaned as his hot, wet mouth captured her nipple. "Seeing those other men put their hands on you drove me wild with jealousy."

Olivia gasped and let out a low, shaky sigh. Had Gabriel just said he was jealous? Impossible. Her thought splintered when he bit lightly down on her nipple, driving everything from her mind save for what Gabriel was doing to her. Weaving her fingers through his dark hair, she arched her back and offered more of herself to him as he sampled her other breast. She inhaled sharply when his hands crept beneath her skirts and up her thighs.

Gathering the tattered shreds of her willpower, Olivia

pleaded, "Gabriel, you must stop. We can't do this. It's indecent."

"What's to stop us?"

"Common sense."

Unfortunately, common sense flew out the window when Gabriel plucked her up and set her down on the opposite seat. One corner of his mouth kicked upward into a half smile as he pressed her back against the leather squabs and lowered himself to his knees.

"Gabriel . . . What . . . ?"

"Don't stop me, Livvy. We both want this."

With a soft moan, she closed her eyes and yielded to the gnawing need Gabriel had created within her.

Hitching her skirt up to her hips, he braced her legs on the opposite seat, placing himself between them. Grasping the coach's looped leather straps, she held on for dear life as Gabriel took her with his hands and tongue. Lifting her hips, she moved with him, her bones melting in the steamy heat they created within the coach. Tension built. She felt herself quickening, her blood pulsing, her head throbbing. She was barely clinging to the edge of sanity.

He moved away so abruptly, Olivia grasped his shoulders to hold him in place. "No! Don't stop!"

His voice quivered, thick with need. "I can't wait. I have to have you now."

"Your coachman will hear."

Rising, he lowered her to the seat and straddled her. "Jenkins is discreet. I instructed him to drive around the park a time or two."

"You planned this?"

"Actually, no. I thought it would be a good oppor tunity for us to talk." He shrugged. "Right now, talk is the last thing I want to do."

"We should stop right now, Gabriel. Lady Leslie is waiting for you."

"I'd rather have you."

"I'll not be your whore."

"You could have been my wife."

Olivia's reply died in her throat when Gabriel's sex prodded boldly between her thighs. She felt his hardness and his need, and felt her core softening in anticipation.

"Open for me, Livvy."

Olivia wanted to resist, to deny her need, but this was probably the last time she would make love with Gabriel. After he walked out of her life, Olivia knew she would never love again, never want a man in the same way she wanted Gabriel. Why shouldn't she let him make love to her one final time? Her legs fell open, and Gabriel slid between them.

The coach bounced and the wheels rattled and the horses' hooves pounded against the roadway; Olivia heard nothing but the harsh mingling of their breath and the pounding of her heart as Gabriel slid easily into her waiting warmth. He was so stunningly aroused, so brazenly full, she felt utterly consumed. The friction of her silken sheath gripping his swollen sex drove them both mad with desire. She felt the shudders that racked him, her own matching them in intensity. She saw the grimace of pleasure that twisted his face, and was lost.

Caught up in the same passionate frenzy she sensed in him, she arched to meet his driving thrusts. His heart thundering against hers, he buried himself deep, the driving force of his strokes shattering her. Her anger was gone; everything was forgotten but the desperate need that opened a floodgate inside her. She closed her eyes against the rising tide of emotions and let her senses carry her away.

"Look at me," Gabriel grated harshly into her ear. "I want you to remember this, remember us, remember what could have been had fate been kind to us."

His dark whisper compelled compliance. Gabriel's features were cast into a grimace of tightly leashed restraint. The cords of his neck bulged and his body was rigid. Submerged in the throes of her own building climax, Olivia was only dimly aware that Gabriel hadn't pulled out of her yet.

A flame caught fire inside her. She felt possessed, eaten alive by passion. The churning thrust of his loins drove her to unimaginable heights. Her mind closed down. She was a bundle of raw nerve endings, each one sizzling with anticipation. Then her body convulsed and gave itself up to pleasure. Vaguely she felt Gabriel's hands sweep down to catch her buttocks, lifting her, the scalding heat of their bodies binding them together. Dimly she heard him shout her name and felt the hot rush of his seed inside her. She closed her legs around him and rode him to oblivion.

Pulling out abruptly, Gabriel collapsed against Olivia, angry with himself for losing control. For the second time during their tumultuous relationship, he had remained with her until the end. Hastily refastening his clothing, he muttered a string of curses. Most of his adult life, he'd avoided what had just happened tonight. The single most important reason for his reluctance to wed Olivia was his inability to control himself when he made love to her. Giving Olivia a child would be disastrous. She would never forgive him if a child of theirs turned out to be . . . God, he couldn't even say the word. If his lapse in restraint resulted in a child, he would never forgive himself. Tonight had proven what

311

he'd known all along. He couldn't trust himself with Olivia. He was finally ready to admit that Olivia meant more to him than a warm body in his bed.

That reality brought him up short. It sounded almost as if he . . . Bloody hell! Could it be? Could he actually *love* Olivia? Was that what this was all about? No wonder she was so dangerous to him. Groaning, he buried his head in his hands.

"Gabriel, what's wrong?"

Dropping his hands, he gazed at her, his eyes revealing his pain. "You know what happened as well as I. I may have given you a child. I don't know what possessed me; I'm not usually so careless. You'll get in touch with me if . . . you find yourself increasing, won't you?"

Her lips compressed, Olivia began putting her clothing to rights. Her motions were jerky, almost frantic, and he realized he had hurt her in a way she would never forgive. Recalling his words, he cursed himself for not telling her he'd wed her if she found herself with child.

He hadn't wanted to hurt Olivia. His feelings were confused, his emotions so raw he couldn't think straight. Loving women came naturally to him, but being *in* love was completely new and frightening.

He had thought he wanted to wed Olivia to stop her from running afoul of the law and to salve his guilt for shooting her. When and how had his emotions become engaged?

"I'm sorry, Livvy. I didn't—"

"Perhaps you should signal Jenkins to return me to your grandmother's house," Olivia bit out, leaving his sentence dangling. "I wouldn't want to keep you from your assignation with Lady Leslie."

The name didn't register. "Who?"

Olivia peered at him. "You look strange, Bathurst. Are you ill?"

"One could say that," Gabriel answered as he thumped on the roof of the coach. Wasn't madness an illness?

Staring morosely out the window, Gabriel realized that the blackness of the night couldn't compare to the blackness inside him. It would have been far better had his brother not confided in him. Ignorance was bliss. How he wished he weren't his mother's son. If only . . . But he knew the truth, and he couldn't change his parentage even if he wanted to.

Aware of Olivia's scrutiny, Gabriel said, "Forgive me, Livvy. Hurting you was never my intention. There's something you should know about me. Something I've never told a living soul."

Olivia stared at him with rapt attention. "You don't have to tell me your secrets, Gabriel."

"But I do. After tonight, I have no choice. This is the second time I gave you my seed. You may already be carrying my child."

Olivia gave him an arrested look. "What are you trying to tell me? Do you have some kind of sickness? If so, it isn't apparent."

"I don't expect to live long," Gabriel explained. "On any given day I could slip into madness. It runs in my family. I suspect my brother drowned himself because he saw signs of it in himself. Should that happen to me, I'd do the same. Ned was wise not to give Cissy a child. Continuing the line would be tragic. That's the reason I tried to take precautions when we made love."

Olivia stared at him as if he had just sprouted horns.

"How do you know madness runs in your family? Your grandmother is perfectly sound in mind."

"My father's side of the family isn't affected. It's the maternal side. Mama was quite mad when she threw herself out the window to her death, just like her mother before her. My father loved Mama too much to put her away in Bedlam when her madness became apparent. She had her lucid moments, but mostly I remember her as a frail wraith who couldn't even remember the names of her children."

"Did your grandmother know?"

"I don't think so. She was abroad during those years Mama was ill. Grandfather was ambassador to Spain at the time. I'm not sure Father told Grandma the truth about Mama, and she's too frail now to be told that her only grandson is likely to go mad in the near future."

Disbelief colored Olivia's words. "If your mother was so ill, when did she tell you all these things?"

"As I said, she had lucid moments. Shortly after Father died, she called Ned into her room and told him about her family history. She advised him not to have children, to let the line die out with him. She jumped to her death the next day."

"Why did she tell Ned and not you?"

Gabriel shrugged. "Who knew how her mind worked? I suppose she thought Ned would tell me, which of course he did. I didn't want to sit idly by and wait for madness to strike, so I fled. My emotions were so raw, I never wanted to see the ancestral estate again. I bought a commission in the army and fought on the Peninsula. Ned's death brought me a title and responsibilities I never wanted. I returned to London and decided to live my life to the fullest.

"Womanizing, drinking, gambling, debauchery; I found my place among the rogues and rakes and was quite happy. Then you came along and turned my life upside down."

Stunned by Gabriel's confession, Olivia couldn't find the words to comfort him. He was so sane, so in control of himself that she couldn't believe he could end up insane like his mother.

"How did I upset the scheme of things?"

Gabriel blinked and looked away. "Need you ask?"

"I want to know, Gabriel." *Tell me you love me.*

"Olivia . . ." Gabriel began as the coach rolled to a stop. Olivia never learned what he was going to say, for the door opened and Jenkins lowered the steps. Confusion warred with compassion; her head was spinning after Gabriel's startling admission.

Olivia stepped down from the coach. "I can see myself to the door, Bathurst. Good night."

"Olivia, wait! About tonight . . . You will tell me, won't you?"

"Good night, Gabriel," she repeated. Lifting her skirts, she ran to the door, rapped once and was immediately admitted by a sleepy eyed footman. Pausing in the doorway, Olivia glanced over her shoulder. What she saw nearly broke her heart. Gabriel stood stiffly beside the coach, his profile stark with an emotion she couldn't define. Stifling a sob, she turned away.

Gabriel didn't blame Olivia for hating him. He'd tried to withhold his seed, but he'd been so overcome by the moment that he'd lost control. It was too late now to tell her he loved her. Too late to say he was sorry for the way things had turned out. He'd give up his title and everything he owned if he could be someone else . . . anyone but Gabriel Wellsby.

\*    \*    \*

Olivia awoke the following morning to a roiling stomach and a headache. When she sat up in bed, her stomach lurched, and she reached for the chamber pot beneath the bed. And just in time. She lost everything she had consumed during the past twenty-four hours. Weak and damp with sweat, she rested her head in her hands, wondering if the knowledge that Gabriel could die before his time had brought on her sickness. Or was it the thought of bringing a child afflicted with madness into the world?

She had no time for weakness, Olivia thought. There was much to be done before she and Aunt Alma moved into their new home, and she needed strength to carry on. Whether or not Gabriel was lying about his family history made no difference. He had chosen the kind of life he wanted to live, and it didn't include her. Had he said he loved her she would be at his side no matter what. Now that she understood his situation, she could have accepted not having children, if that was what he wanted. They could have faced his problems together, but he had chosen to face his fate alone.

Quite possibly, Gabriel would escape the madness. No one knew for sure whether or not his brother had taken his own life. Gabriel's mother could have exaggerated the progression of the disease, or perhaps she wasn't as lucid as they thought when she'd confided in Ned. Why hadn't Gabriel's father mentioned the inherited illness before he died? Nothing was clear save for one thing: Gabriel didn't love her.

Rising cautiously, Olivia dressed and went down to the morning room to eat breakfast with Alma and Lady Patrice. The two women welcomed Olivia effusively.

"Did you have a good time last night?" Lady Patrice

asked. "I heard you come in. It was very late. I hope my grandson acquitted himself well."

"I had a . . . lovely time," Olivia choked out.

"Have some kidney pie, dear," Alma said. "It's delicious."

Olivia took one look at the food on Alma's plate and turned a vile shade of green. She could feel her stomach churning and the bile rising, and she leaped to her feet. "Excuse me." She had to leave before she embarrassed herself.

"Did we say something to upset her?" Lady Patrice asked. "I hope Bathurst didn't do anything to offend her."

"Livvy was absolutely green around the gills," Alma said worriedly. "I don't believe it was due to anything we said or did. Excuse me, Patrice, I must go to her."

"By all means."

Olivia was rinsing out her mouth when Alma entered the room.

"Are you all right, dear?"

"I'm fine, Auntie."

"Almack's is notorious for its bad food. It must have been worse than usual last night."

Olivia frowned. "I didn't eat or drink anything."

Alma laid a hand against her forehead. "You're not feverish. Has something upset you?"

"Please don't fuss, Auntie. Perhaps a cup of tea and a slice of dry toast will settle my stomach."

Alma's eyes narrowed. "It's Bathurst, isn't it? What has he done now?"

"Please, Auntie, don't pry. I don't want to talk about Bathurst. Shall we go down and reassure Lady Patrice that the state of my health is excellent?"

Olivia managed to drink two cups of tea and nibble

on a piece of dry toast without turning green before she returned to her room. Her energy depleted, she sat on the edge of the bed and recalled the things she and Gabriel had done in the coach and what he had told her afterwards.

Living with the knowledge of his potential madness and early demise would have felled a lesser man than Gabriel. He'd barricaded his heart against love, avoided emotional contact, and cut his ties with his ancestral home because he couldn't handle the memories. His plight made her heart ache for him, made her feel ill.

Sick enough to turn green at the sight of food? To vomit? She shifted uncomfortably, her memory jolted back to the first time Gabriel had gotten carried away and lost himself inside her. How long ago had that been?

She let the thought wither and die and went on to another. It was ludicrous to think that madness lurked inside Bathurst. She didn't believe it, not for one minute, though obviously he was convinced of it. She wished she knew a way to ease his mind. Dimly she wondered if Lady Patrice held the key. The thought was worth exploring.

Olivia's sickness passed and she began to feel her old self as the day wore on. Mr. Culpepper arrived with the deed and the key to her home, and Olivia couldn't wait to move into the townhouse she remembered so fondly from her youth.

"You'll find a complete staff in place," Culpepper said. "The previous owners' servants wished to remain, so I took the liberty of hiring them on. Of course, if they are not to your liking, you may replace them."

"I'm sure they'll suit," Olivia said. "Peterson will be

in charge, and I plan on bringing Mrs. Hamilton, our previous cook and housekeeper, to Fairfax House, if she's agreeable. Peterson is talking to her about the position even as we speak. When can I move in?"

"Tomorrow."

"Wonderful!" Olivia cried, clapping her hands. "Neville will be so pleased to have his home returned to him."

Alma and Lady Patrice joined Olivia after the solicitor left.

"I'm going to miss you and dear Alma," Patrice said, wiping away a tear. "I've grown so fond of you both. I hope you'll visit often."

"We will, as often as time allows. Thank you for making us feel welcome here," Olivia replied.

"Forgive me for prying, but where do things stand between you and Bathurst?" Lady Patrice asked.

"Nothing has changed. Bathurst is . . . you must speak with him, my lady. Your grandson is troubled."

Lady Patrice gave Olivia a sad smile. "I've known that for some time, but he won't confide in me." Her smile wobbled. "Admit it, my dear. You love him, don't you?"

Olivia looked away, wishing she could lie, but Lady Patrice had a way of gleaning the truth.

"It's all right, Livvy, dear," Alma soothed. "It's obvious that you love Bathurst. I've known it for a long time." She looked to Patrice for confirmation. When the dowager nodded, Alma said, "We both believe Bathurst loves you and is too stubborn to admit it."

Olivia choked back a sob. "You can't possibly know that. It's so sad. Excuse me, I'm needed elsewhere."

"What do you suppose that was all about?" Alma asked after Olivia rushed off.

# Connie Mason

"Something is going on," Patrice answered, "and I intend to get to the bottom of it. My grandson can fool others, but not me. I know him too well."

"Olivia's illness this morning was puzzling, was it not?" Alma mused thoughtfully. "She seems to have recovered rather quickly."

"Are you thinking what I'm thinking?" Patrice asked.

"Indeed I am."

"You will keep me informed, won't you?"

"Most assuredly, dear Patrice, most assuredly."

# Chapter Nineteen

Gabriel made no attempt to see Olivia again. He hadn't wanted to burden her with his family secrets, but he'd kept them inside him so long, he felt as if he would explode if he didn't confide in someone. Besides, Olivia deserved to know the reason for his resistance to marriage and fatherhood. Now, after divulging his innermost fears, he was too embarrassed to face her.

He would never forgive himself if he had given Olivia a child on either of the two times he'd lost control of himself. Dimly he wondered if she could possibly know yet whether his seed had taken root that first time they had made love. Would she tell him if she was carrying his child?

Cursing his weakness where Olivia was concerned, Gabriel threw himself into the social scene. He drank excessively, lost enormous amounts of money at cards because he couldn't concentrate, and escorted a different woman each night to events he cared nothing about.

Astonishingly, he had bedded none of them. He had even visited a sporting house without sampling any of the women paraded before him.

Today he was to meet Lady Leslie at the races and escort her home. He knew she would expect him to make love to her, and somehow he had to work up the enthusiasm to perform to her expectations. Even though his heart wasn't in it, he knew that bedding Leslie was a test of his ability to carry on without Olivia. He would do what rogues did best despite the fact that another woman owned his soul.

Grimsley was waiting for Gabriel in the foyer with his hat and cane. "A note just arrived from your grandmother, milord. Will you read it before you leave?"

Gabriel stared at the note and shook his head. This was the third summons Gabriel had received, and he intended to ignore it as he had the others. "Place it on my desk. I'll get to it later."

Grimsley said nothing, but his pinched expression spoke eloquently of his disapproval. Though Gabriel hated to disappoint Grandmama, he couldn't face her right now. He was aware, however, that Olivia and her aunt had moved into their own townhouse and that her brother had joined them a few days later. He also knew that Grandmama disapproved of the way he was conducting his life, but refusing to wed and produce heirs was one way, the only way, to put an end to the madness inherited from his mother.

"I'm off to the races," Gabriel said as he sailed past Grimsley.

Lords Braxton and Westmore were on hand to greet Gabriel when he stepped down from his curricle.

"Bathurst," Ram greeted. "You're just the man I wanted to see. Are you alone?"

"For the time being," Gabriel said. "What are you two up to?"

"I'm thinking of purchasing a matched pair for my new phaeton, and you've a knack for picking out prime stock. Will you accompany me and Westmore to Tattersall's tomorrow?"

"Of course. What time?"

"I'll pick you up at three o'clock."

Luc cleared his throat and nudged Gabriel. "I say, old boy, isn't that Lady Olivia? Who's the young dandy with her?"

Gabriel swiveled his head until Olivia came into view. "Her brother, Neville. He's home from the university."

"Now that you and Olivia are no longer an item," Luc said, "she's seen frequently out and about, attending various social functions. I saw her at the Hudsons' musicale and again at the Carltons' fete. She's become the belle of the ball."

"Why wouldn't she?" Gabriel snorted. "Her fortune is as attractive as she is."

"You sound jealous, old boy," Luc chortled.

"Perhaps you should change your policy about marriage," Ram suggested. "Most men *do* fall into the parson's trap sooner or later."

"Keep your unsolicited opinions to yourselves," Gabriel said sharply.

Despite his harsh words, Gabriel couldn't keep his gaze from straying to Olivia. She looked smashing in a military-inspired afternoon dress. Worn over a red linen sheath, her dark blue spencer had tight-fitting sleeves, brass buttons and gold epaulettes. A far cry from the threadbare gown she'd worn during leaner times. She looked as if she was eating better, too, for she looked fuller in the bosom and waist. Upon closer inspection, however, Gabriel thought her face appeared drawn, and he noticed purple smudges under her eyes.

"Bathurst, there you are, you naughty boy." Though the shrill feminine voice grated on his ears, Gabriel turned an engaging smile on Lady Leslie. "I've been looking all over for you."

"I just arrived, Leslie," Gabriel replied. "I was waylaid by Braxton and Westmore."

Both men bowed politely and murmured greetings.

"You'll excuse us, won't you, gentlemen?" Leslie said archly. She tucked her arm beneath Gabriel's. "Shall we stroll, Bathurst? The first race is about to start, and I'd like a place near the fence when my horse takes the lead."

"Are you referring to Karma, the two-year-old gelding you recently purchased?"

"Indeed I am. I hope you wagered heavily on him. He's going to win."

"I rather like Samson, Lord Paulson's gelding. I've seen him race before and was impressed with his speed."

"Bite your tongue, Bathurst!"

They reached the fence just as the horses left the gate. When Samson leaped into an early lead and kept it throughout the race, Gabriel was glad he had placed a hefty wager on the horse. Winning was the first piece of good luck he'd had in a very long time. Leslie, however, was fit to be tied. She protested her loss so loudly, she began drawing unwelcome attention.

"I lost a fortune on that nag!" Leslie raged. "I'm selling him tomorrow. Let's go, Bathurst, I've seen enough. I can think of better ways to entertain ourselves than watching losers."

\* \* \*

Olivia wanted to ignore Gabriel's mistress's outburst, but her shrill, unladylike display of temper made it difficult. What did Gabriel see in her besides the obvious? Olivia wondered.

Gabriel hadn't tried to contact her since that fiasco at Almack's, and it hurt. She wanted desperately to be with him, to help him face the destiny fate had dealt him. She wanted to succor him, to ease his sorrows and allay his fears. She wanted to be with him when the end came, whether it was a matter of months, years or decades. How could Gabriel deny either of them the comfort she offered?

*Rather easily*, she thought disgustedly. He preferred to waste the time he had left in sensual pursuits, to drown his guilt and fears in sexual gratification with women who cared little for his welfare.

"Are you all right, Livvy?" Neville asked solicitously. "I know it must hurt to see Bathurst with another woman."

"I'm fine, Neville. I'm the one who ducked out of the marriage, if you recall."

"You also told me why. I could kill Palmerson for interfering. If he hadn't lied to you, you'd be Bathurst's marchioness now. I wonder where Palmerson has hidden himself," Neville mused aloud. "No one has seen him in weeks."

"Perhaps he is looking for another heiress," Olivia ventured. "Thank God I received your letter before I married him. I shudder every time I think of how close he came to actually having you under his control. I would have wed him to save your life."

"I can't believe that Papa knew about our inheritance and never told us."

"Papa wasn't himself after Mama died. He was grieving and vulnerable, and Palmerson took advantage of him. When Palmerson learned about the inheritance, he urged Papa to try to break the trust, but fortunately for us, he couldn't. I wouldn't even be surprised if he talked Papa out of telling us about it.

"After Papa's death, Palmerson decided I was a likely candidate to fill his empty coffers. No heiress would have him after that merchant's daughter killed herself."

"Thank God for Bathurst," Neville replied. "What *really* happened between you and the marquis, Livvy? There's more to it than you're letting on. You're an heiress now; you should be happy, but you're not."

Olivia darted another quick glance at Gabriel before replying. "There are so many things to be grateful for, Neville. Our money worries are over, for one. When you decide to wed, you'll have no trouble attracting a woman of equal rank. With your looks and fortune, you can choose wisely and wed for love. It's my fondest wish for you, little brother."

"My fondest wish for you is that *your* wishes come true," Neville returned.

Olivia returned her attention to the racetrack. She'd much rather be home with Aunt Alma, taking tea in the drawing room with her feet resting on a footstool and her corset loosened. She'd just recently taken to wearing a corset in order to look well in the fashionable new clothes she'd ordered, and she still felt uncomfortable in the confining garment.

The second race began and the crowd surged forward, pressing Olivia against the fence. The cloying heat, the dust and smell of unwashed bodies doused in perfume closed in on her like an iron fist, stifling her. Her head began to swim, and she swayed against Neville. If not for her brother's steadying arm, she would have fallen and been trampled beneath the surging crowd.

"Livvy, are you all right? You're so pale."

"Get me out of here before I embarrass myself," Olivia pleaded, clinging to her brother's arm.

His brow wrinkled in concern, Neville steered her through the throng of people. "Are you ill?"

"It's the heat and the crowd," Olivia replied.

Concern darkened his brow. "I shouldn't have insisted that you accompany me. Can you manage by yourself while I bring the carriage around? I shan't be long."

"I'm feeling better already."

"Splendid. I'll be right back."

Olivia waited near the road, her stomach churning, her forehead damp.

"What are you doing alone, Olivia? Where's Neville?"

*Bathurst!* Olivia didn't need to see him to know who it was. She'd recognize his voice anywhere. "Neville went to get the carriage."

"Are you leaving already? The races have just begun."

"I . . . I've had enough. Where did you leave Lady Leslie?"

"With friends. I went to collect my winnings and saw you standing alone, looking pale and unwell."

"Why do you care?"

"I care. No matter what you think of me, I do care. I tried not to, but you're not easy to forget, Livvy."

"Don't do this to me, Gabriel."

"You look tired. Aren't you sleeping well?"

"I'm fine."

"I'm sorry about the way things turned out, Livvy.

327

At least now you understand why I've resisted marriage all these years. It has nothing to do with you, and everything to do with me and my family history."

"There you are, Bathurst." Leslie pushed herself between Olivia and Gabriel. "I'm ready to leave, my love."

Olivia closed her eyes and swayed. Gabriel reached around Leslie to steady her. "You're not all right."

"It's the heat, Bathurst," Leslie complained. "I'm feeling a bit faint myself. Shall we go?"

"In a moment. As soon as Lady Olivia's brother arrives."

"Here's Neville now," Olivia said on a sigh of relief when she spied her carriage.

Neville stepped down from the driver's bench to assist Olivia.

"You should take better care of your sister, Sefton," Gabriel lashed out. "She's unwell."

"I'm quite aware of that, my lord."

Neville handed Olivia into the carriage. A frown lowering his brow, Gabriel watched until it disappeared around the corner. He wondered if Olivia was increasing and prayed he was wrong. He wished he knew more about the symptoms pregnant women experienced, but since they had never applied to anyone close to him, he'd paid scant heed to such things. If she was with child, it had to have happened the first time he had failed to withdraw. Counting back, he realized that two months or more had passed since that day.

"Where is your curricle, Bathurst?" Leslie asked impatiently. "I'm bored with the races. It's been far too long since we've been alone."

Gabriel looked at Leslie and saw a predator, a woman whose enormous appetite for sex made her an excellent bed partner for a man like him. He'd sampled nearly every sinful pleasure known to men and no doubt invented a few. Once he was gone, however, she would find another lover to take his place. She wouldn't waste a moment mourning him. Would anyone mourn him? Grandmama, if she was still alive. Perhaps Braxton and Westmore would miss him, but there was no one who knew him intimately. He felt as if his soul had already left his body, as if he were an empty shell with nothing but emptiness to look forward to. The present was uncertain, and he didn't even want to think about the future.

It occurred to Gabriel that he had neither the desire nor the will to make love to Leslie. Not today. Not tomorrow. Not ever.

"I'll take you home, Leslie, but I can't stay."

Angry color bloomed on her cheeks. "How dare you dismiss me, Bathurst! How many times do you think you can put me off and still remain in my good graces?"

Gabriel shrugged, not really caring. "I don't know, Leslie. You tell me."

"This is it, Bathurst. There are others waiting in line to take your place in my bed."

"I don't doubt that. You're a beautiful, sensual woman. Perhaps it's time we parted company."

"Very well, if that's what you want. Don't expect to come crawling back to me, for I've had my fill of your excuses."

"I'm sorry, Leslie. I'm sure your husband will be pleased to know I've removed myself from your bed."

Leslie's expression amply displayed her outrage as she whirled on her heel and marched away. Gabriel knew he'd acted like an unfeeling bastard, but it felt damn good to be rid of the countess. She had never meant more to him than a warm body when he needed one. He probably would have parted ways with her long ago if she hadn't been so blatant in her pursuit of him.

Feeling weary and despondent, Gabriel left the race-course in search of a bottle. He needed something potent to numb his mind and ease his bleak thoughts. If his introspection got any darker, he wasn't sure he would survive it. Madness must be closer than he'd thought. Had it already begun? He had hoped for more time.

Olivia definitely wasn't well. Everyone close to her had noticed her malaise and remarked upon it. She had made light of her illness and continued to do so, but she knew that no one believed her. It was past time to face the truth.

She was expecting Gabriel's child.

Recalling that first time Gabriel had released his seed inside her, Olivia realized she hadn't had her monthly for three months now.

Acknowledging the facts was frightening. *She was carrying a child who might or might not have inherited madness.* What was she going to do?

Telling Gabriel was out of the question. He had enough problems without accepting responsibility for a child he didn't want. It occurred to her that she should purchase a cottage in the country and simply disappear from the London scene. Fairfax House belonged to her brother. It had always been her plan to leave once Neville took a wife, and she had enough money of her own to raise her child alone. Aunt Alma would go with her, of course, and Gabriel need never know about his child.

Olivia had never felt comfortable with her peers after they had rejected her following the scandal of her father's death. Fortune hunters disgusted her, and becoming part of the social whirl did not interest her as it did Neville.

Neville seemed pleased with his new standing in society, and she was happy for him, despite her own misfortune. He had made many new friends among the dashing young blades about town and was taking an interest in young ladies of the *ton*. As for the male callers who showed up at Fairfax House with courting on their minds, she offered them tea, listened to their inane chatter and promptly forgot them after they left.

"How long are you going to sit there and brood?" Neville asked when he came upon Olivia sitting in a window seat in the morning room with a book in her hand.

"I'm not brooding," Olivia retorted. "I'm reading. Where are you off to?"

"Tattersall's. Would you care to accompany me? The horse auction is today, and I'm thinking of purchasing a new mount. Can we afford it?"

Olivia smiled. "Of course. But if you don't mind, I'd rather stay home and read."

"You stay home too much, Livvy. What's wrong? Is there anything I can do to help? Is Bathurst the reason you're avoiding society? I know why you ducked out of the marriage, but Palmerson is no longer a threat. Why don't you tell Bathurst what happened? I'm sure he'll understand."

"There are . . . extenuating circumstances," Olivia revealed. "Bathurst doesn't want a wife; he never did. Don't worry about me, I'll be fine. In fact, I'm thinking of retiring to the country. A cottage in a bucolic setting sounds heavenly to me. You'll be taking a wife soon, and my presence here could be awkward."

"Livvy! I have no intention of wedding any time soon. Getting leg-shackled is a serious business. I intend to take my time. Besides, I won't even come into my inheritance until I'm twenty-five. You'll always have a home with me, no matter what."

Deeply touched, Olivia brushed away a tear from the corner of her eye. "Thank you, Neville, but I really do prefer the country."

Neville grew thoughtful. "Are you sure you're all right? You haven't been yourself lately. If you're ill, I want to know about it." He puffed out his chest. "I'm the man of the family."

"Indeed you are," Olivia said, smiling fondly. "There's nothing to worry about, love. Go to Tattersall's and have a good time."

Neville gave her an uncertain look, then nodded and strode off.

"Why didn't you tell him the truth, Livvy dear?"

"Aunt Alma, where did you come from?"

"I was listening from the doorway. I didn't mean to eavesdrop, but neither did I want to interrupt."

"What makes you think I was lying to Neville?"

"I know you too well, dear. I'm not stupid, you know. You're carrying Bathurst's child, aren't you?"

"Oh, Auntie, is it so obvious?"

"To me it is. What are you going to do about it? Bathurst must be made to face up to his responsibilities."

"Auntie, you must promise not say a word to anyone, especially Bathurst. He has enough to contend with right now."

"Humph! He's not the one carrying a child. You have to tell him, Livvy."

"I refuse to add to Gabriel's woes, Auntie."

Alma's eyes narrowed. "He's rich, healthy and devilishly handsome. Those don't sound like woes to me. What's wrong with him?"

"I can't tell you."

"Is Lady Patrice aware of Bathurst's problems?"

Olivia shook her head. "Gabriel would rather she didn't know. I'm thinking of purchasing a cottage in the country, where I could raise my child in a peaceful setting," she said, abruptly changing the subject. "Will you come with me?"

"If that is what you really want, dear, then of course I will support you."

"I knew I could count on you, Auntie. I don't know what I would do without you."

"My brother let you down, but I won't," Alma said.

Alma gave Olivia a hug and left her to her solitude. She stopped abruptly when she spied Neville standing just beyond the door, looking as if his world had just crumbled beneath his feet.

"You heard," Alma said.

"I'd forgotten my cane and heard you and Livvy talking in the morning room when I returned to retrieve it. I didn't mean to eavesdrop, but the conversation sounded serious. I know everything, Auntie. Damn Bathurst! What are we going to do about it?"

"Nothing for now. I need time to think. You heard Livvy, she's adamant about keeping this to herself."

"It's not right!" Neville blasted. "I should call Bathurst out. The whoreson! He hurt my sister and shouldn't be allowed to walk away as if she were some lightskirt he'd tumbled."

"You must keep a cool head, Neville," Alma cautioned. "Livvy is very fragile right now. We don't want to hurt her."

After Neville left, Alma asked Peterson to bring the carriage around and gave directions to Lady Patrice's townhouse. The dowager received her immediately.

"Alma, how good to see you. I've ordered tea and cakes. You'll join me, of course."

Simmering with nervous energy, Alma wrung her hands, uncertain how to begin. "I didn't actually promise Livvy I wouldn't say anything, so I'm not breaking my word. Oh, dear, where to begin? Have you seen Bathurst recently?"

Lady Patrice gave a snort of disgust. "The young puppy has ignored my summons. Several of them, in fact. He didn't even have the courtesy to reply." She frowned. "Why? What has he done? Is it as we suspected?"

"I fear so. Olivia is expecting your great-grandchild and my grandniece or nephew, and she doesn't intend to tell Bathurst."

Lady Patrice's face sagged, and her skin took on the hue of old parchment. "Whatever are we going to do to get those two together?"

"Livvy said that Bathurst was grappling with some problems we are not aware of, and that she was reluctant to add to them. Have you any idea what she meant?"

"I don't have a clue," Lady Patrice murmured. "But I intend to have strong words with Bathurst as soon as I can pin him down. How is dear Olivia?"

"She's a strong woman, and determined to face this alone. She's planning to buy a cottage in the country and live there permanently with Bathurst's child. Society has ignored her for so long, she cares little for the *ton* or its opinion. All she ever wanted was for Neville to be accepted by his peers."

"Don't let Olivia do anything drastic until I talk to Bathurst," Patrice advised. "I'm sure he'll want to do his duty by her."

Alma wagged her head despondently. "That could be a problem. Olivia isn't likely to settle for duty, and I don't blame her. My niece deserves a loving husband, a man who will be a good father to her child."

"I'm sure Bathurst loves Olivia. It's up to us to bring those two stubborn souls together."

Gabriel couldn't seem to find his stride these days. He was bored, unable to concentrate, and found life generally uninspiring. The excitement had gone out of the usual activities that had amused him before he'd met Olivia. He found himself gambling for outrageously high stakes, drinking too much, and completely uninterested in seduction.

He feared the madness was beginning and wondered if the time had come for him to shun society. Though his mother had never shown violent tendencies, he couldn't predict how the illness would progress in him.

Grimsley, ever vigilant where his master was concerned, approached Gabriel one day with his fears. "Please forgive my impertinence, milord, but I'm worried about you. You're not eating, you're drinking too much, and you seem troubled. Is there anything I can do to help?"

"It's starting, Grimsley," Gabriel confided.

Grimsley appeared perplexed. "May I inquire what is starting, milord? Does it have something to do with Lady Olivia?"

"Not at all. It's the madness, Grimsley. It runs in the family. I want you to keep watch on me, make sure that I do not become violent."

Grimsley looked utterly undone. "Surely you jest, milord. You're the sanest person I know. I see you every day and have observed no sign of madness in you."

Gabriel let out a long, relieved sigh. "Thank you, Grimsley. While I may not show any outward signs of insanity, I must admit my mind lacks stability these days."

"You should wed her, milord. You haven't been the same since you met Lady Olivia."

"I refuse to burden Olivia with my problems."

"There's no guarantee you'll inherit the illness, milord. I've been with you a long time. I've observed your valor in battle and watched you acquit yourself admirably among your peers. I wouldn't call that madness."

"I appreciate your trust, Grimsley, but I cannot wed. I refuse to burden a wife with a future I cannot predict. It wouldn't be fair."

"Can any of us predict our own future?"

"I don't know, my friend. But you're right about one thing. I've been dwelling on this long enough. I'm going to the theater tonight. Don't wait up for me."

Gabriel went through the motions of dressing, but his heart wasn't really in it. Briefly he debated sending a note around to Olivia and asking her to join him, but decided against it. How could she forget him if he kept intruding? Since acknowledging, at least to himself, his love for Olivia, he realized how desperately he wanted to remain sane.

When he'd first learned he might inherit his mother's madness, he'd accepted his fate and tried to make the best of the years he had left. Then he'd met Olivia, and suddenly his future mattered. He wanted Olivia in his life. He wanted . . . Damnation! It didn't matter what he wanted. What would be would be, and he couldn't do a blasted thing about it.

The evening didn't go exactly as Gabriel had planned. He joined a group of acquaintances at the theater and even sent a note around to Lizette, one of the actresses, asking her to join him for a midnight supper. He had intended to bed the woman in a private room he had engaged beforehand, but when he kissed Lizette and eased her down on a divan, he couldn't summon the arousal necessary to complete the act he was usually so good at. He had to be going mad, for he had never failed to perform before. Just the thought of making love to a beautiful woman was usually all it took to make him ready. The alcohol he had been consuming of late could have dulled his senses, but he doubted it.

It was Olivia.

Images of her were with him no matter where he went or what he did. Love was a curious thing. Nothing in life had prepared him for Olivia. She had arrived without warning and imbedded herself in his heart before he could erect barriers.

Gabriel tucked several gold sovereigns in Lizette's cleavage and sent her on her way. Chuckling despite himself, he wondered how soon his odd behavior in the bedroom would became public knowledge.

He arrived home in a strange mood. Perhaps it was the dark fog that swirled in his head, or maybe the sense of his own vulnerability.

He unlocked the door with his key, picked up the sputtering candle sitting on the hall table and slowly made his way to the study to finish off the bottle he'd been working on before he left for the theater. Someone had built up the fire, dispelling the dampness and the shadows, and Gabriel went directly to the sideboard.

"About time you returned home, Bathurst."

Whirling, Gabriel stared at the man who rose from a chair deep in the shadows of the room. When he stepped into the circle of light emanating from the fireplace, Gabriel wasn't at all surprised to see Neville. "What is it this time, Sefton? This is getting to be a habit."

"Your butler let me in."

"Grimsley takes too much upon himself. As long as you're here, you may as well have your say."

Squaring his shoulders, Neville said, "It's time you faced your responsibility to my sister."

"What in blazes are you talking about?"

"Olivia is carrying your child."

# Chapter Twenty

The short but explosive conversation with Neville proved enlightening. Not only did Gabriel learn that Olivia was carrying his child, but he finally discovered why she had bowed out of their marriage. Consigning Palmerson to hell, he vowed to make amends for the damage the bastard had caused. The conversation with Neville had concluded abruptly when the young man advised Gabriel to do his duty by his sister and then stormed out the door.

Mulling over the conversation, Gabriel guessed that Olivia had become pregnant that first time he'd failed to protect her. How long ago had that been? Long enough, he thought grimly.

The concept of bringing a child with an inherited illness into the world horrified him. How Olivia must hate him! They would be wed immediately, of course, but he could never undo the harm he had done her. He never should have touched her when he realized how thoroughly she compromised his self-control.

Poking his head out the door, he yelled for Grimsley. The normally unflappable butler appeared a few minutes later, his sparse hair sticking up from his pink scalp and his robe flapping around his bony knees.

"You called, milord? Did young Sefton leave?"

"Yes, he departed after giving me a bit of distressing news. I find myself in desperate need of liquid fortification. Bring two bottles of my best brandy and see that I'm not disturbed."

Grimsley hesitated. "Is there anything I can do?"

"Not this time, Grimsley. I have to face this on my own."

"Very good, milord." He started to withdraw.

"Make that three bottles, Grimsley. That way I won't have to bother you again tonight."

Collapsing into a chair, he leaned his head against the cushion and closed his eyes. How in the hell had he let this happen? He could go insane at any time and leave a child predisposed to insanity for Olivia to raise. He had made a shambles of his life and dragged Olivia down with him.

"Your brandy, milord," Grimsley said in a voice ripe with disapproval.

"Leave it and go back to bed," Gabriel said wearily.

Grimsley hesitated a moment, then shrugged and shuffled off. Gabriel splashed a generous amount of brandy into a snifter, whirled it around and tossed it back in one swallow. He knew drinking wouldn't solve his problems, but it helped make him forget the horrible injustice he had done to Olivia. He refilled his glass and drank deeply.

\* \* \*

Gabriel woke to the sound of voices drifting in and out of his befuddled brain. His head felt like a ripe melon ready to burst open, and his mouth tasted foul. Disoriented, he wondered why he was slumped in a chair, his limbs askew and an empty glass dangling from his hand. As he stretched out his cramped legs, his feet rattled the empty bottles on the floor, jostling his memory.

*Olivia was carrying his child.*

The voices in the foyer grew louder. A thumping sound and a strident voice created a pain inside his head that nearly doubled him over. Suddenly the door burst open, admitting an irate Lady Patrice and an apologetic Grimsley hovering behind her.

"I'm sorry, milord, but your grandmother insisted on seeing you immediately."

"Leave us, Grimsley," Lady Patrice said imperiously. "I wish a private word with my stubborn grandson."

"Make it fast, Grandmama," Gabriel grumbled. "As you can see, I'm not fit for polite company."

"What's wrong with you, Bathurst?" Grandmama railed. "You have your whole life ahead of you. Why must you waste it on worthless pursuits? Enlighten me, dear boy, so that I may understand."

Gabriel heaved a weary sigh. It was apparent that his tenacious grandmother wouldn't stop hounding him until she learned the truth. Perhaps he had done her an injustice by not telling her why he favored a life of debauchery over marriage and a family.

"Sit down, Grandmama. This may take a while."

Perching in a straight-backed chair, Lady Patrice leaned on her cane and glared at Gabriel. "You're foxed."

He shrugged. "I suppose I am."

"You've ignored my messages. You're not ill; you've

been seen out and about. You owe me an explanation."

"And you shall have it. After hearing me out, you will understand why I can never marry or sire children."

"You were willing enough to wed Olivia."

"I had to, to protect her. She was involved in something that could have sent her to prison had she been caught."

Grandmama stared at him in disbelief. "Are you saying dear Olivia was doing something illegal?"

"That's exactly what I'm saying. I hurt Olivia once, hurt her badly, and I wanted to protect her as well as salve my guilt. That's why I offered for her. But there would have been no children from the marriage."

"Humph! Rather late for that, isn't it?"

It took a few moments for her meaning to penetrate Gabriel's benumbed brain. "You know?" he asked when he found his tongue.

"If you're referring to Olivia's delicate condition, indeed I do. What are you going to do about it, my boy?"

He should have known. Lady Alma must have imparted the shocking news to his grandmother the moment Olivia had confided in her aunt. "Am I the last to know? Neville arrived on my doorstep last night, demanding that I do the right thing by his sister."

"The lad shows promise," Lady Patrice declared.

"I'll marry Olivia, of course, but I'll never forgive myself for the devastation I've wrought. The situation is impossible."

"In what way? It's obvious you care deeply for Olivia. By your own admission, you wanted to protect and care for her. Explain yourself, Bathurst."

"I do care for Olivia, but there are things you don't know about me that place marriage and a family out of my reach."

A wary look darkened Lady Patrice's brow. "Go on."

"You were in Spain with Grandfather when my mother went mad. Father probably never told you about her illness to spare you the pain he was going through. Father loved her too much to make her condition public knowledge. I think the knowledge of her deterioration was what caused his death. I'm glad he wasn't alive to see her leap to her death from the third-floor window."

"But, my dear boy—"

"No, Grandmama, hear me out. In a lucid moment before she ended her life, Mama told Ned that her illness was inherited; her own mother ended her life in the same way when Mama was just a child. She told Ned there was a long history of madness in her family and cautioned him against siring children who might eventually go mad as well."

"Did you not think it strange that your mother chose to relate such disturbing news to Ned and not you?"

"No. Ned and I were close. Mama probably assumed Ned would tell me."

"And you never thought to ask me about Mary's madness?"

"No. I assumed you knew nothing about her illness."

"Pity," Grandmama said. "Had you done so, you would have saved yourself years of anguish."

"You knew about Mama's madness?"

"Had you asked me, I would have told you, but I assumed you already knew the truth about your birth."

Gabriel shook the cobwebs from his head. "What truth? Are you saying I'm a . . . bastard? Papa loved Mama too much to have an affair, and Mama would never have cheated on Father."

"You're not a bastard, Bathurst, though you have

none of poor Mary's blood flowing through your veins. Your mother—your real mother—was my daughter and your father's twin sister, Lenora."

Shock, disbelief, tenuous hope—all those emotions washed over Gabriel. "I knew Father had a twin sister, but I thought she'd died before I was born."

"She died in Spain, where your grandfather had been serving as ambassador. She married a Spanish adventurer without our permission and was left a widow before her child was born."

"This is unbelievable," Gabriel said, clutching his aching head. "How did I become a Wellsby?"

"After Ned's birth, Mary sank into a deep depression. Doctors seemed unable to alleviate her condition, and, fearing that she would end her life like her mother before her, my son brought his family to Spain for a visit. He hoped the change of climate and invigorating sea air would heal her mind."

"It must have helped, for she lived many years after that," Gabriel said. "Her mind was always fragile, but it didn't begin deteriorating until shortly before Ned married Cissy. But go on with your story, Grandmama."

"To make the story simple, Lenora died in childbirth. Before her death, she begged her brother to raise her newborn son as his own. You were legally adopted in Spain and raised as a Wellsby. Everyone assumed your adoptive mother was expecting when she left England and delivered you in Spain. They told no one differently. Mary loved you dearly, and so did my son."

"I never felt unwanted," Gabriel admitted, still in a state of shock. "Why was I never told?"

"I assumed your father had already told you. We will never know why he didn't. The answer went to the grave with him. It's not as if you are the child of a servant; you have Wellsby blood flowing through your veins."

"Do I have relatives in Spain?"

Lady Patrice's expression hardened. "Perhaps, but they were quite willing to give you over to our family's keeping. You weren't pure Castilian, you see. You were far better off with parents who loved you. And no matter what, dear boy, you're still my grandson."

Gabriel's eyes burned with unshed tears. He rose abruptly and knelt at his grandmother's feet, taking her frail hands in his. "Do you know what this means, Grandmama? I will never again have to look for signs of madness in myself. I can have all the children I want without fear or guilt. And to think that I once considered putting a period to my life."

Gabriel felt as if an enormous burden had been lifted from him. "I'm free now to love Olivia. To give her the life she deserves."

Lady Patrice squeezed his hands. "Had you come to me with this years ago, I could have eased your mind."

"Years ago you were abroad with Grandfather. Then there was the war, and after that, I accepted that I would die insane. I saw no reason to burden you with my problems."

"I'll never forgive myself for putting you through this," his grandmother lamented. "It hurt so to mention Lenora's name that I never spoke to you about her." She wiped away a tear. "She was too young and beautiful to die. It doesn't seem right that a mother should outlive her children. But the good Lord left me here for a reason, and now I know why.

"Thank God for Olivia," Lady Patrice said with

heartfelt relief. "Without her in your life, we would never have had this conversation."

"Olivia is carrying my child," Gabriel said with an excitement he'd never thought possible until today. "I'm going to be a father."

Lady Patrice smiled benignly. "You love her, Bathurst. Dear Alma and I knew it all along and figured you were both too stubborn to admit it."

Gabriel chuckled. "Livvy and I make quite a pair, don't we? She's obstinate, opinionated and too independent for her own good. How could I not love an extraordinary woman like her? The first time I met her she was disguised as a highwayman and held up my coach. I lost a perfectly good set of diamond shirt studs and a ring that had belonged to Ned that night."

Lady Patrice's hand flew to her chest. "Oh dear me! Never say it's true, Bathurst. You're pulling my leg."

"I speak the truth, Grandmama. Olivia and her family were destitute, and without a dowry she had no prospects of landing a wealthy husband. She and Peterson became highwaymen, robbing wealthy travelers of their valuables. 'Tis how she kept Neville at Oxford."

"However did you learn this?"

Gabriel had no intention of telling his grandmother he had shot Olivia, so he kept that information to himself. "It's a long story, Grandmama. Remind me to tell you one day." He raised her to her feet and kissed her hands. "I love you very much. Now I think it's time I told Olivia the same thing."

Lady Patrice wrinkled her nose. "Bathe first, Bathurst. You look the very devil."

He herded her toward the door. "Thank you, Grandmama, you've saved my life."

"I'll send a note around to Alma, asking her to call

on me," Lady Patrice said. "It's Sunday. The servants are off today. You and Olivia will have the house to yourselves." She gave him a stern look. "Don't take no for an answer, dear boy. I expect to attend a wedding very soon."

Grimsley saw Lady Patrice to her coach. When he returned, Gabriel snapped out orders in a crisp, clear voice. He couldn't recall when he'd been so happy. It was imperative that he see Olivia immediately. He only hoped she would be as excited as he about the turn his life had taken.

Unable to concentrate on anything but her bleak future, Olivia did little more than nod when Alma informed her that she and Peterson were off to visit Lady Patrice. Olivia was glad she wasn't invited to go along, for she wasn't up to making small talk with Gabriel's grandmother.

"Neville is off with one of his friends for the weekend," Alma reminded her.

Alma gave her a distracted smile. "I remember, Auntie. Have a good visit."

"It's Sunday. The housemaids and footmen are gone as well."

"Don't worry, I'm perfectly capable of fending for myself. Lord knows it's not the first time. I'm content to curl up beside the fire with a book."

"I may be away for several hours," Alma said. "Lady Patrice is feeling poorly and has need of me."

"Bathurst's antics are driving her into a decline," Olivia muttered.

"Yes, well . . . I'm off, then." She paused in the doorway. "Oh, Livvy, I almost forgot to tell you. Mrs. Hamilton is visiting her daughter today, so you are quite alone."

"Auntie, what *is* the matter with you? You're acting strangely."

"Am I? Pay me no mind, dear." She turned and hurried off.

What in the world was that all about? Olivia wondered. Aunt Alma had always been flighty, but she seemed more so than usual today. Whatever the cause, Olivia was too distracted by her own affairs to dwell on her aunt's behavior.

A racket at the front door scattered her dismal thoughts.

Dimly she wondered why her aunt had left if she was expecting visitors. The urgent rapping continued. Being the only person in the house had its disadvantages. She wasn't in the mood for company, and for a brief moment she considered ignoring the summons, but good manners won out. Pasting a smile on her lips, she opened the door.

"Hello, Livvy."

Stunned to see Bathurst on her doorstep, Olivia couldn't find the words to return his greeting. All she could do was stare as he stepped inside and closed the door behind him. The solid click of the latch freed her frozen mind.

"What are you doing here?"

"I had to see you."

"Why?"

"I learned something today that changes everything."

Olivia paled. Had someone told Gabriel she was carrying his child? "What did you learn?"

Gabriel grinned at her. "I'll tell you later."

Olivia searched his face. Something had indeed

changed. Gabriel seemed almost lighthearted, as if a great weight had been lifted from his shoulders. The lines in his forehead had eased, and the corners of his eyes crinkled with laughter. Olivia let out a squeak of surprise when Gabriel swept her off her feet and carried her up the stairs.

"Gabriel, put me down! Where are you taking me?"

"To bed."

Anger welled up inside her. How dare he think he could come to her whenever he wanted to fornicate! "I'm not your whore!"

"Indeed not. You're going to be my wife. If not today, then tomorrow. Which room is yours?"

"Are you insane?" The moment the words left her mouth, she wanted to call them back. Gabriel needed no reminders of his fate.

Gabriel threw his head back and laughed, further confounding her. "Insane? No. Mad with love, perhaps."

Love? Gabriel had indeed lost his mind. "You're frightening me, Gabriel."

Gabriel instantly sobered. "You need never be frightened of me, Livvy. I finally know who I am and what I can expect from life. Now, are you going to direct me to your room or shall I choose one at random?"

Olivia was seeing a side of Gabriel she'd never seen before, and she was intrigued by the startling change. "Last room on the right."

Gabriel carried her to her room, closed the door firmly behind him and set her on her feet. His hands went unerringly to her bosom, searching for the buttons. Olivia pushed his hands away.

"No. What is this all about, Gabriel?"

"It's about us. I want to marry you. I want to go to

bed with you every night and wake up with you in the morning. I want children with you. When I die, I want your face to be the last one I'll ever see."

A shiver of fear slid down Olivia's spine. "Are you ill? Has the madness taken control of you?"

He reached for her. "I'm well. Exceedingly well. I've never been better. I'm going to make love to you, Livvy."

"Something has happened. Please, Gabriel—please tell me. I can take it."

"After we've made love."

His mouth claimed hers, devouring it with such fierce passion that Olivia felt utterly possessed. Hot and demanding, his tongue stroked her lips until she opened to him. With a sigh, she surrendered to the breathless joy of being in Gabriel's arms again. Carried away by a wild surge of excitement, she realized that what she felt was pure and wondrous and eternal.

The kiss he gave her was sweet and deep. She surfaced from it with a delicious dizziness, arching against him as he stroked and explored her as if he'd never touched her before. He moaned her name, molding her so tightly against him, she felt as if they were one soul, one body.

Losing herself in the taste of him, she felt the heat of his lips on hers, the sensuous thrust of his tongue inside her mouth, and nearly swooned with pleasure. Unable to find the will to stop him, she lay limply in his arms as he unfastened her bodice. With a shout of triumph, he shoved the gown and chemise over her shoulders and down her arms.

He stared at her breasts. "You're so beautiful. And you're mine, all mine. I love you, Livvy."

There it was again. That word. The word she'd never expected to hear from Gabriel.

"I don't deserve you," Gabriel continued. "One day I hope you'll come to love me as much as I love you."

A wary joy suffused Olivia. "Please don't lie to me, Gabriel. It would destroy me if you should recant after we had made love. I love you so much it hurts."

"I mean it, Livvy, every word. I would have told you sooner if I had known we had a future. I wasn't even sure *I* had a future. Knowing you return my love makes me the happiest man alive."

Olivia was confused. "Do we have a future?"

"A long and fruitful one, my love. I'll tell you all about it after we make love."

Olivia's lips trembled with emotion. If this was a dream, she never wanted to wake up. "I love you, Gabriel. I always will."

Gabriel groaned something unintelligible and literally tore the clothing from her body, kissing each bit of bare skin as he exposed it. Her eyes glazed with passion, she tangled her fingers in his thick hair and pulled him closer. His mouth closed over the turgid peak of her breast and suckled her, bringing a rush of damp heat between her thighs.

"I can't bear this," Gabriel muttered as he swept her up and lowered her to the bed.

With his heated gaze riveted on her, he tore off his clothing and lay down beside her. She writhed against him, her hands moving wildly over his neck and shoulders, his back, his buttocks. He rose up on his elbows and kissed her fiercely, hungrily, his hands delving between her thighs and his fingers sliding up inside her wetness. A cry left her lips. Her body was pure sensation. She felt as if the blood in her veins had turned to liquid fire.

Consumed by the need to give as well as take, Olivia gently pushed Gabriel onto his back, her gaze transfixed on his aroused manhood. She wanted to touch him, to taste him, to pleasure him until he screamed for mercy.

Gazing into his slumberous eyes, she slowly dipped her head until her tongue touched the tip of his glistening sex. He inhaled sharply, watching her. Opening her mouth, she took him inside. He shouted an oath and pushed himself deep. Savoring the taste and scent of him, she continued to torment him with the sliding friction of her tongue. His back arched, his breath labored, hands clenched at his sides and teeth gritted, he looked like a man in the throes of agony. Several excruciating minutes later he lifted her away and rolled her beneath him.

"Sweetheart, you're killing me!"

She lifted her head and smiled at him. "I want you as wild for me as I am for you."

"You're not nearly wild enough," he said, reaching up and tweaking a nipple.

He lay on his stomach and slid down her body until his head rested between her raised thighs. He spread her apart, and his tongue slid inside her slick cleft. She gasped, her fingers tangling in his hair. His mouth sought out the small nubbin amidst the slippery folds and gently suckled. A cry burst from her lips; intense feeling swelled within the tiny bud and threatened to burst. She thrust her hips forward, forcing his mouth more firmly against her core. He filled his hands with her buttocks, his tongue dancing in and out of her cleft, sending her spiraling madly out of control. She shattered in a burst of shimmering colors.

Hungrily, Gabriel watched her face as she found her release. Hotter, harder, more ravenous for her than he had ever been before, he crawled up her body and thrust inside her.

Her lips parted and her hips arched to meet his; he felt her sweet breath fan his cheek as he plundered her body. He thrust deep, each stroke ecstasy, each withdrawal pure agony. She lifted her legs and clasped his hips tightly. He could feel the need within her rising again, and the clamoring inside him intensified.

"Don't leave me," she gasped. "Please, Gabriel, come with me this time."

"I'll never leave you again," Gabriel promised. Flexing his hips, he drove deeper, his control all but shattered.

Her climax set off his own. He kissed her with all the fervor and intensity of a man in love. For the first time, he felt no guilt at remaining inside her to the very end.

"I love you, Livvy," he whispered as he pulled out and settled comfortably beside her. "You're managing and stubborn, and our life will never be dull or mundane, but you can't imagine how much I'm looking forward to the next fifty years or so."

Olivia stirred and smiled at him. "You're not perfect, either, Bathurst—except in bed, of course. Now will you tell me what happened to change your outlook on life? The last time we spoke, you despaired of your future."

He gathered her into his arms. "Grandmama stopped by today."

"And?"

"She told me the truth about my parentage."

"Never say you're not Lady Patrice's grandson!"

"I am indeed her grandson, but my parents were not

the two people I thought had sired me. Father had a twin sister who died in Spain during childbirth. I am her son. Her death was so mourned that family members rarely mentioned her. I knew my father had a twin sister, but it never occurred to me that she could be my mother. My real father was a Spanish adventurer."

"You're a . . ."

". . . bastard? No. My father's death occurred shortly after he wed my mother. She extracted a deathbed promise from her brother that he would raise me as his own. And he did. I never once questioned my father or mother's love."

"I'm beginning to understand," Olivia said. "Your mother told Ned about the madness because it didn't concern you."

"I could have saved myself years of anguish if I had discussed my fears with Grandmama."

"Do you really think your brother took his own life?"

"That's something we'll never know. I don't even want to think about it."

"We won't. We'll think of other, more pleasant things." She smiled shyly. "Like having a family."

"Exactly. We're free now to wed and have children without the taint of my adoptive mother's madness hanging over them."

"You *do* want children, don't you?"

"Giving you children will be my greatest pleasure." He cocked an eyebrow at her and settled his hand on her stomach. "Is there something you wish to tell me?"

Olivia gaped at him. "You *know!* Who told you? I didn't want to burden you with my pregnancy. I planned to move to the country and live quietly with Aunt Alma and our child."

"It doesn't matter how I found out. We're in love and

we're going to get married as soon as it can be arranged. If you'd like, we can retire to Bathurst Park to await the birth of our child."

"Not as long as Cissy—"

Her words faltered as the door burst open. Aunt Alma and Lady Patrice stood in the opening, grinning like fools. Rearing up, Gabriel pulled the sheet over them.

"There you are," Lady Patrice sang out. "Thank God you've both come to your senses."

"What in bloody hell are you two doing here? Are we allowed no privacy?"

"You can have all the privacy you want," Alma said, beaming. "Dear Patrice has asked me to move in with her after you're wed, and I've agreed."

"Splendid," Gabriel bit out. "Will you please both leave? Livvy and I will be down directly."

"Of course, dear boy," Lady Patrice said. "Give me your arm, Alma dear. Perhaps Peterson will brew us a pot of tea. Don't dawdle, children."

Groaning, Gabriel fell back onto the bed. "I'm sorry, Livvy."

He grew concerned when he felt Olivia's shoulders shaking. Pulling her into his arms, he tried to comfort her. Shock raced through him when he realized she wasn't crying, and that her body was actually convulsing with mirth. His eyes crinkled, his mouth twitched, and against his better judgment, he burst out laughing.

"Shall we join the scheming duo downstairs?" he asked, wiping away mirthful tears with the back of his hand.

Suddenly Olivia sobered. "Do you suppose your grandmother suspects I'm expecting your child?"

"I know she does."

Her face reddened. "Oh my! Just tell me one more time that you love me."

"I love you. Madly, irrevocably, passionately. I even love Ollie, that irrepressible, conniving thief and highwayman. Satisfied?"

Olivia sighed. "Whatever are Braxton and Westmore going to do without their fellow rogue?"

"We can only hope they will find their soul mates, just as I did. Up with you, my love. It's time to face the dragons."

# Chapter Twenty-one

The wedding was held the following day at Lady Patrice's elegant townhouse before a small, intimate group of friends and family. Lady Patrice had convinced the bishop to perform the ceremony, and the kitchen staff had prepared a festive luncheon to celebrate the nuptials.

Lords Braxton and Westmore stood beside Gabriel to lend support as he repeated his vows. But Gabriel needed no support. He was willing, nay, eager to wed Olivia, confounding both of his friends, who clung tenaciously to their bachelorhood despite the abandonment of their friend and former rogue.

Both Lady Patrice and Lady Alma, though beaming proudly, wiped away tears of joy when they saw Olivia walking into the room on Neville's arm. Peterson and Grimsley appeared as moved as the ladies, despite their attempts to conceal their emotions.

The wedding vows were repeated loud and clear by

both Gabriel and Olivia, their gazes locked in loving contemplation of one another. No one witnessing the ceremony could doubt that this was a love match. Gabriel almost laughed aloud when he heard Grandmama's sigh of relief after the bishop pronounced them husband and wife.

After that he remembered nothing but the lushness of Olivia's lips when he kissed her and the knowledge that she was his forever. Then they were separated briefly by guests offering congratulations. From across the room Gabriel watched Olivia, thinking she had never looked lovelier. Her coppery curls had been piled atop her head in a becoming style and covered with a silver-edged veil that flowed over her shoulders to the middle of her back.

Gabriel was amazed that the impromptu wedding had been put together so quickly. Grandmama and Lady Alma had worked miracles to provide a guest list, food, the bishop and flowers. Gabriel wouldn't even hazard to guess as to how they'd produced Olivia's shimmering silver wedding dress in a matter of hours. The ring, he knew, had been his grandmother's. All Gabriel had to do was show up at the correct time to speak his vows.

Gabriel had just decided to reclaim his bride and escort her to the dining room for their wedding feast when Lords Braxton and Westmore joined him.

"Have you heard the news about Palmerson?" Ram asked.

Gabriel's mouth thinned. "Has the bastard returned to London? Where has he been hiding himself?"

"You mean you don't know?" Luc replied in a stunned voice. "We thought you'd be the first to hear, since it involves your family."

"What in bloody hell are you two talking about?"

"Palmerson married your brother's widow a few days ago. Sanford and Fordham couldn't wait to impart the news. If you hadn't withdrawn from society, you would have heard."

Disbelief was slowly replaced by another emotion as Gabriel threw back his head and gave a hoot of laughter. "That's rich!" he gasped, dashing away tears of mirth with the back of his hand. "I can't think of a couple as well suited as Cissy and Palmerson. If Cissy has her way, and I know she will, Palmerson will be kept on a tight leash. He'll get no money from her unless he toes the line. I can think of no better punishment for the bastard. I may still beat him to a pulp when I see him, but I'll probably let him live for Cissy to bedevil."

"What's so funny, Gabriel?" Olivia asked as she joined Gabriel and his friends.

"You'll never believe this, love. Cissy caught Palmerson in the parson's trap."

"They're married?"

"It's true," Braxton assured her. "Sanford said they've left Braxton Park and are now residing at Lady Cissy's estate."

"Is this the first you heard of it, Gabriel?" Olivia asked. "I'm surprised your estate manager didn't inform you."

"He probably did. I haven't been in the mood to read my mail the past several days. Cissy's marriage and her departure from Braxton Park couldn't have come at a better time. We'll leave for the country as soon as I tie up some loose ends here."

"We'll miss you, old boy," Luc said. "London won't

be the same without you. The ladies will be bereft, but fear not, Braxton and I will carry on."

"Don't gloat," Gabriel said. "Both of you may be closer to the parson's trap than you think."

Braxton gave a harsh laugh. "Not me. My motto is love 'em and leave 'em. That's not going to change any time soon. There are plenty of women in this world willing to accept what I offer without demanding marriage."

"I agree," Westmore echoed. He sent Olivia a winsome smile. "Unless, of course, the marchioness has a sister."

Following that conversation, Braxton and Westmore repaired with the other guests to the dining room. Gabriel offered his arm to Olivia, his lips twitching as he said, "Shall we join our guests, Ollie? I can't wait to get this over with so we can be alone. I want our wedding night to be one you'll never forget."

Olivia took his arm, her answering smile warm and inviting. "My dearest rogue, every night in your arms is unforgettable."

*Bathurst Park, six months later*

A scream echoed through the waiting silence. Gabriel leaped to his feet, his face drawn. "I can't stand this! I'm going up to her. What if she's dying?"

Braxton and Westmore, who had arrived at Bathurst Park just that morning to bolster their friend during Olivia's travail, grasped his arms and physically wrestled him back into his chair.

"Have another brandy," Braxton urged. "These things can take a long time. There's little you can do to help Olivia."

"You'll only get in the way," Westmore added.

Gabriel refused the brandy. He glanced at Lady Patric, hoping she would ease his fears, but she appeared to be in a trance. She was perched on the edge of her chair, her gnarled hands clasped over the head of her cane, her knuckles white from the pressure she exerted. Gabriel thought her grim expression was anything but reassuring, and his fears accelerated.

Peterson hovered in the doorway, wringing his hands, his face creased with worry. Gabriel's heart went out to Peterson, for Gabriel knew he loved Olivia like a daughter. Mrs. Hamilton stood behind Peterson, lending support.

No support in the world could ease Gabriel's fears. What if Olivia died birthing their child? How could he go on without her?

Another scream, this one more intense. This time there was no holding Gabriel back. Wresting himself free of his friends, he took the stairs two at a time and burst into the bedroom he and Olivia shared. The midwife looked up, her lips pursed in disapproval.

"You're not needed here, milord."

Lady Alma, who had remained with her niece to help the midwife, hurried over to Gabriel. "You shouldn't be here, Bathurst."

"Yes, I should," Gabriel said, shoving past her to the bed. "Livvy needs me."

"Gabriel, is that you?"

Her voice was weak, her weariness apparent, but to Gabriel it was the sweetest sound he'd ever heard. He knelt beside the bed and smoothed a damp curl from her sweaty brow. "What can I do to help, Livvy? This has been going on for twelve hours; I can't bear to see you in such pain."

She gave him a weak smile. "Hold my hand. It won't be much longer now."

"If you insist on staying," the midwife said, "you might as well make yourself useful. Brace your lady's shoulders when I tell her to push."

Gabriel did as he was told, positioning himself behind Olivia, supporting her with his body.

"Now, milady. Push with all your strength. I can see the babe's head."

Gabriel suffered along with Olivia as she struggled through the intense pain to deliver their child. Her teeth clenched tightly, she squeezed his hand with surprising strength. Her stomach quivered and contracted strongly, and the noise she made pushing out their child tore painfully through him.

"It's coming, milady. You're doing just fine," the midwife encouraged from between Olivia's spread thighs.

"I'm so proud of you, Livvy," Aunt Alma trilled. "You're so brave."

"One more time," the midwife said. "One more push."

Gabriel felt helplessly inadequate as Olivia pushed their child into the midwife's waiting hands.

"You have a fine daughter, milord. Smaller than I expected, but she has all her fingers and toes." She held the squirming infant up by her heels and gently swatted her tiny bottom. The babe gave a healthy cry, and breath rushed back into Gabriel's lungs. Then the midwife handed the child to Alma while she cut the cord. Carrying the babe to the washbasin, Alma sponged her off and wrapped her in a swaddling cloth.

Gabriel felt as if he were walking on air. He had a daughter. He couldn't recall when he'd been so happy.

"I'm sorry I couldn't give you a son the first time," Livvy said weakly.

He kissed her forehead. "I'm more than pleased with my daughter, love."

"You can leave now, milord," the midwife advised. "I've still work to do here."

Gabriel was reluctant to leave until Alma placed his beautiful daughter in his arms. "Show her to your grandmother and your friends. I'm sure they're anxious for news of Olivia and your babe."

"She's so small," Gabriel said, cradling the babe in the crook of his arm. "I'm afraid I'll hurt her."

"Babies are amazingly resilient. I doubt you'll hurt her."

Encouraged, Gabriel headed toward the door, stopping abruptly when he heard Olivia moan. Glancing over his shoulder, he saw the midwife still positioned between Olivia's legs, a frown puckering her brow. "What's wrong with Livvy?"

"Nothing. Everything is as it should be. I suspect the afterbirth is about to be delivered," Alma answered, shooing him out the door.

Somewhat mollified but still anxious, Gabriel left the room, eager now to show off his new daughter. When he walked into the drawing room, Braxton and Westmore jumped to their feet, their worried expressions easing considerably when they saw the swaddled bundle in Gabriel's arms. Beaming, Gabriel walked to his grandmother and held out the babe for her inspection.

"I have a daughter, Grandmama. Isn't she beautiful?"

Lady Patrice smiled delightedly as she reached for the baby. Gabriel kissed the babe's cheek and placed her in his grandmother's arms.

"How fares your lady?" Braxton asked. "All is well, I hope."

"Olivia came through the ordeal beautifully. She's—"

"Bathurst! Come quickly!"

Aunt Alma's voice, coming to them from the top of the stairs, was strident and fraught with emotion. Gabriel's first thought was that something had happened to Olivia, and Alma's frantic words seemed to confirm his fears.

"Oh my God!"

He took off at a run without a backward glance at the others in the room, literally flying up the stairs. Bursting into the bedroom, he fell to his knees beside Olivia and gazed into her pale face. Her eyes opened and she gave him a wobbly smile.

Though his relief was enormous, he couldn't stop the moisture that came unbidden to his eyes. He dashed it away and gave her an uncertain grin. "Are you all right? I thought . . . I thought . . . oh God, I don't know what I thought. I'm not strong enough to go on without you."

Olivia lifted her hand and caressed his cheek. "That's something you'll never have to worry about."

His brow creased worriedly. "Something is wrong, or Aunt Alma wouldn't have called for me."

Alma hovered nearby, her hands fluttering like two birds in flight. "I didn't mean to frighten you, Bathurst. Things were happening so fast, I didn't have time to think."

Rising, Gabriel looked at Olivia for an explanation. For some reason, Alma seemed unable to give one. Before Olivia could explain, however, the midwife appeared, carrying a tiny bundle. Gabriel's first thought was that someone had carried his daughter upstairs while he had been talking to Olivia.

"Your son, milord," the midwife said, rocking the bundle in her arms. Shifting his gaze from the midwife to Olivia, Gabriel said in confusion, "I thought I had a daughter."

"You do," Olivia volunteered. "But you also have a son. He was born moments after you left the room with our daughter."

"Twins?" Gabriel felt in need of a strong drink and a chair. He plopped down on the edge of the bed simply because his legs refused to support him. "We have twins?"

"Indeed you do, Bathurst," Alma said gleefully.

Gabriel held out his arms, and the midwife placed the babe in them. He gazed at his son with rapt adoration. "A son *and* a daughter. How lucky can one get?"

"What's happening?" Lady Patrice demanded from the doorway. Ranged behind her were Braxton, Westmore, Neville, Peterson and Mrs. Hamilton, who was holding Gabriel and Olivia's daughter against her ample bosom. "I couldn't bear not knowing what was going on."

"Come see for yourself, Grandmama," Gabriel invited. "But you can only stay for a moment. Olivia is exhausted."

Grandmama thumped into the room. She stopped abruptly when she saw the bundle in Gabriel's arms. "What have you there, Bathurst?"

"My son," Gabriel said proudly. "Olivia has given me two children to love, a son *and* a daughter."

"My word," Grandmama said in a shaky voice.

"Well done, Bathurst," Braxton crowed as he peered

at the tiny infant Gabriel held in his arms. "You always did have bloody good luck."

"What wonderful news," Westmore congratulated. "And felicitations to you, madam," he added thoughtfully to Olivia.

Aunt Alma collected Gabriel's daughter from Mrs. Hamilton and shooed everyone out the door. She placed the babe in Olivia arms and left quietly with the midwife.

"Have you chosen names for them?" Olivia asked Gabriel once they were alone.

"I'm still in shock," Gabriel said, "but something does come to mind. I'd like to name them Lenora and Ned, after my actual mother and my adoptive brother. Does that meet with your approval?"

Olivia appeared deep in thought. Her eyes glittering mischievously, she grinned up at him. "Would you reconsider? I rather like Pete and Ollie myself."

Gabriel chuckled. "I'm sure Peterson would be thrilled to have a namesake, but Ollie is out. One hellion in the family is quite enough."

Lenora and Ned were christened three weeks later. Though still small in size, both infants were healthy and lively. While their godfather, Neville, Earl of Sefton, looked almost as proud as the babies' parents, their godmother, Lady Alma, and great-grandmother, Lady Patrice, were absolutely glowing.

But nothing could compare with the unconditional love Gabriel and Olivia felt for their babies and for each other.

"Thank you for giving me the courage to challenge fate and take charge of my future," Gabriel whispered after the ceremony. "Had a courageous highwayman not robbed me of my valuables, I might never have found love."

"Thank you for loving me and changing the course of my life," Olivia replied. "You're living proof that even an irrepressible rogue can be tamed."

"Does that mean there's still hope for Braxton and Westmore?"

Olivia laughed. "Love can find a way into the hardest of hearts. Even the heart of a rogue."

# Author's Note

I hope you enjoyed *The Rogue and the Hellion*. Lord Bathurst found his match in Lady Olivia and all ended well despite their rocky road to romance. Eventually the other two rogues will get their own stories, but the books may not follow one another. They will be stand-alone books about Lord Braxton and Westmore.

Because my fans so loved *The Black Knight* and *The Dragon Lord*, my next book will be another Medieval. Look for *Lionheart* in November 2002. *Lionheart* is set in Wales and England in 1255 and has a heroine who would rather don armor to fight the English than remain safe behind castle walls and admit defeat. Lionheart has no idea the mysterious knight who foils his attempt to capture Llewelyn, the Black Wolf of Snowdonia, is a woman, and lovely Vanora isn't about to tell him. Look for a rousing tale of kings and knights and a woman who fights keep what is hers.

I love hearing from readers. For a newsletter and

bookmark, write to me at P.O. Box 3471, Holiday, FL 34690. I can be reached by e-mail at *conmason@aol.com*. Please visit my website for a list of all my published books and news about all my future releases.

All My Romantic Best,
Connie Mason

# Connie Mason
# The Dragon Lord

Renowned for his prowess on the battlefield and in the bedroom, the Dragon Lord has no desire to wed an heiress he has never seen, but he has little choice. When given the option of the three Ayrdale women, he has no taste for the grieving widow or the sharp-tongued shrew, so the meek virgin it must be.

High-spirited Rose knows she is no thornless blossom waiting to be plucked. Her gentle twin longs for a cloistered life, whereas Rose has never been known as a shrinking violet and is more than capable of standing up to a dragon. A clever deception will allow her sister to enter a nunnery while an unexpected bride awaits her unsuspecting husband for the most unforgettable deflowering of all.

___4932-5                                    $5.99 US/$6.99 CAN

# the Black Knight
## Connie Mason

He rides into Chirk Castle on his pure black destrier. Clad in black from his gleaming helm to the tips of his toes, he is all battle-honed muscle and rippling tendons. In his stark black armor he looks lethal and sinister, every bit as dangerous as his name implies. He is a man renowned for his courage and strength, for his prowess with women, for his ruthless skill in combat. But when he sees Raven of Chirk, with her long, chestnut tresses and womanly curves, he can barely contain his embroiled emotions. For it was her betrayal twelve years before that turned him from chivalrous youth to hardened knight. It is she who has made him vow to trust no woman— to take women only for his pleasure. But only she can unleash the passion in his body, the goodness in his soul, and the love in his heart.

___4622-9                                     $5.99 US/$6.99 CAN

**Dorchester Publishing Co., Inc.**
**P.O. Box 6640**
**Wayne, PA 19087-8640**

# THE LION'S BRIDE
## CONNIE MASON

### Winner of the *Romantic Times* Storyteller Of The Year Award!

Lord Lyon of Normandy has saved William the Conqueror from certain death on the battlefield, yet neither his strength nor his skill can defend him against the defiant beauty the king chooses for his wife.

Ariana of Cragmere has lost her lands and her virtue to the mighty warrior, but the willful beauty swears never to surrender her heart.

Saxon countess and Norman knight, Ariana and Lyon are born enemies. And in a land rent asunder by bloody wars and shifting loyalties, they are doomed to misery unless they can vanquish the hatred that divides them—and unite in glorious love.

_3884-6                                    $5.99 US/$7.99 CAN

## "Each new Connie Mason book is a prize!"
### —Heather Graham

Spirits can be so bloody unpredictable, and the specter of Lady Amelia is the worst of all. Just when one of her ne'er-do-well descendents thought he could go astray in peace, the phantom lady always appears to change his wicked ways.

A rogue without peer, Jackson Graystoke wants to make gaming and carousing in London society his life's work. And the penniless baronet would gladly curse himself with wine and women—if Lady Amelia would give him a ghost of a chance.

Fresh off the boat from Ireland, Moira O'Toole isn't fool enough to believe in legends or naive enough to trust a rake. Yet after an accident lands her in Graystoke Manor, she finds herself haunted, harried, and hopelessly charmed by Black Jack Graystoke and his exquisite promise of pure temptation.

_4041-7                                    $5.99 US/$6.99 CAN

**Dorchester Publishing Co., Inc.**
**P.O. Box 6640**
**Wayne, PA 19087-8640**

Please add $1.75 for shipping and handling for the first book and $.50 for each book thereafter. NY, NYC, and PA residents, please add appropriate sales tax. No cash, stamps, or C.O.D.s. All orders shipped within 6 weeks via postal service book rate. Canadian orders require $2.00 extra postage and must be paid in U.S. dollars through a U.S. banking facility.

Name_____
Address_____
City_____ State_____ Zip_____
I have enclosed $_____ in payment for the checked book(s).
Payment <u>must</u> accompany all orders. ☐ Please send a free catalog.

# Viking!

## CONNIE MASON

The first time he sees her she is clad in nothing but moonlight and mist, and from that moment, Thorne the Relentless knows he is bewitched by the maiden bathing in the forest pool. How else to explain the torrid dreams, the fierce longing that keeps his warrior's body in a constant state of arousal? Perhaps Fiona is speaking the truth when she claims it is not sorcery that binds him to her, but the powerful yearning of his viking heart.

___4402-1                                      $5.99 US/$6.99 CAN

*"Her historical romances are the stuff that fantasies are made of!"*
                                                —*Romantic Times*

"Ye cannot kill the devil," whispers the awestruck throng at the hanging of the notorious Diablo. And indeed, moments later, the pirate not only escapes the noose, but abducts beautiful Lady Devon, whisking her aboard his ship, the *Devil Dancer*. Infuriated, Devon swears she will have nothing to do with her rakishly handsome captor. But long days at sea, and even longer nights beneath the tropical stars, bring Devon ever closer to surrender. Diablo is a master of seduction, an experienced lover who knows every imaginable way to please Devon—and some that she has never imagined. Devon knows she will find ecstasy in his arms, but does she dare tempt the devil?

___4366-1                                    $5.99 US/$6.99 CAN

**Dorchester Publishing Co., Inc.**
**P.O. Box 6640**
**Wayne, PA 19087-8640**

Please add $1.75 for shipping and handling for the first book and $.50 for each book thereafter. NY, NYC, and PA residents, please add appropriate sales tax. No cash, stamps, or C.O.D.s. All orders shipped within 6 weeks via postal service book rate. Canadian orders require $2.00 extra postage and must be paid in U.S. dollars through a U.S. banking facility.

Name_____
Address_____
City_____State_____Zip_____
I have enclosed $_____ in payment for the checked book(s).
Payment <u>must</u> accompany all orders. ☐ Please send a free catalog.